PRAISE

D0725482

"A romantic account of unfinished business on a modern one. All becomes clear by the end of the book, including the past identities of key players in the modern story, and both past and present love triangles are resolved. The puzzle of what really happened pulls readers through *The Boundless Deep* to its satisfying ending." —*BookLoons*

"More than lives up to the promise shown by her first novel, *Seal Island*. A stunning tale of reincarnation and self-discovery [set in a] world much like our own, but one where the unknown lurks, just out of sight, in dark corners and lightless depths. Brallier showcases a fine sense of the historical, and obviously did a great deal of research into both the era in general and the whale trade in particular. A great read, *The Boundless Deep* can be enjoyed by fantasy, romance and fiction fans alike."
  —McNally Robinson Booksellers' website, (staff pick)

"Kate Brallier is a talent to watch." —Susan Wiggs

"A delicious gothic feel permeates this debut. . . . Brallier's book-loving heroine is appealing."
  —*Booklist* on *Seal Island*

"*Seal Island* is a distinctive and inspired debut, and Brallier is a welcome new voice in the paranormal genre."
  —*Romantic Times BOOKreviews*

ALSO BY KATE BRALLIER FROM TOM DOHERTY ASSOCIATES

SEAL ISLAND

THE

BOUNDLESS

DEEP

KATE BRALLIER

TOR®

A TOM DOHERTY ASSOCIATES BOOK
NEW YORK

NOTE: If you purchased this book without a cover, you should be aware that this book is stolen property. It was reported as "unsold and destroyed" to the publisher, and neither the author nor the publisher has received any payment for this "stripped book."

This is a work of fiction. All of the characters, organizations, and events portrayed in this novel are either products of the author's imagination or are used fictitiously.

THE BOUNDLESS DEEP

Copyright © 2008 by Kate Brallier

All rights reserved.

A Tor Book
Published by Tom Doherty Associates, LLC
175 Fifth Avenue
New York, NY 10010

www.tor-forge.com

Tor® is a registered trademark of Tom Doherty Associates, LLC.

ISBN-13: 978-0-7653-5809-7
ISBN-10: 0-7653-5809-3

First Edition: March 2008
First Mass Market Edition: January 2009

Printed in the United States of America

0 9 8 7 6 5 4 3 2 1

To my parents,

who introduced me to songs like
"The Greenland Whale Fisheries" at far too
impressionable an age, thus engendering
a fascination with the doomed romance of whaling.

It is one among far too many things that I owe you.
So, thanks!

ACKNOWLEDGMENTS

First off, I owe a massive debt of gratitude to the incomparable Rick Spencer. I bet he never expected, when he offered to answer my questions aboard the *Charles W. Morgan*, that he'd be on the receiving end of a whaling romance, but he took it in stride with skill, panache, and enthusiasm. He is a scholar and a gentleman (and also a Forebitter, so that is my tribute to him within the story) and his knowledge of things historical, whaling-related, and musical is unmatched. Any facts I got wrong are solely the result of authorial stubbornness, and not in any way due to his eagle eye, which kept me on the historical straight and narrow.

Secondly, thanks to Mystic Seaport, the New Bedford Whaling Museum, and the Nantucket Whaling Museum, for letting me get in and among the tools of the whaling trade. One can read about it all one likes, but there is nothing that compares to actually seeing it, and that is the invaluable gift they gave me.

Thanks also to the Nantucket Historical Association in general—and not just for their marvelous museum. I have played extremely fast and loose with their organization in service of my plot and hope I have not offended, because I have nothing but the deepest respect and admiration for the work they do in keeping a vital piece of American history alive. Not to mention their outstanding online resources, which I was never more than a click away from while writing.

Also, a heartfelt tip of the hat to Nathaniel Philbrick, for his riveting book *In the Heart of the Sea*. Of all the books I read on the subject—and I read many—his brought the past alive for me most viscerally. If my historical Nantucket bears any resemblance to reality, it is thanks to him. I encourage anyone interested in the topic to run out and buy a copy straight away.

On the subject of Nantucket history, however, I should warn readers that Obadiah Young (and all his ancestors and descendants) is solely the product of my imagination. There was no infamous murder, and anyone who goes to Orange Street in search of the dueling mansions will find only one: the Levi Starbuck house. But that impressed me so much that I had to use it somehow—if only as the model for Kitty's smaller, plainer dwelling.

I also owe a debt to Rick Ulmer, owner of the Rose & Crown, for both valuable insights into modern Nantucket and for inadvertently giving me a twist of the plot. Not only did I fictionally co-opt the reason for our meeting, but I also blatantly stole one or two of his stories.

Thanks to my beta readers, each of whom helped me to focus some aspects of the book, and made it better for their insights: Mireille Theriault (who also let me swipe her last name), Kara Cesare, Liz Scheier, Marjorie Groell, Jaime Levine, and

David Keck. And, for their eagle eyes during the copyediting phase, Carol Orisko and Arlene Hodges likewise have my respect and gratitude. Also, thanks to Eileen Keck, for publicity efforts way above and beyond the call of duty!

Thanks to Melissa Singer, Jozelle Dyer, Tom Doherty, and all the other good folks at Forge, for kindness, professionalism, the most glorious cover, and for supporting the book in all the ways they do, and for letting me take the extra time I needed to tinker. An extra special thanks goes to Melissa, not only for a superb concept edit, but for a masterful line edit as well. Without her expert guidance, I would have been (wrongly) tempted to stuff even more Cool Facts About Whaling into these pages, but she kept me focused on what was important, and kept me from embarrassing myself with overly enthusiastic info-dumps.

And last—but certainly not least—a big hug and kiss and great whacking chunks of gratitude to my marvelous husband, David Keck. Not only did he allow me to drag him all over the East Coast in search of whaling sites, but he puts up with me when I am deep into work mode and unable to tolerate distractions. Also, he pushes me endlessly to find the darker, deeper, wilder heart of my story, for which I owe him hugely, quite apart from everything else. You make everything more fun, sweetie, so thanks!

Sunset and evening star,
And one clear call for me!
And may there be no moaning of the bar,
When I put out to sea,

But such a tide as moving seems asleep,
Too full for sound and foam,
When that which drew from out the boundless deep
Turns again home.

Twilight and the evening bell,
And after that the dark!
And may there be no sadness of farewell,
When I embark;

For tho' from out our bourne of Time and Place
The flood may bear me far,
I hope to see my Pilot face to face
When I have crossed the bar.

"Crossing the Bar"
—Alfred, Lord Tennyson

THE
BOUNDLESS
DEEP

CHAPTER 1

It starts with the dream; it always starts with the dream. The ship is rocking, the waves slapping iron-fisted against the hull. A cold wind is screaming out of the south, blasted up from the Antarctic, chapping the cheeks and watering the eyes. There is nothing but ocean on all sides, as dark and forbidding as the backs of the leviathans when they finally surface in swirls of water and spouts of steam. Overhead, the sails creak ominously, taut under the strain of the fierce wind. A momentary lull slackens the canvas, then it snaps into place with the sullen crack of a slavemaster's whip.

The ocean, my dreaming mind tells me, is a harsh mistress, hard and unforgiving. But it is also the cradle of life. The cradle . . . and the grave.

From the slender hoops in the mast high above, the lookout gives the call, his voice high and thin in the screaming winds: "Thar she blows! She blows!"

It rises off the port bow like some beast of legend, water pouring off its scarred black back like waves off a rock. Its breath, moist and hot in the chill air, hisses forth: the fires of Hell unleashed.

Frenzy erupts with the lookout's cry. The deck boils with motion as the ship begins its slow, ponderous turn into the path of the whale. The whaleboats are flung from the sides; men pour like rats over the rails. The boatsteerers take up position in the bows, their harpoons flashing silver in the pale light of the morning sun, ropes coiled like torpid snakes behind them.

Senses are heightened at such a moment. The familiar salt-tang of the air now rakes at the throat with caustic fingers. The voices of the crew echo back and forth like macaques in the jungle: all noisy cacophony, devoid of sense.

"Hold fast the course!" the captain cries—a voice so familiar to my dreaming mind that I know it for my own.

Oars are shipped, the whaleboats skimming across the water like bugs across a pond. The rowers are well trained, the oars a poetry of synchronized motion. Rise, dip, stroke, and rise again.

The whale, too, dips below the surface, then rises, blowing. The dark, squarish head, the stubby ridges of its dorsal hump, reveal it to be black gold: the mighty sperm—the fiercest and most valuable of the cetaceans. Kings are anointed with its oils. And under its flukes, scores of whalemen have met their Maker.

Cries go up from the men, echoing eerily in the chill air. The whaleboats gain speed, fleeting after the leviathan. Harpoons are poised for the toss, their deadly points gleaming. And we who are left behind, riding above the waves as the leviathan rides below, wait in taut anticipation, nerves belled out like canvas before the wind.

For myself, watching in a state not quite awake and not quite dreaming, there is a sense of dread inevitability. I know this scene—as well as I know the feel of my own flesh beneath my fingers.

As the captain on that long-ago deck, I don't know it; but *I,* the dreamer, know it. Because it has happened before, this endless dance of hubris and doom. It has happened many times, night after night. Yet still the sun shines above me, and the deck rail, hard beneath my fingers, drives splinters into callused flesh.

Maybe this time, all will be different.

Once again, the whale breaks the skin of the sea. The lead boatsteerer poises, casts. The weapon soars a silver arc, the lines singing out behind it. And then again, in quick succession. Barbed and deadly, the points sink, one by one, into a mountain of black flesh. The lines snap taut. And the monster rises. Not just breaking the surface this time but thrashing upward in a wake of foam, the small eye appearing, and then that ridiculous afterthought of jaw, seemingly so fragile yet with teeth the length of a grown man's hand.

The toothed jaw clashes; the beady eye gleams with rage and pain. Higher and higher the monster rises until it looms over the small boat like a wall of storm-tossed water. Will it drop once more and attempt to flee the harpoon's sting, towing the whaleboat behind it like a child's toy, or will it dive down deep, our last view of it the mocking flap of its mighty tail?

In the former case—on that mad journey named after my homeland: the Nantucket sleigh ride—the whaleboats can be dragged miles from the ship in the fury of the chase. And in the latter, both boats and crews can take the fast path to Davy Jones's locker if the ropes are not cut with enough speed.

But this time, it is the third and most sinister possibility that occurs. The vast, black body twists in midair, and descends on the boat like a hammer on an anvil, crushing it as if it were no more solid than a nutshell.

The toothed jaw clashes, shearing through the second boat so that it falls in halves, spilling human cargo like seeds from a pod. A mighty flap of the tail annihilates the third.

It is hard to see if there are any survivors in that welter of wake and foam, nor is there time to evaluate, for the whale is turning, spying out the larger ship: the ultimate source of its torment. The harpoon juts from its back like a pin, the lines streaming behind it like a banner as it comes.

And then that vast, squarish head is hammering into the side of the ship. I hear the crack of timbers, feel the wallow that lets me know the ship is wounded. It is not enough, though. The whale comes again, striking up into the hull. I can feel the ragged hole it makes, as if my vessel is an extension of my body.

My fault, I think, as the water floods in and the ship founders.

My fault . . .

I have done something, I don't know what, but something terrible. Something that has drawn down the wrath of God, doomed not only me, but my crew as well. I am twisting with guilt like a fish on a line, even as the waters flood in and the ship begins to split. The boards groan, then tear apart with a tortured scream. Soon, the frigid waters will embrace me: the only lover's touch I deserve.

The ship shudders again beneath the beast's assault. It is not, I know now, a whale. It is some avenging demon out of Hell: my fate and punishment for my many sins.

Yea, though I walk through the valley of the shadow of death. I will fear no evil . . .

Except that I do fear. I can smell its stink upon me, sour and acrid in my sweat. I can taste it on my tongue.

For thou art with me; thy rod and thy staff they comfort me . . .

But it is too late for comfort now. Too late for repentance.

The cold waters claim me, and I wake—so drenched with sweat that I, too, might have been swallowed by the sea. . . .

In the bright morning light, my room looks strangely surreal; too squat, too white, too modern. For some reason, every time I awaken from this dream, I expect to be greeted by vines—a stylized tangle of chaos and pattern. I don't know why; it makes no more sense than anything else. And yet, I know that I am in the wrong place, the wrong rooms. Not my childhood rooms either, in that quaint Midwestern house that has comprised most of my life up until now. But something far more distant, with the smell of sea and salt in the air, the mournful cry of the gulls, the sounds of a busy port town rising to go about its business . . .

It is always like this when I first awake: this sense of disconnection, of things not being quite as they should. But gradually reality filtered back around me, and my things ceased to feel so alien. It was just my room, after all: my abstract posters in their artistic black frames, my spare Ikea furnishings—the grad student's standard décor. The morning air streaming in through the open windows smelled of earth and flowers, and a vague sense of something burning, with nothing of the sea in it at all. Which was just as it should be. I had never in my life lived by the water. And I must have been the only English major ever to graduate without reading *Moby-Dick*. I had spent my life ducking the sea—at least, when I was awake.

When I was asleep, however . . .

"You've been dreaming again," Jane said knowingly, poking her head around the bedroom door.

I sat up, pushing a handful of damp, clammy hair out of my face, and sighed deeply. I'd had these dreams all my life; you'd think I'd eventually find another topic. But no; it had to be this. And it had been growing worse over the past few weeks.

Though perhaps this was because I was finally facing my fears. I glanced down at my suitcase, more than half-packed by the side of my bed, then back up at Jane, who had come all the way into my room with her usual blithe disregard for other people's privacy. The burning smell grew stronger as she entered, and I masked a groan. My punishment, it seemed, for sleeping in.

Still, I managed a wry grin. "Was I screaming again?"

"Like a banshee," she informed me cheerfully. "I could hear you all the way from the kitchen." When I raised an eyebrow, she added, "Well, since it is our big day and all, I figured I'd make the breakfast. And since you're such a fan of French toast . . ."

Yup, that explained the burning. "You decided to make it Cajun style?" I teased.

Jane grinned. "Blackened, you mean?" My roommate was all manner of things, but slow was not among them. "That was the first batch. The second batch is . . . Well, you'll see."

I couldn't help it; I laughed. As a distraction, Jane Bryant was first-rate. I had almost forgotten that she had dyed her hair green. Or at least green in virulent streaks, as if her previous copper highlights had oxidized and run.

Still, this look was a definite improvement over last week's red. That had simply looked as if Jane's head had rusted. But then, Jane changed hair color as frequently as other people changed their clothing. In the nine months since I had answered her ad and taken up residence in the apartment's second bedroom, she had sported at least fifty different colors, ranging from almost normal hues to things Mother Nature had never imagined in her wildest nightmares.

Her personality was similarly mercurial. She absorbed fads and trends with the same ease she adopted hair colors—and with as much staying power. There were flirtations with nose rings and henna tattoos, with mysticism and feng shui. Whatever the New Age flavor of the month, Jane was out there sampling it, absorbing the bits she liked and discarding the rest. She was like one of those crazy patchwork quilts my grandmother had been so fond of making: little bits of this and that combining into an oddly cohesive whole.

The only obsession that hadn't gone away in the months I had known her was her intense fascination with my dreams. She had cooked up theory after theory to explain them. I was haunted; I was channeling some sort of universal consciousness. (I scoffed at this. A universal consciousness about *whaling*?)

Jane's latest theory was reincarnation. It remained ridiculous, but at least she was taking it seriously. My mom—in most ways a practical Midwesterner to the core, save for the perilously romantic streak that had led to my ridiculous name—had always put it down to "Liza's fancies."

"So, which one was it this time?" Jane continued, folding herself onto the foot of my bed with the fluid grace of an Indian mystic—for yoga had, until recently, been an obsession as well. She was wearing a pair of old grey sweatpants and a faded black T-shirt cut off just below her breasts, revealing a taut, tanned stomach complete with the inevitable belly button ring. Her bare feet revealed toenails painted a shocking metallic blue. "The bad one? The one where you know you've done something horrible and are being punished for it?" Jane gave a delighted shiver, and I grinned.

"Yes, that one. Again."

Jane bounced a little on the mattress, her dark eyes glowing. "I knew it," she declared. "That is *so* cool!"

Perhaps to her, but normal girls did not dream of whale hunts—especially not in the era of environmental politics and Greenpeace. Couldn't the universal Powers That Be have chosen something a bit more socially acceptable?

"I know we're going to find the answer," Jane said, her eyes bright beneath her emerald bangs. "There's a reason you keep dreaming this; we just have to find out why." She leaned forward and pushed excitedly at my shoulder. "I mean . . . Nantucket! Can you believe we're finally going?"

I couldn't—not even today, when my suitcases were awaiting only the final additions. I was from the Midwest. College had been spent as far away from either ocean as it was possible to get. And now, graduate school as well. So why a small Atlantic island dominated my dreams remained a mystery.

But a mystery, as Jane said, that might shortly be unveiled. I couldn't help feeling that answers really did lie on Nantucket. Which was why I was haring off to the island on a whim, ignoring my mom's eminently practical advice about getting a job and earning some much-needed money over the summer break. Jane's aunt Kitty lived on Nantucket, Jane had gleefully informed me, shortly after she had learned of the dreams. When classes were done and school let out, we would both go visit. Kitty had a huge old house; she would be delighted to have the company. We wouldn't have to pay for board, and as for spending money . . . Well, there were always a ton of jobs on the island: too many rich people, and never enough service staff. It would be fun, an adventure.

The practical, Midwestern part of me balked at the idea of spending two months in a stranger's house, but Jane was adamant—and lavish in her descriptions of the wonders that were Aunt Kitty. Although the thing that probably swayed me most was the fact that, at twenty-four, I was finally ready to stop hiding. Maybe it was Jane's acceptance of my dreams that changed things, making me feel they weren't just crazy idiosyncrasies. That there was a truth behind them—and that maybe, if I discovered that truth, I could stop having the damned things and get on with whatever I was meant to be doing with my life. Or, at the very least, with the education degree I was currently pursuing.

After all, there's only so long you can live with your head buried in the sand before you suffocate, right? So, off I would go, to stay with Jane and the unknown, but apparently marvelous, Aunt Kitty.

Yet, once the decision had been made, I found myself both eager and apprehensive to see this island from which the dreams originated. Eager because sheer curiosity impelled me to see how closely it mirrored my reality. And apprehensive because . . . Well, what if the dreams *were* real? While it would be reassuring to prove I wasn't crazy, the alternative raised even more appalling questions.

"Get up!" Jane said, grabbing my arm and all but towing me from bed. "We've got to get an early start. It's a long drive, and Aunt Kitty is expecting us for dinner on Thursday. You're going to love Aunt Kitty; she's just like me!"

I laughed. "God, now *there's* a thought." I imagined a feisty old lady, her hair sensibly knotted in a viridian-streaked bun.

Jane reached out to swat me, and I ducked.

"Shower first," I told her, shaking out the tangle of my hair and popping out of bed, almost tripping over my suitcase in the process. An auspicious start. Really, it was a good thing I didn't believe in signs and portents. "And then . . . How bad is the French toast, anyway?"

"Frankly?" She grinned. "Lumpy doesn't even begin to describe it. It looks totally revolting! But it tastes okay. I mean, I ate one just before you started shrieking, and I haven't died yet."

"As good a recommendation as any, I suppose." And I set off for the shower, to wash away the salty memory of a sea I had yet to visit.

Chapter 2

We arrived in Hyannis, as expected, at about midday on Thursday—to what must have been the 537th iteration of the Liza Song.

With her usual fierce industriousness, Jane had somehow managed to sneak about three hundred CDs featuring whaling and sailing songs into the car. Okay, there were probably only twenty of the things, but by the third day, it certainly felt like three hundred! And I probably would have been flattered by her efforts if I hadn't been faintly appalled. But then, this was the very thing that made department after department accept Jane's transfer papers, even though students were roundly discouraged from treating said departments like a series of high-end chain stores in the local mall.

But anyway, thanks to Jane, we had our traveling soundtrack. And she kept popping it into rotation despite my efforts to change the music. After all, it was a long way from Wisconsin. But Jane was not to be deterred. Much to her delight, there were quite a few songs that specifically mentioned a Liza, and even one with a Liza Jane which she kept going back to. In her eyes, it was yet another omen from above: a sign from God (or whatever) of the rightness of our mission.

Jane had inevitably chosen one of the Liza songs—something off a Forebitters album called "Blow, Liza, Blow"—to be my personal anthem for our adventures. I have to admit the thing was catchy. The rest of the music was entertaining as well—at least, once I got into the spirit of the thing.

Until the second day, that is, when a rather monotonous, buzzing song about roses nearly made me run the car off the road.

"What?" Jane said excitedly, after I had pulled the car over to a shaky stop on the shoulder and was breathing heavily against the steering wheel.

"Nothing. I just thought I . . . recognized that, somehow." The feeling had been so sudden and so visceral, I didn't feel comfortable sharing any of it with her. The minute the song had come on, my entire body had started tingling, as if it had all gone pins and needles, the road ahead of me vanished, and I found myself instead in what felt like the darkness of a quiet room, flesh on naked flesh, as that voice I knew so well from my dreams sang huskily, softly, and somewhat off-key. The vision was fortunately so swift and jumbled that I regained the road in no more than a few seconds, just before the car's tires actually hit the gravel of the far-left shoulder.

Jane instantly batted the stereo off, and I pulled swiftly right, across both lanes and out of the (fortunately light) traffic. Then sat there parked and panting—as much from shock as the sudden flood of sexual arousal that had accompanied the vision. I mean, I wasn't exactly a sexual innocent, but I had never found myself . . . *wanting* . . . so much. My encounters had always been fine, satisfying in the moment, but not . . . God, not like *that*!

"Are you sure you're all right?" Jane insisted.

"Yeah, I'm . . ." The throbbing in my groin was gradually decreasing. "I'll live. But we're listening to *my* music while I'm driving in future!"

"No argument from me." Jane paused, then grinned. "But we haven't finished the album yet, so does this mean I get to drive for a bit?"

It was, of course, my car, and I had been reluctant to let her behind the wheel. But given that I was the one who had nearly crashed it . . . I made a point of turning off the engine and handing her the keys.

She whooped with delight, and skipped around the front of the car as we traded places. Five minutes back onto the road, she turned the music on again, but this time nothing happened. Perhaps because I was on guard against it?

Nothing else happened all the way to Hyannis, either. Where, in celebration of our arrival, we were back to the "Liza Song" again—followed shortly thereafter by a different Liza song, which also had something to do with a bulgine running. I imagined the creature in question to be a cross between a buffalo and a freight engine, and was chuckling to myself over the image when Jane—in that too-casual voice that always betokened imminent disaster—said, "So, do you think we need the South Dock or the Queen's Dock?"

I groaned. Jane was driving, and I foolishly hadn't been paying attention to the signs. How hard could it be to find the ferry dock in a small town, after all? It had to be clearly marked. In fact, it was. It just happened there were two of the things.

"Dammit, Jane," I exclaimed. "If you'd put half the energy into actually planning this trip as you did into picking the soundtrack . . ."

It was, I felt, a legitimate concern—and the very thing that kept the aforementioned departments from complaining too hard when Jane decided to take her leave again. Motivated, but not so well focused: that was Jane.

But she just laughed. "Oh, stop being such a fusspot! I got us here on Thursday afternoon as promised, didn't I? No more nights in overpriced motels, straining our poor student budgets . . ." She shot me a sly look, and I had to grin back. I had been a bit vocally horrified about our inability to find a truly cheap place to stay east of Chicago.

"Anyway," Jane added blithely, "Aunt Kitty mentioned something about two forty-five at the Steamship Authority. So I suppose we just go to one of the docks and ask."

Of course, we chose the wrong dock, and got turned around trying to find the right one. But eventually—and still well before the 2:45 deadline—we joined the short line of cars awaiting service at the check-in booth. My stomach was doing a little dance that was half excitement and half apprehension. For the eighty-fifth millionth time, I wondered what the hell I was doing, running off to spend the summer in the house of some woman I had never met. But Jane was grinning smugly as she pulled the car up to the booth and scrolled down the window, clearly delighted that she was about to bring me—quite literally—to the land of my dreams. And, damn it, I *really* wanted to see the place.

"Two passengers and car for the next ferry to Nantucket," she told the booth attendant cheerfully.

He seemed unmoved by her sunny, green-haired charm—and Jane could certainly turn on the charm when she chose. Big-time. Despite the hair and the slightly flaky personality, people gravitated toward her. Just look at how quickly we had become friends after we had become housemates. In fact, I often felt I had known Jane my entire life, not just the nine months we had been cohabiting. And while she more than occasionally irritated me, I still adored her.

Not so the dock attendant. "Reservation?" he asked, not a trace of a smile on his long, dour face.

I felt my own face go grey, and my fond musings about Jane suddenly veered straight into irritation. "Reservation?" I squeaked.

The attendant seemed intrigued enough by my response to lean in through the window, though his expression changed not a whit. "You don't have a reservation?"

Jane tried to brazen it out. "No, we don't. Is that a problem?" Optimistically, she gave him Big Eyes: an expression that had melted many a lesser man.

But instead of dissolving, our man looked almost amused. One eyebrow cocked subtly upward. "If you want to get to Nantucket, it is."

Great. Not only were we unprepared, but now he was mocking us for it.

Then again, he probably had seen his fair share of stupid tourists. I just hated being one of them. "So," I managed, brightly, "when *is* the next available departure?"

"Next Tuesday," he informed us.

"*Tues*day?" Jane spluttered.

"I daresay there are no cheap motels in Hyannis?" I added.

I swear, the man almost laughed.

"But I'm Kitty Bryant's niece!" Jane exclaimed. He looked blank. "She owns, like, one of the most famous houses on the island!"

He remained unmoved.

As for me, I felt like I was sinking into a big black hole. I should have known not to trust the practical details of the trip to Jane, though she had sworn she had everything taken care of.

"And how much would it be to take that Tuesday reservation?" I asked.

"Three hundred and fifty for the car. Twenty-eight each for the pair of you. Round-trip."

Well, so much for our cheap journey. We could probably have flown for less. I looked helplessly at Jane, but she had that clenched, determined, bit-between-her-teeth look that I knew too well. "This is ridiculous!" she declared. "I'm calling my aunt. She'll sort this out!"

Our man seemed unconvinced, but waved us out of the line. "If you change your minds, you can make your reservation at the office," he told us, pointing. "Or leave your car in our mainland lot, and just go over yourselves at two forty-five."

"And how much does the lot charge?" I inquired.

For an instant, I felt a flash of sympathy from our attendant. "Twelve dollars a day," he said. Of course.

Caught between laughter and despair, I glanced again at Jane, but she was determinedly steering the car to the side of the lot. She parked, then dug her cell phone out of her bag. "Don't worry," she told me, with what seemed unfounded confidence under the circumstances. "Aunt Kitty will sort this all out."

Unless Aunt Kitty was God, I somehow doubted it. But Jane was dialing.

"Hey, Aunt Kitty," she said. "Yeah. Yeah, we're in Hyannis. Except . . . No, really? You did? Man, you're the best! I owe you. . . . Really? That, too? You totally rock! Then we'll see you at . . . what? Yeah, that sounds great. Thanks again. And . . . Hey! I didn't come all this way to get insulted!" She laughed. "Yeah, well, you may have a point there. See you soon, then."

She shut off the phone and turned to me triumphantly. "Ha!"

I grinned. "Let me guess. She figured you'd forget, so she made us a reservation for the ferry?"

"Et tu, Brute?" She grinned back. "But she did us one better. She paid for the damned thing, too! So let's go make our little man swallow his words, and get on our boat."

The attendant didn't seem overly impressed when Jane sailed back up to the window and declared: "Reservation for Bryant. One car, two passengers, for the two forty-five ferry." He checked his list—no doubt unchanged since the last time he had consulted it.

"Names of passengers?" he said.

"Jane Bryant and Liza Donovan," Jane responded, no longer trying to charm him.

"ID?" he asked.

I had no idea if this was standard procedure, but he probably had reason to be suspicious. We dug out our driver's licenses. I passed mine to Jane, and she dutifully handed both over. He examined them, peering cursorily at Jane's and more intently at mine. The name again, no doubt. I had done what I could to normalize it a bit, but surely even he knew that Liza was a viable nickname for Elizabeth? And at least the last name matched.

Eventually, he passed them both back. But Jane—no dummy—had caught his preoccupation, and took a moment to study mine before she passed it on. A grin quirked the corners of her mouth, but she managed to hold on to her curiosity until we were actually on board the ferry. My car was stored on the lower deck and we had planted ourselves on the open upper deck, with the harbor stretching out around us and an expanse of slate-blue water in the distance. More water than I had ever seen in one place in my life.

"So," she said coyly, "what's the R. for?"

"Not telling," I replied stubbornly.

" '*R*. Elizabeth Donovan'?" she parroted. "C'mon, you've got to tell me!"

"No, I don't."

"Why not?"

"Because it's bloody awful, that's why!"

She kept at me for a few more seconds, but I can be as stubborn as Jane when my back is up, and she's smart enough not to pursue a losing game. And before long, the ferry gave a deep, rumbling bellow—accompanied by a deafening blast on the air-horn—and we were off, the shores of Hyannis retreating and the wide waters beckoning as the great ship churned away from dock.

The wind whipped up as soon as we were under way, blowing our hair about wildly—or at least, blowing Jane's about. Mine was longer, and I had used a band to tie it back. It had a tendency to be unruly, even without the wind. My hair was thick and dark, with reddish lights, and fell to just below my shoulder blades: a riot of waves and semicurls that never pointed in the same direction at once. Jane enviously called it the "just out of bed" look and was wildly jealous of it; I, in turn, coveted her neat, glossy bob that never seemed to fall out of place—in spite of (or perhaps because of) all the colors she dyed it.

We sat out in the wind as the ferry rumbled along, and I was so excited, I could barely sit still. My stomach was churning nervously, and I had all the attention span of a three-year-old as I swiveled my head about, trying to see everything at once. I had never been on a boat before. This wasn't the ocean proper, I supposed, more some sort of a bay. But it was vast and alien: a strangely cohesive surface that at times looked like sculpted glass, and at others was thrown into lacy waves of spray by the fierce wind. I particularly loved leaning over the side to look at the boat's wake, waves cut into a milky foam shot through with the palest green, as if a deep emerald light were trying to penetrate an opalescent sheet of crystal.

While the day had started out sunny, the clouds rolled in as we progressed, dimming the light and darkening the waves to a slate grey. The sea grew rougher, and the huge ferry rolled and wallowed in the swell. But perhaps there was something to Jane's reincarnation theory after all, because I didn't get sick. Instead, I reveled in it, feeling again that odd, tingling familiarity in the swell of the waves under my feet. And, had a whale risen, spouting, off the side of the boat, I wouldn't have found it at all amiss.

But eventually, not even my enthusiasm could save us from the cold wind, so we retreated into the enclosed spaces of the lounge—where, of course, all the good seats had already been taken. We had to jam ourselves onto the end of a large table full of screaming children, where we sipped hot chocolate in an effort to warm up and tried to ignore the shrill, piercing cries that surrounded us. I endeavored to read my novel, while Jane dutifully scribbled in her journal—the one religion she had never abandoned since I had known her. And before long, the curve of the Nantucket coast materialized—grey against the grey horizon—and we went back out on deck to gaze at it.

I don't know quite what I expected from the land of my dreams, but it wasn't this. There was no sizzle of recognition as we rounded the point that led into the harbor. I had been expecting something warmer—a rich, brick-red womb of a place—so the cold, grey-on-grey landscape caught me strangely off guard. The houses all seemed to blend into the sky, their weathered, shingled sides giving them an austerity sometimes at odds with their grandeur.

"Do you recognize anything?" Jane asked eagerly, at my shoulder.

"I don't think so. I . . ."

My voice trailed off, and she turned to me suspiciously. "What?"

The more I looked and the less I thought about it, I did

know this landscape. At least, at some level. The cold, grey ranks of houses held no familiarity, but as I gazed across the sweep of harbor, I caught sight of the white points of two steeples poking above the massed dwellings. My limbs went all tingly and a cold wave swept over me. I didn't black out— quite—but I knew those white buildings, bracketing the grey: the silhouette of my homeland.

I *had* been here before, listening to the wind snap the canvas taut overhead as a ship tacked into the harbor. And the feelings that swelled through me then were much the same as now: excitement, apprehension, uncertainty. . . .

The feelings of a whaling captain returning home, or was I just projecting?

Unbidden, words popped into my mind, and I found myself murmuring them out loud: "They that go down to the sea in ships, that do business in great waters. These see the works of the Lord, and his wonders in the deep. . . ."

I came back to myself in time to see Jane staring at me incredulously. I shook off the strange spell that had gripped me. "What?"

"What the hell were you on about?"

I grimaced ruefully. "I have no idea. But . . . I have a feeling this may be a more interesting trip than either of us intended."

Jane just laughed. "Speak for yourself. This was precisely what I intended! You're home now, aren't you?"

Somehow, I suspected I was.

CHAPTER 3

Despite—or perhaps because of—my experience on the ferry, I was fiercely on guard as we pulled the car out of the hold and emerged onto Nantucket soil. Jane was driving—both as a precaution against any more blackouts on my part, and because she knew the way. She had spent a few summers here with her aunt when she was younger, and though she hadn't been back in a while, apparently some things were easy to remember.

"You can't miss Kitty's place," she said cheerfully as she maneuvered the car along the crowded, narrow streets choked with tourists and SUVs. "I'll let her tell you the history. But, like I told the guy at the ferry terminal, it is one of the most infamous houses on the island."

I felt another shiver at her words—but probably only because of the deliberately ominous tone she was using. So instead, I distracted myself by peering about me, taking in the town. It looked like any tourist seaside town, all souvenir shops and eateries. Perhaps there were more bike rental places than usual, but what was a seaside resort without at least three ice cream parlors?

Though this particular seaside resort also happened to have a whaling museum, I noted as we drove past it. I resolved to visit as soon as possible. As long as I was dreaming about the damned business, I might as well see what it was all about, right? And hopefully learn how wrong I was in every essential detail. . . .

Still, I have to admit our first entry into the town was a bit anticlimactic. Maybe because I was rigorously guarded against any shock of recognition, but I didn't see anything that called out to me. It was too new, almost self-consciously quaint— cobbled streets mixed with high-end boutiques that said nothing to me of history or tradition.

"So, what do you think?" Jane asked, turning up yet another shop-laden street. "Feel like home yet?"

I shook my head. "Not even close. I . . ."

"What?"

She had turned again, and my fingers started tingling as we passed a building that gave me a strange jolt of recognition. This was just too weird. Could Jane be right? Reincarnation? That was just Cleopatra coming back in the body of some beautician, or people coming back as slugs. I didn't buy that sort of stuff for an instant; I never had. So why was I reacting as if I were the poster child for life reincarnate?

It had to be nerves; that was all. I had been dreaming of Nantucket for as long as I could remember, and now I seemed determined to convince myself there was some reason for it.

"Liza?"

I shook myself out of my fugue. "I'm fine. Really. When . . . Oh!"

This latter was a pure, involuntary exclamation. We had turned up yet another street—this one solely residential—and it almost corresponded to my previous expectations. As we had progressed deeper into the town, I had noticed the occasional grey-shingled house fronted cheerfully with white or yellow clapboard. On this street, almost every house bore a jaunty white façade over its grey expanse, giving the severe town a more lively air, and the slight curve of the road seemed anchored by two vast Georgian mansions—the near one much grander than its farther neighbor.

"I told you you couldn't miss it," Jane said smugly.

"You mean . . . the big one?" It was certainly the grander of the two, covered with frills and furbelows, in contrast to its more ascetic cousin—if you could call a grand mansion ascetic. The nearer was enhanced with columned detailing and elaborate embrasures over every window, which, like frosting on a cake, were layered in white over plaster walls that had been painted just the faintest shade of pink. Yet it was the smaller of the two that drew my eye. It bore its elegance more simply, with a minimum of frills, its walls a soft, creamy, uniform white. And, like the harbor, I suddenly knew that I had seen this house before. Seen the bones of its construction, even. For a sudden shard of a vision wavered before me, fluttering like a veil over reality: an open structure, dotted with workmen. . . .

I felt the blood drain from my face, and ground my nails into my palm, hard, to drive back the wave of dizziness. Fortunately Jane seemed oblivious to my reaction.

"Heavens, no!" she exclaimed. "That gaudy pile?" Her

voice was contemptuous. Then she grinned at me, and took on her Lecturing Tone. "When Obadiah Young became a captain and married the young socialite Lucy Dalton in 1824, he was determined to build her the grandest house in the neighborhood—and so he did. He finished his creation in 1834, and it was the pride of Orange Street. Only then, in 1838, that upstart, Captain Levi Starbuck, had to—"

"—one-up his neighbor," I concluded softly. "Build an even larger, better one for himself."

Jane glanced at me, startled. "How did you know?"

I flushed. "It, uh . . . seems the logical conclusion," I managed.

"I've always wondered," Jane continued musingly, "why he felt the need to compete like that."

"Well, because Obadiah married a foreigner," I said, as if it were perfectly obvious. "And fell away from the Friends. And because he . . ." But the memory, like a whale, had surfaced only briefly, and now sank deep below the troubled waters of my subconscious again.

Jane was staring at me oddly. "The logical conclusion again?" she asked sharply.

I shrugged with a studied casualness—probably thoroughly unconvincingly. "Yeah, why not?" But I could not tear my gaze off the smaller of the two mansions. There was an incipient tingling in my limbs, which I tamped down firmly. If this was indeed the house in which I was to spend the summer . . . Well, I also didn't believe in such coincidences. As far as I was concerned, this was definitive proof I was making the whole recognition thing up. "So, are you telling me your aunt actually *bought* that one?"

"Yup," Jane confirmed gleefully. "Though probably at a discount, 'cause it's rumored to have a bit of a curse on it. But I'll let Kitty tell you the details; I always forget all the good bits."

And that alone had to account for the shiver that went through me when she pulled my car into the short drive that fronted the house.

Obadiah Young—and why did that name send a wave of heat zinging through me?—and Levi Starbuck had built their twin mansions with vast porticoed front entries, but neither faced the main street. Instead, they were turned at right angles to the road. Obadiah's house had been rotated left, with its right side facing out, whereas Starbuck's—yet another facet of his one-upmanship?—was rotated right.

Thus, the two grand entries seemed locked in a perpetual face-off, bristling at each other across the intervening yards with columned mouths gaped wide.

"Pretty swank, huh?" Jane grinned as she parked and handed me the keys. "Did you ever think you'd be spending the summer in a real captain's house?"

I shook my head mutely, trying to tamp down my reaction to the place's seductive song of welcome and recognition. *Coincidence,* I told myself firmly. *Coincidence.* I was *not* going to pass out in Kitty Bryant's gracious porticoed entry.

Fortunately, I was distracted by the front door opening. A woman stepped out. "You made it!" she declared in a warm, confident voice.

"Oh ye of little faith," Jane countered, then launched herself at what had to be her aunt for an enthusiastic hug. After a moment, the two broke apart, and the older woman surveyed me. I studied her in turn.

Quite contrary to my initial fantasy about the veridian-bunned matron, Kitty Bryant had nothing of the matron in her at all. Tall and elegantly clothed, she carried herself with the supreme confidence of a woman who knew exactly what she wanted out of life—and who had achieved it. She had Jane's dark eyes and thick, equally dark hair cut in a sleekly stylish coif. Her features were more rounded than Jane's and her expression was friendly and welcoming. I found myself warming to her at once—much as I had to her niece nine months earlier.

What was more, I loved seeing someone so wholly at one with herself. I wondered if Kitty had always possessed this level of self-confidence, or if it was something she had come to later. Either way, I admired it. She was every inch the type of woman I wanted to become.

"You must be Liza," she said. "Welcome! I'm so glad you could spend the summer with us; Jane has told me all about you."

I flushed slightly, wondering how many of Jane's crazy theories had been bandied about for Kitty's benefit. But dignity before all, right? "I wouldn't put faith in everything Jane says," I countered dryly.

Kitty laughed. "Yes, she said you were a fighter, too. Good, I can see we're going to get along just fine. Now, come here and give me a hug; I feel like I know you already."

It was mutual—and any lingering doubts I had about the wisdom of spending an entire summer with someone else's relatives blew away like dandelion seeds in the wind. This wasn't only going to be tolerable; this was going to be *fun*!

I collected my hug, then added, "And thank you for making the final leg of our journey possible." I glared darkly at Jane. "We owe you *big*-time for that one, I expect."

She just laughed. "Nonsense. It was my pleasure. And besides"—she grinned at Jane—"I've known my niece most of her life; I had a feeling my intercession might be needed. I'm just glad you arrived on the promised day. Knowing Jane as I do, I admit I had an anxious moment or two on that score."

Jane flushed.

"What?" Kitty said shrewdly.

"Yeah, thank Liza for that," Jane mumbled.

Kitty laughed. "Then I shall. Thank you, Liza—and I suspect that makes us more than even! How many side trips did she want to make?"

"At least five."

"Liza . . ."

"The llama farm was the weirdest."

"Well, come on, how many times in life do you get to visit a llama farm?" Jane countered in a tone that made her whim sound totally reasonable. "But, no, Liza kept me on the straight and narrow, and here we are, safe and sound—albeit unllamaed."

Kitty grinned. "Come on in, both of you. Don't worry about your luggage for now; we'll have that brought in later. What?" she added, catching sight of Jane's drop-jawed expression.

"Don't tell me you've added a butler, or something?"

Her aunt looked vastly amused. "No, not as such. Just an extra pair of hands—though I doubt he'd be flattered by that description. Come on; I'll show you to your rooms."

Jane was looking rebellious—no doubt dying to pump her aunt for details of the mysterious stranger—but I for one was dying to see more of the house. We had progressed only as far as a gracious opening foyer, but from what I could already see, the house was a study in symmetry, with large gracious rooms, high ceilings, and sculpted moldings. And it was probably that very symmetry—with rooms mirrored across a central hall— that made me shiver again with that uncanny sense of recognition. No doubt, I felt as if I knew where every room in this place was just because it was so orderly, because it was built on a plan that was common to its day and time.

Still, I must have been rubbernecking like a tourist, because Kitty said, "Let me give you the penny tour first, just so you can orient yourself in this great pile, and then I'll show you both where you are sleeping."

The house was light and airy inside, with big windows and fairly modern, though comfortable, furnishings, its walls painted a series of subtle shades. Kitty had clearly not been a slave to period detail, but instead had made the house her own: a home rather than just an historical showplace. In form, I recognized nothing, which gave me the same odd, off-balanced feeling I always had when waking from my dreams. As if I were expecting things to be different than they were.

Though large, the house was comparatively simple, with a living room and more formal parlor to the front, then a hallway that forked around the stairs, leading to an open kitchen/ dining area on one side, and a library/office complex on the other. A largish bathroom was tucked behind the stairs, scattered with the detritus of a resident male, and I saw Jane raise her eyebrows.

But I was more concerned with the odd thing that happened as we headed to the second floor. The stairs were configured in a fairly standard design, going up at one angle, turning on a generous landing, and continuing upward on the opposite cant. Yet no sooner had we reached the landing than a sudden shiver of dread went though me—the proverbial icy hand, reaching from the grave.

I must have made some involuntary sound, for Jane turned and said, "You okay back there?"

I manufactured a bold smile. "Fine. Lead on, Macduff."

I was almost afraid to see what awaited me upstairs, but everything seemed perfectly normal. At first. Kitty showed us her master suite, then opened the door to the room across the hall—a big, airy corner chamber. "I thought we would put Liza here," she said, and that's when the weirdness erupted again. I felt an instinctive denial, followed almost immediately by Jane's whine of protest: "But that's *my* room!"

"Jane . . . ," Kitty began repressively, but I quickly broke in.

"No, that's okay, really. I'll take the other room." Then suddenly wondered what I was letting myself in for, if my reaction to *this* place had been so extreme. But I needn't have worried. For the moment Kitty opened the door to my designated room, an instant sense of peace and belonging rushed over me, so strong that I nearly collapsed.

Which was an odd reaction to have, since, although it was a lovely room, it wasn't in any way unusual. It was another corner chamber, although smaller, and light flooded in from the wide windows. The lace-topped canopy bed was covered with a sprigged comforter and sheet set in light green and white. There were pale green towels set out at the foot of the bed, matching the even paler green of the walls—which were so faint and icy as to be almost white, and added an elegant coolness to the place. The moldings and ceilings were pure white, and there was a desk and chair on one side of the room; a dresser with a large mirror atop it on another; a large free-standing cheval mirror; and a big, comfortable armchair next to the window.

Which was all very well and good, but still didn't explain my absurd reaction to the place. But then, people did talk about idealized forms, so maybe it was just the proportions of the room that felt so pleasing to me.

Jane turned to Kitty and grinned. "See? Didn't I tell you that Liza would be fine in the smaller room?"

Kitty pursed her lips disapprovingly. "I still think you two should trade—"

"But I want *my* room!"

"And I love this one," I insisted. "Really. Thank you."

Kitty surveyed us both for another second, then seemed to mentally throw up her hands. "Fine, then. You'll be sharing the bathroom across the hall from Liza's room"—she pointed—"and I've left you each a set of house keys on your dressers, so you can come and go as you please. But if you wouldn't mind staying in tonight, we'll have dinner here. I have some chicken marinating, and I baked your favorite cookies, Jane."

"Ooh, bribery," Jane exclaimed happily. She turned to me confidingly. "Kitty's an amazing cook when she takes the time for it, so I'm sure we're in for a treat."

Her aunt smiled. "Flattery will get you nowhere. And

don't think I'm cooking for you every night, young lady. Wasn't there a mention of both of you getting jobs?"

"Of course! But give us at least a week to get settled and have a *shade* of vacation," Jane wheedled. "Two busy, burned-out graduate students deserve that much."

Kitty laughed. "No doubt. Also, I plan to keep up the Sunday-evening tradition of family dinner, so make sure you're around for that. Both of you," she added, smiling at me. "Liza's family this summer. But otherwise, you're on your own. Don't fill the refrigerator with too much junk, Jane, and try not to burn down the kitchen."

I laughed. "Don't worry, Ms. Bryant," I assured her. "I do most of the cooking for us at home, and I'll be happy to do so here, too. Save us all from Jane."

"Then for that, you have my gratitude again," she said with a twinkle. "Though it might take more than culinary intervention to truly save us from my niece—"

"Hey!" Jane protested.

"But for heaven's sake," Kitty continued, unmoved, "don't make me feel my age! Call me Kitty; everyone else does."

After some parting words, she was gone, and soon Jane departed as well. I shut the door and sank down on the lace-topped four-poster, put my head in my hands, and started shaking. This house was freaking me right out, and I desperately needed some time to talk myself back into rationality. There were too many damned coincidences. But get real, I told myself firmly after a few minutes. The house I was to randomly spend the summer in was the very one I had lived in all those years ago? As I had told myself before, I was simply projecting, trying to fit my dreams into a recognizable context. And right now, the only context I had was this house. Otherwise . . .

No, it didn't even bear thinking about.

Fortunately, shortly thereafter Jane knocked briefly on my door, then bounded in without invitation as usual, beaming excitement. She had, I noticed, changed out of her warm and functional ferry clothes into something far more kicky, and looked every ounce the picture of green-haired, gamine charm. She was towing my suitcases with her.

"Jane, you didn't have to lug those up for me," I began, but she just laughed.

"I didn't. I found all our stuff in the upstairs hallway. Clearly Kitty's mysterious houseboy at work."

"Jane!"

"What? More power to her. I hope he's young and hunky." I raised an eyebrow. "For her sake," she added, sounding offended.

"Of course." I ran a hand over my hair, which I had pulled from its ponytail on the way off the ferry, but which was still a tangled mess. "Damn, I must look a wreck."

"A bit," she admitted. "Wear that green thing and your brown trousers; that brings out the color of your eyes."

"Yes, ma'am," I said, saluting. My eyes were the exact color she had described: green and brown combined. And she had, uncannily, suggested the very combination I had been thinking of myself.

If I had ever had any modesty (debatable, according to my family), nine months of living with Jane had cured me. I shucked jeans, boots, and sweater, and—clad only in my underwear—dug the requested outfit out of my suitcase.

"I'd forgotten how much I love this house!" Jane now declared, bouncing on my bed. "And isn't Aunt Kitty divine? This summer is going to be *fun*!"

It was so nearly my thought from earlier that I laughed. Besides, as I had always maintained, there was no one like Jane for a good bout of distraction. "Amen. I adore your aunt, and this house is fabulous!"

That certainly wasn't a lie—despite my ambiguous feelings toward it.

"When's dinner?" I added, feeling my stomach rumble.

Jane consulted her watch. "Well, it is six fifteen now. We should probably go down, see what we can do to help. Or at least, snag a drink. Aunt Kitty always has the most amazing wine."

"That sounds like a plan." I dressed hastily, then grabbed one of the pale green towels and padded across to the bathroom to throw some water over my face. I ran wet fingers through my mess of hair and grimaced at my reflection in the mirror.

"You look gorgeous, of course," Jane called from across the hall, knowing my routine almost better than I did. "What about shoes?"

I returned to my room, adding some strappy bronze sandals to complete the ensemble. The water had managed to tame my hair, and Jane was right about the floaty, emerald chiffon top bringing out the green in my eyes. For an instant, we examined our reflections in the cheval mirror, and I felt a certain satisfaction at the sight. Jane had an unwitting tendency to upstage the world, but tonight I more than held my own. She might be thinner and with slightly more unusual features that added a piquancy to her look, but I was taller, and my boobs were bigger. That counted for something—or so I'd been told.

Jane grimaced.

"What?" I said.

"My hair clashes with your shirt," she replied. And, laughing, we clattered downstairs.

Or, at least, such was the plan. But I had forgotten my weird reaction to the stairs. No sooner had I started down than:

Help me, I heard someone pleading in my mind, voice high and tight with fear. *Help me!*

And I was gripped by such a strong wave of guilt and panic that I lost my footing and almost tumbled straight down.

"Jesus!" Jane exclaimed. "Are you okay?"

I gathered myself with an effort. "Yeah, fine. It's just . . ." I was still slightly breathless. "Apparently spiky heels and wooden stairs are a lethal combination."

Jane shot me a dubious look, but I moved quickly past the landing and made it the rest of the way down the stairs without incident. After that, the kitchen was a welcome refuge—and delectable smells were indeed issuing forth.

Kitty, wrapped in an apron splashed with vibrant colors, was bustling around, chopping and sautéing.

"Smells fabulous!" Jane exclaimed. "See? I told you," she added, sotto voce to me.

"And don't you two look lovely," Kitty said, looking up from her cutting board with a smile.

"Can we help with anything?" I asked.

Jane scowled at me. "Great. Liza just stole my line."

I smirked at her. "First of many, babe."

Kitty laughed. "You found your bags all right, I take it?"

"Yes, thanks," I said.

"Tell the houseboy we owe him," Jane added, grinning.

"The houseboy?" Kitty laughed. "I think Luke would be even less delighted by that than my 'extra hands' comment."

"Luke?" Jane exclaimed. "You don't mean—"

"Speak of the devil," a deep voice said from the doorway. "Hello, coz."

CHAPTER 4

To my surprise, Jane was scowling ferociously. "Irish," she spat. "What are *you* doing here?"

"Spending the summer with my dear godmother, same as you."

"Kitty, did you—?" Jane began, affronted.

Kitty raised an eyebrow. "He asked, and I agreed. After all, it *is* my house. And I love my godson every bit as much as my niece."

"Don't know why," I thought I heard Jane mutter.

As for me, I was barely aware of the exchange; my attention was firmly fixed on the young man slouched in the doorway. He was . . . Well, not traditionally handsome. His features were too sharp, and he was looking about as unhappy with his current situation as Jane, which gave him a sullen cast. But he was tall and lean, his hair was thick and dark, and his eyes were a piercing light grey. And the sight of him just about took my knees out from under me. Again.

Damn it! This was getting ridiculous.

I snuck a hand behind my back and gripped the counter

to keep myself upright on my spiky bronze shoes. But he seemed oblivious, still leaning with a too-studied casualness against the wall, his gaze fixed resolutely on Kitty and Jane.

I sensed a tightness around his mouth, a kind of storm brewing behind those startlingly light eyes, but I had no idea of its cause. Just that there were uneasy waters here I couldn't begin to fathom.

The silence stretched out for a moment; then he seemed to gather himself with an effort and refocus his attention. Onto me. But I still had the feeling he wasn't quite seeing me; his face was tight and shuttered. With a studied deliberation, he detached himself from the wall and stepped toward me.

"I don't believe we've been introduced yet," he said. His voice held the faintest hint of an accent I couldn't identify. "I'm Kitty's godson, Lucian Theriault." He extended a hand.

I had the sudden feeling that if I gripped it, the current that passed between us might well shoot me straight across the room, eyebrows singed and hair smoking. Never one to back down from a challenge, however, I steeled my expression to make sure none of my absurdly overblown reaction to him was visible, and advanced.

I shook the proffered hand and did indeed feel a jolt that rocked my whole body. But because I had anticipated it, none of my reaction showed. Instead, I just said, with what I thought was commendable poise, "Liza Donovan. Nice to meet you."

"Are you going to be here *all* summer?" Jane added.

To my intense relief, Lucian's silver eyes shifted off me and focused on Jane instead.

"Jane!" Kitty said reprovingly. "I know the two of you

have had your differences, but you're both adults, and you can behave civilly for a summer. Now, say hello to each other properly."

A moment of silence. Then, "Hello, Irish," Jane said tautly. "Thanks for playing houseboy."

Something that wasn't quite a smile touched the corners of Lucian's mouth. "Hello yourself, Moonbeam. Who are you trying to channel this time, Poison Ivy?"

Kitty threw up her hands. "Well, on your heads be it. If you want to make each other miserable all summer, go right ahead. But in my opinion, you should have started dating years ago, and saved everyone the bother."

"Kitty!" both of them exclaimed hotly, horror and disbelief mingled equally in their voices. Then Lucian started to laugh, Jane joined in, and the tension swelling in the room seemed to burst.

Still, I felt a kind of depression at Kitty's words. That level of mutual antipathy had to spring from something, and sexual tension seemed as good a cause as any. But it figured that the first guy I'd seen who had literally rocked my world belonged to Jane.

I steeled myself further to the charms of Lucian Theriault, and accepted one of the glasses of wine that Kitty handed around.

As Jane had promised, the wine was fabulously good—clearly, more expensive by orders of magnitude than the cheap plonk Jane and I usually sprang for—and it did seem to mellow my friend out a bit.

"So," she said to Lucian as we all clustered around the table watching Kitty work—because she refused to accept help from any of us, despite repeated offers—"what *are* you doing here? Last I heard, you were looking for work in Montreal."

Lucian shrugged one shoulder with affected casualness. "Oh, you know me," he said.

"That I do. Lucian," Jane confided to me, "is a professional dilettante."

"Takes one to know one," he replied in a lazy drawl.

"Hey!" Jane protested. "I'm not a dilettante!"

I actually laughed. "How many different majors have you declared this year alone?"

To my amazement, Lucian shot me a conspiratorial glance that might have dropped me again had I not already been sitting. It wasn't a smile—not quite—but it was a half quirk more than I had seen out of him before, and his light eyes were dancing with amusement. I found myself wondering what he would look like if he *truly* smiled . . . then fiercely crushed the thought.

Jane's, I reminded myself.

"Three," she admitted sheepishly, then laughed. "Okay, you both win that point." I swear, Lucian winked at me—but the drop of eyelid was so slight, I might have imagined it. Jane turned back to Lucian. "So, you were saying, fellow dilettante?"

He shrugged again. "I found a job or two, hated them, and quit. So I thought I'd spend the summer bumming around the island of my birth. What about you? Why have you decided to subject your friend to your crazy family for the summer?"

"You're not my family," she replied promptly.

"Thank god," he responded, equally fervently.

I glanced over at Kitty, who was shaking her head fondly at the exchange, but I began to wonder if her instincts were right. Granted, she knew Jane better than I did, but this seemed more like rivalry than repressed lust. I'd have to ask Jane later.

"Hell, Liza's the reason we're here," Jane replied, and I suddenly froze. I don't know why I didn't want Lucian to know of my true reasons for coming. Maybe it was that somewhat cynical look in his eyes, or the crack he had made earlier about channeling. Lucian might be a dilettante, but he was clearly a sophisticate—and just as clearly contemptuous of Jane's New Age dabbling. I had almost busted up laughing at the Moonbeam comment—damn, it was going to be hard not to call her that myself—and now *my* odd delusions were about to be revealed.

Everyone was looking at me: Jane proudly, Kitty knowingly, and Lucian with that cool reserve back in his enigmatic silver eyes.

"Yes, Jane mentioned you'd been having dreams about Nantucket and whaling," Kitty said, joining us at the table while things simmered delectably behind her. "For how long?"

"Most of my life, really," I admitted, feeling profoundly stupid.

"And what do you think of the island?" Kitty continued. "Is it anything like your expectations?"

I looked around the table for a minute—two pairs of dark eyes, open and eager, and one pair of light, completely shut down—then shrugged noncommittally. "Yes and no," I said.

"Meaning?" Kitty persisted.

I hesitated.

"Don't force her to talk about it if she doesn't want to," Lucian interjected. His eyes were still deeply shuttered; no doubt he was as embarrassed as I by the entire topic.

"But she came here for answers," Kitty said mildly. "And how can she find them if we don't discuss it?" She appealed to me. "You don't mind, do you, Liza?"

"No," I lied. "It's just . . . I don't know how to respond."

"Nonsense," Jane said. "I've been watching you. It's like you recognize some things, then draw a complete blank on others. The town was a mystery to you, but you know this house. And what about that moment you nearly fell down the stairs? If that isn't significant, I don't know what is."

"I tripped!" I protested, probably too firmly.

"Maybe you are sensitive to ghosts," Kitty said.

That was going way too far. "Ghosts?" I yelped.

Lucian glanced my way with a look of sympathy in his eyes.

"Look," I insisted. "I don't believe any of this! Really. It's just dreams. I'm going to the whaling museum tomorrow to find out just how wrong I was, and then I'll settle down and get a sensible job for the summer, and that will be that!"

"So what about all that stuff you were spouting on the ferry?" Jane persisted.

"What stuff?"

"That thing about going to the sea in ships and great waters; I don't know what it was."

The answer came from an unexpected quarter. " 'They that go down to the sea in ships, that do business in great waters.' " Lucian's deep voice rolled through the room, with almost a growl behind it. For an instant, my fingers tingled and the room wavered around me, and I was in another place, another time—another voice reciting those same words.

" 'These see the works of the Lord, and his wonders in the deep,' " I continued, half-tranced.

"That's it!" Jane exclaimed. "But what is it?"

"What, were you raised in a barn?" Lucian countered. "It's the Bible, Moonbeam. You know, that thing people read in churches?"

"I know what the Bible is," she snapped. "I'm just amazed that *you* do. Being such a confirmed heathen and all."

He cocked an eyebrow. "Ever heard of the Bible as literature?"

She stuck out her tongue.

"Hey, unpierced," he countered. "When did you get so conservative?"

"Kids," Kitty chided, "behave."

"So how did Liza know it?" Jane continued, undeterred.

Lucian raised an eyebrow.

"I don't know," I said, feeling ambushed. "I don't even know what comes next!" Only I did. Half-hypnotized, I felt the words pouring out of me:

" 'For he commandeth, and raiseth the stormy wind, which lifteth up the waves thereof. They mount up to heaven, they go down again to the depths: their soul is melted because of trouble. They reel to and fro, and stagger like a drunken man, and are at their wit's end. Then they cry unto the Lord in their trouble, and he bringeth them out of their distresses. He maketh the storm a calm, so that the waves thereof are still. Then they are glad because they be quiet; so he bringeth them unto their desired haven.' "

There was a long moment of silence when I finished.

"See?" Jane said at last. "Now, where did that come from?"

"I have no idea," I confessed. "I don't even know what part of the Bible it is from!"

"Psalm one oh seven," Kitty said softly, and we all turned to stare at her. She rose to stir the soup. "Verses twenty-three to thirty." And when she found us still staring: "This is an old Quaker town, my loves. The Nantucket whalemen—even those who strayed as far as Obadiah—knew their Bible. The whole town's history is steeped in it."

She turned to me then. "And speaking of history, I daresay Jane did no more than hint at the history of this house?"

"And very enigmatic she was, too."

"Well, then, dinner's almost ready. Let's get the table set, and then I'll tell you all about Obadiah's tragedy while we eat. Here, I'll put out the mats. Can someone—?"

"I'll do it," I said, going to the cupboard and getting down the dishes. I was in the midst of laying out the silverware when I noticed that everyone was staring at me. Kitty was smiling slightly, Jane was looking triumphant, and Lucian seemed slightly freaked. "What now?"

"Amazing how she knew where everything was without being told, isn't it?" Jane said.

A sudden chill washed over me, and I dropped the rest of the silverware onto the table with a clatter. Kitty scooped it up.

"Here, I'll finish that for you," she said.

"Is this some sort of weird setup?" Lucian accused her, angrily.

Kitty seemed genuinely baffled. "I'll admit," she confessed as she quietly finished my job, "that Jane had told me Liza's story before they arrived. I'm sorry if this upsets you, Liza, but I always have credited Jane's theories on the matter. I've always believed that there is more in Heaven and Earth, Horatio, and all that."

"So, what *are* Moonbeam's theories?" Lucian countered, still surly.

"Why don't we just ask Liza?" Kitty replied instead. Everyone looked at me. "What do *you* think is going on, Liza?"

I shrugged. "Half the time, I think I used to be some whaling captain. One who died when a whale rammed his ship."

"And the other half?" Lucian said dryly.

I turned to him, and met his gaze, determined not to let him intimidate me. "The other half," I responded, equally dryly, "I think I'm going insane. Fun, eh?"

If I had ever wanted to know what Lucian looked like when he let himself go, I knew now. His sudden grin was as brilliant as it was—I suspected—completely spontaneous.

"My sympathies," he said, sounding as if he genuinely meant it.

"Soup's on," said Kitty. "Luke, why don't you sit across from me? Then Jane and Liza can sit to either side. And who wants more wine?"

Over a truly fantastic crab bisque (which Kitty claimed was an old local recipe), the subject—of course—came up again.

"So," Kitty said, "what intrigues me is how specific these dreams of yours are, Liza. You say your ship was sunk by a whale?"

"Yeah," I confirmed. Buoyed by wine and haute cuisine, I felt less self-conscious about the whole thing—maybe because at least two people at the table were taking me seriously. However, the more the discussion continued, the spikier Lucian became, as if he couldn't believe he was sharing a table with such a bunch of freaks. But given that he was sitting to my right, I didn't have to pay attention to him. I just canted my body away and focused on Jane across from me, and Kitty to my left.

"The dream starts on board a ship, when the lookout sights a whale. Three boats go out after it, and it crushes them all. Then it comes after the ship, and sinks that as well. And as it happens, I feel this tremendous guilt, as if this is all my fault."

"Three boats, do you say?" Kitty sipped at her soup thoughtfully. "The whale crushed all three boats? Are you sure?"

Suddenly, I wasn't. "I think so," I said, "but maybe not. Why?"

"For a moment, I thought we might have your captain. Have you ever heard of the *Essex*?"

I stared at her blankly.

"The whaleship *Essex*," Lucian supplied. "Sunk by a whale. The true life story on which *Moby-Dick* was based."

I flushed slightly. "I've never read *Moby-Dick*," I confessed.

"And you an English major?" Kitty chided. "You must read

it; it is a remarkable book. But, regardless . . . Well done, Lucian! You've picked up some local history, after all. Lucian was born on Nantucket," she told me, "and I've tried in vain to get both him and Jane interested in the local history, which is both rich and fascinating. For example, do you know that the guy who started Folgers coffee was a native Nantucketer? As was Benjamin Franklin's mother?"

"Kitty," Jane protested with a groan.

"Sorry, pet subject. But I'm delighted to see that at least one of you has absorbed a few things. And maybe I can get you interested, Liza; I'll lend you my copy of Nathaniel Philbrick's *In the Heart of the Sea.* It's a truly remarkable book. It's about both Nantucket and the whaleship *Essex,* which was Nantucket's second most infamous tale. On Thursday, August twelfth, 1819, the *Essex* sailed out under the command of Captain George Pollard, Jr. It was Pollard's first command; he was twenty-eight at the time. He had a crew of twenty-one. The *Essex* was an older ship, and small, with only three whaleboats. Almost two years later, on the morning of February twenty-third, 1821, Captain Zimri Coffin of the *Dauphin*— another Nantucket whaleship—spied a derelict craft that looked like a modified whaleboat drifting in the Pacific Ocean. The sides had been built up, and two makeshift masts had been rigged. Squatting within it were two men surrounded by human bones."

I shivered.

"Pretty gruesome, huh? The *Essex,* according to the survivors, had been sunk by an enraged sperm whale. None of the whaleboats were wrecked in the attack, and the men used them to escape when the *Essex* went down. Before they were rescued, they'd sailed something like five thousand nautical miles across the Pacific. Which, if I remember my figures correctly, is about a fifth of the way around the earth.

"The details of your dream differ in some respects from the reality of the *Essex* disaster. And Pollard survived and returned to Nantucket, where he was given command of the *Two Brothers*. But when that ship ran aground on a reef off the Hawaiian islands, he was said to be under a curse, and never commanded a ship again. Instead, he became the island's nightwatchman, and died in 1869."

So, Kitty was right; I probably wasn't Pollard, haunted by shades of the *Essex* disaster. Still, the fact that a Nantucket whaling captain really did have a ship destroyed by a whale . . . Well, how cool was that? And how scary?

"So, if that is Nantucket's second most infamous tale, then what's the first?" I couldn't help asking.

"Why, Captain Obadiah Young's murder of his wife, Lucy, of course," she said, smiling serenely.

To which Jane added, "Right there on the very steps you nearly tumbled down earlier."

CHAPTER 5

∞

Another silence met her words. Then, "Really, Kitty," Lucian exclaimed, "need you be so dramatic? And why is everyone so quick to blame Obadiah?"

"Defending your namesake?" Jane taunted.

I swear, he growled at her in response.

Kitty chuckled. "Well, at least I won't have a boring summer with you three in residence! And Lucian has a point; no one knows who killed Lucy Young. The circumstances were certainly suspicious, but Obadiah's guilt was never proved. On the morning of November sixteenth, Obadiah sailed off on his bark, the *Redemption,* on that dawn's tide, never to be seen again. Several hours later, Lucy Young was found dead on the stairway landing by the housemaid, when she arrived for her morning duties. No one knows what happened to the *Redemption,* but sailors are a suspicious lot, and the townspeople held that the loss of the ship was Obadiah's sentence from on high."

"And what about all those other souls who sailed under him?" Lucian persisted, his voice still tight and angry. "Were they guilty as well? The *Redemption* had twenty-eight men aboard her. Who was passing sentence on them?" He glared at each of us in turn, then threw up his hands in disgust. "Sorry, Kitty, but I've heard this story eighteen million times, and don't feel inclined to hear it again."

His godmother shrugged, clearly disappointed. We discussed more neutral topics throughout dinner—which was, again, excellent. If this was an indication of what we were in for every Sunday night, then this whole visit to Nantucket was looking better than ever.

There was only one odd incident toward the end of dinner. We had polished off our meals, and Lucian and Jane had fallen into a somewhat snippy reminiscence about a mutual summer spent at Kitty's house—which, unsurprisingly, consisted of them trying to one-up each other with tales of the other's embarrassments—while Kitty bustled about making coffee and laying out a plate of cookies. Satiated from the meal, and somewhat exhausted from the events of the day, I was drifting a bit. I was thinking about George Pollard Jr., whose ship was sunk by a whale, and Obadiah Young, who might or might not have murdered his wife, and how it all connected to me.

And then, before my sleepy eyes, the kitchen wavered a bit, and I saw in its place an older room, complete with hearth and iron range, and an old tub sink with an iron pump mounted upon it. Through my haze, I heard Kitty saying, "I think I'd like iced coffee instead of hot tonight. Liza, can you fetch me some ice?"

It wasn't until I came out of my trance with my head inside an empty, musty wooden box set into the wall and turned to find everyone staring at me again, that I realized how odd the request had been in the first place.

Kitty was looking subtly triumphant, Jane as confused as I was, and Lucian—no surprise—thunderously angry.

"What the hell, Kitty?" he exclaimed. "Another of your tests?"

"Yes." She seemed unabashed. "And I'm sorry, Liza, but this just proves my point."

"What point?" Lucian insisted.

"That she lived in whaling days. That hatch you have open," she added to me, "is what used to be the icebox."

I closed it again hastily, masking a surge of anger. I didn't like being forced to face this, but I had to admit it was seeming increasingly likely that there was something to face.

To add to the surreality, I suddenly had Lucian as my defender. "I cannot believe," he said to Kitty, "that I am witnessing this behavior! Since when have you made a point of humiliating guests this way?"

Humiliating? Okay, I felt minorly stupid, but calling it humiliation was going a bit too far. "Don't you think *you're* overreacting?" I shot back.

Those grey eyes swiveled back to me, shot through with a mixture of shock and anger. I straightened my spine, noting idly that my eyes were exactly level with his own, and was startled to see the sudden burgeoning of what might have been respect in that silver gaze. Followed by a brief flash of . . .

Dear God! Was *that* what raw desire looked like?

But it couldn't be, because it was gone the moment I noticed it, shut up behind a once more inscrutably light gaze. Except that my insides had turned to liquid, and I was almost panting. From a look!

"Fine," he said tightly. "If that's the way you want it. If you all want to revel in your lunatic theories, go right ahead. Just don't include me." And he stomped out of the kitchen—though I did notice that he paused long enough to scoop up half a dozen cookies on the way.

"I'm sorry about all that," Kitty said when he was gone. "He's not normally this testy, but he just turned twenty-eight, and I think his lack of direction is starting to bother him. He's been working a lot of stuff out this summer, and I do hope he's able to reach some sort of peace at the end of it. He's such a smart boy that I hate to see him so directionless."

"Well, he certainly has snarky down to an art form," Jane opined.

And devastating, I thought, though I didn't say it.

"I hope you don't mind decaf?" Kitty asked, changing the subject. "I never drink high-test at night."

"Fine by me," I said, accepting a cup. I snagged a few cookies from the plate Jane passed me. "So, what's this about Obadiah?" I asked, to avoid the topic of Lucian for a while. Just then, a murderous whaling captain seemed the lesser of two evils.

Kitty beamed; clearly, she relished the history of her house. The narrative took a while, but the salient facts were these:

Obadiah Young was born to one of the old Nantucket whaling families—one of the founding families of the community. Coffin, Macy, Folger, Starbuck, Young: these were the equivalent of the Nantucket ruling class. They owned the ships and the warehouses and the suppliers, and received the lion's share of the profits. Their younger sons trained to rule the empire by sailing the ships—first as boatsteerers, then as mates, and finally as captains.

Obadiah Young was born into this Quaker bastion, and was raised to the sea. But unlike them, when his fortunes rose, he married not a local girl, but a beautiful young socialite from off-island: Lucy Dalton. Which, somehow, I had known earlier.

Lucy came to live on Nantucket, but she never settled into the highly insular Nantucket society.

With the men frequently out to sea on voyages that lasted an average of three years, women ran the industries and kept the island economy flourishing. But Lucy was not raised to work. She was raised to be beautiful and frivolous, and in conservative, Quaker Nantucket, she stood out like a parrot among rooks.

She had been seduced by Obadiah's position and power, and now she was trapped. He built her a grand mansion, but that made no difference. She even brought a cousin to the island as her companion, a cousin who was rumored to be on the verge of an engagement to Obadiah's second mate, Matthew Phinney, when Lucy died and the *Redemption* was lost. The cousin was left to raise Lucy and Obadiah's son, Owen—a child of three at the time of his mother's demise.

It was rumored that Lucy had died a grim, embittered woman. Years of struggling to conceive a child before Owen's birth had driven a wedge between her and the husband who had once adored her. Even more insidious rumors held that Lucy became addicted to opium, a common component of a ship captain's chest in those days.

Still, Nantucket was shocked when Lucy Young was found dead on the landing, her back broken and her head split open in her fall. The incident might have been dismissed as an accident, save for blood and hair discovered on the newel post at the head of the stairs. But forensic techniques in the 1840s were not as sophisticated as today. When the servants were questioned, no one knew anything. And besides, the only man who might have had motive in her death was gone, beyond questioning, on a voyage from which he never returned. Suspicious timing, certainly, but that was it.

So in the end, Lucy's death was ruled an accident—until the court of public opinion seized it. And in that court, Obadiah was tried and convicted.

I have to admit, this tale struck more of a chord with me than Kitty's story of the *Essex*. "What happened to the *Redemption*?" I asked, wanting to see if that ship's fate matched my dream.

"No one knows," Kitty answered. "About a year and a half into the voyage, Obadiah bespoke the *Lucinda* out of New Bedford, and was reported to have half a hold of oil, but that was the last anyone heard of him."

We lingered over coffee for a while longer, and then—as even Jane had started yawning—retreated to our rooms. It was only nine thirty, but I felt as if it were well past midnight. Still, I knew the day was not quite over—a suspicion that was confirmed when Jane knocked briefly again, then breezed in.

I had already washed up for bed and changed into my pajamas and was not surprised to see her in a similar state. "Just like a slumber party," she said, flopping down on the foot of my bed with a grin.

I smiled, settling cross-legged against my pillows. "You were right about the cooking."

"Yeah, wasn't I? But I'm sorry about Lucian. What a brat! I had no idea he'd be here, wrecking our summer."

"Well, he'll only wreck our summer if we let him," I told her stoutly.

"Amen!" she agreed. "Death to Lucian."

"Well, I wouldn't go that far. He must have a few redeeming qualities—"

"What, you mean because of the Secret Weapon? Anyone who can smile like that can't be all bad? Trust me, he knows the power of that grin only too well. And has used it to great effect, on multiple occasions."

"Oh, really?"

"Okay, I admit, there was a time when I had a bit of a crush him. But for heaven's sake, I was twelve at the time, and he was a lofty sixteen, so give me a little credit! No, I've just heard the rumors. Quite the slayer of hearts, our Lucian. Any number of girls—both here and in Montreal—left in the lurch. Commitment and Lucian don't exactly see eye to eye. So don't let yourself get sucked in by him—despite the pretty smile."

"So, I take it Kitty's suspicions about you and Lucian are unfounded?"

"Entirely!"

I felt a profound relief at her words—though God only knows why, given that Lucian had not exactly left the best impression on me this evening. "Why do you call him 'Irish'?" I asked instead.

She grinned. "If there's one thing Lucian resents Kitty

for, it's saddling him with his middle name. It's Obadiah," she said with a smirk.

"Obadiah?"

I think she mistook my shock for horror and nodded smugly. "Dreadful, isn't it?"

"But why did Kitty pick *that*?"

"Well, you see, Lucian was actually born in this house. His mother was French Canadian, here for some kind of summer position, and she got herself into a bit of trouble. Her family was positively Victorian about such things, and disowned her when she wanted to keep the baby. So, there she was, penniless and pregnant. Kitty took her in. The two became great friends, and Kitty became Lucian's godmother when he was born—in the middle of a huge storm, I might add, which was why they couldn't get his mom to a hospital in time.

"Which," she added, somewhat maliciously, "probably explains why Lucian is deathly afraid of storms, though he'll deny it strenuously every time. Anyway, in gratitude to Kitty for getting her through it all, Lucian's mom allowed her to pick the child's middle name. I bet she regrets that now! So he became Lucian for his great-grandfather, and Obadiah for the Nantucket house he was born in, poor beast. He lived here for about five years, until his mom moved back to Montreal. When she married Paul Theriault, he adopted Lucian, and Lucian took his last name."

"But still . . . why 'Irish'?"

"Well, since he hates the name, I always try to remind him of it without actually saying it. So Lucian O. Theriault is kind of like Lucian O'Theriault, you know?

"Hence Irish?"

"Hence Irish," she agreed. "He retaliated with the Moonbeam thing several years back . . . which, of course, is not even remotely accurate!"

"Of course not," I declared loyally, masking a grin.

"So, there you have it. The despicable Lucian in a nutshell. Stay well clear of him. I saw you go a bit googly when you first saw him, but there are plenty of worthier fish in the sea, trust me."

"No worries," I said. "He did seem a bit of a brat, and Angry Young Man has never been one of my triggers." Which was entirely true, though Lucian seemed to get around that a bit. But never mind. I was woman enough not to go falling for every hot young thing I saw, no matter how much he sent my libido into turbodrive.

After Jane left, I found myself thinking about it all: Lucian, Obadiah, Pollard, Nantucket. Somehow, there was some obscure connection there, tying one to the other. And tying them all to me. But what? Or was it just my imagination?

I tried to read, but my mind kept spinning. This house, too—there was something about it. . . . The silverware thing had been compelling, but it was scant evidence of anything supernatural. Like the layout of the house, I must just have made a damned good first guess. Otherwise . . . Coincidence again. Coincidence, too, my finding the old ice chest. Just a fluke.

After a while, I turned out the light and fell into an uneasy slumber, and from there into another dream. Not the old familiar dream, either. A new one, just as startlingly visceral, and surprising. . . .

It is night, and moonlight is pouring in through my windows—the windows of the very room I now occupy. Around me, the house lies silent and still, but that is deceptive, for I know that he waits. And that he may come to me, tonight.

I shiver, a strange mix of apprehension and desire, and clutch the covers more tightly around me. I have wanted him for so long now that it muddles my mind, sings through my senses, obliterating all else, save fear. I am too ignorant, in all the ways of flesh and the world. . . .

I hear the creak of his steps in the hall, then a soft tap on the door.

Can this really be happening? I hesitate in an ecstasy of indecision, and for a moment I wonder if he has retreated in the face of my apparent indifference. Then I rise swiftly from my bed, clutching a shawl around me as much for warmth as for protection. I draw the door open, terrified that he will be gone—even more terrified that he will not—but he has only raised his hand to knock again. He looms: a dark, black bulk in my doorway.

I step back, and he enters. He draws me into his arms. I lay my head against his chest, so as not to have to look up into his face, and I know he feels my trembling.

"Are you cold?" he asks, his voice a deep, gravelly rumble beneath my ear. The intimacy of it makes me shiver anew.

"No," I say.

"Scared, then," he guesses.

"Yes . . . No . . . I don't know," I stammer.

But his body feels so right against mine, how could this

possibly be wrong? Emboldened, I turn him into the moon-light, gazing up into a lean, bearded face that could have been harsh had its angles not been softened and transformed by pas-sion.

The part of me that is still Liza gasps. I don't know who I had expected to see, in this atmosphere drenched with sex and longing. Lucian, perhaps. But in comparison to this man, Lu-cian is a mere squall against a full-blown gale. Dark, dark, dark is my impression. Hair a deep, unrelenting black, shot through with the faintest trace of silver. Eyes like two deep holes in the night, dark as obsidian. Dark as sin. And yes, there is sin here somewhere, I know that. Sin and love and fierce desire.

I gaze up into the sleepy, heavy-lidded eyes, thick with passion, then survey the generous, sensuous mouth that no amount of beard can disguise. The scarred, hard-planed body missing one small finger—legacy of a tangled line and a whale.

"Obadiah," I whisper.

"My love," he whispers back. "Bride of my heart."

I feel a wave of panic, but already his hands are moving over me, warming me, dulling the terror, and I burrow closer, feeling the heat flaring from his skin. I breathe in the scent of him, give in to the desire to let my hands go exploring in turn. He is leaner and harder than I expected, under his dress-ing gown. This is a whaleman's body, spare and hard.

But his hands . . . his rough, callused hands are gentle, as is his voice. "Do you know how many times I have dreamt of this? Of touching you, feeling you?"

I wonder if it is as many times as I have pictured it myself, in my naïve, dreaming mind. But the hard thrust of him against me lets me know how wrong my imaginings have been.

"I would almost believe this was still a dream," he continues, "and I still aboard the *Redemption*." Then, gripping me tighter, "Please, convince me that this is no dream!"

I am paralyzed in the face of his desire . . . until he leans in and kisses me breathless. His mouth plunders mine, and I have never imagined kisses could be like this: so bold, so daring.

He leads me to the bed and unwraps my shawl. I shiver again.

"I know this is your first time," he says. "I'll be gentle, I promise."

The words scare me. He is so large, so hard. Is there ever a time when it is not gentle, this act?

"You have no reason to be scared," he promises, but I hear the hollowness in his voice. For some reason, he is scared, too, and this comforts me. I let him slowly ease my nightgown off, for an instant uncaring of the cold. His warm hands wander over bare skin, leaving a trail of fire behind, warming me despite the chill air.

I gasp as he touches a breast, grazes the nipple, which tightens into a hard, needy peak.

"I want to see you, all of you. Can you light the candle?"

Is this customary? I don't know. But I light the candle with shaking fingers, because suddenly I want to see him, too.

His face—all hard planes and angles—looks even more forbidding in the trembling light of the lone flame. Even as I watch, he drops his dressing gown to the floor. I can barely breathe. I have never seen a man naked before. His body is whipcord lean, dusted with black hair, and his organ juts out of a nest of darkness like the prow of a ship, hard and angry with need.

I swallow audibly.

But at the same time, a treacherous warmth is filling me, my body throbbing in time to the rapid beating of my heart, of his. I am filled with an inchoate longing I can't explain. He eases me back onto the bed, he runs his hands all over my body—taunting, teasing. I part my legs instinctively as his hand moves lower, amazed at the wanton woman who has overtaken me, but uncaring, because it feels so good. A gift from God. And when his fingers delve into my molten core, I find myself moaning aloud and writhing against his touch, wanting more, faster, harder. . . .

"Shh, quiet, sweetheart," he says, and for a moment I remember who and where we are. I start to stiffen, but then he touches me again, just *there,* and it is so exquisitely sweet that I bite back another cry. Only this time he does not stop, but keeps touching and stroking me, until a pressure builds so high that I think I must explode, and he is sweating and trembling above me. And then something does explode, like fireworks inside my head, and I'm shaking all over with the glory of it, wanting it again, wanting more. . . .

"Oh," I say, and, "Oh," again, at a loss for words. How can the Bible say this is wicked? It is a piece of heaven, here in the dark with us.

His face, hanging above me, is awed, transformed. "What?" I ask, suddenly self-conscious.

"Dear God, I never knew it could be like that. You are so wet, so willing. So responsive. . . ."

"Then is it over?" I ask, almost disappointed.

He rumbles a laugh. "Do you wish it to be over? Or would you have more?"

"More, please," I find myself begging, and his harsh face softens in a smile. His love washes over me, like a warm summer tide, and I feel myself glowing with happiness. It is good, it is right. God has not struck us down.

"Then, sweetheart, there shall be more. Do you think you are ready to take me inside?"

I glance down between us. He is right; it is not over. And if anything, he looks even larger, his organ almost purple and glistening with moisture at the tip. It looks so fierce. . . .

"Touch me, if you want," he says. "Only . . . gently, if you don't want this to be over too quickly."

Tentatively, I reach out. I expected this flesh to be cold and hard, but I am astonished by how warm and sleek it feels, like velvet over iron. I stroke it once, and again, before he groans softly and stops me.

"Later. For now, I need to be inside you. Will you let me be inside you?"

I nod, not knowing what else to say, and he moves on top of me, poised for the thrust. I feel the head of him probing me where his fingers had been before, and I feel myself tense— whether in fear or anticipation, I can no longer tell. Then his kiss smothers my cry as he plunges deep. And there is a brief pain, and then, the pleasure mounts again. He seems to sense, what I need. When to move with a languorous slowness, and when to imbue his motions with a greater urgency. An unbearable pressure is building inside me—stronger, deeper than before, reaching down to the depths of my womb—and . . .

I wake, coming as strongly as I ever have in my life.

For a few baffled moments, I lay there in my bed, sweating and throbbing. I didn't know quite where I was—especially since the dream-room seemed to mirror reality. Windows, door, bed, all were in the same place—save that there was no four-poster in that room of yore. Or room of fantasy— whichever it had been.

No, I was just in Kitty Bryant's Nantucket house—a place that once belonged to the murderous captain, Obadiah Young, of whom I might just have dreamed. With Jane next door and Kitty down the hall, and Lucian who knew where.

My treacherous body still throbbed. As if that orgasm hadn't been enough, damn it!

I tried to ignore it for a while, concentrating on the less heated moments of the dream. What the hell had it been about? As near as I could tell, I had just seen Obadiah's wed- ding night—but why from Lucy's perspective? My dreams up until now had been a captain's dreams, not those of a stay-at- home wife.

Still, if that had been Obadiah and Lucy—and not just the fevered imaginings of a Lucian-inspired brain—then they cer- tainly hadn't started their marriage estranged. There had been heat and passion there aplenty. Heat and passion that still seemed to coil through the air, like smoke from a suddenly extinguished candle.

This was neither my house nor my bed, but the night was tight and dark around me, wrapping me in a quiet shroud of anonymity. And I was no stranger to silent self-gratification in the dark, though I had also never wanted—or needed—it quite so badly before. Which scared and aroused me further.

Restlessly pushing off my pajama bottoms—the bed was getting too hot, anyway—I used my fingers to imitate the touch I remembered from the dream until I came again, hard. And if it was Lucian's face I saw as my physical release flooded over me, that was a secret between me and the warm, deep darkness.

At last, exhausted, I drifted back into sleep, and again into dream. Where I could almost hear the wind whistling through my hair, the creak of the boat's timbers beneath my feet. And taste the fear and excitement combined, welling up at the back of my throat with the lookout's cry. . . .

CHAPTER 6

T here blows, blows!"

"Where away?" Captain Taylor cries. He is my first captain, and this my maiden voyage, but his ship, the *Wampanoag,* is not unknown to me. She is a small craft, shipping only three whaleboats, but lithe and fleet on the sea. It was aboard her decks, at dockside, that I learned the ways of a ship; it was her lines that cradled me when I first scrambled up a ratline and into the rigging.

Barzillai Taylor has known me since I was a lad. And, when the choosing came, he picked me for his very own boat—for, in those days, the captains still headed their own boats, in the main.

And so, at sixteen, here I am: a young man upon the sea, about to encounter his very first whale. For it is this cry that will seal my doom or prove my worth.

I will never forget the feeling that arises at the lookout's call: a fierce, sharp excitement, undercut with the gnawing bite of fear. Will I be worthy? Will my arm cast strong and true? Or will I shame Captain Taylor for his choice?

There is little time to worry as I bark the orders to ready our boat. Then, easing off my shoes—for any loud noises on the surface of the water can gally the whales—I leap into the boat beside Captain Taylor, and together we lower it off the davits, dropping it gently into the sea while the men scramble down the lines after, settling into their positions as silently as possible.

I have heard of chases in inclement winds and tossing waves, but God is smiling on us today, for it is propitious weather for a whale hunt. The sun is shining from a cloudless sky and the playful breeze has put only a mild chop on the sea. We five seamen, in silent concert, extend our oars, engage the blades with the water, and pull. In a low voice, Captain Taylor gives us the count until we can hold our own rhythm, stroking in silent unison, fleeting the whaleboat toward our quarry.

"Sounded!" comes the cry from the ship, where only cook, cooper, and cabin boy remain, and I feel disappointment lance through me, as sharp and painful as my irons were to have been to the whale. My first time out, and we have lost the beast already?

But no; the captain and the cooper are conferring, for the creatures are reliable in one thing, at least. When they rise for breath, if you count the spouts, you can estimate how long they may be down. And this time, it is a bit over a quarter of an hour that our captain guesses.

So, under his direction, we row out as smoothly and silently as we can to the place where he suspects the beast will resurface, the other two boats following after us like ducklings in a line.

This is the magic of the captain, that some have and others do not: the feel for their prey. Captain Taylor has a reputation for knowing the whale's mind better than the creature itself. I wonder if he will prove himself to us again.

Eventually, at the captain's silent signal, we stop, wait. Four oars are poised above the surface of the water, while I ship my oar, stand, take up the first of my harpoons.

My trial by wave and fire.

My heart is hammering under the hot sun as, like the captain, I scan the water. The sea is a deep blue, and the planks of the whaleboat grow hot under my bare soles. The wind whisks tauntingly through my hair as I press my thigh into the rough canvas pad over the clumsy cleat.

A trail of sweat snakes down my backbone as the tension swells.

Then the leviathan rises—a vast expanse of scarred black flesh, so huge compared with our tiny boat that, for an instant, my knees go to water, and it is only the notched brace of the cleat that keeps me upright. My hand tightens convulsively around the hilt of my iron, but sweat slicks the wooden grip, and I'm not sure if I can hold it, let alone dart it as I should. My thigh is pressed so hard into the cleat that I will have bruises for days. . . .

"Fasten on!" the captain cries, even as the warm mist of the whale's breath envelops the boat. Reflexive obedience raises my arm, darts the iron—hard—into the wall of dark flesh rising beside me.

And then, after a moment of suspended animation that seems to stretch on for years, my soul snaps back into my body, and I am myself again. I watch my iron sink hard and true into the whale's side. And, flush with triumph, I grab up the second harpoon, and dart that in, too—even as I marvel at how high the whale rises, at the depth of anger in that ridiculously tiny eye. . . .

The remaining four oarsmen are backing us off hastily as the beast begins to thrash and bellow, churning the water to a white froth with the mighty sweeps of his tail. He is a big one, my first whale—eighty barrels or more. A great, scarred mountain of a creature who could crush our boat to kindling if we get too close.

He begins to dive, in a fury to escape us. Oars are hastily shipped as the line coiled in the first of the tubs begins to unscroll. There is smoke coming off the loggerhead, and Enoch Cotton is frantically throwing water over it to prevent a fire, and still the whale goes down, faster and faster. . . .

One tub, two . . . and then Captain Taylor is frantically gesturing the neighboring boats in, and the first mate lets us fasten on to his line as down and down the whale goes. Three tubs, four . . . and we are fastening on the drogues: the square planks whose sole purpose is to slow the whale's descent.

And still it dives, and if we did not have the contents of three boats to keep fast to it, we would have been forced to cut the lines and lose it forever. But the great creature eventually slows its descent at what we later reckoned to be twelve hundred fathoms below our planks, and begins to rise again. With all hands working at top speed, the line is recoiled as it goes slack. And, finally, with only one hundred fathoms between it and us, it breaks the surface.

But the beast is not done with us yet. Before the captain and I can change positions, it begins to speed away, towing our boat—the only boat still fastened to it.

The boat is pounding against the waves, which hammer against us, rattling the timbers. The sea pours over our bows, drenching me as I cling to the rope for dear life, spitting salt water out of my mouth. Enoch must be bailing with all his worth, though I cannot see him, and Captain Taylor is yelling encouragement, calling us stout lads and true. And still the whale drags us, until the *Wampanoag* is gone from our sight, and it is just us and the beast, alone on the merciless ocean.

Finally, it slows, lolling on the waves with its vast sides heaving, as we haul ourselves toward it hand over hand. I give up my place to Captain Taylor, and take his in the stern. When we are beside the beast, the captain raises his lance, the sunlight gleaming off its razor-sharp point. He drives it into the mighty creature just behind the fin, churning the blade into the whale's life until the brute goes fin-out.

I have survived; I have proved Captain Taylor's faith in me. My future shines, as bright as the sun that beams over-head.

A deep satisfaction fills me, and then . . .

I wake to sunlight flooding in through gauzy curtains and fil-tering down through the lacy canopy above my bed. When I open my eyes, there is no sense of disorientation. The vines I've been missing are present in the wallpaper, crawling up-ward in a riot of pattern and color. Then I blink, and . . .

The walls are back to the pale, icy green of Kitty's day. Of mine. I reach for my watch, which I had left on the bedside table.

Eight forty-five. Good Lord! Jane wouldn't be up for

hours, yet. In fact, I hadn't been up this early myself since high school—unless I had class. But I felt amazingly rested despite my interrupted night.

I rose and donned my robe, then peeked into the hallway, which was empty save for beams of sunlight pouring in through the window. I padded across to the bathroom, where I showered quickly, then finger-combed my hair into some semblance of order. Back in my room, I dressed casually in jeans and a teal-blue top. Then, still barefoot to avoid waking Jane, I headed downstairs—and nearly fell over again on the landing.

Help me, the voice pleaded, this time accompanied by a flash of vision: ice-blond hair, drifting in a growing pool of blood. *Help me!*

I felt a sudden surge of anger. "Stop that, Lucy," I declared, and almost listened for an answer. But the house was calm and silent around me.

I shivered slightly, then continued downstairs.

Jane had never said exactly what Kitty did for a living, but for all I knew, I could have been the only one awake. It was not to be. When I entered the kitchen, which was bright and cheerful in the morning sun, Lucian was there, lingering over a book and cup of coffee, a crumb-covered plate pushed to one side.

He looked up as I entered, and one brow crooked upward in amused surprise. Remembering last night's excesses, I wasn't quite able to mask my blush. He was every bit as devastating in daylight as he had been last night; no wonder he had haunted my dreams. Or, at least, influenced them. But I was determined to play it cool.

"Morning," I said.

His eyes filled with mischief. "That it is," he confirmed. "So, you don't share Jane's vampiric tendencies? More power to you."

I was in too good a mood to rise to his baiting, however cheerfully it might have been offered. "What, does rising early impart some sort of moral superiority?"

Signs of that deadly grin flickered in the corners of his mouth. "Well, wasn't it the descendant of our own Abiah Folger—the infamous Benjamin Franklin—who went on about making a man healthy, wealthy, and wise?"

"What, you mean 'Early to bed and early to rise?' "

"That's the beast."

"Only . . . I'm a woman, in case you hadn't noticed."

He actually chuckled. "I had kind of picked up on that. I'm fairly brilliant that way. But does that mean you get a whole different set of rules, just for you?"

"Of course," I replied complacently, pulling out the chair across from him and plopping myself down. "Comes with the equipment. Don't tell me you hadn't figured *that* one out yet?"

"Much to my detriment, yes." He flashed The Grin at me again, leaving me wondering if he wasn't one of those Jeckyll-and-Hyde types, totally different after the sun went down. He was actually approachable today, his porcupine quills retracted. "What do you want for breakfast? There's cereal, toast, eggs . . . Coffee on the counter."

But transformations went only so far. "You're not offering to get it for me, are you?"

"Hell, no! I do have some reputation to maintain as a

misanthrope, after all. Kitty just told me to tell you to help yourself to what you wanted. Toaster's on the counter, next to the breadbox. Cereal in that cupboard. Eggs and milk in the fridge, pans under the counter. But then, you probably know all that with your Spidey sense already."

"Ha, ha," I said, rising. But damned if I didn't get the coffee cups on my first try. I poured, then considered my options.

"The eggs came fresh from a farm yesterday morning," Lucian said.

That decided it. I grabbed a pan and a bowl, then milk, eggs, and butter from the fridge. "Nice attribution, by the way," I added, cracking two eggs into the bowl. The yolks were a vibrant orange, unlike the pallid specimens Jane and I bought at the store.

"What, you mean the Franklin thing?"

I nodded, adding a shot of milk to the bowl.

"Well, we academic dilettantes do manage to pick up a fair amount of trivia along the way."

"I know," I said. I'd lived with Jane for nine months. It was sometimes amazing what obscure details her magpie brain retained.

"That's right," he said, echoing my thoughts, "I forgot you lived with Moonbeam. She's even worse than me. You'd think we were related or something. How many majors did you say she'd been through this year?"

He was starting to annoy me again. "Don't you have somewhere to be?" I asked pointedly as I sorted through Kitty's spices, adding a dash of this and that to the eggs.

He laughed and leaned casually back in his chair as I dumped the mixture into a pan and began cooking. "Nope, free as a bird. One of the great advantages to the dilettante's life. What are you up to today?"

"Why do I have to be up to anything? Who's to say I'm not a dilettante, too?"

"You don't have it in you," he said lazily.

He was right, but why did it sound like such an insult coming from him?

"I do, too," I protested—then muffled a shriek as I turned to find his jawbone bare inches from my nose. He must move like a cat; I hadn't even heard the floor squeak.

Without my heels, we were no longer of a height. He topped me by about two inches. Not too humiliating for him; I was a healthy five foot eight. But he was also, damn him, so lean that he probably weighed no more than I did. He smelled of fresh soap, undercut by something more musky and male.

There went my hormones again. Swallowing down memories of last night's dream, I scowled. And demanded sharply, "What are you doing?"

He ignored me, leaning over my shoulder to sniff at the pan. "That smells amazing. What did you put in it?"

"A bit of this, a bit of that."

He took a few steps back, and I could breathe again. "Want to make some more?"

"Why?"

I swear, the man had no shame. Clutching both hands around the brim of an imaginary hat, he made Big Eyes at me, as pleading and piteous as Puss In Boots in *Shrek 2*.

I started laughing so hard, I nearly dropped my spatula. "Why? Because you're a cartoon cat?" I managed.

He abandoned the pose with an even more melting grin. "No, because I'm hungry."

"But you just ate."

"That was first breakfast. This can be—"

"—second breakfast," we chorused together, in a broad Scottish accent.

Okay, just because we liked the same movies did not mean . . .

"Don't think I'm making a habit of this," I said, getting out more eggs.

"God forbid," he responded, returning to his seat. "I'll even wash the pan," he added magnanimously.

"That's more like it. And the dishes?"

"Dishwasher," he said, nodding over to a subtly disguised front by the sink. "Why do any more work than you have to?"

"Another advantage to the dilettante's life."

"What, not working?"

"No, mooching off others."

"A much maligned art, mooching," he said with another pale cousin of The Grin. "And you still haven't told me what you're up to today."

I peered at him suspiciously over one shoulder. "Why?"

He gave an exaggerated shrug. "Curiosity won't suffice?"

"Hmph. You know what they say about curiosity," I said, tipping the new egg mixture into the pan.

"Yeah. Only . . . not a cat," he told me, in such an eminently reasonable tone of voice that I swallowed a chuckle.

"Mmm. I had kind of picked up on that," I told him. "You know, I'm fairly brilliant that way."

He gave a shout of laughter loud enough to wake the dead—or at least Jane. "Right. Round one to Liza."

"Really? I didn't know it was a competition," I lied, feeling absurdly pleased with myself.

He gave me the full-wattage grin. "You know, you're nothing like . . . ," he began musingly, then broke off, looking stricken.

"What has Jane been telling you?" I demanded.

"Nothing. Nothing, really. I just . . . made assumptions. Mistaken, as it turns out."

"You mean that I was another New Age flake like Jane?"

He flushed. "Well, something like that."

"Believe me, I hate this as much as you do. As for today . . . I'm going to the whaling museum to prove to myself that I've made this whole damned thing up!" I sized him up for a moment, then added, impulsively, "Want to come?"

Regardless of my dreams, the offer had been pure whim—but his face shut down so fast, I felt like I'd been slapped.

"I don't indulge in foolish quests," he said coldly.

I had a sudden urge to hurl the contents of my pan at him. Like I needed further reminders of his contempt for my delusion!

Fortunately, he must have correctly interpreted my expression—and saved himself from having to wear his breakfast—by adding, "Sorry, that was uncalled for. Sometimes I think Kitty is right, that I *was* born in a barn. Forgive me?"

I considered for a moment. But I still had to share a house with him for the summer, so I swallowed my angry rejoinder, and served his eggs on a plate, instead of on his shirt. He made toast, as compensation. By the time Kitty appeared, we were almost back on a companionable footing again.

"Good morning, you two," she said. "I'm glad you found everything, Liza." Then taking in the whole scene, she added, "Luke, haven't you already eaten?"

"Yup," he declared, unabashed, scooping up another forkful of eggs.

"Don't tell me," she said. "He did Big Eyes?"

I grimaced slightly, and she rolled her own. "Don't make a habit of it," she told me.

"I don't intend to."

"Good. I'm going out for a couple of hours. Luke, can you stop by the store? I've left a list on the fridge."

"Sure—"

"Well, will wonders never cease?" Jane drawled from behind us. "Maybe I wasn't so far off in my houseboy comment."

Lucian looked pointedly at his watch. "Will wonders never cease?" he parroted dryly. "Crack of nine forty-five. Is the world coming to an end?"

"Don't you wish?" Jane fired back.

Kitty shot her a look. "Don't be smug, young lady; it'll be your turn soon. I expect everyone to pull their weight around here this summer."

Lucian grinned. Jane growled, gripping the ends of the belt that cinched her robe closed.

"When does the whaling museum open?" I asked.

"Ten, I think," Kitty said.

I started to rise. "Then I'll . . ."

"No way!" Jane said, "I'm not missing this for the world! It won't take me long to get ready, so if you can just make some more of those eggs, we'll go together." She dashed back upstairs.

I sighed and turned to the fridge for more eggs. Kitty departed, then Lucian snuck away without washing the pan when my back was turned. Granted, I had been using it at the time, and at least he'd loaded our dishes into the dishwasher before he left.

And Jane must have been hurrying, because she took only forty-five minutes to get ready instead of the usual hour. By the time she finished her cold eggs and we were out the door, it was only an hour past the museum's opening time.

CHAPTER 7

The Nantucket Whaling Museum was back by the ferry terminal, but Jane insisted on walking instead of taking the car, since parking, according to Jane, was a bitch.

It wasn't a long walk, maybe ten minutes at the most. And it was a lovely day, though it was still early June and temperatures hadn't remotely hit their summer heights. It was somewhere in the sixties, with a stiff breeze, but the sun was shining brightly, the sky was a brilliant blue scattered with puffy white clouds like itinerant sheep, and the air smelled of the sea.

Somehow, I had the feeling the island was putting its best foot forward. Surely, the air could not always smell this fresh and clean. There were times, I recalled . . .

"What's with you, Liza?" Jane said, tugging on my jacket.

"Huh?"

"You went into this fugue state and nearly walked into a tree! What did you recognize?"

"Oh, God. I didn't. That is . . ." It had been a sort of recognition, but not of anything specific.

From up close, the town was not so relentlessly grey as it had seemed from the sea. True, most of the houses were cedar-shingled, the wood weathered from sea and salt to a pale silver color startlingly reminiscent of Lucian's eyes. But more buildings than I expected were fronted with clapboard in white or yellow, or completely constructed of a warm red brick that, oddly, made me think of home, though I'd grown up in a white wood house.

I couldn't say I recognized anything in particular, although Jane took us on a tortuously winding route that I couldn't have replicated on my own—and which, I suspected, was nonetheless the most direct path; these old towns never did run straight. But before long, we arrived at the Whaling Museum—an airy, modern structure that was somehow not at odds with the old-style charm of the town.

I felt incredibly nervous as we pulled open the two huge doors and entered a lobby dominated by a huge prismatic structure that sparkled and shimmered in the morning sun. And I might have assumed it was some amazing modern sculpture, had Jane—who always managed to find the informational plaques—not exclaimed, "Cool! This is the lens from the old Sankaty lighthouse: a Fresnel lens, circa 1849."

Yes, I could picture those curves and facets of glass refracting and beaming light deep out to sea.

From behind the nearby information and ticket-sales counter, a grey-haired woman hailed us cheerfully. "It's a beautiful thing, isn't it?"

"That it is," Jane declared fervently. This was what I loved most about Jane; there wasn't a deceitful bone in her body. She was genuinely interested in things, and she loved learning. It didn't matter what, or where; she was always pulling interesting facts out of even the most boring places, and always asked insightful questions.

I almost regretted keeping her away from the llama farm. God knows what we could have learned!

"Are you here to see the museum?" the woman asked.

Jane peered up at the board above the woman's head. "Hey, walking tours!" she exclaimed. "We should do one of those, Liza."

"How long are you here?" the desk clerk asked.

"All summer," Jane said, crossing to the counter. "Why? What do you suggest?"

"Well," the woman replied. She was wearing an ID card from the Nantucket Historical Association on an NHA lanyard; her name was Martha MacRae. "You've just missed our ten thirty whaling lecture." I heard an enthusiastic round of applause from a neighboring room and felt a surge of disappointment. "But we have another one at one thirty. So if you have some time to spend on the island, I'd devote today to the museum, then do the walking tour another day. We have a special treat today. We're still gearing up for our summer season, and are currently a bit understaffed, so one of our curators is doing the lectures. And he's a genuine font of knowledge. So if you buy a museum pass for today, you can go through the museum yourselves for the rest of the morning, then get some lunch, and come back for the afternoon lecture."

"Sold," Jane said, and handed over the fee for both tickets before I could stop her. She grinned as she handed me mine. "So, the grand voyage of discovery begins. Try not to pass out too dramatically, or anything."

The first sight that greeted me—at least, the first that really snagged my attention as we progressed down the long hall that led into the museum proper—was a black iron harpoon twisted into a curious pretzel shape, mounted on a dark red field.

"Cool," Jane said again, at my shoulder. "That harpoon was bent out of shape by a whale." She had, of course, been reading the card; I had just been staring at the object, which sent a strange chill through me. It seemed to symbolize all the violent uncertainty of a trade that pitted men against beast in such a primal way. Briefly, I recalled my second dream and the fearsome struggles of the great beast against my harpoon. All of which now seemed caught up in this barbed and twisted piece of metal.

"You're not going to pass out, are you?" Jane said, tugging on my jacket again. I shook my head. "Good. Then come on; let's explore this place."

A second long hall, at right angles to the first, contained historical information on Nantucket; I promised myself I'd read all of it later. A larger room beyond was calling to me. I could see a scattering of weapons on the wall, the curved prow of a boat. Leaving Jane studiously reading the information in the hall, I entered the room.

The floor was partially filled with rows of chairs from what had to have been the whaling lecture, and the few people still in the room were scattered about, peering at the various exhibits. The roof was curved into a wave, mirroring the line of what had to be a whale skeleton depending from the ceiling. And beneath it . . .

I didn't need a whaling lecture, I suddenly realized. It wasn't just that I had seen this all in my dreams; I knew it all in my blood. I always had.

For beneath the whale skeleton, raised up from the floor and tilted slightly, was a full-sized model of the six-man whaleboat that was lowered off the davits to chase the beast. The tilt enabled the viewer to see inside; it was fully loaded. And I knew it all, from clumsy cleat to loggerhead—and not just from my dream last night. The lines lay coiled in their tubs; harpoons and lances stowed at the thwarts. God, I could even name the positions: harpooner's oar, bow oar, midship oar, tub oar, after oar, and steering oar. I whispered them under my breath; each had their own wielders, their own reputation. . . .

"You seem to be boning up on your whaling," a voice said from behind me.

I turned slowly, as if hypnotized.

"I'm sorry, but I couldn't help but overhear you reciting the oar positions. And it's lovely to see people interested in the subject. If there is anything I can tell you . . . Jesus, are you all right?"

I had completed my turn and was face-to-face with one of the most gorgeous young men I had ever encountered. Okay, perhaps his features were a bit boyish, but if I had a type, he was it. He was tall and broad-shouldered, and quite simply *built*. Somewhere between six feet and six-two, he was solid and well-muscled under his jeans and sweatshirt, I could tell. As for the rest . . . Chestnut hair, which was thick and curly without being effete. Green eyes, cheekbones to die for, wide mouth built for laughter.

Really, a guy custom-built to push every button I had, and

here I was the midst of an emotional meltdown. I was staggering under the realization that there really was more in
Heaven and Earth, Horatio, and I was doing so in front of
this lovely man who was staring down at me with concern
and a hint of alarm in eyes as clear and bright as sea-washed
glass.

Life can really be the shits sometimes.

"I . . . ," I managed.

"Here, sit down," he said, guiding me to one of the now-
vacant seats. "Do you need me to call somebody?"

"No, I . . . Unless you know a priest or something," I
said, and burst into slightly hysterical laughter.

A quick look at his face confirmed that I was totally
freaking him out. Welcome to the club; I was freaking myself
out as well. I made a concerted effort to control myself, but
of course Jane chose that minute to burst into the room like
a green-haired whirlwind.

"Liza, where did you vanish to? Oh, there you are; you
had me worried. You . . ." Then she noticed the guy—
because, really, who wouldn't? And . . . "Oh, I'm sorry. I . . ."
She started backing away, but by that time I had finished turning toward her, and she got a good look at my face. "Jesus!"
she exclaimed, sinking to her knees beside me and grabbing
my hand. "What's wrong? Did you pass out?"

"No, it's just . . . It's real, Jane. It's all god-damned real!"

"What's real?"

"The dreams. All of it. I know this stuff. I shouldn't, but I
do. Look!" I pointed—somewhat wildly, I'll admit—to the
whaleboat. "Harpooner's oar, bow oar, midship oar, tub oar,
after oar, steering oar."

"Is she right?" Jane demanded.

I glanced at my hunky Samaritan, who was looking relieved to delegate his responsibility to someone who clearly knew me. Jane, of course, had noticed the one detail I had not: the Nantucket Historical Association ID card, strung on an NHA lanyard around his neck. Jane was always good at details.

The name on the card was Adam Gallagher.

He looked no older than me, probably a fellow grad student on a summer internship. "About the oars? Yes, she is. It's why I came over in the first place," he admitted with a faint flush. "I'm always thrilled to see people interested in whaling."

"Yeah, but I know it better than most," I countered bitterly, which just went to show how completely unrecovered I was.

Adam shot me a startled look, but Jane was triumphant. "I knew it!" she said. "You really did live all this before!" She appealed to my companion. "I mean, how else could she have known those names?"

At the oblique reference to reincarnation, his eyes went cold as stones. Jade, I thought idly. Or agate. But then, who could blame him? It did sound totally nuts, even to me.

"She could have read the sign?" he said dryly. "They are all listed there."

Jane just dismissed this. "Liza doesn't read signs; that's my job."

"Or maybe you were at the morning lecture . . . though, no, I'd have remembered you." And he flushed again.

Green hair, I thought. *Can't miss it.*

"I can do it backwards, too," I said, half-ignoring them.

"Steering oar, after oar, tub oar, midship oar, bow oar, harpooner's oar. Also called the boatsteerer's oar, by the way, depending on whom you ask. Which is kind of odd, since the only time the boatsteerer actually steered the boat was when the mate was lancing the whale. Otherwise, he was up front, with his harpoons."

There was a moment of silence.

"Could she have done that just by reading the sign?" Jane finally demanded.

Adam looked baffled, then rallied. "If she has a photographic memory, she could."

"A photographic memory? Some days she can't even remember where she left her car keys!"

That jolted me out of my trance a bit. "Hey," I complained, "that only happened three times. And the first time I was drunk. Which, I might add, was entirely your fault." I glared at her.

She grinned in return.

"Okay, what the hell is going on here?" Adam exclaimed angrily. "Is this some sort of joke?"

I turned back to him. Those green eyes could shoot some truly impressive sparks, but part of him was still intrigued, I could tell. I tried to appeal to his rational side. "I don't blame you for thinking I am completely nuts. Right about now, *I* think I am completely nuts! How can all this be true? But I've been having this dream about whaling all of my life. I thought it was just a delusion—I mean, how could it not be? But I know things I shouldn't. And I don't know how I can convince you that I've never studied the subject, except to tell you that I haven't. I haven't even read *Moby-Dick,* for

Christ's sake! The damned dreams made me want to avoid the whole topic. But then Jane brought me here, and . . . I find myself remembering things I shouldn't possibly remember, and knowing things I shouldn't possibly know. And it's making me crazy!"

Adam was silent for a long moment. "You know, I don't believe a word of this . . . ," he began eventually, his voice hard and tight.

"I don't, either!" I burst out, affronted.

Abruptly, he started laughing, his whole face shifting from suspicion to a twinkling openness that almost took my breath away. "Now, *that* I believe," he admitted. "You look righteously pissed."

"I *am* righteously pissed! I mean, why me? I just wanted a normal life. I would have made a good normal person. But no, I had to have these stupid dreams."

"Okay, tell me about the dreams," Adam said.

"Gladly. And if you can prove to me that I'm somehow making this up, I'll be eternally in your debt. In fact, I'll even buy you dinner at the fanciest restaurant on this island—and I'm only an impoverished graduate student!"

He smiled faintly. "The fanciest restaurant on the island is pretty damned swank. Do you know how many billionaires there are on Nantucket?"

"No," I admitted, thrown by the change in topic.

"Twenty-five," he said. "On an island only fourteen miles across."

"Damn," Jane said. "That's a lot of billionaires. Are any of them single?"

Adam shot her a bemused look.

"Kidding," she said.

"Anyway, there are a lot of really nice restaurants here," Adam continued.

"I don't care," I said stubbornly. Proving this was a delusion was worth more to me than the cost of a good meal. Plus, we grad students had to stick together.

"So. Dreams?" Adam prompted.

I took a deep breath, then outlined the salient facts for him: the hunt, the chase, the whale ramming the ship. I didn't mention last night's novel outing—if indeed that was even real. I mean, Barzillai? What self-respecting woman names her kid Barzillai? "So, you seem to know this stuff. Poke holes in it for me. Please."

"I can't believe I'm even considering this," he said after a minute. "But okay. And if this is really one of my colleagues testing me, I'll pry that name out of your cold dead hands, and then kill him myself!" He measured me again for another long moment. "Describe the whaling vessel. What kind is it?"

I closed my eyes, the better to focus on the dream. "A ship," I said. "Not huge, but not small, either. Four boats on the davits—"

"Wait," he said. "What do you mean, a ship? Are you speaking generically, or specifically?"

I looked at him blankly. "Huh?"

A look of triumph formed on his face. "Wait here for a moment, both of you. Don't move. I think I'm about to win myself a dinner!" And he raced off.

In the sudden silence, I peered at Jane. Whatever other people had been in the room had departed now, off to other rooms or gone completely. For the moment, we were alone in the great space.

"Damn, he's cute," she said at last. "And could he be any more your type?"

I stared at her. "I'm having a philosophical crisis of epic proportions, and all you can talk about is my type?"

She grinned, unrepentant, and I laughed.

"Okay, I admit, he's pretty damned gorgeous. No doubt, he has some model-caliber girlfriend, but there's no harm in looking, right?"

"No harm, indeed," she admitted. "What, is he like the bastard love-child of Rufus Sewell and Ioan Gruffudd?"

Two of my top crushes. I sighed, and we were silent for a minute, contemplating the gorgeous Adam. But I couldn't help adding, "Jane?"

"What?"

"Doesn't it bother you at all that this might be real?"

"What, your dreams?"

"Exactly. I mean, what does it do to your world-view to know that reincarnation may actually exist? Or that something, at least, goes on beyond death? I mean, isn't that a pretty earthshaking idea?"

She contemplated that for a moment in silence. That was the thing about Jane; she took it all equally seriously, from cute guys to the big, burning questions of life, the universe, and everything. Or maybe, equally casually.

"Not really," she said eventually. "At least, not for me."

"Why not?"

She shrugged. "What's the difference? The world's always been incomprehensible in the corners. This is just one more incomprehensible fact among many. Why you? Why whaling? It doesn't make a lick of sense, so why stress about it?"

I stared at her for a long moment. "You're a real piece of work," I said at last, admiringly.

She grinned. "Thanks. Now, straight face, no panting—here he comes."

And indeed, Adam had returned with a blue vinyl binder in his hand. He seemed almost surprised to find us still there, but quickly gathered himself.

"Right," he said, rotating a chair from the row ahead to face us. He opened the binder and showed me a reproduction of an old nautical painting of a ship under full sail. He was, I noticed, holding his hand over the bottom of the picture. "What's this?" he demanded.

"I have no idea," I said testily, except that suddenly I did. Damn it. "A barque."

"And this?" He flipped to another clear vinyl sleeve, holding another picture.

I didn't know where the answers were coming from, but they were coming, fast and easy. "Barquantine."

"This?"

"Brigantine."

"This?"

"Schooner."

"And this?"

"Ship. Hey, that's the one from the dream! Well, not exactly, but close."

He was frowning deeply by now, and Jane was looking astonished.

With a sudden bang, Adam snapped the notebook closed.

"What?" I said into the sudden silence. "Did I win?" And the sheer sass in my voice was probably a good measure of just how badly off balance I was feeling.

"Okay, so that clearly didn't work," he said, frowning. He seemed to be thinking something over.

"What did that all mean?" I persisted.

"I have no idea," he answered. "Yet. So, tell me, what do *you* think it means?"

I still couldn't believe I was thinking this, let alone saying it. "I think that, for whatever reason, I'm having some old whaling captain's dreams. Or that my dreams are his memories." I couldn't even bring myself to say the dread word "reincarnation"; it just sounded too silly.

"What captain?" Adam persisted.

"This is ridiculous!"

"I can't help but agree," he said with a faint grin. "But indulge me."

"Aunt Kitty wondered if it might not be George Pollard," Jane put in helpfully. "Because of the whale."

"And you?" he asked me.

"Obadiah Young," I confessed. "Maybe . . ."

He looked disgusted again. "God, are you *sure* this is not a setup?"

I scowled at him. "Hey, *you* asked."

"True, but do you know how many crackpots we get each year claiming to be the reincarnation of the mysterious Obadiah Young?"

"No, how many?" Jane asked.

I think he'd intended the question to be rhetorical, so was

thrown by Jane's response. In fact, it took all the wind out of his sails, which had, until then, been swelling with a righteous indignation. "I . . . Well, maybe one or two a year. There was one quite famous one in about the 1940s, I think, who was desperately trying to clear his name. But no matter the number, they always annoy me. Why does everyone claim to be the most infamous captain? What about all the thousands of others who don't have famous stories behind them?"

I had no answer to that one, and he was probably right. I had latched on to Obadiah Young only because I was staying in his house, and—apart from Pollard—his was the only name I knew. "You may have a point there," I said. "But I'm having someone's damned dreams!"

"What do you do about these so-called 'crackpots'?" Jane asked logically.

"Well, there is a little test we can give them," he admitted.

"So? Give it to me," I insisted.

"Really?"

"I've told you already, I'd be delighted to have this over and done with. Test away."

He measured me again for an instant, then said, "Okay, follow me."

Jane and I meekly tailed him to the wall behind the whaleboat, where he shot a look at Jane, then slapped the notebook over a set of labels on the wall. From under the notebook, a serried rank of harpoons peeked out.

"Right," he said, pointing. "What's this one called?"

"Single-flued harpoon."

"And this?"

Duh. "Double-flued." And my voice must have reflected a

basic contempt for the line of questioning—which did seem ridiculously obvious, even to me. Only Adam shot me a hard look that quelled my cockiness in its path.

And rightly so. Because, when he pointed at the next harpoon—a far more complicated piece of engineering, complete with pinned-on moving bits—I drew a complete and utter blank. "Uh . . . I don't know. Wiggle harpoon?"

And, for the first time, Adam actually looked shaken.

"What?" Jane said, picking up on his confusion. "What does that mean?"

"Nothing," he said tersely—but he didn't look as if he truly believed it.

"And that's it?" Jane persisted, her voice almost contemptuous. "That's the extent of the test? So is she Obadiah, or not?"

Adam scowled again, and said, "Okay, you want the critical test? Come on." And he marched out of the room. We trailed him like dutiful ducklings as he led us back through the main lobby and up the stairs that curved so grandly about the lighthouse lens.

"Nice ass," Jane whispered to me as we trailed him up the stairs. "I think he likes you."

"Are you nuts?" I whispered back. "He thinks I'm a complete crackpot! And I don't blame him in the slightest. I think I'm a complete crackpot, too!"

"But he's listening, isn't he?" she said, raising one eyebrow.

And she was right; he was—albeit reluctantly. And he did have a pretty fine ass, as well; I couldn't help staring at it as we went up the stairs.

He led us around a corner, down a small hallway, and out into a sunny gallery with golden pine railings looking down over the lower room and the whaleboat. At the far side of this room, a glass door led into another chamber, adorned with portraits and old furnishings.

Poor Adam didn't even have a chance to slap his binder over the labels; I saw the picture right away. A harsh portrait, the grim, unsmiling face so suited to its monochrome dark background. Those dark eyes seemed to stare out at me know-ingly. It was a face of hard angles, the dark beard hiding what I knew lay beneath: the wide, sensual mouth that had kissed me so thoroughly last night in my dreams.

I knew that face as intimately as I knew my own, and see-ing it so starkly before me was the psychic equivalent of step-ping on a land mine. Not that I've ever stepped on a land mine, but if it is like having your knees catapulted out from under you while something smashed into your brain pan like a blacksmith's hammer. . . . Well, then, maybe the analogy wasn't a bad one. Because all that happened. And the last thing I remember hearing was Jane squeaking, "Catch her!" before blackness descended.

CHAPTER 8

I don't know how long I was out, but I came to to see both Jane and Adam leaning over me, identical looks of concern on their faces.

"How's your head?" Jane asked.

I reached out a tentative hand. It was indeed aching, and felt a bit tender to the touch in back.

"Sorry," Adam added. "I couldn't get to you in time. I've never seen anyone go down quite that fast before!"

"Boom," Jane added cheerfully. "Like someone had punched you. I didn't mean for you to take my passing-out comment quite so literally, Liza!"

"You should know by now not to put anything past me," I retorted, attempting a smile.

"See?" Jane turned to Adam triumphantly. "How many of your other crackpots had that spectacular a reaction?"

"They're not my crackpots," he protested. "And I'm more worried about Liza's head right now. How *are* you doing? Can you follow my finger?" He moved it slowly in front of my eyes.

"I'm not concussed," I said. "Really, I'm fine. Just a bit embarrassed is all."

"Are you sure?"

I nodded.

"Can you sit up, then?" He sat beside me and slipped a gentle hand under my head, lifting it onto his jean-clad thigh. And he expected me to breathe normally like this? I hadn't been wrong about him being built; I could feel rock-hard muscle under my cheek. And his hand was still cupping the back of my neck.

I caught Jane's eye. She gave me a faint grin and raised both eyebrows fractionally. I couldn't help it; I started laughing.

"I'm okay, really," I told Adam, because otherwise I'd be tempted to stay welded forever to his leg. He might not scramble my senses like Lucian, but I was quickly becoming disenchanted with sense-scrambling, anyway. At least when it made my head hurt this badly.

I let Adam help me up, but only as far as a sitting position. And if I feigned a bit of dizziness at that point, who could blame me? His chest was about as sculpted as his thigh; I could feel it, because he kept an arm around me as I sat there for a moment, leaning against him.

But eventually, it was only pure indulgence on my part that kept me there, and we were beginning to attract attention from the few other visitors to our wing of the museum. So I pushed away from him and stood, turning my attention to the portrait once again.

I still recognized it—though I felt no inclination to faint anymore.

"So, who is it?" I asked.

"Who do you think?" Jane replied smugly.

The answer seemed inevitable. "Obadiah Young?"

"Got it in one," she said. "And isn't it a neat coincidence that you're actually staying in his house?"

Too much of a coincidence, I still thought. And Adam was looking suspicious again.

But Jane, as usual, was oblivious. "So, did he do it?"

"What?"

"Murder his wife, of course! If you're Obadiah, you should be able to answer that question. So, what happened?"

"I have no idea," I confessed.

"Why not?"

"Because," I said, feeling the concept through slowly, "I don't think it works that way. So far, I'm just getting odd flashes of things, like the house. At times it looks familiar, and at others utterly alien. The same with this whole island. Whatever's going on, it hasn't even come close to resolving itself yet."

Adam's face was bathed in disapproval. "I should go. We don't have enough people minding the museum today. Are you going to be okay?"

Well, so much for that one, I thought sadly.

"Of course. Hunky-dory. Obadiah and I both," I couldn't help adding, bitterly.

Adam fled.

"Bugger," I said to Jane, when he had left us alone in the glass-enclosed gallery. "I told you that he thought I was nuts."

"Oh, he'll be back," she said blithely.

"And what evidence do you have of that?"

"I saw his face as he was holding you."

I sighed deeply. "You're as crazy as I am, just for different reasons. Damn it, I need a drink. What time is it?"

"Eleven fifty-five," she said. "If we do lunch now, we'll definitely be back in time for the one thirty lecture. And then, maybe after that, we'll actually have a chance to look around the museum. If you promise not to keep passing out like that. . . ."

"I think I'm done fainting for the day," I told her. "Now, get me some beer, woman!"

We stopped at a place called the Rose & Crown across the street—which, according to the menu, used to be an old livery stable. To my profound relief, I didn't recognize it. Or perhaps my body was allowing me only one shock a day. If so, thank God—or whatever—for small favors.

And while Jane felt compelled to order me a Whale's Tail, a local brew, my only reaction to that was that it was, blessedly, beer.

I sucked down one, quickly, and then a second more slowly.

"Well, that's been one hell of a day already," Jane said as we munched our burgers.

"I don't want to talk about it," I said, and I didn't. I didn't much want to think about it either, but I couldn't help recalling last night's dreams. In one of them, at least, I had decidedly *not* been Obadiah. My cheeks flushed in memory . . . but the truth was that I had known Obadiah's face, and not from any mirror. So did that make me Lucy? Yet how was I having dreams of whaling if I had been Obadiah's wife? It was whaling I knew, as today's outing had just proved, and Lucy was no whaler.

None of it made any sense.

We managed to discuss more neutral topics over lunch, and when we returned to the museum at shortly past one, I was definitely feeling calmer. Or perhaps just drunker. I tried to focus on the exhibit, but I just couldn't wrap my mind around it, so instead I stared blankly while Jane tried to interest me in tales of the community's founders—the Coffins, Macys, Starbucks, Folgers, and Youngs. But it all bounced off until a voice behind me said, "Liza."

I turned; it was Adam. His expression was still wary, but at least he was looking at me without overt condemnation in his gaze. And that alone made me feel so happy that I grinned broadly back at him. Or maybe it was just the beer again. "Hey, Adam!"

"Can I ask you one more question?"

"Fire away."

Jane had, by now, noticed his appearance, and had diplomatically drifted several feet to the left. She appeared absorbed in a display about candles, though I knew she was listening keenly to our conversation.

And I suspect Adam knew it as well, for he put his hand on my arm and drew me off to a quieter corner of the main room. Probably in anticipation of the one thirty lecture, more people had gathered than before, and the hall was far from deserted. But Adam still found a relatively unpopulated nook.

"I'm amazed you're still talking to me," I said frankly.

"Truth to tell, so am I. But tell me one thing. You said before, in your dream, that the lookout had sighted a whale. Was he standing in the crow's nest as it happened?"

"Crow's nest?" I said, frowning. "You mean that baskety thing up on top of the mast?"

He nodded, and I felt a surge of excitement go through me. "Oh my God, I must have been making it up, after all, because there was no crow's nest! Just . . ." I frowned slightly, trying to dredge up the images from the dream again. "Just two metal hoops, mounted toward the top of the main mast. And there was this sort of feeling every time I looked at them, as if they were some odd, newfangled thing; that they hadn't always been present. Oh, and there wasn't just one lookout; there were two, one per hoop. So I must have had it wrong—" And then I caught sight of his face, and my sudden enthusiasm waned. "Unless it was a trick question, of course. It was a trick question, wasn't it?"

He nodded sheepishly.

"I don't blame you; I'd ask me trick questions, too." I sighed. "So, I got the right answer?"

"There were actually two right answers, and you kind of got them both. In the earliest whaling ships, the lookouts just balanced on the topmost yard and hung on to the mast. In about the 1820s, the hoops were added, and by the 1850s, the hoops were pretty much universal. The more formal version of the crow's nest we know today was developed in 1807, but it was restricted to the Arctic trade, because the lookouts needed the extra structure to keep them warm in the teeth of the northern winds. So, the fact that you saw hoops was right—as was your feeling that they didn't quite belong. I can't remember offhand on which ships Obadiah did his stints as boatsteerer and mate . . ."

The *Wampanoag,* I almost said, but fortunately stayed quiet.

". . . but I'd say it was likely he spent his early watches without the hoops. So there you have it."

He looked oddly resigned, and I was silent for a moment. But I couldn't help asking, "So, what made you believe me enough to come back and ask that?"

He sighed deeply. "That last harpoon I asked you about, the one you didn't recognize? It's called either the toggle harpoon or the Temple harpoon, because it was invented by an African-American blacksmith named Louis Temple, working out of New Bedford in 1848." And when I was silent, he added, "Obadiah Young set out on his final voyage in late November of 1843. The last time he was seen again was in the spring of 1845, in the Pacific. So if you really were Obadiah, it would make sense that your memories would stop around that time. The coincidence seemed . . . well, hard to ignore completely."

"I know what you mean," I confessed. "This whole damned thing seems fraught with too many ridiculous coincidences. Like the fact that Jane's aunt owns Obadiah's house."

"You mean . . . Your friend's aunt is Katherine *Bryant*?"

"You know her?" I said.

"Know of her, anyway," he replied. He looked more impressed by this than anything else I had told him. "Damn. I'd love a look at that house! I've seen a number of the other captains' houses on the island, but because that one's in private hands, I've been reluctant to intrude."

"I'm sure something can be arranged. And I'm sorry. I hadn't realized when Obadiah went missing."

He smiled faintly, then abruptly checked his watch. Great. My charm was apparently working overtime again. "Hey, if you're staying for the lecture, you should probably grab a seat. They seem to be filling up fast for a Friday in June. Oh, wait; your friend's already got you one."

And indeed, Jane was waving at me from a seat down near the front. I waved back.

"Are you staying?" I said to Adam.

He looked amused. "You could say that."

"And you promise not to accuse me of knowing information in the future just because it was mentioned in the lecture?"

"No, but if you let me buy you a coffee later, I'd love to see how much of it already seemed familiar to you. Because— unbelievable as it sounds—if you really were Obadiah . . . Well, that's a resource no researcher could pass up!"

So, that explained his interest in me. Ah, well. I wondered how gorgeous the model-slash-girlfriend was. "If you like," I said.

"I would. See you later, then?"

"Later," I agreed, then went back to Jane, who was beaming at me.

"What did I tell you?" she whispered. "I told you he was interested."

"Yeah, in my brain. He's decided that if I'm not lying to him, then I'm a terrific research opportunity."

"He's probably right. But that's just an excuse; you'll see."

"Right, sure. He wants to see Kitty's house, too."

"That can be arranged."

"That's what I told him. But I still think you're totally off.

I mean, just look at him! There's got to be a girlfriend some-where."

Jane just rolled her eyes. "Here we go again. I will never understand why you don't realize how gorgeous you are—"

"Because I have eyes! And I've seen those damned maga-zines you always leave lying around the bathroom."

"Liza—"

"Shh, I think they're starting. And . . . Oh my God!"

Jane grinned. "Okay, I'll admit. That I did *not* expect!"

"Shh!" I hissed again as Adam stood up in front of the crowd. How old *was* he? And how the hell had he managed to become a curator at his age? The very word conjured visions of aging academics in tweed, not—

"Good afternoon, folks. As you have already probably heard, we're running a bit understaffed today, so you've got me instead of one of our regular docents. And I hope you'll forgive me if I don't have the spiel exactly right, since I don't usually do these talks. But I'm Adam Gallagher, one of the as-sociate curators of this marvelous museum, so I do know a fair bit about the place. Feel free to ask me questions at any time during the talk, but for now, we'll start with the movie."

Sometime during the movie—narrated by John Shea and about a sperm whale that washed up on the Nantucket beaches sometime in 1998, and whose skeleton now hung above us—I got over my shock about Adam. By the time he started his lecture and slide show, which both featured some his-tory of the island and related the experiences of a fictional novice sailor aboard his first whaler, I was hooked. He was a fascinating, dynamic speaker, and his face glowed with enthusiasm. And if I—and every other female member of the audience— paid special attention to the topic due to the attractiveness of the speaker, I suppose we can be forgiven.

The first residents of Nantucket were the Wampanoag Indians—a name that perked my ears right up, let me tell you, as well as engendering an increasing sense of doom. I mean, how many more times did I need to be whapped over the head with the fact that I knew things I shouldn't? Anyway, these Indians had long been in the habit of processing the "drift" whales that washed up on the beaches. The first English settlers were determined to do what they knew best, and started off by farming. But soon that proved impossible—the soil was very poor, and while sheep did well, there were no rivers on Nantucket to run the wool-processing mills.

So, eventually, they, like the Wampanoags, turned their attention to the sea. The right whales—so called because they were the right whales to hunt: slow, placid, and they floated when killed—were pursued in twenty-foot boats crewed by six men, five Wampanoags and one Nantucketer on the steering oar. Dead whales were dragged back to shore to be processed, or "tried-out."

Rendered whale oil was used in oil lamps. The baleen strips in the whales' mouths were long and flexible, and were used for such things as carriage and sofa springs, as well as for the infamous corset stays.

In 1712, Captain Hussey was blown far out to sea by an unexpected gale, where he and his crew encountered a type of whale they had never seen before. Despite the bad weather and the whale's aggressiveness, Hussey managed to kill it and tow it back to Nantucket. It was a sperm whale, and while it had no baleen, the islanders quickly realized that this whale's oil was far superior to that of the right whale, being both cleaner-burning and brighter. Plus, the sperm whale had an even purer reserve of oil in its head—the spermaceti—which could be ladled directly into casks.

From that time onward, Nantucket whalemen devoted themselves exclusively to hunting the sperm whale. By 1760, they had virtually wiped out the local whale population. They had also developed large-draft whalers capable of processing whale oil out on the open ocean. No longer needing to return to port to try-out the whale, they could range farther and farther in search of their prey, eventually sailing around the deadly Cape Horn and into the Pacific Ocean. Voyages lasted for two or three years—and in some cases as long as eleven. The whaling trade put places like Hawaii on the map, and ships often reached Japan, Australia, and New Zealand. Whalers' crews became incredibly diverse as the harshness of the whaling life drove many men to desert, replaced by natives from the widely flung lands the whalers visited.

Adam laid out the conditions—rat- and roach-infested ships, wretched food, and the hardest work on the sea. His descriptions of the hunt matched my dreams down to the smallest details, like my bare feet. But I had not known, or "remembered," that though they called it the whale's life, they were aiming for the lungs.

When the whale began to spout blood—or "fire in the chimney," as it is called; and why did I not remember that part? From Adam's description, it sounded pretty memorable—the whaleboats drew back as the whale went into its death throes, or flurry.

"Actually," Adam said cheerfully, "one of my favorite facts about whaling is that when a whale goes into its flurry, not only can it smash boats in its violence, but it can also vomit up chunks of giant squid the size of Volkswagens that can crush the boats all by themselves."

The more impressionable women in the audience squealed, and I grinned.

Whales also vomited ambergris—a waxy substance that was literally worth its weight in gold. Whalemen would collect it from the surface of the ocean once the whale was dead—or "fin out." Then they had to tow the dead body of the whale back to the ship, which could be miles away since a whale could drag a boat at up to twenty-five miles an hour. Rowing back was slow and arduous, and once they got back and the whale was fastened to the starboard side of the ship, the men got no rest until every inch of the whale was processed.

First vast strips of blubber called "blanket pieces" were cut off the whale's body and lowered into the hold of the ship, where they were cut up into small pieces that were then put into the huge cauldrons of the try works and boiled down. It was a greasy, smoky, revolting-smelling process.

Sharks fed off the whale's carcass even as the head was cut off and brought on board. The spermaceti was bailed out into casks. The lower jaw was cut off, its teeth useful for scrimshaw.

Adam's description of all this was vivid and awful—the fires of hell unleashed. And I was, frankly, astounded to remember none of this on a visceral level. The whole time Adam was talking, I had this odd, niggling feeling that I knew all this, but more as some sort of intellectual exercise. There was no bone-deep recognition, as there had been with the whaleboat.

Adam talked for a bit longer—something about the death of whaling—but by that point I was no longer listening, too busy reflecting on what had come before.

When Adam managed to detach himself from his adoring fans, and join Jane and me as we worked our way around the exhibits, I begged a rain check on coffee. I had to reconcile my lack of memory, if I could. And I wasn't sure I wanted Adam to think of me as only a research subject, anyway.

He looked disappointed, but took my refusal in good grace, and left with both my cell phone number and Kitty's house number in his pocket.

"What, are you crazy?" Jane declared after he had departed. "A cute guy wanted to take you out!"

"Only because he wanted to pick my brain. And unless he wants to violate my body as well, what fun is that? Now, come on; let's see the rest of this museum."

CHAPTER 9

Jane and I prowled the museum, going through both the reconstruction of the candle factory—at the time, spermaceti candles were some of the best light around—and the scrimshaw gallery upstairs. My previous incarnation had not contributed to the collection, to my profound relief. So I was free to marvel at the elaborate whalebone structures, some of which were incredible feats of engineering.

By four o'clock, I was ready to go home and sleep, but Jane was wired, so we went shopping instead. And I have to admit that poking through the overpriced shops, admiring objects that we couldn't possibly afford and making fun of others we wouldn't ever want to, woke me right up.

Then, since we had yet to provide ourselves with any food, we went to another of the local restaurants for dinner. This one was called, ironically, Obadiah's, and had both fabulous food and a hip, trendy atmosphere that Jane fell instantly in love with. But it also had some of the worst service I had ever encountered. Okay, I admit the place was badly understaffed, but our waitress forgot to put in our dinner order, and an hour and a half later, we were still unfed. At that point, even the easygoing Jane began to make noises.

About five minutes after our food finally arrived, the owner of the restaurant came over to our table to apologize, and that was when the evening turned around. He was a laid-back guy somewhere in his forties with sandy hair and an outdoorsy look, and when neither of us showed any inclination to tear him a new one, he took a seat and ended up chatting with us for most of the meal.

His name was Rob Winter, and he had come to the island from San Francisco about two years ago and fallen in love with the place. Since he had worked in a whole series of restaurants in California, he decided to open his own place here—which was, like any number of the local places, both restaurant and night club.

"Well, you've done a great job with the place," Jane told him. "I adore the décor." She would; it was very hip, in a way that missed being self-conscious by the slightest hair. It was, you could tell, designed to be the happening place for the over-thirty set. A demographic that Jane had always felt herself very much a part of—despite her measly twenty-five years.

"Thanks," Rob said, beaming proudly—clearly the author of said décor—and I grinned. Jane was up to her usual tricks. Her best male friends in Wisconsin were all gay, and it seemed she had found her new soul mate.

I had a feeling we'd be eating here a lot this summer.

"It's a strange place, this island," Rob admitted. "I adore it—especially off season—but sometimes it can get a bit much. Do you know how many billionaires live here?"

This was the second person who had asked us this today. "Twenty-five?" I hazarded, remembering Adam's answer.

"More like a hundred," he confessed. "I have a friend who works for the town council; she's seen the census rolls. There are a lot of really rich people here who expect a certain level of treatment."

Jane just grinned. "Well, fortunately, that's not us. We're both poor as dirt."

"And I'm sorry again for the confusion over your dinner," Rob repeated, "but thanks for being so nice about it! We've had a bit of a problem this year finding help that lasts. I'm down two waitresses, and I just lost my bartender last night. You don't happen to know a good local bartender, do you?"

I laughed, and Jane tossed her viridian locks. "As it happens, I do," she said smugly. She had earned extra money for the past few years bartending in one of the local campus establishments. It was the natural job for night-owl Jane. She loved the hours, loved the clientele, loved the access to a whole variety of eligible men. The bar clientele was Jane's sexual smorgasbord, and she was never without her regular admirers. Not to mention a great many more one-night stands than I could ever have contemplated. She went through men as fast as she went through hair colors and majors. There had been one memorable week when I'd encountered a different guy in the kitchen each morning—but then, Jane was never at her best right before finals.

"What's the pay? And when do you want me to start?" she continued.

Rob's whole face lit up. And some quick and stiff negations

later, all was settled. She'd have Sundays and Mondays off, would work 7 P.M. to closing Thursday through Saturday, and do day shifts on Tuesday and Wednesday. And she would start this coming Tuesday.

When we left the restaurant, she was still beaming. "Damn, this will be fun! Gainful employment. And maybe I'll even meet one of those twenty-five to a hundred billionaires! Hey, are you sure you don't want to take one of those waitress slots Rob mentioned? Billionaires in the offing. . . ."

I laughed. "Only if it is the last job on earth! I waitressed once; never again. Not even for billionaires, not if I can avoid it. Besides, I have a feeling something better will come up soon."

"Amen, Ms. Optimist. But damn, it's been a day chock-full of Obadiahs! Fun, huh?"

I made a noncommittal noise, but I couldn't help but agree. A day of Obadiahs, indeed.

It was close to ten by the time we arrived back home. Rob had not only given us our late dinners gratis, he'd bought us a round of drinks. Which was fine by me. I still wasn't sure about how I felt about returning to a place I had clearly once lived, but I needn't have worried. I was feeling no pain by the time the big house hove into view, and even Lucian couldn't shock me when we found him ensconced in the living room on our arrival, reading.

"You're back late," he said as we closed and locked the door behind us. "Big day?"

"You could say that," Jane said, advancing into the room.

I followed. Lucian was sprawled in one of the big leather armchairs, his feet up on the ottoman. He closed his book and surveyed us.

I surveyed back. He seemed almost approachable again, as he had been during our breakfast, and the sight of him still scrambled my senses. But, objectively, he couldn't compare to Adam. Against the memory of those brilliant green eyes, glossy chestnut curls, and cheekbones to die for, Lucian seemed a bit too lean and ascetic. Too Puritan.

"What were you up to?" he asked.

"Museum," Jane replied. "Where's Kitty?"

"In bed. So, how was it?"

"Interesting. Cute curators. Right, Liza?"

"Mmm," I agreed wholeheartedly, and Lucian's face tightened a bit.

"Anything else?"

"Oh, it's been a day full of revelations," Jane answered blithely. "Kitty would be so pleased. Liza discovered that she's the reincarnation of Obadiah, and I got a job."

Lucian's jaw dropped open. He looked utterly poleaxed—though whether from the revelation about my putative discovery or Jane's gainful employment, I have no idea. But never one to let a good bombshell go unwasted, Jane breezily added, "Good night," before Lucian could recover, and we made good our escape.

I had hoped for a night free of dreams, but I was not to be so lucky. Instead, as sleep grips me, I find myself on my back, in what can only be a bed. The night is so black, I cannot see more than shadows and rough block-forms of shapes, but he will not let me light the candle. Not tonight. So instead I must listen. The bedropes are loose and will soon need tightening, but that is only of minor concern, for I hear by their creak that he is in motion. Every sense seems heightened as my eyes struggle for vision, and I am exquisitely aware of my body, naked and exposed in the darkness, tingling with longing for what I know comes next. A touch, a caress, against my aching skin. . . .

Which, when it comes, nearly arches me off the bed with desire—though he has touched nothing more intimate than the curve of my hip. My ears strain, trying to discern when his next motion will come, and where. But he is silent as a cat when he wants to be, and I do not know where or what the next caress will be, and that is part of the game, the torment.

I feel my lips curve in a grin, then bite down hard to mask my groan as lips tease a nipple, teeth nibble up the inside of my thigh, the brush of his beard electric in his wake. It continues for what feels like a mindless eternity, this teasing of touch, as every inch of my wanting skin receives his attention until I am almost mad with need.

Yet so well does he know me, my response, that just as I am about to cry out with longing for a firmer touch . . . one long, strong finger slides up inside me with such sweet inevitability that I almost shatter from that alone.

But no; he knows me better. And in this game that we play, he won't let me seek my release until I am much further gone than this. It is as vital to him as to me, this knowledge, this shared need.

In my mind—the part that retains a shred of rationality—I feel a sharp spike of jealousy. For if I again am Lucy, it seems she had the one thing I have never achieved: a lover so completely tuned to me and my needs that we might as well have been of one flesh, one mind. This, I know, is the kind of sex all women dream of, but which I have never experienced, despite a successive chain of boyfriends.

And yet I also know I am somehow wrong, that I am missing some vital part of the equation.

Then all rational thought disperses as my lover's mouth dips between my legs, his tongue dancing over the heated core of me until I am writhing under his touch, and all that exists is pure sensation. Between the hot pant of his breath, the light, flicking caresses of his tongue, and the tickling brush of his beard against my thighs, I am close.

Even as the waves of my release again begin to gather in the base of my womb, he shifts, moving up to taunt my nipples, claim my mouth with fevered kisses, until the throbbing in my lower body decreases. His back under my hands is familiar terrain, all whipcord-lean muscle and sinew. And then—and only then—do his fingers again find my core, as his mouth courts first one breast, and then the other.

One finger slides back inside, and then another, caressing that area so deep and secret that only he seems to know or find it, but which turns every bone in my body to liquid. And all the while, his busy thumb strokes outside, until the combined pressure raises me to the peak again.

I drop fevered kisses on his neck, his shoulder, licking away a trickle of sweat. It tastes of his other mistress, the sea. He touches himself for me, he has confessed, at night in his rocking bunk. He fattens and groans and spills his seed in guilty secret, all for me. He does not know if the other men abuse themselves this way, but he cannot help it. He burns for me, even when I am away.

I, too, have learned to imitate the movements of his hands on myself—and all for him. I, too, pass the long years alone with only my fingers for company, dreaming of him.

But now he is here, and he will not let me sleep while I am still wanting. I am panting, my body sleek with sweat, but still no release is granted. Instead, he pulls back yet again, shifting his weight until only the tip of him is teasing where I most need him.

My lips form a sound—mindless, aching—and with a motion as sudden as a whale rising beneath a whaleboat, he rears up, pulling me up and around until I am on my knees. And he, standing behind me, finally sheathes himself in me with a force that takes my breath away. His thighs are clenched, hard as iron, against mine, and his chest drops to cover my back as his hands roam freely across breasts and belly. I can feel his heart hammering against my ribs, his breath hot and fast across my neck.

"Now?" his rough voice rasps out.

"Now," I confirm, as breathless as he, and one hand drops back to my core as he thrusts harder and faster, stimulating inside and out. The beautiful tension gathers yet again . . . and this time, my climax takes me so explosively that I grab the pillow one-handed and shriek into its depths. And . . .

Pain. Oh, God, pain like black and red waves, breaking over me. I cry out again—loud, uneven, my voice as ragged as broken glass.

Was there ever pain in the world like this? I shall be rent in twain. . . .

"You must stay with me, mistress. Mistress, you must push!"

The woman's voice whines in my ear like a mosquito—a constant, irritating drone. I want to slap her; I want to rend her. I want to rend them all.

"Yes, Lucy, push!" another voice says, sharp and overeager.

"No!" My denial is strong, instinctive, but before I can say more, another wave of pain seizes me, lifts me, and I bear down hard against it, screaming.

Sweat is streaming down my body, my hair a damp tangle in my face.

Someone brushes it back—not the hand I want. The injustice of it wrings a sob from me.

"That's it, mistress. You're doing fine."

Dear God, the irony.

The pain is too strong; I cannot bear it. Blackness wavers at the edge of my vision.

Then the midwife's face is thrust into mine. Her breath smells of cabbage and onion, and I gag. There is a mole on her chin, sprouting three coarse hairs.

"Once more, mistress," she says. "Just once more."

"Yes, once more," her faithful shadow echoes, and I am filled with a wave of such sudden, sharp hatred that I cannot draw a breath. She is my salvation, and yet I loathe her.

But before I can examine this feeling any further, another wave of agony grips me, and I scream my rage, pain, and hatred into its jagged maw. I bear down, fueled by anger, by injustice. By love. Yes, there is love there, too. And then . . .

. . . A sudden surcease of pain, so blissful, I almost cry out again. A long silence . . .

Then a lusty cry splits the air—a wailing, raging sound so full of indignation that I have to laugh though my tears. Joy wells up in me, so strong, I might break.

"A son, mistress!" the midwife says, triumphant.

"A son," says her echo, awed.

"What will you call him?"

I cannot speak through my tears, but it does not matter. She says it for me.

"Owen," she says. "His name is Owen."

Wrung out by my dreams, I did not wake until after ten, by which time Lucian was long gone from the kitchen. I poured myself a bowl of cereal, then stared fixedly at the kitchen walls. So much for revelations. I was more confused now than I had been yesterday. Those were Lucy's dreams, without a doubt. I mean, how much clearer could it get than witnessing the birth of Lucy's son?

I shuddered, suddenly glad for the protection of my small pack of little white pills. No way was I going through that in anything like the near future!

Then I snorted a laugh and tidied away my dishes. It was high time I started thinking about the future, not the past. At my request, Kitty had left the local paper on the table, and I spent the hour until Jane awoke reading the want ads, mindlessly circling employment possibilities. It was a depressing list.

Waitress, waitress, shop girl, sales clerk. Nothing I couldn't have done equally well back home. Not that I had really expected anything better, but still . . .

I couldn't bring myself to dial any of the numbers, so instead I phoned my parents, assuring them that I was safe, that I was not being an imposition, that I was looking for a job, that Jane was fine, that I wasn't subsisting solely on junk food. . . .

It was such a normal conversation that it actually cheered me up, and I was grinning by the time Jane wandered down and snagged the cell phone from me, offering her assurances in turn. Which I'm sure did more to ease their minds than anything I could have said. Like everyone else, my parents adored Jane.

I hung up as she was crunching her way through a bowl of cereal, and she grinned at me.

"So, now that we've set parental minds at ease . . . Errands today?"

I nodded, and before long we were driving my car to the big market on the outskirts of town, where we stocked up on food and supplies, so we would no longer be dependent solely on Kitty's hospitality. Then, once we had unloaded our groceries and made lunch, I started making noises about a library, since I was nearly out of books to read. So Jane introduced me to the Atheneum.

It was only a short walk from Kitty's, and if a few carefree hours of errands had led me to believe I was free from the grip of my other life, the Atheneum soon disabused me of this notion. For no sooner had I seen its whitewashed Grecian façade than my limbs began to tingle and I almost blacked out again. I had a sudden vision of carrying an armload of books into this building, and it felt like an old, familiar routine.

I recalled its big doors, the curving stair to the second-floor meeting hall on the left-hand side of the foyer, the wide, gracious room before me. And for some reason it saddened me, as though the memory were shot through with grief.

"What's wrong?" Jane exclaimed, grabbing my arm as I tottered.

I shot her a wry look. "What do you think? It seems I was once here, too. God, this is getting old."

But at least I was able to get a pile of books to take home with me, as well as some informational pamphlets. Because, apparently, the Atheneum maintained a tradition that had dated back to whaling days: community meetings. Now these were of a literary bent, and followed by a free wine-and-cheese reception. And once the librarian had established my credentials as a bona fide book person, she told me gleefully of all the big names they had lined up for the coming season.

I gawped at her. "You've got to be kidding me!" I mean, even I had heard of these guys. Some were local, but a surprisingly large chunk were *New York Times* bestsellers—the heaviest of the heavy hitters.

She smiled proudly. "Pretty good for such a small island, huh? But of course, this has become a very affluent island now—probably even more affluent now than when it was the whaling capital of the world—and people expect a certain caliber of entertainment." That sounded close to what Rob had said last night, and indeed she followed it up by adding, "Do you know how many billionaires we have on this island?"

I almost laughed—and wondered how long it would be before I was asking this of others. At least I had stopped trying to guess. "I have no idea. How many?"

"Thirty-seven," she said proudly, and I made the expected noises of shock and surprise, trying madly not to pop her bubble by giggling.

"What?" Jane asked me, seeing my amusement as we proceeded home, my arms full of books.

"Billionaires again," I told her. "This one said thirty-seven."

She grinned and rolled her eyes. "Hell, I'd settle for a lowly millionaire. Wonder how many of those there are here? I mean, beyond the obvious. . . ."

After I had deposited the books in my room, it was cooking time. I had been so seduced by all the gourmet variety at the local stores (the billionaires again, no doubt) that I had gone a bit nuts at the market. Granted, it had been a bit of a strain on my poor student budget, but it was worth it, I felt. In part because any truly civilized society deserved a cocktail hour, but also because the admonitions of my parents still echoed in my ears. Kitty was giving up her home to me for the summer; I could at least do something nice for her in return.

Jane had entered enthusiastically into the idea. In our current mood, we agreed that sherry sounded very elegant—and besides, we knew we couldn't outdo Kitty for quality of wine. We debated over dry versus sweet, and ended buying a bottle of both: amontillado for me, because of Poe, and manzanilla for Jane, because she was the sophisticate who had actually been to Portugal and Spain.

I whipped up a quick olive tapenade, we baked some frozen phyllo/spanakopita pockets, and decanted some bottled taramasalata. Jane, with her usual stylish flair, laid it all out on a series of platters, arranged the crackers, and even placed four small crystal glasses on a silver salver, surrounding the two bottles of sherry. "In case Kitty and Lucian come home early," she said. "What do you think?"

"Elegant in the extreme," I told her. "Are you sure you never trained as a caterer?"

She grinned. "I meant about Kitty and Lucian."

"The more the merrier," I replied, suddenly acutely aware of the cell phone tucked in the back pocket of my jeans. Not that Adam had called, yet. I don't know why I was surprised. *Model-slash-girlfriend,* I reminded myself. *Plus, he thinks you're insane.*

"You know," Jane added as we carried our bounty into the more formal parlor—because, as she said, someone had to use the room, and elegance deserved elegance, "we probably should have gotten ouzo instead of sherry."

"Ick! Why?"

"Just look at our food: all Greek."

"I hate ouzo."

"Fair enough. Have a puff."

I helped myself to a teeny spanakopita. "You know, we're still missing something."

"What?" Jane said, raising an eyebrow.

"Just look at us." We were both wearing jeans and sweat-shirts. "We hardly match the ambience."

Jane grinned. "Good point. Race you?"

We tore upstairs. I did a quick change in my room—basically into a variant of the outfit I had worn on my first night here—then nearly lost both the race and my balance be-cause I was so busy trying to beat Jane that I forgot to steel myself against the horror of the landing, as had become my custom. And this time, the vision was worse. Not just a flash of hair and blood, but eyes, wide and panicked, yet still celestially blue against the sheet of blood that poured down her face. Her mouth, forming the plea:

Help me. Help me!

I scrunched my eyes shut and pounded the rest of the way down the stairs, shaking. Only to discover Lucian bent over our trays.

He looked up as I entered, and I thought I saw a flash of approval in his eyes. But if so, it was quickly masked. And it was probably only for the food, anyway. "Can anyone partake?"

"Well, anyone in the house."

He raised an eyebrow. "So, no street people?"

"Not unless they're billionaires."

He burst out laughing. "I see you've discovered our local pastime."

"What, counting billionaires?" I grinned. "It does seem to be a bit of an obsession. How many do you think there are?"

"Frankly, I couldn't care less," he said airily. "So, what can I get you to drink?"

"You're pouring? Amontillado, then," I replied. It seemed the elegant setting was having a salutary effect on Lucian's manners again.

"And who are you planning to brick up in a wall afterwards?" he asked as he decanted.

"Oh," I said as airily as he had about the billionaires, "I haven't decided yet. Female prerogative, you know."

"I'll make a point to be nice to you, then," he said, raising an eyebrow and waving me to a seat.

"Heavens, I never thought I'd hear that from you," Jane commented from behind us. "What did you do to get him so compliant, Liza?"

"Threatened to brick him up in a wall."

She laughed and flopped into a chair. "I'll have to remember that. Hey, Lucian, can you pour me a manzanilla?"

"Pour it yourself," he replied nastily. "I'm not *your* houseboy."

"But you poured Liza's."

"Only because she didn't presume. Besides, she's the founder of this feast."

"How do you know?"

"Because I do. Her idea, your layout. The homemade tapanade is wonderful, by the way," he added to me.

"Thanks!"

Jane scowled and fetched her drink. Lucian, I noticed, was drinking the manzanilla as well.

We heard a key in the door, then, "What's this?" said Kitty, entering the room. She was still in her jacket and was carrying several anonymous parcels. "Liza, what a lovely idea! And Jane, what a beautiful layout. Give me a few minutes, and I'll join you." And she bustled off.

"See?" Lucian said into the silence, smirking at Jane.

She scowled back at him.

I ate a cracker of tapanade.

Lucian poured amontillado into the remaining glass.

"So, what's on offer?" Kitty said as she returned. "I'll have a . . . Ah, thanks, Lucian. That's perfect!" She happily sipped the sherry he handed her, then snagged a spanakopita off the plate and sat. "We should do this more often. Plain civilized, this is."

"Did you have a good day, Aunt Kitty?" Jane asked.

"Very. But not as exciting as yours yesterday, I hear. What's this about a job?"

After Jane had explained, Kitty turned to me. "And you, Liza? I understand you had a bit of a revelation as well."

I glanced briefly at Lucian, who—predictably—was scowling again. I really hated talking about this in front of such an unappreciative audience, but I didn't want to be rude to our hostess, either.

"Well, I don't know if you'd actually call it a revelation—"

"She passed out cold in front of Obadiah's portrait in the museum," Jane crowed. "Adam said he'd never seen anyone go down so fast before."

"Oh, dear," Kitty said. "You weren't hurt, were you?"

"Who's Adam?" Lucian asked, simultaneously.

"Banged my head a bit, but I'm fine," I told Kitty with a smile.

"The cute museum curator who was with us," Jane answered Lucian. "I don't think he believed us at first—I mean, about all the reincarnation stuff—but he seemed more convinced after he'd given Liza a few tests."

"Tests?" Kitty said, sounding concerned.

"He showed her pictures and stuff, to see if she recognized things."

"And did you?" Kitty asked me.

I nodded sheepishly. "It was weird. He was showing me all these different rigging patterns. And one part of me had no idea what they were. But I could still name all of them." I shuddered. "Truth to tell, Adam probably convinced me as much as I convinced him. I still think this is nuts, but I also can't deny the fact that I keep recognizing things. I almost passed out in front of the Atheneum today."

"Really? Are you sure? Because I could have sworn the Atheneum burned in the fire."

"What fire?"

"The Great Fire of 1846. Didn't Adam mention this? We lost a huge portion of the town—a bunch of the wharves, and most of Main Street. Plus a few side streets as well. And Obadiah sailed years before the Great Fire. So if you are really Obadiah . . ." Her voice trailed off, but even I could complete that thought by myself.

If I were really Obadiah, then I couldn't possibly know the Atheneum—at least, not the version I had recognized today, as that couldn't have been built until after 1846. The same if I were Lucy. So how could I be having these dreams, and also know I'd been in that very same library before?

On the other hand, it was fuel for the fire, so to speak. I hadn't had the slightest idea that half the town had burned. You'd think if I really had lived through something like that, I'd have remembered it. And yet, hearing of it caught me completely off guard. As it would, if my memories of Nantucket ended in 1843.

So maybe Kitty was wrong about the Atheneum.

And maybe all this supernatural crap *was* just a delusion.

My musings were interrupted by the ringing of the phone, deeper in the house. Kitty rose to answer it, then returned to the room, grinning. She extended a cordless handset to me.

"For you, Liza. Someone named Adam."

CHAPTER 10

Since I hadn't really expected him to call, I found myself taking the handset with a strange detachment. I retreated into the living room for greater privacy, then put the phone to my ear.

"Adam?" I said, as if to confirm that it was really him.

He picked up on the distraction in my voice right away. "Is this a bad time?"

"No, it's just . . . Can I ask you a question?"

"Of course," he said. "Actually, that seems more than fair, considering how many I asked you yesterday."

"Did you mention anything about the Great Fire in your lecture?"

"Of course I did. But I had a feeling you'd tuned out by then."

"So the town really burned in 1846?"

"Large chunks of it, anyway. Why? Did you suddenly remember something about the fire?"

"No, but I almost passed out in front of the Atheneum today. I remember the place—I'm sure I do—but Kitty said it was destroyed in the fire. Is she right? And if so, how can I possibly recognize it? I mean, unless this whole thing is a crock."

Adam was silent for a long moment, and I wished I could see his face. "I don't know," he finally confessed. "It did burn—but it was also the first thing rebuilt after the fire, which just goes to show how important reading and education were to the Nantucketers. They were among the first to educate women, did you know that?"

"No, I—"

"I'm sorry." He laughed. "Occupational hazard. If you talk to a Nantucket historian, you get too many Nantucket facts. But maybe it was the idea of the Atheneum you remembered, more than the building itself."

"Maybe," I said. "Was the building put back just as it was, or not?"

"Mmm, that's another point," Adam said. "I have to admit, I can't recall. But I'll check on that for you, if you'd like."

"I would. Thanks, Adam."

"However," he added, "I take it from all this that you haven't had a chance to do a walking tour yet? I was calling to see if you wanted to do that coffee, but if you are more interested in a tour, I can offer a good one of those as well; I've been on enough of them myself to remember most of the details. You can invite Jane, too."

So not a date, then, I thought. Just another attempt to probe my brain.

"Sure," I said, somewhat glumly. "When?"

"Monday? If I spend most of tomorrow catching up on everything I didn't get done last week, when I was filling in for the docents, I should be able to get off work on time, for once. Would that work?"

"Sure. And I'll tell Jane. What time?"

He was silent again, and I began to wonder just what I'd said wrong now.

"Adam?"

He seemed to gather himself into briskness. "Sorry. I was just thinking." Another pause. "I . . . Well, would you be free for dinner, after? Not Jane, or anything. Just, you know, you and me—"

"You mean, like a date?"

Another, longer pause, and I could have kicked myself. *Model-slash-girlfriend,* I reminded myself sternly. Now the poor man was going to have to find a way to let me down gently.

"Yeah," he said. "Just like a date. I mean . . . if you want. I have to admit, your whole reincarnation thing caught me off guard, but I was actually trying to pick you up yesterday, before you freaked out on me."

"What? You . . ." *Pick me up?* I thought. *Me?* Then I started laughing, as the absurdity of it all struck me. "God, Adam, and I'm sure it would have been a lovely pickup, too. I'm sorry I ruined it. But I'd love to have dinner."

"Really?"

Was this paragon of manhood actually shy? "Really," I insisted, as forcefully as I could, even as I was thinking: *Hallelujah!*

"Shall we make it five o'clock, then, outside the museum? We'll do the tour, then . . ."

"I'll ditch Jane, I swear. And thanks, Adam. I can't wait!"

"Me, either," he said, and hung up.

When I returned to the parlor, still feeling slightly bemused, Jane pounced. "So? What happened? Did he ask you out?"

"Amazingly, yes."

She whooped loudly. Kitty was smiling at us, and Lucian was looking shuttered again.

"See? Didn't I tell you? I knew he was into you!"

"Congratulations," Kitty said. "He sounded like a charming young man."

"He is," Jane confirmed. "And dead gorgeous, too! So, when is it?" she asked me.

"Monday. He's actually offered both of us a free walking tour first, if I promise to ditch you after."

"Cool! Consider me ditched."

"What time?" Kitty asked.

"Five o'clock, outside the museum."

"Do you think he'd mind an extra? I'd love to see what a museum curator knows about the town."

"I'm sure that'd be fine. As long as you don't mind him bugging you about the house. He wants to see it."

"And I'd love to show it off. Well, that's settled, then. More sherry, anyone?"

I have to admit, I spent the rest of the night in kind of a haze. Adam had wanted to pick me up? Me? What about the model-slash-girlfriend? And poor boy; I doubt many men out to pick up a girl expected to get whomped with a big old reincarnation story.

I was still amazed he had taken it as well as he did. But

then, was that simply because—amazingly—he wanted to get into my pants, or was there really a core of truth that he believed? I knew things I shouldn't, but then, as the Atheneum had proved, that was just the problem. I knew things I shouldn't.

Had I lived through the fire or not? Was I Lucy or Obadiah? Or was I deep into delusional territory, making stuff up out of whole cloth?

With all these unanswered questions swirling through my head, it was no wonder I had a series of strangely disturbed, disjointed dreams that night.

It started on board a ship, but a ship that suddenly was Kitty's house; I could see the waves tossingly wildly through the windows as the wind screamed around us. Grey waters surged against the glass, and I knew one of the windows would soon break under its onslaught.

"Here," Kitty said, handing me a board, but as I tried to nail it over the window, it squirmed and writhed in my hands.

"How could you?" Kitty shrieked at me, but when I turned to face her, I saw another woman instead: one whose gaunt, pale face still showed signs of what must once have been a staggering beauty. Her pale blond hair, the color of spun moonlight, was pulled back in a bun with a few ringlets falling across her cheeks, and her crystalline blue eyes were large and wide-set. But the cheeks—which must once have been cream and roses—were now too sallow, and those eyes seemed somewhat wild, the pupils too wide and black.

"Stop!" the woman insisted, her voice high and taut with panic.

I glanced down at my hands. To my horror, the writhing board I had been trying to nail in place was a baby, pink and squalling from the marks I had left in its hands and feet.

"It's all your fault!" the strange woman railed at me. "You've destroyed everything!"

She flew at me, and I glanced around wildly. Lucian, who had been tending a rosebush that twined wildly up one wall, tried to leap between us, separating us. "Lucy!" he cried. "No!"

But I couldn't tell whom he was addressing. Was she Lucy, or was I?

My head reeled, and the house shuddered as if it had been hit. Outside the windows, Obadiah stretched a hand out to me, drowning in the storm-tossed sea. I tried to reach for him, but then the scene shifted, and Lucian was taking me hard against a wall. We were both still fully dressed, and my skirts were rucked up between us as he groaned and thrust into me. And a husky voice around us was singing of roses and I wanted to melt against him, but I knew it was too dangerous. And indeed, when I turned, there was Jane, her face pulled into lines of hurt and confusion.

"I thought you loved *me*," she accused, as Lucian pushed into me, and then . . .

I am standing at the head of the stairs. The white walls of my day are no more; instead, a florid wallpaper of twining vines covers them, clashing wildly with the patterned carpet on the upstairs hallway floor. It is dark outside. Oil lamps flicker and I find myself wondering if this is the sperm oil with its pure, clear light that I have heard so much about in the past few days.

I have come upstairs, but Lucy is not here. She is in Owen's room, comforting our scared son. But before long, the door opens; she emerges, the woman with the white-blond hair. Her cheeks are sallow, sunken. Her eyes wide and haunted, filled with pain. I can see the tracks of tears on her cheeks— and the ghost of girlhood in her features, the pallid remains of that once-staggering beauty.

"How?" she asks pitifully. "How could you do this to me? I trusted you. I . . ."

Her voice breaks, and guilt washes over me like a wave.

"Lucy . . ."

"How?" Her voice cracks, breaks. "Traitor! Viper!"

There is, I notice now, a storm raging around the house— a companion to the one in my head.

Her lips draw back in a snarl; her fingers hook into claws. And she flies at me—kicking, flailing.

I am stronger than she is. I cannot fight her. Besides, I understand her pain, her rage. Her helplessness. It is, I know, one too many losses, one too many betrayals. She is coming apart before my eyes.

She has, remarkably, stood up to everything else. But not to this.

Whatever love there was between us lies dead. Our twisted bond is too broken to fix.

And so I stop fighting, because I deserve her blows, her hatred. My guilt rises, so strong it might choke me. I let her beat her fury against my flesh, because it is no more than I deserve.

"Go away!" she is crying, her words punctuated by her weak, ineffectual blows. "Go away, and never come back!"

It is fair; she is right. Only . . .

A door flies open, framing a small anguished face. Owen—my tiny dark-haired son, so small and vulnerable in his white bedgown. His eyes are wide with horror, at this sight no child should see.

"Mama!" he cries. "Mama, no!"

And we both freeze.

Lightning flashes outside; thunder booms. I did not think it was possible to feel any greater hatred, any greater loathing, for myself than I already do, but it rushes in like a wave, drowning me. I am choking in a sea of bitter gall. For in all my desire to make amends—to do the right thing, at last—the one person I somehow never considered was my son.

His eyes are fixed on me—desperate, pleading.

If I leave, it will break him, irreparably; I know this now. And suddenly, all my thoughts of nobility look foolish and self-serving. We have entered into a devil's bargain, Lucy and I, one we can never untangle. Not without someone paying the price. But dear God, please let that not be Owen!

Not my boy, my son. Flesh of my flesh, blood of my blood, bone of my bone.

Why must she make me *choose*?

And suddenly, blindingly, my hatred flies outward, burning like an inferno at the edges of my vision.

If only she were dead, I find myself thinking. She, alone, is the root of all my troubles. If only she were gone!

The rain pounds down around us. Lightning; thunder. I step forward, and then . . .

With a wrench, I am elsewhere—on a sea as storm-tossed as my emotions. I am somewhat older now, I know that, in that unreasonable way one knows things as fact within dreams. This is not the first whale on the end of my line, nor will it—God willing—be the last. But this is no neat, orderly chase, and it is only now that I realize how lucky I was, on that first day, for such a placid day, such a calm whale.

This is chaos, pure and simple.

All three boats are down, at the mercy of the battering waves, and rain sheets from a leaden sky until it is hard to tell which is the whales' domain and which is ours. Nor is there one whale in the water, but a whole host of them: mothers and calves together. It is often thus—the lone whale the scarred male, while the females travel together in flocks like crows.

And they are tenacious in defending their offspring—though how tenacious, I do not realize until today.

I have fastened on to a large cow—maybe sixty-five barrels at the outside—and she thrashes madly on the end of my line. William Stockton, in the second mate's boat, has taken a slightly smaller cow, maybe fifty barrels, and she, too, creates a white spume on the water as she fights the irons. And now begins the battle: not only to tire the whale, but to make sure the lines do not tangle, the two boats become hopelessly fouled.

With half an eye, I watch to see what Obed Perry, in the first mate's boat, will do. It has been somewhat of a joke, throughout this voyage: Obed and Obadiah, the twin boatsteerers—though of course we look nothing alike. Sunny

Obed, with his hair that shines like a golden beacon in the sun, his eyes like two slices of the summer sky. And me, the dour, dark one, my fires banked so deep that none seem to see them but me and, maybe, Captain Taylor.

Not so different now, though, with both our hair dark from the rain, our faces taut with concentration.

I see Obed maneuvering after another cow, larger even than mine—for it seems our fate is to always outdo the other, as if each wants to claim the name, and the glory, for his own. It is as if sharing the name has brought us too close, and we must each strive to gain a distance, an identity, despite it.

And, if so, Taylor chose wisely, for each of us rises to heights, when pitted against the other, that we would never have attempted alone. Still, I think, when it comes down to the choice, it is Obed who will get a second's berth on his next voyage, and me the third. For the men love Obed far more than they love Obadiah. . . .

Just as Obed is about to cast at his cow, a calf rises into his path, and he is forced to take that instead. A fierce exultation rises in me—swiftly quelled—that it is I who now have the better beast. Until the large cow sees the frantic thrashing of what must have been her offspring, and falls on Obed's boat like a demon from hell. The sturdy boat falls into halves like a walnut, shedding men into the raging sea—now boiling with whales.

I see Obed vanish beneath the surface, and then there is no more time to think on his fate, for amidst this host of panicked whales, it is only my own survival that matters.

Bodies bump and batter our boat, threatening to swamp it, as the cow I am fastened on to fleets away, burying herself deep in the herd. I glance hastily back at Taylor, wondering if

I should cut the line, when I see his mouth open in horror, and that alone is what alerts me. I duck quickly as William's line comes singing across our bows, too fast for Taylor's shout, as his whale crosses the path our own has taken.

I feel the hot graze of rope across my scalp. Samuel Bradshaw is knocked into the boat, and Enoch Cotton is flipped out, as the line cuts on past our stern. But before I can draw a breath of relief, I realize the lines have crossed. Our boat swings about, jostled by a panicked whale, and the kink in the line comes flying back toward me. And I am yelling at Taylor, anyone, to cut the line, cut the line, but they are too busy pulling a spluttering Enoch back out of the sea's cold embrace, and by then it is too late. The crossed lines reach me, and I try to let go, but my smallest finger is trapped in the kink, and there is a hot, nauseating burst of pain as the digit is sheered off, and . . .

I wake, feeling the nausea boiling up my throat, and am halfway across the hall to the bathroom before I even realize that I have left the bed.

After I finished throwing up, I huddled on the bathroom floor in my sweat-soaked pj's, shaking as hard as if I had been on a bender. My finger was still throbbing, and I looked down at it in amazement, stunned to see it still on my hand.

I took a deep breath, then another, pressing my cheek to the porcelain, which was hard and cool against my skin.

"Liza? Are you okay?"

I looked up. Lucian was peering at me from beyond the half-open bathroom door. I scraped back my hair and managed a smile—though I wasn't so far gone that I didn't notice he was clad in only a pair of silk pajama pants, his lean, tanned torso a marvel in the faint light that spun in through the hallway window.

"Liza?"

"I'm fine, really," I said, all-too-aware of the foul taste in my mouth. "I must have eaten something that disagreed with me."

I felt the lie sounded credible, but he was still staring at me, curiously. As I started to struggle to my feet, he seemed to remember how to move, and extended a hand to help me up. His right.

I stared at it for a moment in turn, wondering why I was surprised to find it as whole as mine. But then, perhaps I was just obsessed with missing fingers right now. After a moment, I reached out and grabbed it, and he pulled me upright with a minimum of effort, clearly stronger than he looked.

"Can I get you anything?" he said. "Some water? Tea? Whiskey?" This latter with a faint quirk of grin.

I shook my head. I had no desire to torment myself further with a half-naked Lucian. I was close enough to him already that I could feel the heat of his body. And those pajama pants were so flimsy that I was hard-put not to stare. "No. I'm just going to brush my teeth, go back to bed. Sorry for waking you."

"Not a problem," he said. "I'm just next door, if you need me." And he jerked his head at the door between my room and Jane's.

I started a bit; I hadn't realized he'd been sleeping so close. Had he heard me, the other night? But even as a flush crept up my cheeks, he added, with another quirk of grin, "Hey, someone had to take the nursery."

The nursery. Of course, I thought, suddenly remembering.

That poor little room, kept in a constant state of readiness for the baby that never came. Year after year, until Owen . . .

My knees dipped, and suddenly there was an arm under my elbow, and entirely too much naked torso pressed against me. I muffled a gasp and pushed away, before I embarrassed myself still further.

"What did you say?" I demanded instead.

"You mean, that someone needed to take the worst room?" He was frowning down at me now—a more familiar expression, and I felt my equilibrium returning. Perhaps he had said "worst room" after all; it was an easy mistake to make. But I still knew that I was right.

The nursery. God. What devil's bargain *had* Lucy and Obadiah made, regarding Owen? And why was I back to Obadiah's dreams again?

"Brush your teeth," Lucian said curtly. "I'll be right back."

I complied, numb, then examined my reflection in the bathroom mirror. I looked like I had been dragged backwards through a bush.

When Lucian returned, he was well-wrapped in a robe, with a glass in hand. He passed it to me and I took a deep mindless gulp—then sputtered and nearly choked as the harsh whiskey burned down my throat.

"Lucian! Good Lord . . . ," I gasped, and was treated to a full-flowering of The Grin.

"See? Now you're feeling better. Night, Liza." And, with the quirk of one eyebrow, he vanished into his room.

But he was right. I *was* feeling better. Still, I downed the last of the whiskey before falling back to sleep.

CHAPTER 11

I managed to stay fairly silent about my dreams for most of the following day—especially since it was a quiet one. Lucian was off doing whatever Lucian did, and Kitty, I suspect, spent the morning at church. I would never have put her down as the religious type, but perhaps that explained why she knew Psalm 107. Which left Jane and me rattling around the house, and the closest she came to my secret was to ask, "So, did you dream about Adam last night?"

I managed to mask a shudder, but was able to deny it quite truthfully.

When Kitty got home, she started cooking for the Sunday meal, and soon the house was filled with glorious smells. Before long, Jane and I had drifted down. While Kitty had Jane kneading dough for the home-baked rolls, I took the opportunity to peruse the pamphlets I had gotten from the library.

"Hey," I said to Jane at one point, "did you know Thomas Moreland is coming to town?"

"Really?" she said, perking up. A popular writer of extremely well-crafted legal thrillers, he was a particular favorite of hers. "When?"

"July eleventh. Wednesday. Want to go?"

"Absolutely! I can't believe he's actually doing appearances, now. . . . Oh, wait. What time?"

"Eight."

She exhaled: a deep sigh of relief. "Good, that's my early day at work. And I'll make sure Rob lets me out on time. Thomas Moreland, cool! He's almost as cute as Adam."

Kitty laughed, looking up from her cutting board. "Isn't he a bit old for you?"

"Not to mention married?" Jane retorted. "But I like them older."

It was true; I'd seen the guys she brought home.

"Speaking of marriage," I said casually, though we hadn't been. "Kitty, what did Lucy look like?"

"Lucy Young?" she asked in surprise. "Why?"

I managed a casual shrug. "Just wondering."

"Gorgeous, apparently. White-blond hair, big blue eyes, and one of those perfect porcelain complexions. I believe there's a portrait of her in the museum, too."

"Really?" I must have missed it; I'd have to ask Adam to show me.

"I wonder what she thought about being married to that old stick, Obadiah," Jane said.

"Why do you say that?" Kitty asked.

Jane shivered slightly and punched her dough harder. "I saw that picture of him; he looked like a total cold fish."

"People have hidden depths, you know," Lucian said, entering the kitchen on his preternaturally silent feet.

"Please!" Jane declared. "If you can't smile, you can't fuck."

"And who says he couldn't smile? Obadiah was hardly the first person in the world to get swayed by a pretty face and marry the wrong girl."

"Can we not argue about Obadiah now, please? At least, not about his sexual prowess?" Kitty said, sounding exhausted. "That should be good, Jane; you can let them rise, now. And Lucian, can you set the table in the dining room? For five, please."

"Five?" he asked, with an arch of eyebrow.

"That's what I said."

"But—"

"Just do it, okay?"

He rolled his eyes behind Kitty's back, and Jane grinned. The two exchanged a meaningful look, then, "Don't leave that up to him, Aunt Kitty," Jane said. "He'll just make a hash of it. Liza and I will do it. So, who's our fifth?"

Kitty seemed wary. "Just a friend. Why?"

"Well, I wanted to know whether to set to impress, or set for family," Jane said breezily.

Kitty gave her a sharp look. "Look, I'm not exactly withered on the vine," she exclaimed after a moment. "What do you want me to say? That James and I fuck like bunnies when you three are not around?"

There was a moment of silence. My face was flaming, but Jane and Lucian started laughing so hard, I thought they would burst.

"Well?" Lucian said.

"Do you?" Jane echoed.

I thought Kitty would chastise them, but instead she just smiled serenely. "Of course. What fun is independent womanhood if you can't fuck like bunnies when you want?"

"Amen!" Jane declared, clapping. "When I grow up, I want to be just like you, Aunt Kitty!"

"I suspect you already are," her aunt responded dryly. "Now, table."

I admit that Lucian, Jane, and I did some wild speculation out of Kitty's earshot. Lucian had predicted white-haired and proper. Jane had scoffed at this, saying Kitty had far more taste, and conjured up a flamboyant creature who sounded half gypsy and half aging hippie, complete with ponytailed hair. Lucian had snorted at that, saying she had far more sense; then they both turned to me.

"I don't know," I said desperately. "Probably just some guy, you know?" But they wouldn't let me get away with that, so I ultimately weighed in on the side of the aging academic: grey hair, well-trimmed beard, tweed.

But James Musgrove, who told us to call him Jim, was really closest to my initial prediction: just some guy. He was shorter, rounder, and balder than any of us had expected, but I adored him on sight. As, I think, did Jane. It was only Lucian who had an odd reaction—perhaps because Jim's sudden appearance in the kitchen, bearing two bottles of wine, had startled him. He gave a sort of involuntary grunt, and then, as if to cover, he grabbed the glass of water he'd been nursing, took a big gulp—and immediately started choking.

"Excuse me," he managed, then escaped to the downstairs

bathroom, from where I could hear him coughing—or laughing hysterically; it was hard to tell.

Poor Jim looked a bit flummoxed. He put down his bottles of wine, then hesitated, looking at Kitty—clearly unsure how to greet her in company.

"It's okay," she said with a flash of humor. "They know all about us."

"Really? Well, in that case . . ." And he gave Kitty a resounding kiss that actually had Jane whooping.

"Thank you, young lady," Jim said with a twinkle, when he came up for air. Kitty was blushing fiercely. "It's good to know one's talents haven't entirely gone to waste over the years. You must be Jane; your aunt mentioned the hair. It's very becoming." Jane preened. "And you must be Liza. I'm delighted you could join us for the summer. Like Kitty, I'm another huge fan of the island, so feel free to ask me any questions."

By this point, Lucian had returned, looking rather red in the face. The two men measured each other for a moment; then Jim said, "And you must be . . . I'm sorry, do you prefer Luke or Lucian?"

"Lucian," Lucian said—and suddenly shot Jim such an open, joyous smile that I went all wobbly again, even though the expression hadn't been remotely aimed at me.

Jim grinned back. "Well, then, lovely to meet you all. Kitty, everything smells wonderful! When do we eat?"

Jim's presence was like oil on troubled waters. He didn't have an ounce of flair, but his eyes were blue and full of a sort of twinkling joy, his round face just beamed when he looked at

Kitty, and he seemed so amazingly . . . nice. And I know that is supposed to be a sort of lukewarm word, but it shouldn't be. And, in Jim's case, it definitely wasn't. He really was, genuinely, nice.

Jane and Lucian hadn't fought once, and I was actually enjoying the latter's company again. When he wasn't being an ass, Lucian had a keen wit and a good sense of humor, and we kept finding things in common. I already knew he had good taste in movies, but in books? TV? Jane and I so rarely agreed on shows that we had gotten separate televisions.

It was both lovely and frustrating all at once. Why did I have to have so much in common with someone I could rarely stand? I wondered if Adam and I would find as much to agree on; I certainly hoped so.

Jim owned a combination antiques and rare book shop, and was every bit as keen an amateur Nantucket historian as Kitty. He told us about the *Beaver*, which was the first American ship to round Cape Horn—after it had achieved an earlier moment of fame as one of the original Boston Tea Party ships. But eventually, the conversation turned to the island's favorite topic: the insanely rich.

"So, how many billionaires *are* there on the island?" Jane asked.

"Why?" Kitty said, amused. "Are you out to land one?"

Jane shrugged cheerfully. "If he's cute enough, sure. Why not? But it's just that everyone seems obsessed with the question, and we've never gotten the same answer twice. Does anyone actually know?"

"Mmmm, I suppose someone must," Kitty said. "I've heard about sixty, sixty-five."

"Nonsense," Jim countered. "There are only forty-six." He said it with such authority that I laughed. I might even have believed him, had the librarian not been equally forceful—and likewise specific—with her thirty-seven.

Kitty raised an eyebrow. "I think you're wrong, James."

"Are you sure you're not thinking millionaires?" he returned.

"Billionaires," I said dryly. "As mysterious and uncountable as unicorns."

Lucian laughed.

"What I want to know," I added, "is why everyone cares so much. Is it just some sort of status symbol?"

"Perhaps in part," Jim said thoughtfully. "But I suspect it's mostly jealousy and resentment. Do you have any idea how expensive real estate is here, now?"

I shook my head.

"I saw an ad the other day for a four-bedroom place on the outskirts of town with two acres and a view, going for nine million."

"Nine *million*?" Jane gasped.

Jim nodded. "It's criminal. So many rich people want to come here that us average folks can't afford it anymore. Even ten years ago, Kitty wouldn't have been able to buy this house. Do you have any idea what this place is worth today?"

"Fifteen million?" Lucian hazarded.

"More like thirty," Kitty countered. "It has historic value on top of everything else."

We moved on to other topics, but as we were clearing the table later, Lucian said to me, softly, "Quite a piece of work, my godmother."

"What do you mean?"

"Have you noticed that Kitty doesn't call Jim anything but James, yet insists on calling me Luke half the time?"

I had noticed, and acknowledged it by smiling. "I take it you don't like Luke, then?"

"Hate it."

"Why?"

He shrugged slightly. "Who can say? It's just never felt right."

His voice was serious, and I had the feeling I was seeing a corner of the real Lucian for the first time ever. And that was followed by a second shock, as I found myself thinking: *Lucian, Lucy.* Good Lord! I had never even considered the idea that maybe I was not the only one here who had lived before. Maybe the reason that Lucian kept ruffling my emotional feathers was that I knew him in the same odd way that I knew the town. And maybe the reason he was so prickly about the topic was that some corner of him suspected he was part of this, too.

And that wasn't an easy revelation to accept—as I knew only too well myself.

"What?" Lucian said. "Why are you staring at me like I've suddenly grown two heads?" He made a point of patting his neck. "Have I suddenly grown two heads?"

"No, sorry. Momentarily distracted." I'd have to think about this whole thing some more before I even began to consider it seriously. After all, I was still convinced, half the time, that *I* was Lucy! I kept my voice casual. "You were saying about Luke?"

He grinned, and added flippantly, "What's the point of having a cool French Canadian heritage if you can't trade on it? Girls can have Lukes aplenty, but how many get a Lucian in their lives?" He pronounced it with a French inflection, and I felt another little shiver—a completely different kind—go through me.

"Oooh, do it again! Say something else."

"In French?" he said, and when I nodded, added, "See? Proves my point right there." And he reeled off something way too fast for me to follow, then peered at me with an odd tentativeness on his face.

"Cool! What did that mean?"

A fleeting grin appeared, with a certain self-deprecating twist. "You don't speak French?"

"No. I did Spanish in school. So what was it?"

That familiar look of cynical amusement was back on his face. "Oh, something unspeakably obscene. What fun is speaking a second language if you can't curse in it? Here, give me those plates; I'll take them back to the kitchen."

Long after dinner was done and I was tucked back up into my room, I couldn't help thinking of the Lucian/Lucy connection. If I was Obadiah and he was Lucy . . . God knows, there had been passion between them, so maybe that explained my odd reaction to Lucian. Yet what had gone so wrong between them, and how had it involved Owen? I had felt Obadiah's rage, his desire to wound.

God, none of it made a lick of sense. And I was so tired of thinking about it all. Better to think about my date with Adam. Gorgeous, eligible Adam, the bastard love child of Rufus Sewell and Ioan Gruffudd . . .

I grinned, then rolled over and turned off the light. I was trying to keep Lucian from invading my thoughts of Adam when I became aware of an odd, rhythmic noise in the darkness. It took me a minute to identify it, since it was so out of context in this house. Kind of a ghostly moan, and a creaking . . . For a panicked instant I actually thought that Lucy's ghost was manifesting on the landing, then recognition kicked in. I hadn't lived with Jane for nine months for nothing.

But good Lord, I thought to myself in some amusement, I would have thought that bunnies would be quieter than that.

I actually managed to fall asleep halfway through, but I do wonder if what I heard didn't have some salacious effect on my dreams, because . . .

I am back to the wall, only it is not Lucian that holds me, but Obadiah. And somehow, I know this is the true version of events. His hands are hard and demanding on my waist, and he is thrusting desperately into me as if he might find his redemption within.

His breath is hot and ragged on my neck, and my shoulder blades grind uncomfortably into the hard wall behind me, but I clutch him, trying to absolve him in the only way I can, for what he cannot help but see as a betrayal.

We are caught in a trap neither one of us can escape.

There will be time to be slow later, but he needs this now: this hot, rough urgency.

My skirts are bunched around my waist, crushed between us; my legs are twined about his waist. He holds me up with the strength of his arms alone. He hasn't even bothered to let down his breeches, just unfastened the front. I feel the rough fabric scrape against me as he thrusts, and his need for me ignites an answering fire.

There is a reckless danger to this that thrills me, even as it scares me. But my need for him has become too great to deny. I wrap my arms around him, urging him on. . . .

And I awake to the sounds of Jim and Kitty, yet again.

CHAPTER 12

Jim was sitting at the breakfast table when I came down the next morning, looking surprisingly bright-eyed and well-rested, and I have to admit I wasn't sure what to say to him. What did one say to a guy who had been doing the horizontal tango half the night?

Fortunately, he took matters out of my hands. "I hope we didn't keep you up too late," he said, sounding slightly sheepish, but not in the least repentant. "I kept forgetting we had company."

It was strange to realize that this really was more his house than it was ours; I had settled in so completely, it was like I had never lived anywhere else.

"No, it was fine," I said, then couldn't resist adding, "You only woke me up once."

Jim laughed, then flushed, and we dropped the subject. But as Jane commented, later, "That was kind of creepy. I mean, I'm delighted to know that old people can still get it on, but that was *Aunt Kitty,* for Christ's sake!" She shuddered, then poked me. "So, are you ready for Adam today?"

I had actually been feeling a bit guilty about Adam, as if it were somehow disloyal to keep dreaming about other men. But I think part of me was hoping that a night out with a normal man would help stabilize the crazy ride that had become my life. I wanted this to be a nice, normal summer fling, with no whales whatsoever. And no sudden moments of recognition during our walking tour.

No passing out, I told myself firmly. *Not today.*

Indeed, everything went brilliantly . . . at first. Jane, Kitty, and I got to the museum at about ten minutes before five, and when Adam came out to meet us—bang on the dot of five—his eyes lit up at the sight of me. (But then, I had put particular care into my outfit; Jane and I had spent about an hour going through my closet, trying on different combinations. I felt like I was in high school again, but it seemed the time spent was worth it.) He leaned over to kiss me on the cheek in greeting before turning to Jane, and I flushed in pleasure.

Kitty, who caught my eye, grinned and raised an appreciative eyebrow. I was still finding it a bit hard to meet her gaze since last night, but this helped.

As introductions were performed and questions raised about houses, a voice behind me drawled, "So, are we walking, or not?"

I whirled. It was Lucian, his silver eyes filled with a certain cynical amusement.

Jane scowled. "Who invited you, Irish?"

"What, it wasn't an open invitation?" He turned to Adam. "You don't mind an extra body, do you? Kitty has always been bugging me to learn more of the land of my birth."

The two men measured each other. I could tell Adam was

a little suspicious, but Lucian seemed more amused than anything.

"Of course not," Adam said politely.

"My godson, Lucian Theriault." Kitty made the introductions. "Lucian, this is Liza's friend, Adam Gallagher."

I thought there was a slight emphasis on "Liza's friend," but Lucian seemed oblivious.

"Nice to meet you," he said, holding out a hand. He and Adam shook, and that seemed enough for Adam.

He began by telling us how Nantucket was a glacial island, and followed that up with the Native American creation legend, which told of a giant named Maushop who slept on the shores of Cape Cod. But he didn't like sand in his moccasins, and so threw them out to the sea in a fit of pique; the moccasins then became Nantucket and Martha's Vineyard. Nantucket, meant "far off place" in the Wampanoag language.

Adam went on to repeat some of what Jane and I had read about in the museum: the history of the early settlers, many of whose direct descendents still lived here. The earliest settlers had formed their first community on a different site from the present town. When that harbor had silted in, they had physically moved the town to its new location.

"They were Quakers, you see, and thus very frugal. And to them, it made more sense to take the houses apart and put them back together elsewhere than to start again from scratch," Adam explained. "Between 1700 and 1800, the island was a totally Quaker island, and it was probably this fact alone that made them such good whalers. The Quakers didn't see that making money was in any way contrary to worshipping God. As they saw it, it was their duty to God to do everything as perfectly as they could—including making money and being successful.

"In fact—despite the brutality of the slaughter of the whales, and the creatures' obvious suffering during the process—they used the Bible to justify their work."

" 'And God said, Let us make man in our image, after our likeness: and let them have dominion over the fish of the sea, and over the fowl of the air, and over the cattle, and over all the earth, and over every creeping thing that creepeth upon the earth,' " I found myself quoting, dreamily.

Adam looked startled, but Lucian, I noticed, was smiling enigmatically again. "Exactly. Genesis 1:26. The old dominion thing," Adam continued. "The early whalers had a number of mistaken ideas—including the thought that, as the old, traditional whaling grounds were tapped out, the whales were simply moving on to more fertile areas. They didn't realize that sperm whales are highly territorial creatures, and that they were wiping out the local populations. Destroying their own livelihood, as it were. How's that for irony?

"The Quakers were also a very tight community. The island, in those days, was like a gigantic extended family. It was said that if you arrived on the island looking for a specific man, you could ask anyone you encountered where he was, and they could not only direct you to the house, but also tell you if he was home.

"The downside to this was that Nantucket became a very insular island. Nantucketers wouldn't believe a piece of information unless it came from another Nantucketer. In fact, they were extremely suspicious of outsiders in general, called them—"

"Coofs," I inserted again, caught up in his narrative.

This time, Adam's glance was more rueful. "Again, Liza's right. 'Coofs' was a bastardization of 'Cape Codder'—regardless of where the foreigner actually came from.

"In the early 1800s, Nantucket was the acknowledged whaling capital of the world. But by the 1820s, neighboring New Bedford began to rise in prominence. Then, in the 1840s, Nantucket was dealt three fatal blows that rang the death knell for whaling."

"The fire?" I said.

Adam smiled at me. "That was one of them, in 1846. But the first was the sandbar that lies across the entrance to our harbor. By the 1840s, the whaling ships had become so big, in order to accommodate the longer voyages, that they could no longer clear the bar easily. Then the Great Fire destroyed most of the commercial part of town—docks, warehouses, and many ships. And the third cause? Anyone have any idea?"

There was a moment of silence; then Kitty said, "The Gold Rush."

Adam grinned at her. "Precisely. After gold was discovered in California, the whalemen fled in droves to become prospectors. It was said that, in the early days of the Gold Rush, the San Francisco harbor was littered with the abandoned hulks of old Nantucket whaleships.

"The last whaler sailed out of Nantucket harbor in 1869, and out of New Bedford in 1925. The only surviving whaler in the world is the *Charles W. Morgan*. She's docked at Mystic Seaport, just down the road. It's worth a trip down to see her; she's a lovely old ship. Though"—he grinned at me—"for Liza's sake, I should probably say 'barque.'"

I smiled back at him. And damn me for knowing exactly what that meant.

We wandered the streets as Adam pointed out various historical buildings. He showed us where the Great Fire started, and told us of that dreadful night, when flames from the hat shop spread to the wharves and ignited the barrels of whale oil, then swept back up Main Street. No lives were lost in the blaze, but all but two brick buildings on Main Street were destroyed, as were several structures on the side streets.

Despite Adam's vivid description, I had no sudden visions of blazes, no tingling of recognition from the few structures that remained. Whoever I had been, I hadn't lived through the fire; that much was certain.

And a blackout-free day was just peachy by me. It was a beautiful late afternoon. The sun was shining brightly and there was an actual hint of summer in the air. And if I found myself tuning out Adam's commentary to admire his jeans-clad ass or boyish grin, then who could blame me? It was exactly what I had been hoping for—a day fully grounded in the here and now.

Which was an odd way to think of an historical walking tour, but there you had it. As we wandered back toward the museum, Jane asked, "So, Starbuck. Is that, like, Starbucks? Did the family make good?"

"Not that way," Adam confessed with a smile. "It's undoubtedly where Melville got the name for his novel, but no. The famous coffee baron among us was another one entirely."

"Folger," Lucian said.

"Exactly. Mr. Good-to-the-Last-Drop himself. The Folger brothers went out to the Gold Rush to be prospectors, but

James Athearn Folger kept noticing how all the men had to hand-roast their beans, and thus made bad coffee. So he started a San Francisco business that pre-roasted beans—which grew into the industry we know today.

"And there is, of course, one other really famous Nantucketer. Care to guess?"

There was silence. Kitty was smiling; clearly she knew the answer, but she wasn't saying. Eventually, Adam said, "Has anyone ever shopped at Macy's?"

Jane wrinkled her nose; Macy's was well below her average style. But I had certainly darkened their doors in my pre-Jane days.

"Really?" I said. "Macy's? Cool!"

"It gets better," Adam confided. "Do you know what the symbol of Macy's is?"

I thought for a minute. "A red star?" I hazarded at last.

"Precisely. Rowland Hussey Macy, like any good Nantucketer, went a-whaling aboard the *Emily Morgan*. In the South Seas, he got a red star tattooed on each hand. When he founded his department store, it became his symbol."

It was odd, I reflected, for one who had spent her life dreaming of whaling, not to realize how widely the tendrils of that industry had touched her world. It was about more than chasing whales in boats. It had, in a sense, molded our land.

And suddenly, I felt as if my dreams were far more noble.

Whaling was odd—a bold and romantic trade until you started looking into the grim and awful details of it. But then, just when you thought it was brutal and vile, it turned the tables on you again.

So maybe it was because of my oddly reflective mood that what happened did. Or maybe it was just inevitable, given my history with this place. Because no sooner had Adam brought us within sight of what had been Nantucket's first wharves than the world slid and twisted before my eyes, and . . .

I am standing before the busy piers. As usual, they swarm with activity in the summer sunshine. Not that it is true summer yet; it is too cool, and the women that pass me clutch shawls around them as they hurry about their business, but still I feel an absurd pride in the place. At its prominence, its vitality.

Whaleships by the dozen line the docks, their masts bristling like a forest of winter trees against the cerulean sky. A cacaphony of voices bounces among the spars: some trading friendly insults, others barking commands. One ship is retarring its rigging, and the sharp scent of the pitch twines in the breeze, an acrid undertone to the oil.

Small boys by the dozen swarm among the vessels, their voices high with excitement. Some are running errands for the mates; others scurry up the ratlines like monkeys. Another group—older and more sober than their fellows—clusters around a mate who shows them how to load a whaleboat. One of the boys swings recklessly from the davits until one of his companions pushes him off, and he splashes loudly into the water.

That one, when he takes up his first oar, will need some discipline, I can tell. But this is where the new talent is judged and forged. Some of these lads know these ships as well as their masters; know the name of each line and cross-beam.

It was so in New Bedford, and so it is here. And I have been here long enough now to know our fleet. Look, there is the *Prudence Coffin,* and there the *Chili*. And the *Aurora,* at last returned from seven long years at sea.

The only thing that still looks strange to me are the citizens—all clad at the height of fashion, and yet all in black, like a gathering of crows. . . .

Liza?"

I blink, amazed to find myself still standing.

"Are you okay? You went blank there for a minute." Adam's face, near mine, was pulled into lines of concern, and I cursed, mentally. Was it so hard to have one vision-free day?

At least I had stopped falling over. That was something, I supposed.

"I'm fine. Honestly. Probably just getting hungry."

I could tell he didn't quite believe me, but Jane was quick on her cue.

"And I think we all have somewhere to be. Kitty? Lucian?"

Kitty thanked Adam for the tour; Lucian looked at us and said, "Behave, you two."

"Pay no attention to him," Jane countered. "Have fun. Misbehave."

And, with a grin, she towed the group away.

CHAPTER 13

Adam smiled as Jane departed. "I like a girl who knows how to take a hint. How long have you known her?"

"Nine months. But it seems like I've known her for years!"

"And the others?"

I did a quick calculation. "Five days." Which seemed almost more unbelievable than nine months. "Jane and I are roommates. Grad school."

"Really? I suddenly realize I know next to nothing about you. What are you studying?"

"Education," I said, with a slight wrinkle of my nose, which Adam immediately picked up on.

"Don't you like it?"

"No, I do. It's just that it always sounds like such a complete cliché. I mean, what else are you supposed to do with a BA in English? Except that . . . I don't know, the idea of teaching for a living has always felt right to me."

He flashed me a grin. "A vocation?"

"Well, I don't know if I'd go that far," I said, embarrassed.

"For all I know, it could just be a fundamental lack of imagination on my part." But I had a feeling he knew all about vocations. So young, and already an associate curator. Which reminded me. . . .

"Adam, can you . . . Oh, damn! The museum's probably closed already, isn't it?"

"And you don't think I have keys? Don't sound so glum. All fantasies fulfilled here."

"Excuse me?"

"What, you've never had any fantasies about being alone in a museum at night?"

I'm afraid I just stared at him, and after a minute, he added, sheepishly. "So, that's just me, then. Fair enough. Caroline never got that one, either."

"Caroline?"

"My ex. Sorry, not the best way to start our date. Let's start again. What can I show you in the museum?"

"Well, Kitty said you had a portrait of Lucy Young."

"We do. Right next to the one of Obadiah."

"Can I see it?"

"Of course," he said, then peered at me with a slight quirk of a smile. "As long as you promise not to pass out again."

"I swear."

"Are you sure?"

"Not even close," I said cheerfully. "But shall we risk it anyway?"

He laughed, and let me into the darkened museum. And I had to admit that Adam might have had a point about after-hours museums. Everything was silent and shadowy. Exhibit cases loomed like ghosts in the darkened rooms, and the whalebones gleamed palely overhead.

I edged slightly closer to him, realizing how delightfully illicit this all felt. Kind of sexy, really. We could do anything here, and no one would ever know.

As if sensing my growing intrigue, Adam shot me a sly, sidelong glance. "Fun, huh?"

"Certainly . . . different," I conceded.

"Told you. Now, let's go see Lucy."

I shivered at his words, and he used that as an excuse to drop an arm around my shoulders. I leaned into him. His body, beneath his jacket, was hard and warm against mine.

And, I swear, he took me the long way around, too.

But soon we were back in the room where my earlier humiliation had taken place, and there was Lucy, as promised, right next to Obadiah. She was every bit as beautiful as Kitty had described her. Her skin glowed with a rosy health, and her large, wide-set eyes were a pure, crystalline blue. She wore her white-blond hair in a chignon and ringlets. And she was every bit the woman from my dreams.

"She's lovely," Adam said.

"She was," I admitted. "Then."

"So you've seen her?"

I nodded. "I know Jane thinks I was Obadiah, but it's not that simple. It's like . . . sometimes I'm him, and sometimes I'm her. Which convinces me even more that I'm just making things up." But I suppose there was one way to tell—or, at least, to test my theories further. "Hey, Adam, you have access to the records and things. Can you find something out for me?"

"Absolutely! I mean, if I can. What are you after?"

"The name of the person who was Captain Barzillai Taylor's boatsteerer aboard the *Wampanoag*. That is, if the *Wampanoag* was even a ship, and Barzillai Taylor even its captain. I mean, who'd name a kid Barzillai?"

"Actually, it's a good old Nantucket name," he said, and I felt my spirits sinking. "But yeah, I can find that out for you." His green eyes were curiously bright. "Why?"

"Because, in my whaling dreams, my first time at sea was as boatsteerer, aboard the *Wampanoag*. At least, if the dreams are anything to go by. . . ."

"A recent dream?"

"A few nights ago." I flashed him a rueful smile. "If I'm right, the first mate's boatsteerer was named Obed Perry. It was kind of a joke among the crew: Obed; Obadiah . . ." My voice trailed off lamely, and then I added, "You think I'm nuts, don't you?"

He laughed faintly. "Maybe a bit. But I like you. You're funny and cynical—and you seem to believe in all of this as little as I do, which ironically convinces me all the more. Besides . . ."

"What?"

He moved a little closer, and ran a light finger along my cheek, pushing back a strand of hair. "You have other charms."

I felt myself grinning, and my heart started pounding faster. "I do?"

"I noticed you right away. For a moment, you reminded me of . . ."

"What?"

"Sorry, dangerous ground," he said hastily. "But didn't I already mention I was trying to pick you up?"

"You might have said something to that effect," I agreed.

And then he kissed me. He tasted cool, and slightly sweet. I twined my arms around his neck, letting one hand sneak up into his dark curls, which were as thick and soft as I had imagined.

I pressed tighter against him, and felt definite stirrings of arousal pressing back against me. Damn! He really did want me. . . .

We were both slightly breathless by the time we broke the kiss.

"Sorry," he said. "Deserted museums always get to me. I usually don't jump the girl until after I've bought her dinner. I mean, I don't even know your last name yet!"

He didn't know my first name, either, I thought, and laughed. "Donovan. And no apologies needed. I was kind of ripe for the jumping."

He surveyed me, a twinkle in his eyes. "Well, then, have you ever made out under a whaleboat before?"

"Uh, no, I don't think so. I mean . . . not that I remember, anyway."

He started laughing. "Yeah, that suggestion might have a different meaning for you than for others."

I raised an eyebrow archly. "Why, is it a suggestion you make to the girls often? I mean, the nonreincarnated ones?"

"Actually, you're the first."

"In which case, I'm honored." I moved closer, tilting my face back up to his, and whispered against his mouth, "The whaleboat it is, then."

Only my stomach chose that moment to betray me, rumbling loudly.

Adam didn't let that distract him from the kiss, but he did say with a grin, after he released me, "After dinner, though, I think. Come on, I've got the perfect place in mind."

It was, of course, Obadiah's—and he seemed a little surprised when Rob greeted me at the door by name.

"You know this place?" he asked after we were escorted to our table.

"You could say that. Jane and I had dinner here the night you and I met. Plus, she starts working here tomorrow."

"Working?"

I grinned. "Don't let the green hair fool you. Or the devil-may-care attitude. Jane's a natural bartender. And this definitely isn't a vacation for either of us. Like I told you, I'm a graduate student. I can't afford to spend a whole summer unemployed."

"So where are you working?"

I grimaced. "Well, that's the issue. Rob offered me a waitress spot here, but I'd rather cut both my feet off. I'm a dreadful waitress. But nothing else seems to grab me—despite my combing the paper. I don't suppose you have an opening at the museum?"

I meant it as a joke, but he didn't laugh. Instead, he studied me seriously. "Well, you do have teacher training. Tell me a few facts about the town."

"What, from my memories?"

"No—though we'll get into that a bit later. From my tour today, I meant."

I shrugged, then recited the facts about the fire. At least I had been listening, then.

"Very impressive!" he said when I had finished.

"Not really. You're a good speaker."

He flushed. "And I already know that you know your whaling. Besides, it could be neat to have people getting a lecture from someone who'd actually been there before—not that we'll tell them that, of course!" he added, and I laughed. "I do have a reputation to maintain. But, yeah, if you want, I can pull a string or two. The pay's not great, and there will be a bunch of training first, but . . . It's a good place to work. What do you think?"

"God, yes, please! That is . . . if you mean it. I don't want anyone thinking it's like . . . nepotism, or something."

"Well, given that you are not my nephew, I think we can rule out nepotism right there."

"Adam . . ."

"Kidding," he said. "I mean, I'm hoping you see me as more than the path to a decent job, but let me talk to Marian tomorrow morning. She's the head of the NHA, so all hires ultimately go through her. But my word will carry weight. Now, tell me all about Liza Donovan. You know, just in case Marian asks."

I smiled, but it didn't take me long to provide the essential facts. Apart from the dreams, my life had been boring. It didn't even get us through the appetizer course.

"Boyfriends?" he asked.

"A few, here and there, but nothing earthshattering. You?"

"Nope, no boyfriends," he admitted, grinning.

Over the entrées, I learned that he was thirty-four (which

astounded me, and I think he was thrown by my own tender twenty-four) and his middle name was Stephen. He was born near Mystic, Connecticut, and had spent his childhood playing aboard the *Morgan,* thanks to an uncle who worked at the Seaport. That had started his lifelong love affair with whaling. He had done both his undergrad degree and a Ph.D. in History at Yale, and a year at the New Bedford Whaling Museum before taking the job in Nantucket—where he had helped to set up the newly redesigned museum just a few years ago. A few ex-girlfriends, but only one who counted—the aforementioned Caroline. They had been dating for a year and living together for three before she left him, extremely unexpectedly, about three years earlier.

"Don't take this wrong," he said, "but you kind of look like her. Her hair is straighter—"

"Lucky dog," I interrupted.

"—and her eyes are a bit darker, but . . . Well, not that I'm looking for Caroline again," he hastened to add. "It's just that I seem to have a type, and—"

"I'm it? I'm flattered. And surprised, I admit. Most people seem to go for Jane instead."

"Jane?" he said, in such genuine amazement that I almost kissed him again, just for that.

"Well, don't say it that loudly or with such horror in here after tomorrow; she might take offense. But yeah; it's kind of like rooming with a human magnet. It's quite impressive, actually."

"And what about Lucian?"

"Lucian? What about him? Kitty thinks he's pining for Jane, but I think they really can't stand one another—and I can't exactly say I blame her. I've never really seen the appeal of the moody, sullen type, myself, but I suppose we'll see what the summer brings. Why?"

"Just the way he was looking at you. I was kind of wondering . . ."

"What, if there's something between us? God, no! Besides, he thinks I'm insane. So, points to you on that one."

He made a vaguely noncommittal sound, adding: "And speaking of which . . . You saw something today, didn't you? When you went all quiet."

I cursed silently. Apparently, my acting abilities weren't as formidable as I had hoped. I was debating what to tell him when Rob interrupted. "Dessert's on the house," he said, offering us menus, "so indulge yourselves."

"Thanks, Rob. Do you know Adam?"

He didn't, so I performed the introductions; then Adam ordered a berry crumble and I treated myself to a wicked-sounding ice cream sundae. But, of course, after Rob had left, the question still hung between us.

"If you don't want to talk about it . . . ," Adam said.

"No, it's just . . . I still feel a bit of a fool for believing any of this, even as it's happening," I confessed. "But I see this stuff, and . . . Well, you're probably one of the only people who can tell me if it is real or not. I mean, I could be seeing the historical equivalent of giant monkeys roaming the streets and not know the difference."

"If you saw giant monkeys," he said, "I really would worry. But . . ."

With a little mental shrug, I told him the lot. He sat in silence for a long moment after I had finished.

"Well?" I finally asked. "Were the *Chili* and the *Aurora* even Nantucket whaleships?"

"Yeah," he said. "And even scarier . . . Oh, thanks," he added to our waitress as our desserts were placed in front of us. "Even scarier," he said, when she had departed again, "is the fact that I can pretty much date your vision."

"What?" I exclaimed, with a spoonful of sundae halfway to my mouth.

"The thing about the *Aurora* returning from the seven-year voyage? It did, in June of 1837. So . . . Liza, you're not going to faint again, are you?"

"No," I said, putting down my spoon, but he didn't know what a near thing it had been. "So, I saw June of 1837?"

"It seems so. And damn, I wish I could have seen what you saw! Just to know what the place really looked and felt like, apart from historical accounts." True academic that he was, he pulled himself together with effort.

We moved on to more mundane topics as we dug into our desserts. We ended up lingering over drinks, and by the time we paid the bill, it was well past eleven. Adam had to work tomorrow, plus make an early phone call on my behalf. So we decided to call it a night.

"Ugh," I complained as we walked back out into the night, "I should *not* have eaten that whole sundae! I can barely move."

"So, no whaleboat?" he said suggestively, then spoiled it by yawning.

I laughed. "Rain check?"

"Absolutely."

Gentleman that he was, he walked me home, though the

streets were more crowded than I had anticipated late on a Monday night. We were certainly not the only couple out for a stroll. There were also far more teenagers than I had expected—and even a few families.

"Tourists," Adam said. "You'll get used to it in time."

At least the back streets were more deserted, and darker. And there was some most satisfactory kissing beneath the overhanging branches of a sheltering elm.

So what if it wasn't like my dreams? A connection like that took time to grow. And Adam and I were just getting to know each other. There was potential here, in spades.

In the dark shadows beside Kitty's portico, he kissed me again. "I'll call you tomorrow, about the job," he said. "And to set a new date for . . . other things."

"I can't wait," I replied. And it was true.

Chapter 14

I had forgotten how much fun dating was. It was a good ten minutes more before I actually let myself into the house—ten blissfully breathless minutes. And I had also forgotten how much fun the deconstruction afterwards could be. For no sooner had I shut the door to my bedroom than it sprang open again and Jane whirled in.

"I only heard one set of footsteps," she said, "so I figured it was safe. Well?" And she peered at me.

I stared back, and she started grinning. "Clothes slightly disordered, hair nicely tousled, and . . ." She peered closer. "Ah-ha! Well-kissed, unless I miss my guess."

I laughed and touched my lips reflexively. "Yeah, definitely well-kissed."

She whooped loudly and flopped down on my bed. "So? Tell me all!"

"Jane!" I exclaimed. "You'll wake Kitty."

"So?" Jane said callously. "She kept us up most of last night. Now, was it amazing?"

I smiled and she whooped again. Then, while I got ready for bed, I told her everything.

"Really?" she said. And, "The whaleboat? Oh, Liza, this is excellent! I'm so happy for you. A great date and a job, too!"

"I don't have the job yet," I reminded her.

"No, but you will. Ooh, and just think of all the possibilities! Misbehavior with the boss. Well, not the boss, exactly, but you know what I mean. You are going to have so much fun! We both are. What a summer so far, eh?"

"Yeah, I owe you for this one. Now, vamoose. Some of us actually need some sleep."

She obliged, but apparently couldn't resist poking her head back around my door as she left and adding, with a waggle of eyebrows, "Hey . . . Blow, Liza, Blow!"

"Well, not yet," I temporized, "but hopefully soon." And, with a little ghost of a laugh, she vanished.

I turned out the lights, then, with a little smile, sank into sleep—and dreams. . . .

The sea is slate grey—light beneath a night-black sky for all that it is still day. The winds are howling, and the sails are all reefed on the yards as we bob about like a cork on the waves. The walls of water loom high above our bows—solid, glassy sheets rising thirty feet or more, with spray flying off their peaks to crash against the deck.

I have rarely seen a storm this fierce. For a full twelve hours it has raged, and it is all we can do to keep our ship afloat. Water sheets from the yards and the rigging, spilling like blood across the decks and over the gunwales. We mount the great crests of waves, then fall off until we lie again in the dark valley between the walls of water—which, in some places, are a thin, translucent green, like frosted sea glass.

Rain pours down, and the sea sluices the decks, and poor George Dawes nearly goes overboard until Stockton catches and steadies him. There is no time for thanks in a storm, only survival. The gratitude will come later, when we are all warm and dry. But for now, we are wet and cold and there have been no whales, not for nigh-on a month. Our hold is not yet a quarter full, for all that we have been at sea for more than half a year.

But God works in mysterious ways, and sometimes He sends a sign of beauty and hope in the midst of misery. I will never forget how each man who saw it went soft and silent, how his face smoothed of fear in the midst of the blast, glowing instead with an awed wonder.

We shudder down the face of a wave, and there they are. Whales, gamboling in and out of that high wall of water like children at play: wheeling and diving and sliding down the wave side. At times, they float above and around us, as we plunge below the glassy wall.

We cannot lower the boats in such a blow, so all we can do is watch the sheer joy in motion of these great beasts, the innocent exuberance of a day uninterrupted by our harpoons.

It is as if, in their joy, they give us hope for our future, and remind us that there is always salvation, even in the midst of terror. . . .

———

The ringing of my cell phone woke me the next morning. The room was washed in sunlight as I fumbled the phone off the nightstand and answered.

"Did I wake you?" said Adam's voice, in my ear.

"Mmm-hmmm."

"Oh," he said. "Wow." Another moment of silence, then, "Sorry, I was just processing the visuals. I had intended this to be a strictly business call—at least at first—but the thought of getting you all warm in bed . . . You are in bed, aren't you?"

"Yup," I confirmed.

More silence, then, "What are you wearing?"

"Adam!"

"Sorry, only human. So, what *are* you wearing?"

"A big furry ape suit," I replied tartly. "Did I get the job?"

"God, that's a mood-killer," he said with a laugh. "But yes, Marian wants to see you at two o'clock at the NHA offices on Fair Street. Seven Fair Street. She gets the final say, but she's happy to interview you. Do you know how to find the place?"

"I'll figure it out," I said.

"Good. Oh, and one other thing. I did a little digging this morning, and you were right; Barzillai Taylor was indeed the captain of the *Wampanoag*. And want to guess who his boat-steerer was in 1807?"

"Obadiah Young?" I said with a shiver of inevitability.

"Got it in one."

"And the first mate's boatsteerer?"

"Obed Perry. Only . . ."

I remembered my dream, how the cold waves had swallowed him. "He died, didn't he? Aboard the *Wampanoag*?"

"Damn, you keep stealing my thunder. Yup. October twenty-fourth, 1809." The day Obadiah lost his finger. "So, what happened?"

"A whale happened; what else?" I was silent for a moment, then said, "Thanks, Adam. I owe you."

"I can think of a few ways for you to pay me back."

"So can I," I admitted. "Starting with celebratory drinks tonight?"

"Damn, I can't tonight; we have a staff thing. Wednesday?"

"Done. And Adam?"

"Yeah?"

"In answer to your previous question . . . Not very much at all."

I laughed and hung up while he was still strangling.

My interview with Marian went very well. She quizzed me extensively on the information that Adam had related both in his whaling lecture, and in his walking tour, and seemed quite impressed by my responses.

"Adam said you were smart and a quick study," she said, "and it seems he was right. But I still want you to spend at least a week listening to other people's tours and lectures before we let you out on your own. Our whaling lecture is fairly standard, thanks to the accompanying slide presentation, but everyone chooses slightly different facts and a slightly different route for their tours, depending on their interests. Obviously, some things we always mention, like the Great Fire, but there is some room for freedom. Does that all sound good to you?"

It did. Adam was right that the pay was not stellar, but my expenses were also pretty minimal; I would come out all right. For the first week or so, I'd be working admissions and—as Marian had said—observing other people's tours and lectures. But once the summer crunch really started, I'd be on my own.

I signed a raft of paperwork, had my photo taken, and Marian gave me some local history books. I'd have my official ID badge soon, and I started on Thursday.

And not once was any past affiliation with Nantucket mentioned.

"She doesn't know, does she?" I said to Adam after, when I phoned him to thank him again and tell him the news.

"God, no!" he responded fervently. "And she never should."

When I arrived home, Kitty said, "Congratulations on your job, Liza! That is excellent news. I spoke to Marian this morning—did I mention we were friends?—and recommended you wholeheartedly. I didn't, however, mention your little, um . . . thing. Marian's a doll, but she wouldn't understand it. She's a fabulous researcher, but way too literal-minded."

I smiled. "My lips—and Adam's—are sealed."

"Good. And you've got books, too. Excellent." She held out her hands, and I handed the volumes over. She looked through them. "I've read all of these myself. Fascinating stuff. So, do you have any plans with Adam tonight?"

"Not until Wednesday. Why?"

"James is coming over tonight to cook dinner, and he does a terrific lasagna. We'd love to have you join us if you are free. He always cooks enough for a small army."

"Thanks, that sounds wonderful."

Lucian was nowhere to be seen, and Jane was at work, so I distracted myself by diving into the first of my books. And by seven o'clock, the house had indeed filled with the most delectable smells.

I drifted downstairs to find everyone but Jane assembled in the kitchen. Lucian, his back to me, was opening a bottle of wine.

"Ah, fabulous timing," Kitty exclaimed as she saw me. "I was just about to send Luke upstairs to fetch you, so you've saved the reprobate a trip."

"Reprobate?" he said, turning to shoot me an ironic smile over one shoulder. "What have I done to deserve that?"

"Everyone else in this house is now gainfully employed. Or at least justifiably busy," she countered.

"Hey!" he protested. "I'll figure something out. Eventually. . . ."

She measured him, but he forestalled her comment, adding, "Yeah, I know. You push because you love. Now, stop it." He poured four glasses of wine and handed me the first. "I take it you are the newly employed paragon who has brought this diatribe down on my poor, jobless head?"

"Yeah, sorry."

He waved a dismissive hand. "It's my lot in life to be slighted. So, where are you working?"

"The NHA," I admitted.

He raised an eyebrow and plopped himself down at the table. Someone—probably Kitty or Jim—had assembled a plate of tiny appetizers: tomato and mozzarella squares toothpicked between a basil leaf. Lucian reached for one and ate it reflexively. "Impressive. And what have they got you doing there? Channeling the past and writing down your observations?"

"Luke!" Kitty said sharply. "Did your mother raise you in a barn?"

"She raised me right here, as you well know," he said archly, raising the other eyebrow for effect.

"Then clearly Montreal was a bad influence. No one at the NHA—save Adam—knows the slightest thing about Liza's experiences. And no one is going to tell them, either," she added sternly.

He frowned, then turned back to me. "So, what *are* you doing?"

I took the seat across from him. "Right now? Working the admissions desk at the museum. But eventually, they'll have me doing tours and lectures. Want me to tell you how the Lily Pond disappeared?"

He put his hands over his ears. "God, no more Nantucket history, please! Someone, change the subject."

Someone did, and before long I forgot to even miss Jane. It was amazing how fast these people had become like a second family to me. Jim and I got into a grand political debate, and we were all laughing by the time Jane returned around eight. She had already eaten—"Rob made me this huge burger; I couldn't resist!"—but sat down to join us nonetheless. And soon enough, the smell of Jim's lasagna got to her, and she accepted a generous plateful, tucking into it with enthusiasm. "Call me first, the next time you are doing this," she said, "and I'll skip the burger. Hey, Liza, did you get that job?"

"Yup. So how was Obadiah's?"

"Fun as hell!" She grinned. "You and Adam should come in for a drink next time you go out. I'll comp you some stuff. All of you," she added magnanimously. "I mean, what's the fun of knowing a bartender if you don't take advantage?"

When I met Adam the next night in front of the museum and floated the idea, he was amenable. "I never say no to free drinks," he told me cheerfully. "Still too close to my days as an impoverished graduate student, I suppose." And then he kissed me properly.

Jane was bustling behind the bar like a green-haired dervish when we entered, utterly in her element, pulling pints and mixing drinks with panache, flirting with male and female customers alike. She waved at us cheerfully as we entered, and pointed to a free spot at one end of the bar.

We took our seats, and didn't have to wait long for service—another advantage to knowing the bartender.

"So, any billionaires?" I teased as she materialized before us, planting her elbows on the other side of the bar and regarding us.

"Not yet, but I remain hopeful. And damn, do the people around here tip well!" I suspected that had as much to do with Jane's personality as the local affluence, but said nothing. "So, what can I get you?"

We ordered two Whale's Tails, and Jane added a bowl of spicy mixed nuts and pretzels. And all was going brilliantly, until a voice from behind us said, "Hello, you two."

I whirled. Surprise, surprise: it was Lucian.

"Mind if I join you?" he added, indicating the free seat beside us.

"What are you doing here?" I demanded.

He shrugged elaborately. "Well, Jane said to stop by, so I did. I won't stay long, but I figured I'd know at least one person here. Lucky me, knowing three."

Adam seemed to take the coincidence at face value, but I knew what had been said at dinner last night. "Are you chaperoning?" I said to Lucian in an annoyed whisper, while Adam tried to catch Jane's attention.

He grinned at me sardonically. "Just making sure he's good enough for you."

"Surely that's my decision? And not to worry; he is."

He raised an eyebrow but had no time to respond, because by that point Jane was planted in front of him.

"What are you doing here?" she demanded.

"I've already been through that with Liza. I'll have one of whatever they're having."

She vanished and returned, plopping the pint down in front of him with a scowl, but he just smiled charmingly back, and proceeded to be the perfect bar companion—at least, as perfect as anyone can be who knowingly interrupts a date. He asked Adam about his job and his background, so maybe he was only doing the vaguely paternalistic thing, as he had claimed. And he certainly could be personable when he tried. He had both of us in stitches at several points, and Jane started spending more time at our end of the bar and only called him Irish once.

As for me, I found myself thinking about the two sides of Lucian's personality. How could someone be so obnoxious one moment, and so normal and charming at others? Maybe my previous suspicions were right; maybe he really hated the reincarnation topic because he was somehow involved. I resolved to ask him, and seized my chance when Adam excused himself to go to the bathroom, and Jane was down at the other end of the bar, flirting with a white-haired gentleman.

"Lucian," I began.

"You were right; I like him."

"Huh?"

"Adam," he confirmed. "He's a good guy. Nice, grounded. I like him."

"Well, I appreciate that," I said, somewhat tartly. "But, like I told you, I'd already made up my mind."

"Just trying to help."

"I don't get you, Lucian. One moment I like you, and the next you're biting my head off. What have I done—I mean, besides having these dreams which seem to disturb you so much?"

"Me?" he protested. "I'm not disturbed."

"No?" I raised an eyebrow. "I think maybe you're annoyed because you're part of it."

"Part of it?" he parroted, his voice virtually cracking. "What do you mean, *part* of it?"

I surveyed him for a moment. "Lucian," I said seriously, "are you Lucy?"

He nearly choked. "What?" He looked utterly incensed. "I can't believe this!"

"So you're not—"

His face tightened. "I'm not anyone, all right? I'm just me, just myself. And what the hell is wrong with that?"

"Nothing. It's just . . ."

"Just what? Do you have any idea how ridiculous you sound? I hate to see perfectly intelligent people making utter fools of themselves!"

And when I gaped at him, he stood abruptly and threw a twenty down on the bar. "That should take care of the last round," he said. "I can't do this anymore. I can't." And he stalked out.

"Where did Lucian go?" Adam asked when he returned.

"He remembered he had somewhere to be," I said tightly.

He looked concerned. "Did you guys get into a fight, or something?"

"No. Hey, are you hungry? Want to go somewhere for dinner?"

We adjourned for food and it took Adam only half an hour to pry the substance of the fight out of me. I left out my suspicions of Lucian as Lucy, but asked: "Do you think I'm making a fool out of myself with this Obadiah thing?"

To Adam's credit, he thought about the question a long time before answering. "Seriously? I still find it all a bit hard to believe, but . . . You've seen things and dreamed things neither of us can explain. And belittling your intelligence—or your experiences—does no one any good. You're trying to find an explanation that fits all the facts, and what's wrong with that? I mean, who knows what your ultimate answer might be? It may be very different from anything you expected. But that doesn't mean your quest is any less valid."

"And you don't feel stupid hanging around with me?"

He smiled. "I'm still here, aren't I? And if you didn't have to start work bright and early tomorrow, I'd show you just how seriously I take you."

"Really? I can risk a little exhaustion."

But he shook his head, a smile playing about the corners of his mouth. "I'm not talking just a little exhaustion, Liza. If we're doing this, we're doing it right."

He was looking at me so intensely, I found myself getting a little breathless. "Oh, really?" I managed. "Meaning?"

"Meaning," he said, deadly serious, "that I want the whole night, not a few measly hours. Does that suit?"

It suited, all right—and suddenly my fight with Lucian seemed extremely unimportant. I smiled at Adam across the table. "It's a date."

CHAPTER 15

Adam got his wish on Friday night—and I probably would have been even more nervous had I actually had time to think about it. But I started work on Thursday morning, and they kept me running. Much as Jane had predicted, Adam stopped by the front desk more than chance alone dictated, and we ate lunch together on the observatory deck on the roof of the museum both days, looking out across the grey roofs of the town when we weren't canoodling. But those were the only quiet moments of an otherwise hectic few days.

Martha McRae—the woman who had greeted us on our first day there—was in charge of the tour and museum staff. And when Adam introduced me as the newest employee, she immediately began showing me the ropes.

Soon, information was coming at me hard and fast from a variety of sources. To make things worse, on Thursday nights the museum was open until eight instead of the usual five, so by the time I got home, it was all I could do to eat dinner and collapse into bed. If there were any dreams, I didn't remember them.

So any nervousness I might normally have felt about expectations vanished into a haze of facts and details and procedures. I think I was a little grey around the edges when I met Adam outside the museum a little past five on Friday. Forget sex; all I was longing for was a drink. But my gratification would have to wait, because Adam rented a small house on the outskirts of town and usually biked to work. So, in lieu of slinging me over the handlebars, we decided to walk his bike back to my car, so I could drive us both to his place. And also stop to pick up a few things for the evening, like a toothbrush and a change of underwear.

Once the logistics were decided, however, my nervousness came flooding back—in spades. I wished I had time to talk to Jane properly, but she was buzzing about getting ready for work, and Adam was downstairs loading his bike into my car, so all I got was a wink and a thumbs-up—which didn't exactly calm me down.

God, I was so much better with spontaneous flings. This much advanced planning made me sweat. How good could things be when there was this much anticipation going in?

Worse, my mood seemed to have affected Adam, who had made an utter hash of stowing his bike. My car's trunk was partially open and spitting out bicycle tires, netted with an elaborate web of bungee cords. When I raised an eyebrow, he laughed awkwardly, and said, "I know; it looks awful. But I think it will hold."

I hoped it wasn't emblematic of the night ahead. "Right, I'll drive slowly, then. So, where am I going?"

We got to his place without incident, and it was indeed far out on the outskirts of the town. But it was a quaint little house, complete with requisite white picket fence and a huge tree in the front yard. It had a cozy front porch, and dormer windows on the second floor.

He extracted his bike from the trunk as I examined the house.

"Cute," I said.

"Well, come see the rest," he said, and unlocked the front door, ushering me in. He left his bike leaning in the front hall as he gave me the tour. It wasn't quite so tiny on the inside as it appeared from the front, but it was close. Still, it was a comfortable place, the furnishings clearly secondhand, but not hideous. Downstairs, there was a living room, a kitchen–dining area, and a bedroom that had been converted into a study and office, complete with attached bath. Upstairs, under a sloping roof, were the bedroom, second bathroom, and another room well-filled with junk.

"Most Nantucket houses don't have proper basements," he said apologetically. "And this place is too small for an attic. So I just make do."

"No," I said, "it's nice. I like it. Very cozy." But I was studiously not looking at the bedroom as I spoke.

"Yeah, well," he said awkwardly. "None of the furniture matches, but after Caroline left, I didn't want any of our stuff around, so I had to do a hasty replacement. I haven't given it much thought since, I'm afraid."

"Hey, at least the couch isn't orange-and-brown plaid, so you're a step classier than the average bachelor."

"True," he admitted, with a flash of the old Adam in his grin. "I did have the option of a truly awful chintz one, though. So, come down and have a seat on my comparatively tasteful couch, and I'll get you a drink. I think we could both use one."

The rueful tone in his voice brought a genuine smile to my lips, and I felt some of my panic evaporating. "God, yes. Please."

He laughed as he led me back downstairs. "I noticed you were looking a bit fried. Tough few days at work?"

"You have no idea! Though, in fact, you probably do. Sorry."

He flashed me a grin over his shoulder. "Better than most. It's an awful lot of information to swallow in a chunk, I know. But trust me, three weeks out, and you'll forget it was ever a problem."

"I'm holding you to that," I said.

"Feel free." We had reached the living room. "Beer okay?"

"More than."

"Right. Have a seat. I'll be right back."

Adam went off to fetch the drinks, but I didn't take a seat. Instead I wandered the room, peering at his stuff. There were a few photos on the fireplace mantel. One was of a curly-haired sprite who could only be a very young Adam with his parents. In another, a sunburnt Adam mugged amidst a bunch of guys. They were all standing on board a ship, a mast and rigging rising behind them, and looked like they were having a ball.

In a third, he stood on top of what had to be a mountain, with a bay and small islands behind him in the distance, with his arm around a gorgeous brunette. There had clearly been a fierce wind that day, for their hair was blowing wildly about, and Adam was grinning brightly, as if he could want no more in the world than this. And initially, the beautiful brunette— she was the model-caliber woman I had been worried about earlier, with perfect skin, perfect features, and perfect, silky hair—looked much the same. Until you looked a bit closer, and saw the shadow in her eyes, as if you could read the future of their breakup in this moment.

I wondered if Adam had ever noticed that look, or if that was why he still had the picture on display.

"That's Caroline and me, on top of Cadillac Mountain in Acadia," he said as he came back into the room. "She left me three days after we got back from that vacation." He seemed vaguely embarrassed to find me looking at it. "I don't even know why I still keep that around. Here, have a beer." And he handed me a frosty bottle.

I put the picture down and took the beer instead. Once again, the tension soared, thick and palpable. When he gestured me toward his comparatively tasteful sofa, I took a seat, and he sank down beside me.

"Look, Liza," he said, "I'm not usually as forward as I was the other night. I mean, nothing has to happen here tonight if you don't want it to. We can just order in a pizza, watch a DVD, whatever. The couch even pulls out into a bed. So it is pretty much whatever you want. Not that I'm not interested," he added, "because I am. But you seem a bit freaked, and if you want to take it all slower, then that's okay, too. I mean, it's been a long time for me—I haven't been with anyone since Caroline left, and—"

Suddenly, I felt a hundred percent better. I started laughing.

"What?"

"You're cute when you're being earnest," I told him.

"Great," he said dryly. "Condescension."

"Not at all. It's just . . . You're right that I was nervous. And it did seem a great big whack of expectations." Though probably not for the reasons he expected. There were some dreams Adam did not need to know he was competing against. "But now . . ."

"What?" He shifted closer, looked down at me, and damn, his eyes were a brilliant green. I don't think I'd ever seen eyes so vividly green in my life.

"Now," I whispered, "I'm kind of curious to see what you come up with. Um . . . so to speak."

His mouth curved into a brilliant grin that almost rivaled Lucian's for sheer wattage. "Then let's see what I can do," he said, before bending his head and kissing me with a gratifying thoroughness.

I indulged myself, letting my hands wander over what was proving to be some truly spectacular anatomy. And if my exploratory touch did eventually descend into more sensitive regions . . . Well, I had said I was curious. And, unlike the proverbial cat, I was clearly suffering no negative consequences for that sentiment.

An involuntary smile curved my lips as I measured the growing contours of my gift.

When I pressed more firmly, Adam groaned and proceeded to undo the button on my jeans. Then he eased down the zipper and looked at me, as if waiting for permission to proceed.

I kicked off my shoes and jeans and presented him with my most sexy pair of underwear—deliberately chosen for the occasion. His eyes went hot green, and he groaned anew. A moment later I echoed the sound as his fingers began moving, seeking my clitoris.

I shifted to give him better access, leaning back against the breadth of his chest and parting my legs. I wanted him to continue there forever, but instead he shifted me toward him and leaned down to kiss me, his hand roving up under my shirt, cupping a breast.

Okay, there were definite advantages to real sex over dream sex, in that I was actually *having* it. And to hell with expectations. I reached down and, while we were still in the midst of our kiss, popped the button on his jeans and yanked down his zipper in turn. Then I slid my hand inside. He was hard as rock, soft as velvet.

"Liza," he groaned. "It's all going to be over too soon if you continue that—"

"So what?" I said recklessly. "We have all night."

"True. But I wanted the first time to be perfect. . . ."

I endeavored to raise an eyebrow.

He groaned. "All right, you win. But at least let me see you, first." He moved away from my hand and stripped me out of my blouse, and then out of my sexy, lacy bra without even looking at it. But my breasts he did look at—reverently— and then he dipped his head and took first one nipple into his mouth, and then the other, rolling them between lips and tongue until I groaned.

"God, you're beautiful," he said, running a hand along my stomach, and I shivered.

He stood, suddenly—and with what intent, I had no idea, but whatever it was was foiled when his pants plummeted down around his ankles. I couldn't help it; I started to laugh, and he smiled back ruefully. He looked hilarious with his jeans puddled around his feet and his Fruit-of-the-Looms tenting out authoritatively.

"Right, I challenge you to do better," he said.

"I already did," I said, but just to drive the point home, I pushed my panties down until they caught on one toe, then flipped them nonchalantly across the room. Thoroughly naked, I vaulted to my feet and struck a pose.

His eyes devoured me; then he bent over to work hastily at his shoes while I took the opportunity to admire his butt. It was even more impressive out of the jeans than in them. As was his whole body, when I finally got him out of his clothes. He could have had his own swimsuit calendar. Just as I had suspected, he was built: smoothly tanned, satiny skin stretched taut over a glorious array of muscles that were neither too big nor too wimpy, but just right. *Go, Goldilocks,* I thought, and grinned.

But, in truth, his whole body was perfect. Chest and arms covered with a light down of hair, legs slightly furrier. Dark nest of curls at his groin, and then . . . Wow. Lucky Caroline. Lucky *me.*

"What?" he said, a bit self-consciously, as I surveyed him.

"You're not so bad yourself, either," I said, trying to keep my voice light. "So what are you going to do, now that you've got a naked girl in your living room?"

I don't know what I expected—maybe a fireman's carry, or some other sort of caveman maneuver—but instead he only stepped closer, pulled me to him, and began kissing me again, hungrily, as if he might devour me. His erection was pressed firmly into my belly; I could feel it twitching eagerly against me. And my hands had an impressive array of muscles to roam across.

To hell with Lucy and Obadiah. I was growing all breathless again, my body tight with wanting.

He began walking me backwards to the couch, and I went eagerly, falling back with him on top of me. His pace was faster now, more eager; his hands were everywhere, and that suited me fine. When his fingers went back between my legs, I nearly cried out with joy. I arched against his hand as his mouth went to my breast, suckling urgently. My body clenched, tightened . . . But just as I was about at my peak, he pulled back.

"What?" I said desperately.

"Condoms," he said, the regret palpable in his voice. "Upstairs."

"Any ideas?" I asked him.

The head of his penis was as swollen and purple as I had ever seen, and beaded with a clear fluid. His chest was heaving like a bellows.

I couldn't help myself. I started laughing. And with kind of a mindless growl, the caveman came out. He scooped me into his arms, lifting me as if I weighed no more than a feather, and lurched up the stairs. To give him credit, he only banged my feet against the wall once.

And then, blessedly, we were on his bed—where there were condoms. He sheathed himself—and then *sheathed* himself, his long, hard heat stroking deep within me.

Fortunately, the reality of him inside me sent me right over the edge, because he didn't last much longer. To more strokes, and a deep groan of, "Oh, God, Caroline!" and he was done.

To his credit, Adam was deeply apologetic about both his physical and verbal gaffes, but he didn't have the chance to make it up to me, because the stresses of the week came crashing in and I was out like a light about five minutes later. The next morning, I had to work. It was Saturday, and weekends were the museum's busiest days—and would get more so once July arrived. I was currently the low woman on the NHA totem pole, so my days off were Monday and Tuesday.

I woke Adam with a kiss—still feeling slightly resentful about being mistaken for his ex—got a sleepy mumble about a rematch in return, then drove back to Kitty's, where I showered and dressed for work. My phone vibrated around noon, but I was in the middle of about ten things at the time, and couldn't answer. An hour later, Adam showed up in person, with sandwiches, and extracted a promise that I'd let him do it all again properly, tonight. He'd even supply a home-cooked meal. And not mention Caroline once.

I grinned and agreed—then called Kitty and Jane to advise them of developments, promising the latter full details soon, and the former that yes, I'd invite Adam for Sunday dinner.

Adam lived up to his word. The pasta with homemade sauce and garlic bread was delicious (Caroline's favorite, he confessed sheepishly, breaking his promise but I could see why), and the sex was lovely. Okay, so the earth didn't move, but at least he knew who I was, and what did my dreams know, anyway? They had yet to give me more than annoying hints about what was going on, and the lack of a coherent perspective was starting to seriously piss me off. Obadiah, Lucy. Lucy, Obadiah. It was enough to make you want to scream.

Still, I got satisfyingly little sleep on Saturday night, and arrived at work on Sunday duly exhausted—which was both a good thing and a bad thing, depending on your perspective.

Adam came for dinner on Sunday and, to his great delight, got his tour of the house from an enthusiastic Kitty, while Jane hauled me off to my room for a more thorough deconstruct.

"So, dish!" she said, slamming my bedroom door shut and bouncing down on my bed. "How was it? How late were you up?"

"Until three," I admitted.

"Oh my God! And how many times did you two . . . Well, you know."

I chuckled. "Three, again."

"Jesus, I think I'm jealous!" she said, then added, "So, was it everything you had hoped it would be?"

I considered this. "I don't know. I guess."

"You guess?" Jane seemed horrified. "What went wrong?"

"Nothing," I said. "Honestly! It was fine. It was more than fine. It was lovely! But . . ."

"What?" Jane asked, her brow furrowing in concern.

"Well, this is going to sound stupid, but . . ." I thought back to my dreams, to the tides of sensation and deep currents of emotion that made them so powerful. "I mean, isn't the earth supposed to move, or something? You know, when it's right?"

I figured if anyone would know this, it would be Jane. It sometimes seemed she'd slept with more guys than I'd had hot meals. But to my relief—or maybe chagrin—she just broke out laughing.

"Oh, honey, you've been reading too many romance novels. I don't think it ever is earth-shattering. I mean, fabulous, yeah, but . . . You know how many guys I have had. Statistically, you'd think one would have shattered something by now—and I don't mean the one who shook the bed so hard, he broke my bedside lamp. But none have yet. That's just an impossible romantic cliché. And while I know you're a closet romantic—" She shushed my reflexive protest. "—promise me you won't set the bar so high, you can't enjoy Adam for what he is. Overthinking always messes things up. So just relax and enjoy it. Hell, any guy who can manage three times in one night is hardly to be sneered at!"

I grinned, feeling better.

"And what about the equipment? Because I assume you're not buying any of that 'size doesn't matter' crap, either," she persisted.

"Worry not. The equipment is prodigious. And—"

Jane's happy whoop was forestalled by a knock on the door, which then opened to reveal Kitty and Adam. "And here we are," she told him. "Liza's room."

"Oh dear God!" Jane exclaimed. "You haven't actually shown him *my* room, have you?"

Kitty raised an eyebrow, and I grinned. I'd been living with Jane for nine months, after all; no one knew the condition of her room more intimately than I. "Sadly, I know better. And I suppose you are too old for me to tell you to clean up your mess, young lady?"

Jane, at least, had the grace to flush—though how much of that was due to actual remorse and how much to being shown up in front of strangers, I had no idea. But still, she said, with credible insouciance, "You can tell me whatever you want; it is your house, after all. But bear in mind that it is a hopeless cause. Just ask Liza. Every few months I vow to clean up my life, tidy up all my detritus, and then, two months later, I'm just back in the sty again. I'm afraid it's reached the level of a pathology now, and we'll all just have to live with it. Hey, when's dinner? I missed lunch, and I'm starving!"

Dinner—with Jim once more in attendance—was lovely, and Lucian in particular displayed a mellowness I hadn't seen in him before. I wasn't sure if I was more amused by his anecdotes or by Jane's baffled looks as she tried to figure out what alien race had taken the real Lucian away.

Even Kitty remarked on it, at which Lucian shrugged and said, "Just in a good mood, I expect."

"What's her name?" Jane shot back.

He looked almost offended. "Why does it have to be about a woman?"

"Because, with you, it's always about a woman!"

"That's slander," he retorted, laughing.

"Amber?" she said. "Charlotte? Normandy? Or was it Brittany? Oh, and Lauren. And . . . what was that other one's name, the one that always looked like someone had just shoved a huge pole up her ass?"

"Jane!" Kitty exclaimed.

"Well, it's true. . . . Oh! Right, Stephanie. And those are only the ones I know about. God only knows how many others there are that I know nothing about—"

"Jane, enough. Lucian can make his own decisions—no matter how misguided they may be."

"Kitty!"

"Well?" She grinned. "Let's be honest. Stephanie really did look like she'd just sat on a fence post. Lauren was cute; I liked Lauren. But did Charlotte actually have a brain in her head, or just poodle fluff? I swear, that girl made porch swings look intelligent."

Jane was laughing so hard, she choked on her wine, and even Lucian was looking amused—if a tad affronted. While poor Adam was not sure quite which way to look, and had that expression generally worn by people first encountering the terminally insane.

"Don't worry; it's normal," I whispered to him, stifling a laugh at his quiet distress myself. "You'll get used to it."

"Really?" he whispered back.

"I wasn't dating her for her brains," Lucian said, dryly.

"Well, obviously," Kitty said scornfully. "And I admit, she had nice tits. Pity they were fake, though."

"Hey . . ." But Lucian's pro forma protest died quickly beneath a nascent grin. "How did you know?"

"The wisdom of age and experience," Kitty said, reaching over to pat his hand. "Well, that, and a certain inevitable familiarity with the effects of gravity."

"Nonsense!" Jim said stoutly, and it was Kitty's turn to blush.

"All right, enough," she said. "Adam, I hope we're not embarrassing you."

"It's always like this around here," Jane added cheerfully.

Adam made demurring noises, but I could tell he was relieved when we finally made it back to my room.

"Are they really always like this?" he asked, when I had shut the door behind us.

"Some variation thereof, anyway. Why?"

He shook his head in a bemused fashion. "Not that I minded," he said, though I think he was fibbing it, "but I grew up in a family who would never mention sex publicly, let alone—I suspect—have it. And Caroline . . ."

"What?"

He flushed slightly. "Never mind."

"Well, anyway, it's a good thing you rebelled," I said.

"That's just the point; I didn't rebel. I just sort of . . ."

"What?"

He looked faintly embarrassed. "Nothing. No, really; forget it. They're a fun crew. I can see why you're enjoying your summer here."

I cocked an eyebrow at him. "They are not the only reason I am enjoying my summer here."

"You see what I mean? I . . ."

"What?"

"Nothing. Go get ready for bed before you force me to ravish you again."

With Lucian next door, and Jane, Kitty, and Jim down the hall, we were definitely on our best behavior—as were (fortunately!) Kitty and Jim. But, although things were more sub-dued, fun was had by all. (Well, I'm only assuming about Kitty and Jim.) And I, for one, fell asleep almost instantly after. And again into dreams . . .

And screams. Desolate, heartbreaking screams.

"No!" a voice cries. "Dear God, no, no!"

I am down in the parlor. As I tear toward the stairs, I have a sudden horrible feeling I will see Lucy sprawled dead on the landing, but there is no broken body on the stairs. Instead, the cries are coming from above.

I feel a wave of dread rise up, almost choking me. I fear what I am going to see, more than I can say.

Not again, I find myself praying. *Dear God, not again.* How many times can she go through this and live?

I run for the nursery, hoping—praying!—that it is just Rachel, that she has merely found another mouse, scampering from beneath the bed. But no; it is Lucy. I had left her in the nursery not ten minutes ago, rocking placidly in her chair, sewing garments for the child with her loose, erratic stitches. Now she is crouched on the floor, huddled around herself, weeping.

I catch myself on the doorframe, halting my mad dash.

"Lucy?"

She raises her face to mine. Her eyes are brimming with pain and despair. Tears course down her cheeks; her lips are drawn back in something that is half snarl, half gasp.

She has been so happy these past months, with the child growing inside her. The roses were almost back in her cheeks.

Now her face is as pale as the tiny gown that lies abandoned at her feet.

It is a moment before I see the blood, thick and bright on her skirts.

"Help," she pleads, voice small and lost as a child's, and then cries out again, doubling over.

I kneel beside her, embracing her as best I can. "I'll fetch the doctor . . . ," I say.

She clutches me tighter. "No! Don't leave me. I can't . . . I can't bear it! I can't go though this again! I can't do this alone. . . ."

Her voice breaks. She is weeping so hard, she can barely speak, her face a slick of snot and tears.

"Rachel!" I call, desperately. "Rachel!"

Lucy burrows against me, her damp face pressed to my breast. I tighten my arms around her as the maid peers anxiously in.

"The doctor, now!" I order, and she flees.

"I can't . . . I can't . . . ." Lucy is choking, gasping, her fists pummeling me helplessly.

Not knowing what else to do, I sit on the floor and, oblivious to the blood, pull her into my lap, cradling her against me. Unsure of what to say, I just rock her as emotions flow though me: guilt, pain, sorrow. She is such a child sometimes, her wants so simple. Safety, comfort, love.

She was meant for a gentler life than this. Balls and parties, frivolous pursuits. She will never understand the life of the sea and the demands it makes. She deserves better. Different. A simpler husband—less complex, less passionate. We are not evil people; we have just made mistakes.

"Why?" Lucy weeps. "What have I done?"

Nothing, I want to say, *other than be yourself.* God help us all.

A child might have helped, though she is still but a child herself. But that is the one thing God has denied her. Repeatedly, and cruelly.

"How many times?" she sobs. "How many *times*?" And screams again, as another wave of pain seizes her.

I hold her tighter, whispering mindless nonsense syllables into her ears. Each new loss tears a tiny chunk out of her soul. I see that in her eyes, in quiet moments, when she thinks I am not looking.

How many more losses can she shoulder without breaking?

When the doctor finally arrives, we are both covered with blood and tears. He almost has to pry her from me. My arms have gone numb, and her hands are clenched so tight, they will not open.

She has not stopped screaming, in all the time we waited, and now her voice is raw, ragged, broken.

There is only one way to calm her, now: milk of the poppy. And then she will wander about the house dull-eyed and dazed, only half a person, until her grief subsides and she is ready to rejoin the living.

We have done this dance before, Lucy and I. And each time, it is harder to wean her back to life. Harder still, when a large part of me wishes she would stay gone. . . .

But ties of love and guilt and blood bind us, and I know my duties.

Still, when I am alone in the house, with Lucy in drugged

slumber, I bury my face in my pillow and weep for what could have been, and what isn't. . . .

And start awake with tears streaming down my face, muffling my sobs in the pillow.

A body bumped against me: Adam.

"Caro?" he muttered, sounding still half-asleep. He rolled to face me. "What's the matter? Are you crying again?"

Again? I thought, dashing tears from my eyes. "I'm fine," I said with a strangled laugh—ignoring the Caroline part for the moment. "It was just a dream, Adam. Nothing to worry about. Just a dream."

"One of the . . . *dream* dreams? I mean, one of the ones from the past?"

"Why?" I replied, more tartly than I intended. "Is it research time now?"

It was still dark enough in the room that I couldn't see the subtleties of his expression, but I think my sharp tone had hurt him.

"Sorry. I didn't mean . . ."

"No. It's okay. I wasn't pushing. I just . . ." He paused for a long moment, then added, "I didn't know they were that bad. Are they always that bad?"

"No," I admitted. "Not always. Go back to sleep. I'll be fine. Really."

I tried to back my words up with a smile, and must have succeeded—at least marginally—for he did eventually turn away from me and lie back down. But instead of maintaining my distance, I found myself burrowing against his back, seeking the comfort of warm skin against skin. Because, despite my words, I was still shaking. And when he rolled over and enfolded me in a tight embrace, I did not complain.

Before long, his breathing softened back into sleep, but I stayed awake, peering into the dimness, feeling the aftermath of guilt and sorrow reverberate through my body. And, like Lucy, the one question on my mind was, *Why me?*

CHAPTER 16

Why me? It was a feeling that only deepened as the weeks went by. Superficially, everything was great. As Adam had promised, work swiftly became easier as the great wodge of information filtered into the correct corners of my brain, and I forgot why I once found it so intimidating. The hours were routine, but the tasks were endlessly varied, and while I still did stints on the front desk, my reputation as a quick study soon had me wandering the rooms of the museum available for questions. By then I'd heard the whaling lecture enough times that I could do it with my eyes closed, though I was still occasionally trailing along on other people's tours, learning those ropes.

After July Fourth, when the tourist season truly took hold, I'd be on my own. And while the prospect made me vaguely nervous, I also knew my information cold—as I proved by dragging Adam along on some sample tours during our lunch hours. And if he objected to being carted from one end of town to the other while being lectured about facts he already knew perfectly well instead of scarfing sandwiches and making out on a quiet corner of the roof deck, as had been our wont, he never said a word.

Late one Saturday evening, we even got in our session under the whaleboat—which, I have to admit, made it a little hard to concentrate during the lecture on Sunday.

Evenings, too, fell into a routine. In addition to our Sunday dinner, the denizens of Obadiah's house had taken to gathering on Wednesdays as well. On that day, we each, save Jane, took a turn at the cooking. Even Lucian, on his night, grilled up some very credible steaks. Monday—our mutual day off—was Girl's Day, and Jane and I had developed a tradition of loading two plastic beach chairs and a big umbrella into my car, and driving out to Dionis, Surfside, or Madaket Beach, depending on our mood (and the availability of parking). And there we would spend a highly satisfying day basking, reading, swimming, and gossiping.

Tuesday, Thursday, and Saturday were Adam's nights, and Friday was kind of up for grabs. On Fridays, we had all taken to meeting at Obadiah's after work—Lucian included—and sometimes I would head home with Adam afterwards, and at others, wander back to Kitty's with Lucian.

Actually, the biggest surprise in all this *was* Lucian, who had undergone a sea change as soon as I started dating Adam. The snarkiest bits of his personality had vanished. He became a genuine friend I truly came to enjoy spending time with— though I admit to spending a fair amount of time puzzling out the reason for his change. In the end, all I could come up with was that he must have—embarrassingly—registered my initial crush on him, and then tried to cure me of it by being as obnoxious as humanly possible. Once I had proved myself firmly off the market, he had allowed himself to relax again.

It was a prospect that alternately mortified and infuriated me. I mean, the ego of the guy! And . . . Well, who wants to be caught out that baldly in a lust attack?

But through all of it, the dreams continued—mostly. At Adam's house, I didn't seem to spend any time dreaming—although, to be fair, I also didn't spend a lot of time sleeping, either. But at Kitty's house . . . Every night it seemed, brought new dreams—and still no answers. Lucy, Obadiah. Obadiah, Lucy. By this point, I could practically have told you what they ate for breakfast, but I still knew no more about how their relationship had faltered so badly, or how Lucy had died. Or even who I was.

And then there were the dreams that mingled both worlds into an incomprehensible whole. I remember one slightly more peaceful dream of sailing, in which I was astonished to find Jane up in the rigging and Jim by my side. I mean, how weird were things getting if I was dreaming of *Kitty's* boyfriend and not my own?

A month had passed. In mid-August, Jane and I would have to drive back to school and resume our regular lives. And I was beginning to wonder if I would ever get solid answers.

A part of me kept feeling there was some vital factor I was missing, some piece of information that, once I had it, would make everything fall into place like a key turning a lock. On the other hand, there was another part of me that was increasingly doubtful. Maybe I was just making it all up. Maybe, despite the shreds of evidence, my dreams had no significance at all.

Most frustrating of all was how isolated I was starting to

feel. I had a great job, great friends, the most gorgeous boyfriend of my life, and yet I was increasingly involved in this world that no one else shared. A world that could appear without warning, sucking me out of the here and now as greedily as a child grabbing after sweets.

Once I was walking up Main Street with Adam on our lunch hour. We were holding hands, our arms idly swinging between us. Then, suddenly, the modern shops were gone and Lucy was beside me, her hand on my arm, saying, "I'm so glad that you are here. It is so much better when you are here!" her face as guileless as a child's, her eyes as blue as the summer sky as she smiled at me.

When I came back to myself, Adam was looking at me strangely.

And then there was the day in the kitchen. Lucian and I were eating breakfast, and he was chuckling over something in the morning paper. He opened the paper out to show me . . . and suddenly I was shoulder to shoulder with Obadiah—a more animated Obadiah than I had ever seen. A series of plans was laid out before us—plans that my modern mind realized, with a shock, were for the very house I was currently sitting in. His voice was eager as he pointed out features and alternatives, and I remember sneaking sidelong glances at him as he chattered, thinking . . .

Whatever the thought was, it fled as Lucian poked me.

The flashes of Lucy dead on the stairs were also growing more detailed as the weeks wore on. Where once I had seen glimpses of hair or eyes, I now saw the full-body vision: Lucy, lying unnaturally twisted on the landing like an unstrung marionette, her head cracked and bleeding in two places. Blood

sheets down her face, and more pools beneath her cheek, pud-
dling for a moment before cascading down the first stair: a tiny
crimson waterfall. And her back must be broken, for her lower
body is unnaturally still. Only her hands scrabble helplessly. And
her eyes, wide with such terror as her ragged voice claws at me.

Help me. Help me!

Living through things deeper and darker than my twenty-
four years should have encompassed was seriously starting to
affect my moods. One afternoon, I was sitting in the living
room, flipping idly though one of Jane's magazines, when the
magazine vanished, the wallpaper went mad, and Lucy came
skipping in, wearing a sprigged muslin gown that did little to
hide the growing curve of her belly. She grabbed my hand, laid
it across the swell of her stomach, her face alight and joyous.

"Can you feel him kicking?" she crowed.

I felt a surge of joy and wonder as tiny feet battered at my
hand. She was glowing, so full of hope, that I laughed.

"Are you so sure it will be a boy, then?" I teased.

"I know it is! It's got to be. . . ." And her face momentarily went dim, no doubt remembering the four less fortunate
ones that had come before. But then she rallied. "I've never
felt one kicking before. This time it's going to be all right, I
know it!"

That very night, I had to witness her grief as she lost the
child at seven months. I saw the tiny, cold blue body as the
doctor wrapped it: a girl.

Was it any wonder I was short-tempered and snarky for
the next two days?

Lucian kept trying to draw me aside and talk to me, but I

was in no mood to have my delusions ridiculed still further, so I ducked him assiduously.

The Fourth of July came and went quietly—most of our celebration was on the third, as both Jane and I had to work on the actual fourth. (Though it was a Tuesday and technically my day off, I had been bribed by extra pay to take a shift.) Adam had taken off both the third and the fourth, so I was actually able to sleep late at his place for once, and woke to an empty bed, and amazing smells of something breakfasty drifting up the stairs. French toast or muffins or pancakes; I couldn't tell. But something homemade, anyway, and remarkably uncorrupted by the stench of burning that invariably accompanied any of Jane's forays into the kitchen.

I grinned and stretched, feeling an ache in muscles that had gotten a good workout the night before. Then I rose and pillaged through Adam's drawers until I located an old grey T-shirt that covered me to midthigh. I liked the feel of the soft, well-worn cotton against my skin, and when I buried my nose in it, it bore the clean, fresh odors of both laundry detergent and Adam.

I started down the stairs, then paused and reconsidered, and darted back up again. After all, a guy cooking breakfast deserved a bit of a reward, didn't he? And never mind if that sounded more like rationalization than desire. Quickly raiding a different drawer, I secreted a foil-wrapped packet into my palm. This was the one problem with wearing nothing but a T-shirt; no place to hide anything.

When I arrived in the kitchen, Adam was standing in front of the counter, wearing nothing but a pair of silky boxer shorts in a rich jewel-toned blue green, and he looked even better in them than his usual Fruit of the Looms, if that were possible. His tan, smoothly muscled back was a sight to behold, tapering beautifully into the waistband of his shorts, and his hair caught the sun with a dark sheen of auburn fire deep in the curls. It was clearly his I'm-lounging-about-waiting-for-my-sex-kitten garb, and I felt another surge of unreality as I masked a grin, looking quickly about the kitchen for hiding places for my package.

Adam had already set the table—complete with napkin holder. I stealthily lifted the bar that held the paper napkins in place, and slid the condom in among the pile. Then I snaked my arms around his waist, laying my cheek against that smooth expanse of back.

He was so involved in his task that he jumped slightly at my touch, but it didn't take him long to turn and welcome me enthusiastically to the day.

"Hope you don't mind me raiding your drawers," I said, when he released me.

"Hell, no. Besides, you do things to that shirt that I never could." He traced my curves briefly under the cloth, then added, with a pat to my rear, "Now, be a good girl and stop distracting me. Breakfast is nearly ready."

"Mmm. What are we having?"

"Waffles," he said.

"Waffles!" I echoed, in the exact tone that Donkey used in *Shrek*.

Adam grinned. "So you are as much of a waffle freak as I am? Good!"

He turned back to his waffle iron, and I took my seat at the table, feeling oddly discouraged. Lucian would have gotten that reference, I was sure.

But I couldn't stay disappointed long, as Adam laid some truly fine-smelling waffles before me, followed by a truly impressive array of syrups—from the traditional maple to blueberry, strawberry, and blackberry. He had even made coffee, and had placed a pitcher of orange juice on the table—and how many bachelors actually had their own pitcher?

I grinned, and divided my waffle into neat quarters.

"What are you doing?" Adam said.

"Deciding which one is my favorite," I replied, and proceeded to anoint each quarter with a different syrup.

Blackberry, as it happened.

"So, I talked to my parents yesterday," I said as we ate. "They want to know if you are a nice young man."

"And what did you tell them?"

"That maybe someday they'll meet you and see."

He grinned. "Bring it on! I'm good with parents. They always like me. Except . . ." His face clouded.

"What?"

"Nothing," he said, shaking his head as if clearing bad memories.

"Caroline's parents didn't like you?" I persisted.

"I never met them," he said tersely.

Huh? "You were together four years and never met her parents?"

He smiled tightly. "Should have been a clue, right?" He eyed my empty plate. "How decadent are you feeling?"

"Why?"

"I have enough batter for two more waffles," he answered. "And vanilla ice cream in the freezer."

"Bring it on!" I echoed, and he grinned.

We polished off every scrap, and he even washed the dishes after.

"Well," he said when he had finished. "What do you want to do now?"

I had moved my chair away from the table, to better watch him as he tidied up. Remembering the condom I had stashed away, I very slowly and deliberately crossed my legs, uncrossed them, then crossed them again in the other direction.

His eyes bugged out.

"What?" I said innocently.

"Well, if you're going to pull a Sharon Stone on me . . ."

I laughed. The boxers hid little, and my ploy had had the intended effect.

"Upstairs?" he said.

I shook my head. It wasn't really even a conscious decision, just a split-second impulse. "Nope. Have a seat."

"Why, what are you planning?" he said, a certain amount of suspicion in his voice. But he pulled out his chair and complied—and the impressive tenting in his shorts was all anticipation.

I stood and went to him, then flung a leg over his lap and straddled him, suddenly wanting to know how it would feel with clothes between us. It had been a while since my dream of Obadiah and the wall, but I was suddenly tempted to replicate it. I stroked him through the silky fabric of his boxers for a moment, then found the flap in front and freed him. I resisted his efforts to unseat me and strip, and likewise his attempts to remove my shirt. Instead, I pressed closer, teasing up and down the length of him.

He was breathing heavily by the time I was done, as was I—though how much of that was due to Adam and how much to the semi-reconstruction of my dream, I couldn't have said.

"Here?" he said. "Like this?"

"Here, like this," I confirmed, and arched back to retrieve the condom from the napkin holder. I came back with it—only to find that he had a similar packet in his hand, retrieved from a drawer behind him.

We looked at each other for a moment, then started laughing.

"Well, yours or mine?" I said.

"It depends," he replied. "How many do you have?"

"Um, just the one," I admitted. "Why? How many do you have?"

He grinned. "After our experience on the couch? I figured it was best to seed the house, so I did."

"The whole house? I'm impressed! And flattered. That shows foresight well beyond mine."

"But of a sort of nonspecific kind, I have to admit. And since this was clearly your specific seduction—" He leaned back and replaced his condom in the drawer, shut it. "—the honors go to you."

"Well, then . . ." I sheathed him, then lowered myself in the condom's wake, straddling both him and the chair.

It wasn't quite how I had imagined it in my dream. For one thing, the silk of his boxers was cool and sensuous on my skin, not rough and chafing, and the fabric of the T-shirt bunched between us hardly formed a few folds, let alone a roll. Nor were Adam's movements so harsh and urgent as Obadiah's in the dream. Besides, we were sitting, not standing. But still, for an instant, I felt as if I were in that hallway again, pushed up behind the stairs, the heat of an oil lamp against my skin rather than the warmth of the afternoon sun. And, when I came, it was strangely like coming home.

Fortunately, Adam didn't seem to notice my distraction, or the fact that, though I was joined to him, I was miles away. Instead, he drew a deep breath when we had finished, and said, "You may be the death of me yet, woman."

I pulled my head out of the clouds and grinned. "How so?"

"I have a feeling you're more adventurous than me. Ah, well; I'll just have to rise to the occasion."

I chuckled, and wriggled slightly against him.

"Good Lord," he exclaimed, "give a guy a break, Liza! I need at least five more minutes for that. Besides, don't we need to be at Kitty's in, like—" He consulted his watch. "—fifteen minutes?"

I erupted from his lap in a flurry of curses, but we made it. Almost. I drew some consolation from the fact that Jane wasn't even out of the shower when we arrived. But once we were all sorted, the whole gang—Kitty, Jim, Lucian, Jane, Adam, and I—piled into Jim's Jeep and drove out to Great Point, where we picnicked and basked on the beach. And the advantage to celebrating a day early was that we had the place almost completely to ourselves.

Still, even in the midst of the celebration, I couldn't help feeling that same creeping sense of isolation, looking at everyone's happy, smiling faces. What must it be like to just be yourself, unfettered by someone else's existence?

I suddenly wanted that, more than I could say. And again found myself thinking, as I had so often of late, *Why me?*

Chapter 17

My salvation, when it arrived, came from a completely un-
expected quarter. For the Wednesday following the Fourth of
July week was Thomas Moreland's talk at the Atheneum.
Some curators from another museum were in town, and
Adam was playing host and couldn't attend. But Jane was still
keen, and even Lucian seemed willing to give it a go. Since
Jane was coming straight from work, we had agreed to meet
her there—and Lucian had offered to take over the cooking
for that night, though I suspected it was my turn, or maybe
Jim's. It was a lovely evening, so he threw some dogs and
burgers on the grill, and set us all up with beers at the table on
Kitty's postage-stamp side yard. It was still too early for the
mosquitoes to be out in force, and he had provided a wonderful array of condiments, from blue cheese and jalapeños to the
more traditional ketchup and relish, so we had fun mixing and
matching.

Best yet, because we had to meet Jane at seven forty-five,
Kitty and Jim offered to take care of the cleanup. It wasn't a
long walk to the Atheneum, and it was a gorgeous evening, so

Lucian and I took it at a leisurely stroll, occasionally bumping shoulders on the narrow streets. The sun was slanting low over the houses, washing everything in that glorious late-afternoon golden light. The white walls of Levi Starbuck's mansion looked almost burnished, and the trees that shaded Orange Street filtered the sun through their leaves, dappling the sidewalk. I felt completely at peace with the world as I strolled along at Lucian's side.

Until the parked cars vanished and I found myself beside Obadiah, one hand resting on his arm as we proceeded. Yet, for all our decorous posture, I was—as always—infinitely aware of him. I could feel hard muscle beneath my gloves, the warmth of his body like a promise beside me. He shifted his arm and heat flared between us—even after all these years.

The quality of the day seemed much the same, but unlike Lucian's jeans-clad form, Obadiah was in full-dress blacks, topped by a shiny black beaver hat. With his dark beard and eyes, he should have looked intimidating, but he had long since ceased to scare me. Instead, I could see what few others could: the gentleness in the dark eyes, the generous curve of mouth beneath the beard. A beard that, I suddenly noticed, was threaded more solidly with silver.

He looked down at me; our gazes locked. And, as usual, he seemed to sense my thoughts.

His mouth twitched in a smile. "I'll be an old man soon."

"We're neither of us getting any younger," I chided.

"Ah, but I'm a year past the half-century mark. Too old for all the absence, all the killing. I will sail once more, but I mean this to be my last voyage."

I felt a surge of joy. To have him home, all the time . . .

"But what will you do?" I asked, instead.

His lips curved into that smile I had come to know so well. "I thought some creation, after a lifetime of destruction. I want to build things," he said. "Houses, buildings—something. I flatter myself I have a talent for it."

"You do," I assured him with a slightly firmer pressure on his arm—all the intimacy I could display in public.

"William and I discussed it extensively, on our last voyage," Obadiah continued. "They're not commissioning ships as frequently as they used to, and he'll probably never make captain. And like all of us"—a faint flicker of a smile, here—"he's not getting any younger. After this next voyage, we both want to retire, go into partnership together."

I smiled, remembering Obadiah's joy in constructing the house on Orange Street. The endless hours he and William sat in our old parlor, in perfect companionship, poring over the plans—each of them spawning ideas and, improvements.

"Young and Stockton," I mused. "It's a wonderful plan, Obadiah."

That rare smile of his flashed out. "Actually, Stockton and Young. After all these years, it seems only fair to let William take the lead. Besides, I don't want to miss Owen's whole childhood at sea. I want to be there as he becomes a man."

I felt a rush of love for him, for our son.

"Well," he laughed. "That's decided, then."

I could see the recklessness in his eyes, and tried to forestall him. "Obadiah! No. We're in public."

"Not for long," he muttered. Then he was yanking me into a dark alley, kissing me fiercely, as if his life depended on it . . . and I came back to reality to find that I had walked into the side of a building.

Lucian raised an eyebrow.

"Sorry," I said sheepishly, and cursed the universe again, bitterly.

As we turned up onto India Street, a crowd was already gathering in front of the Atheneum, and Jane was clearly visible in their midst, bouncing up and down impatiently as more and more folks filed inside, claiming the available seats. I shot a brief glance at Lucian, and we speeded up our pace.

"About time!" Jane greeted us. "We're going to be stuck all the way in the back. Come on!"

"We would have been earlier if Liza hadn't decided to try to tunnel through solid concrete," Lucian told her, and I glared at him.

At Jane's continued urging, we filed in with the other latecomers, and made our way up the curved wooden staircase to the second floor. The meeting room was a gracious, classical space, with white-painted walls, fan windows, and a raised stage with a podium at one end. Between a rank of low bookshelves that bracketed the room to either side, the center of the floor had been filled with chairs—the majority of which were already taken. At the back, some representatives from Mitchell's Books across the street were setting up a table, complete with cash-box and stacks of Moreland's latest hardcover, plus a selection of his paperbacks.

It was an interesting crowd, ranging from teenagers to senior citizens, and equally mixed between what had to be the furiously rich and the year-round locals. Groups of people who clearly knew each other were chatting in clusters, and there did seem to be a level of true camaraderie in the room.

"I wonder how many billionaires are here tonight," Jane whispered in my ear, and I grinned. "Do you see any seats?"

I scanned the room, since I was taller than she was. "There are a few right down in the front row," I reported.

"Perfect!" she declared. "Enough for all of us?"

"Yeah, I think there are . . . Oops! No, wait. Only one left now. You grab it. Lucian and I can lurk in the back."

"Are you sure?" she asked, subconsciously giving me Big Eyes.

"Absolutely, go," I assured her, and she darted off gleefully. I turned back to Lucian, who had gone pale and was endeavoring to hide behind my back.

"What is it?" I whispered, scanning the room again in an effort to see who or what he was reacting to.

"An ex," he whispered back. "Bad breakup."

"Which one?"

"Dark curly hair, behind the Mitchell's table," he said. "Liza, stop staring!"

I had been, totally curious to see what Lucian's type would be. If you had asked me yesterday, I would have expected a tall aristocratic blonde, but this girl was short and slightly rounder than the norm, with a very pretty, open face. She looked extremely nice, and I found myself surprised. This wasn't what I would have expected from Lucian at all.

But there was no doubt it was she, for, catching my stare, she smiled tentatively at me—that is, until she caught sight of Lucian behind my shoulder. Then her face went pale and pinched, as if she had just been slapped, and she sat there staring at Lucian as if he were a big juicy steak and she a starving dog.

"Jesus," I hissed. "What did you *do* to that poor girl?"

"Nothing!" he whispered back, aggrieved. "We just had different expectations, is all."

"What, you wanted a fling and she wanted marriage?"

His expression said it all.

"So, am I supposed to be your beard?" I continued, arching an amused eyebrow. "Cling to you like the next devoted conquest?"

He looked amused at the suggestion. "Do you think you could carry it off?"

"Probably not," I confessed. "I don't think I'll *ever* be that desperate for someone. But perhaps I could vamp it up a bit?"

His lips curved up in the start of that devastating grin, and for a moment I could almost understand the poor girl's pain. I wondered which one she was; Lauren, most likely, based on Kitty's comments.

"Perhaps," he began, and then his voice trailed off as the tall aristocratic blonde I'd been expecting turned toward us and began shoving her way through the crowd, clearly intent on annihilating the upstart newcomer: me. She was undeniably beautiful, from her fall of pure gold hair to her trim, athletic body, but I could see what Kitty and Jane meant. Beneath the cool, aristocratic iciness, she did indeed look like she had just sat on a very large fence post.

"Perhaps coming here was not the wisest of ideas," Lucian amended dryly from behind me.

I laughed. "Stephanie, I presume?"

"None other. Mind if I . . ." And he gestured idly at the door.

"Not a problem. Run away, little rabbit. Jane and I will report back later."

He grinned broadly. "You're the best. Thanks, Liza." And catching me completely by surprise, he leaned down and kissed me quickly on the cheek before fleeing.

Leaving me kind of numb in his wake.

Okay, so I had offered to be his beard, but . . . God damn. Apparently whatever sexual magnetism Lucian exuded so successfully was still working on me. How come I never reacted this way to *Adam's* kisses?

I shook my head slightly in bemusement, then looked back around the hall. Lucian's abrupt departure had deflected Stephanie, and the girl who had to be Lauren was pointedly not looking at me. I peered around for a seat, but the program was due to begin in about five minutes, and there wasn't a free chair to be seen. So instead, I drifted over to stand at the back with a few other stragglers, ending up next to a truly beautiful woman of the kind who put Stephanie to shame—if only because she looked so nice, in addition to everything else. Her hair was a deep burnished gold, falling thick and straight around her shoulders, and her eyes were an arresting greenish bronze. She was also very pregnant.

She noticed my scrutiny and smiled. "This is a beautiful old building, isn't it? Have you been here before?"

I couldn't help the wry grin that curved my mouth. "Several times before, I suspect." And when she gazed at me, slightly puzzled, I smiled and added, "It's a long story. So, are you here for the summer, or just . . ." I let my voice trail off, hoping she'd fill in the blanks.

She did. "I wish for the summer! This is a lovely place. I don't usually accompany my husband on tour, but I've always wanted to see Nantucket, so I seized the opportunity." And she grinned at me in such a friendly way that I wanted to hug her before her words sank in.

"Wait! Your husband? Are you—?"

"Cecil Moneghan," she said, holding out her hand. "Tom's wife."

"Liza Donovan," I said. "Lovely to meet you."

"Are you a fan of Tom's work?"

"I do like it, yeah," I confessed, "but the really enormous fan is my roommate, Jane. She's down in the front row, the one with the . . . green hair." Even as I said it, I realized how unusual it was for Jane's hair to be the same color, almost a month later. "She'll be totally jealous that I met you."

Tom's wife laughed. "Well, if you want, I'll introduce her to Tom later. I can't believe how much he's come out of his shell recently. He actually enjoys meeting his fans now. And frankly, I've been so busy with my own business these days, I'm almost never home. So I'm glad he's got something to keep him from missing me. Though I suppose things will all be different soon." And she ran a hand over her belly—which gave me permission to mention it.

"Yes, and congratulations. When are you due?"

"October. Off-season, fortunately."

I grinned. "Boy or girl?"

"Boy," she said. "We're thinking of calling him Ronan."

"That's lovely! Is it a family name?"

She looked faintly embarrassed. "No, just . . . someone we used to know. Someone who brought us together, actually."

"Oh." I couldn't help noticing the past tense, or the way her vibrant face closed down at the mention of his name. "So he's . . ."

"Dead, yes." Her voice was flat.

"I'm sorry."

"Don't be. It's . . . Well, it's complicated, really." She smiled at me then—a genuine expression. "Whoops, it looks they are about to start."

The head librarian gave an introduction, and then Tom took the stage. He was even better looking in person than in his author photos. His dark hair was not quite so curly as Adam's, but it had a decided wave, and there was a rough-cut ruggedness to his looks that wouldn't have been out of place on one of the old whaling boats. He was also far more down to earth than I would have expected—especially given his level of success. His smiles were ready and self-deprecating, and he was clearly madly in love with his wife—although perhaps I was the only one who realized at whom his frequent, warm glances toward the back of the room were directed.

I found myself envying her. Those two had a bond I could feel even from here, like a cord stretching out between them. I had the absurd feeling that, if I could just reach out and pluck it, it would sing—like a perfectly tuned harp, only rich with harmonies, all layered into a pure, clear tone.

It was what Lucy had had with Obadiah, as I knew from my dreams, and suddenly I wondered if I would ever find that as me, as Liza.

I thought briefly of Adam, wondering why the idea of us heading together toward a grey old age felt so unreal. But then, who said a summer of discovery had to end with me riding into the sunset with my knight of choice anyway? I was only twenty-four—far too young to be married, and a liberated woman, besides. I had my whole life ahead of me, so why worry about this now?

But then, as I shot a surreptitious glance at the woman standing beside me, her eyes glowing as she listened to her husband's speech, I found myself thinking: *There. That's why.*

Fortunately, my companion hadn't noticed my lapse, and I was soon able to focus on her husband's speech. He spoke for about half an hour on the writing process and his history as a Boston ADA, then opened the floor to questions. And half an hour beyond that, he surrendered the stage and was promptly mobbed by fans.

As, for a briefer instant, was my companion. Clearly I wasn't the only person who knew who she was. I started to move off, but she cast me such a desperate glance that I remained at her side.

"Thanks," she said when the crowd had thinned somewhat. "I've been to enough of these events that if one more person calls me Mrs. Moreland, I think I'm going to scream. But you I feel I can talk to."

"I'm flattered," I said. "So, you were a refreshingly liberated woman and didn't take your husband's name?"

She laughed. "Oh, no, I was decidedly unliberated. I took his name, all right. I just didn't take his pseudonym. Thomas Moreland is a brilliant writer, but Tom Moneghan is an even more amazing and complex person. Three years into the marriage, and I'am still learning things about him. It's been an incredible journey."

"Yeah, you guys seem really happy together. That's wonderful."

"You have no idea!" she said, then blushed. "Or maybe you do. Sorry, that was a rude assumption. *Is* there anyone special in your life?"

I thought of Adam. "One guy who's pretty amazing, but . . ."

"What?"

"Oh, I don't know. I'm too young to make these sorts of decisions, anyway."

"Why? How old are you? I mean . . . if you want to tell me, of course."

I found her bluntness oddly refreshing. "Twenty-four."

"Really?" She looked surprised. "You carry yourself like you've seen a lot more than twenty-four years."

"You have no idea," I said dryly, and she peered at me curiously.

"Now, this sounds like something I want to hear," she said, only at that moment we were interrupted again by a bit of a scuffle across the room as the Mitchell's folks tried to coerce the clot around Tom into a more formal book-signing line. Jane, I noticed, was buying a copy of the book.

"You don't have to leave immediately, do you?" Cecil asked me.

"No. It looks like my roommate will be pretty far back in the line, anyway."

"Good," she said. "These things can be a bit of a trial without someone to talk to. If you'll excuse me for just a moment . . . and don't go away, whatever you do! Though it looks like they are putting out some fruit and cheese, so if you feel like loading up a plate for us . . ." She grinned and patted her belly. "I'm using every excuse I can these days for gluttony."

"You've got yourself a deal."

"Fabulous! No vanishing, then. Which one did you say was your roommate?"

"Green hair, looks like a pixie." I pointed her out.

"Excellent; I'll be right back." And she scooted across the room to her husband, leaning down to whisper something in his ear as the signing line was corralled into order.

I grinned, went to tell Jane I'd be waiting in the back, and loaded up a plate with fruit and cheese—enough that I got some rather nasty looks from the folks presiding over the refreshment tray—then snagged a plastic cup of red wine. I retreated back to our corner, and was joined a few minutes later by Cecil, whose face lit up at the sight of the laden plate.

"You," she said, "are a goddess!" And she appropriated a wedge of cheddar, biting into it enthusiastically. "I told Tom to write something nice and personal in your friend's book, since you were entertaining me. He promised he would."

"God, Jane'll love you!" I said. "Thanks."

"Not a problem. Ooops, here comes another of those Mrs. Moreland types. Quick, over here." And she dragged me back behind a layer or two of bookcases, to an even quieter corner where no one was likely to disturb us. There were even two wooden chairs, with a small table between them holding a cloth-shaded lamp. Cecil gestured me to a seat, and sank into her own with a sigh like steam escaping a kettle. I slid the plate of goodies between us and reached out for more cheese.

"Heaven help me, I'm only six months pregnant," she said, "and already I'm acting like this! Still, we have been on our feet all day, taking advantage of our time here to do a little sightseeing. That walking tour was fascinating . . . but you *do* do a lot of walking, don't you?"

"Well, it depends," I said, with a grin. "Whose tour were you on?"

Her brow furrowed. "I think . . . Nancy something-or-other?"

"Nancy Villard? Yeah, you were lucky. She does a good tour. Patricia Cavanaugh is the best, but Nancy is damned good. And I should know. I've been on most of them!" And at her raised eyebrows, I added, "No, I'm not a history geek—not entirely, that is. I'm working for the NHA this summer, giving tours and so on."

We chatted for a bit about various island attractions and what I thought she should see in her remaining day here, and then she got me off into some minor point of history and all my geeky impulses came out and the poor woman got a mini-lecture, and . . .

"Wow, you really know your stuff," she said. "You describe thing so vividly, it feels like you actually lived here back then."

I grimaced. "Well, that depends on who you—" I cut myself off abruptly. I had gotten so caught up in the discussion, and those gold-green eyes were just so frankly inviting that I nearly spilled the whole deal . . . to a complete stranger!

Worse, her face had gone very serious. God, she definitely thought I was a freak now.

"Just joking," I hedged, trying to force a smile.

"No, you weren't," she said, "*Do* you think you lived here before? That is there some force that continues on, no matter how small?" I just stared at her, and this time it was she who flushed. "I'm sorry; I didn't mean to pry. But what you said about that, and feeling older than your years . . . Well, this may sound stupid, but I, too . . . I mean . . . How does one go about saying something like this?"

"What, that you don't think I'm terminally insane?" I snorted a laugh. "Jane doesn't think I'm insane, either—but then Jane believes in auras, and probably fairies, for all I know. I'm not sure what Kitty believes, and Adam's probably only in it for the research potential anyway, and—"

"Tell me," she said gently, and to my amazement I found myself relating the lot. "God, you must think I am totally nuts!" I said when I had finished.

"Not if you'd been through what I have." She ghosted a laugh. "I knew there was a reason I felt like I could talk to you. What's that phrase?"

"Takes one to know one?" I said dryly.

"Well, that, too. But I was thinking more about that other one. There are more things . . ."

". . . in Heaven and Earth, Horatio?" I finished.

"Yeah, that one. Horatio's infamous thing. Well, let me tell you, I've seen Horatio's thing—or one of them, anyway . . . and ick, doesn't that sound like we're discussing an old boyfriend, or something? But yeah, I know Horatio's thing far too well."

"So you've . . ."

"Brushed up against the unexplained?" she said, and shivered, curving an almost unconscious hand around her belly. "Damned straight."

It was like a spark shot between us. Impulsively, I reached out and grabbed her hands, and she clutched back, a lifeline. "I know it seems overwhelming when you're in the midst of it . . . ," she began.

"Like a boat in a storm," I said, half-tranced. "Tossed this way and that, never knowing if you're going to go under or survive. . . ."

She squeezed my hands. "Exactly. But you *will* survive. Take it from one who knows." In the slanting light of the lamp, I suddenly noticed a faint tracery of scars across her cheek. "You have the strength to get through it; I can tell." There was a certain darkness in her gaze that let me know she spoke the truth.

And, strange as it was, I suddenly felt like the sun had come out, and I could breathe again. Which sounds odd, since no one save Lucian had been outwardly condemning. But suddenly, I felt far less alone in the universe. Just knowing someone had come out the far side of such an experience gave me hope.

"So, what was yours?" I couldn't help asking, curiously.

She made a dismissive sound at the back of her throat. "Erch. Doesn't even bear mentioning. I mean, at least yours is reasonably mainstream! Pretty much everyone has heard of reincarnation. But—"

"Oh, there you are, Liza!" Jane exclaimed, bursting around to our side of the shelves like a green-topped whirlwind. "Look at what Thomas Moreland wrote in my book!"

CHAPTER 18

Whatever Cecil Moneghan had been about to say was swallowed by Jane's arrival, and for once I could have cheerfully killed my irrepressible roomie.

Ever intuitive—or perhaps responding to my glare—Jane seemed to sense that she had interrupted something vital, for she became flustered as only Jane can be flustered. "Oh, I'm sorry," she said, her eyes going big and round and liquid. "I didn't mean to . . . Hey, you must be Cecil Moneghan!"

"Points to her," my companion muttered dryly to me as she stood to greet Jane and I struggled to hold back my laughter. Jane was always good at points.

"Man, it's a pleasure!" Jane was gushing. "I love your husband's books—and I've heard it's you we have to thank for getting him out on tour at last, so thanks! And . . . Hey, congratulations! When's the little muffin due?"

After that, there was no going back—although I was dying to know what Cecil's completely non-mainstream experience had been; I wondered if it didn't have something to do with that Ronan she had mentioned. Maybe he had died, and they had seen his ghost. But then, ghosts were pretty mainstream as well, as such things went. Vampire, maybe? Ooh, what if he was a vampire? I pictured her for a moment, stake in hand like Buffy, her straight gold hair swinging as she pivoted for the kill. . . .

But that was a silly piece of fiction. There were no such thing as vampires. There were no such things as ghosts, for that matter. Or reincarnation. But still . . .

Just hearing that one voice in the wilderness that said, "No, you're not crazy; I've seen it, too," made all the difference in the world.

We said our good-byes, but neither Jane nor I really wanted to go home. Jane was flying high from her momentary brush with fame, so we ended up at Obadiah's—where Rob brought us free drinks and duly admired Jane's signed book. Repeatedly. In fact, he even abandoned his duties and sat with us for a while. And it was nice getting to know him better, even if Jane was acting increasingly manic as the evening progressed.

Clearly, I would have to keep her away from famous authors in the future. I finally pried her out of the bar a little past midnight, and we headed home through the quiet back streets—though Jane herself was far from quiet.

"Wasn't he the coolest, Liza?" she crowed. "Didn't I tell you how cute he was? I liked that wife of his, too—though, you know, I hate her on principle, of course. But she was awesome! And you two really seemed to have a bond going, too. Oooh, which reminds me . . . What's the deal with Lucian? Did he even stay for the talk? I saw Stephanie headed his way."

"Nope, he scampered before the introduction."

She snorted. "What a coward. Steph's a total bitch, anyway.

Totally not worthy of him. And hey, wasn't it cool that Rob came by for a while? Don't I have the greatest boss?"

There was something kind of rushed about the way she said the last part that made me think she was hiding something. And what was that about Lucian being worthy? It was so contrary to her usual sentiments that it drew me up short.

Had she suddenly decided that Lucian was her man? But I couldn't be bothered worrying about it, not tonight. Because I was not alone in the universe.

And maybe someday soon I'd actually stop grinning.

"You look different," Lucian greeted us as we walked in the door. "More relaxed." He was ensconced in the living room as he often seemed to be on these nights, almost as if he were waiting for us.

Almost as if he were master of the house. And just why *that* thought caused a shiver to run through me was something I simply wasn't thinking about.

"Relaxed? Me?" Jane replied.

"Heaven forfend," Lucian answered mildly. "You just look drunk. I was talking to Liza."

"Liza, is it?" Jane responded. "And I am so *not* drunk! And how would you know, anyway? Hey . . . what are you drinking?"

"Scotch," he said with an indulgent smile.

"God, is this what Steph drives you to?" she said, and yawned broadly, flopping down on the couch across from his. "So, what are you waiting for? Pour!"

Those silver eyes met mine, and I was too tired to deny the shiver that went through me. He arched an eyebrow. "Drink?"

"Sure." I was going to regret this tomorrow, but I was still feeling giddy tonight—albeit in a quieter way than Jane.

Lucian rose with his usual catlike grace and splashed Scotch into two more glasses; I could smell the peaty strength of it halfway across the room. He handed Jane hers first, and then delivered mine.

Our eyes met, locked.

"What happened?" he said, his gaze not leaving mine.

I felt a coy smile curve my lips. "Nothing. Just a good evening."

"Don't tell me you have a crush on our famous author, too?"

"Oh, nothing so mundane."

"Hey!" Jane protested. She raised her glass and downed a swig of the smoky liquor. "Damn, this is good. Thanks, Irish."

"No sweat, Moonbeam," he said without rancor.

I sat down beside him; at least that way, he couldn't keep staring at me with that oddly speculative yet vaguely knowing look on his face, as if he were determined to ferret out my secrets. Or Cecil's. No, tonight I was hugging my membership in the secrat club of two close.

"So, how was the talk?" Lucian asked Jane eventually.

"Awesome!" Jane responded. "Liza stumbled into a friendship with his wife, and look how he signed my book!"

The signed copy was again duly admired.

"So, went running from Stephanie, did you?" Jane added, once her book was back in her hands.

Lucian snorted a laugh. "Stephanie *and* Lauren. One alone I could have handled, but both together?" He gave an exaggerated shudder, and Jane grinned.

"Poor Lauren. She was the nicest of the lot. Still, I can't see you settled down with lots of round happy babies."

"I'll drink to that," he said, and did.

I thought of Cecil and Tom, and their obvious bond, and suddenly felt depressed.

I stood, setting down my still-full glass. "If you'll excuse me . . ."

"What's the matter, Liza?" Jane asked, her eyes as speculative as Lucian's had been a minute ago.

"Nothing. Just contemplating the ungodly prospect of waking up before eight tomorrow morning. And working until after eight at night."

"That's what you get for turning down Rob's job offer," Jane declared.

Fortunately, I didn't have to fake my answering yawn; I really was tired. "Perhaps. But it's way past my bedtime."

I picked up my Scotch glass and drained it, feeling the liquid trace a path of fire down my throat. I heard the murmur of voices behind me as I climbed the stairs; no doubt they were discussing my weird behavior. Or else Jane was following up on her "worthy" comment and was finally putting the moves on Lucian. There was something genuinely strange about the two of them not fighting.

I have no idea how long they stayed down there. I didn't hear Jane came up to bed, and I was awake for a good hour after I turned off the lights, just staring into the darkness and thinking about Cecil, who had also seen Horatio's thing. And who had come triumphantly out the other side—although not without her scars. And I wasn't talking about the faint tracery on her cheek.

But eventually sleep claimed me—and to my delight, it was dreamless.

G lad the salutary mood is still holding," Lucian said to me on Friday night as we anchored our traditional end of the bar at Obadiah's.

"What do you mean?"

He arched an eyebrow. "Come on. You've been wandering about like a corpse for weeks, all grey and shut down. That is, until Wednesday night. Then suddenly you're all energized and perky. What gives?"

"Nothing. Honestly."

The eyebrow stayed up. "So are you really trying to tell me that the lovely Adam hasn't called you on the mood swings?"

"The lovely Adam," I responded, more tartly than I intended, "pretty much hasn't called me at all."

"Oh-ho! Trouble in paradise, then?"

"No, for your information, he's been busy squiring foreign dignitaries."

"Foreign dignitaries? I thought he was a curator, not in the diplomatic corps."

I shrugged. "Well, what else do you call a bunch of curators from other museums? And you needn't look so smug about it, anyway."

"Who, me? Smug?" And I have to admit, Lucian did innocent to perfection. Still, it did highlight how irrationally upset I was with Adam. I'd had a major week, and he was busy with men in tweed. Or so I assumed . . . but then, I had been wrong about Adam. Maybe they were all hunky specimens of manhood, but even so . . . What it came down to was that Adam was missing. Sure, he had called me, frighteningly late on Thursday night, saying all the right things about how he missed me and wanted to see me, and could I come right over? So I did, only he fell asleep in the interim and didn't hear my knock, and I turned around and went home in disgust— though at myself or him, I really couldn't say.

"I slept at home last night," I told Lucian, fairly self-righteously, "or so you would know if you got back yourself before a quarter to dawn."

"How do you know when I got home?"

"Because Jane woke me, banging in a few minutes before you did. And who else would be sneaking in that late at night? Or, that early in the morning, depending on how you looked at it? So, what were you up to?"

"Oh, the usual sorts of no good," he said airily. "Just because your social life is on the fritz doesn't mean the rest of us have to suffer."

"My social life is not on the fritz!"

He shrugged with that supremely Gallic indifference he did so irritatingly well. "What, are you jealous?"

"Of you? Dream on!"

"Yes, of course. You have the luscious Adam. Well, don't take my head off for trying to make sure our gallant curator isn't about to break your heart irreparably."

"Not a chance in hell," I said, trying to match his airiness and succeeding admirably.

But Lucian was not so easily deflected. "Mmm. Of course, this doesn't answer the primary question, which was why you've been looking so pale and wan—and I will refrain from making the joke about Mexican men here."

I grinned. "Yeah, because—if you hadn't noticed—not so much a man. And pale and Juanita just doesn't carry the same impact."

He chuckled. "Actually, I rather like it. Pale and Juanita. Yes, so there you were, all pale and Juanita. But since you're not the type to go all swoony from neglect—"

"Hey! How do you know?"

" 'Not a chance in hell'?" he parroted back to me sarcastically.

"I could have been lying."

"Except you weren't," he said, and I was shocked to realize he was right. Adam was fun, and gorgeous, but . . . something was missing. Something I saw reflected in dreams. Something I suspected he still felt for Caroline. "Which brings us right back to your *Corpse Bride* impersonation, and the primary question: What the hell happened at the Atheneum, anyway?"

"I told you, nothing." It wasn't entirely my secret to share, so I'm not sure if I would have told even Adam, had he been around to tell. But I sure as hell wasn't telling cynical Lucian!

Besides, this wasn't the time for analysis . . . not on a lovely Friday evening, when the air was crisp and cool, and the sun was slanting golden across the harbor, gilding the crisp white hulls of the yachts and fishing boats that lay at anchor outside the restaurant's back window.

Just for an instant—and with only the faintest of tingles—I beheld a misty overlay of the old docks, with the graceful big-bellied whalers rocking at anchor, their masts rising bare against the sky like a forest in winter. And, for the first time, the sight comforted rather than scared me. I knew this world; I did. I still didn't have the whole of the picture, but maybe soon the rest would come. And I would survive the process. . . .

"Liza?" Lucian said, waving a hand in front of my face.

"What?" I blinked, and the gorgeous old ships vanished.

"You were miles away."

"Or years."

The eyebrow shot up. "Again?"

"Come on, you have to admit. There is nothing more beautiful than one of the old wooden ships under sail. These new things"—I waved a hand at the harbor—"are a travesty!"

"Tell that to the billionaires," he said with a grin, but then his eyes grew unfocused and misty, as if he were seeing what I had, mere moments before. "But I have to admit," he added softly, "I'm with you. Those ships did have a grace and beauty. The snap of the wind in the canvas, the ship cutting through the waves. . . . Or so I imagine," he finished hastily, and I blinked, for the sudden practicality of his voice had broken an odd sort of spell—as if I had lived this moment before. But when I tried to reach for the meaning of it, it eluded me, like a shiny fish squirting out of my grasp.

"So, I take it this means Adam won't be joining us tonight?" Lucian added.

"Nope. It's just us. And our erstwhile bartender, which reminds me . . . Empty down here!" I called to Jane, who was over at the other end of the bar flirting with a trio of distinguished gentlemen with silver in their hair. And doubtless in their pockets as well, I thought cynically.

She grinned and winked, and I masked a chuckle, thinking again how well I was coming to know this mercurial creature who was my roommate. For gone was the viridian hair, and in its place was a smooth cap of jaunty jet black—which made her look more like a 1920s starlet than ever.

"Have I mentioned how much I love the hair?" I told her, when she finally extracted herself from her conquests to bring us our drinks.

"Only about thirty-five times." She smiled. "But thanks."

"Getting conservative in your old age, Moonbeam?" Lucian teased her.

But instead of taking offense at Lucian's words, Jane just flipped her pert, perfect hair. "Perhaps."

"Why conservative?"

Lucian grinned. "Shall I tell her, Moonbeam, or do you want to do the honors?"

"Knock yourself out, Irish," she said, and retreated jauntily back down the bar.

I turned to Lucian. "Well?"

"Don't forget, I knew her when she was toddling about in nappies—and the cutest black-haired moppet she was, too."

I started laughing. "Do you mean . . . No, wait, you can't be saying that. . . . Are you telling me that's her *natural* color?"

"Or as near as makes no never mind. And her looking every bit as darling as she did at four years old."

"I heard that!" Jane accused from partway down the bar.

"I think you were intended to," I replied, still grinning. "Is that *really* your natural color?"

"I hate you both!" she said.

Lucian and I looked at each other, then dissolved into laughter. Jane made a point of turning her back dramatically, but I could see she was smiling.

The light had faded slightly by the time we had finished our second beer, washing the quaint old streets with a mellow golden glow. Beside me, Lucian sighed deeply.

"What?" I asked, turning.

He still had the power to surprise me with that silver-grey gaze. Every time I looked at him, I somehow kept expecting night-dark eyes to match his hair, and every time, his quicksilver gaze caught me completely off guard.

"*Je suis fatigué,*" he said.

"Excuse me?"

"Right, you don't speak Frog. Liza, my sweet, I will be the first to admit that Rob makes a lovely burger, but after several Friday nights running, I am heartily sick of the things. I want real food. Will you indulge a poor, bored Frenchman and let him take you out for a proper meal for a change?"

"Take me out?"

"Not as a date, or anything," he added. "I know the glorious Adam already has dibs on your bodacious self, but you are on a budget, and I am not. Besides, I want a proper night out on the town and can't think of a finer companion."

"Except for the one you were with last night?"

He actually blushed. Amazing! But, "Not even close," he managed, with absolute gallantry.

"Damn straight," I teased, "because I'm not putting out at the end!"

He grinned and arched an eyebrow. "No? Are you sure?"

"One hundred percent," I fired back. Except . . . Damn him for that half-teasing, half-sultry look! He was only pulling my chain, I knew—Lucian loved nothing better than to provoke—except he had stuck this image in my mind that wasn't quite going away. . . .

What *would* it be like to sleep with Lucian? There was a wild streak to him, and I sensed unplumbed depths behind that glib exterior. Not to mention that string of girls who had never quite gotten over him. Plus, French, and . . . Damn! He was probably a total demon in the sack.

I'll bet he even . . .

No! I firmly tamped down the rampaging images and added, "Real food sounds lovely, then. Where to?"

"I'll show you."

CHAPTER 19

We walked along through the golden half light, feeling the streets coming alive with their usual Friday-night electricity. The storefronts and restaurants glowed with a warm, welcoming light, and the breeze whispered along lanes that seemed to have changed little in the last one hundred years—though I probably knew better than anyone how erroneous that truly was. But for an illusion, it was a good one.

We walked along South Water Street in a companionable silence, then—at a signal from Lucian—turned left up Broad Street, past the now-darkened museum. We passed what I was convinced were the only two Victorian houses on Nantucket, shoulder to shoulder in all their turreted, gingerbread glory, as if defiantly allied against the Quaker simplicity that surrounded them. And at the top of the block, king of all it surveyed, the Jared Coffin House loomed in austere majesty, typifying everything that was Nantucket.

Though built in the simple boxlike structure of all the Quaker houses, it was nonetheless a mansion: three stories tall and correspondingly wide, its gracious, perfectly proportioned windows glowing gold in the fading light. Unlike its humbler, shingled neighbors, it was constructed of a rich, red brick. It had been built in 1845 by Jared Coffin, one of the most successful ship owners of his day, as a family home. Now it was one of the island's premiere hotels, and the site of two restaurants: a pub-style one, which stretched between a basement room and the outdoor patio, and another distinctly high-end establishment, inside the building itself.

I thought Lucian was aiming for the outdoor patio, which gleamed with festive lights and white iron tables, but instead he guided me up toward the house itself. At which point, I balked. Badly.

"Lucian . . ."

"What? I did say real food, didn't I?"

"But this is way more expensive than I agreed to! I mean . . . I can't let you pay for this, and I'm not exactly in a position to contribute. And besides"—I indicated my jeans and fairly casual top—"I'm not even remotely dressed for the place!"

He grinned at me. "First, may I remind you of the billionaires—not to mention their more paltry millionaire counterparts? The more money you have, the more you are willing to pay for a high-end restaurant that will let you appear in your yachting togs. Nantucket is used to casual gourmet dining, trust me. Besides, I have never seen you look anything less than beautiful, and tonight is certainly no exception."

It was the oddest compliment I had ever received, uttered in such a nonchalant tone that I wasn't even sure it was a compliment and not just some statement of fact. And since I suddenly felt too self-conscious to look at Lucian directly and see if he were joking, I didn't know how to respond. So, of course, I cracked a joke.

"What, even in my pj's, looking like I'd been dragged backwards through a bush?"

"And hugging the toilet? Most especially then," he countered with a grin, and then I *really* didn't know what to say.

"Shall we?" he added, gesturing at the door.

"I . . . Are you sure? The pub will be fine, really."

He shook his head mischievously. "No, you forget what this is about. This is about my French soul being in withdrawal. I want some genuinely good food, and I want you to eat it with me. And I am willing to pay for the privilege. Besides," he added, cocking one eyebrow at me, "have you ever considered that half the reason I don't have a legitimate job is because I don't actually need one?"

And as I gaped at him stupidly, he took my arm and led me into the restaurant.

I figured it would be a cold day in hell before we got a table on a busy Friday night, but apparently Lucian knew his island dining. The place would be closing in under an hour and a half, and while they didn't generally like seating for such a late shift, Lucian just smiled charmingly, and we suddenly had a table. And I had to admit that Lucian had also been right about my level of dress. Despite the general swankiness of the surroundings, I was not, by a long shot, the most casually garbed in the place. The hostess certainly didn't bat an eye as she led us to our table—though I did notice her eyeing Lucian speculatively.

And him eyeing back. But what the hell; it wasn't like this was a date. He was free to look if he wanted to. Just so long as he didn't make me feel totally superfluous.

I needn't have worried. No sooner had we sat down than Lucian was the perfect gentleman, giving me his undivided attention and encouraging me to order whatever I wanted. (And, never one to look a gift horse in the mouth, I did: a Cajun-spiced prime rib, the mere thought of which made my mouth water, along with a warm spinach salad.)

Over dinner—which was every bit as fabulous as Lucian had claimed—he eventually explained his earlier comment.

"So, how much do you actually know about my background?"

"Other than the fact that your middle name is Obadiah because you were born in Obadiah's house . . . Wait, does that mean actually born, or just kind of generally born?"

Lucian laughed. "I don't know. Can you just be generally born?"

"Brat," I said, wrinkling my nose at him. "You know what I mean."

"Yeah," he conceded. "And that would be actually born, complete with violently stormy night and sudden labor and pails of hot water, right out of some nineteenth-century novel. Pretty ridiculous, really."

"Complete with unwed, disowned mother. God, you're right. What century are you from? You're not some sort of vampire or something, born in the late 1800s and still around?"

"Well, if I am, then Kitty is one, too."

I grinned. "Ah! I knew there was something too perfect about her. So does that mean Jim is her evil minion?"

"What, her undead, converted lover?"

"Well, he certainly screams a lot during . . . uh, you know."

Lucian grinned. "Damn, why do you put these images in my head? I'm never going to be able to look at the poor guy in the same way again! No, Kitty and I are as mortal as you are," this with a look I couldn't interpret, "despite the rapher picaresque nature of my conception and birth. Sadly, my personal story could literally begin: 'It was a dark and stormy night.' " When I laughed, he added, "Yeah, people always say that explains my unholy fear of storms."

"You have an unholy fear of storms? Really?" I vaguely remembered Jane telling me the same thing, but I believed it no more from her than from Lucian. It seemed somehow inconceivable that this overly confident, suave creature could be scared of anything. Or, perhaps more accurately, would let him himself be seen to be scared.

His face tightened slightly, and I thought he shuddered. But all he said was, with his usual insouciance, "What, you actually expect me to answer that?"

"Hey, you brought it up."

"True—but I nonetheless claim the testosterone privilege of male posturing." He grinned—that deliberate, knee-melting one—and changed the topic. Or, rather, returned to the original one. "So, yes, the dramatic origins of Lucian Obadiah Theriault. Born and bred on Nantucket, of a French Canadian mother. Nantucket—the land to which all the wealthy gravitate. And eventually, my mom caught the eye of a Quebecois industrial magnate, who had come down as part of a business retreat and ended up spending the summer. That was Paul Theriault—and yes, I can see you noticing the names. Paul adopted me when he married my mom, and treated me as every bit his own son. I was only about five at the time, so he was pretty much the only father I ever knew. And he was a genuinely lovely man—adored both me and my mom, and we adored him in turn. And even though she was never able to give him a child of his own, none of us were ever made to feel that mattered. I still miss the guy."

"Oh! Then he's—"

"Dead? Yes. About three years ago. Not that it came as any great surprise. He was about thirty years older than my mom to begin with, so he had a good, long, rich life. And no"—his eyes twinkled briefly—"I didn't mean that in the sense of filthy lucre, though he had plenty of that as well. He split his estate equally between my mom and me—which, frankly, made her furious. She was convinced that if I had too many financial resources too early on, I would never make anything of myself. And I'm afraid she now sees me as rather a self-fulfilling prophecy. I still don't know who she is angrier at this summer: my dad, for leaving me the money, or Kitty for indulging me in my continued life of indigence. But my dad always said that I was a smart kid, and would figure things out in time. I guess we're still waiting for me to prove him right." He shrugged. "But in the meantime, yeah, man of means, here. And at a kind of embarrassing level, if the truth be told."

"Embarrassing?" I leaned closer, almost whispering. "You're not saying . . . I mean, you're one of those mysterious, uncounted billionaires are you?"

"God, not even close! My net assets are somewhat lower than that."

"Really? How much lower?"

He raised an eyebrow and gave me a look that would have done my mother proud. "Liza!" he exclaimed, laughing, and my face went bright red.

"Oh my God, I'm sorry! That was totally crass of me, wasn't it?"

He grinned. "Well, at least I know you don't have designs on my cash—especially since we've got this no-putting-out policy in place. Providing the policy *is* still in place?" And he raised a wicked, teasing eyebrow at me—his expression so flawless that for a moment I wasn't even sure that he *was* teasing.

"Lucian!" I fired back, in much the same tone—though fueled as much from panic as indignation. What game was he playing—and why did I always get the sense that he *was* playing some unknown game, trying to get some reaction out of me that I never quite understood? It was frustrating and infuriating, and . . . Why did I have the sudden feeling I was, like Eve, being taunted to reach for that apple?

To hell with that; I already had my Adam. And anyway, Lucian was dissolved in laughter at my response, so clearly it had been one of his weird jokes, after all.

"Pick a number, any number, between one and a hundred," he said as soon as he had stopped laughing.

I peered at him suspiciously. "Why? What do I win?"

"Don't know; it depends. What do you want to win?" he asked provocatively, and I decided to ignore that one as well.

"Forty," I said.

"You want to win forty? Forty what?"

"Don't be obtuse. That's my number: forty."

"Ah." And from his gleeful expression, I could tell he knew exactly what I had meant all along, irritating boy. "In that case, warm."

Okay, I was beginning to get an inkling of his game. "Twenty-five."

"Cold."

"Okay. Eighty-two."

"Positively frosty."

"Fifty."

"Simmerin'," he drawled.

"Fifty-six."

"Now notch it down a degree."

"Fifty-five?"

"Good. Now multiply that by a million."

"What?"

"In answer to your previous question." He grinned. "So, are you sure you don't want to put out?"

Okay, so perhaps I was insanely naïve, but that was genuinely the last thing I had expected from his little numbers game—if only because no one I knew was ever that forthcoming about personal details. Except, of course, for Jane. Maybe it was Kitty's influence on the pair of them.

But I was not going to dignify the moment by gaping at him, so instead I said, with what I thought was commendable aplomb, "Perfectly sure. But I sure as hell am no longer going to worry about you paying for the meal!"

He shouted with laughter, no doubt attracting the attention of several of our fellow diners, and beamed at me. "See? That's why I like you. You're damnably irreverent at the best of times, and you don't let anyone intimidate you. And let me say, that's not at all what I expected when Jane first plunked you down upon my doorstep."

I attempted an arch look, although I wasn't sure I succeeded. "I don't think it was exactly your doorstep that I was, as you put it, plunked down upon. You just happened to be living there at the time."

"See what I mean?" he asked rhetorically, as if to the room in general. "But I think you're wrong in one important respect. I think it was indeed my doorstep . . . but whether it was Jane or Fate doing the plunking, who is to say?"

His voice held a whimsical tone, and I peered at him suspiciously again. Damn him and his games again; what *was* he after? "What do you mean about Fate? What is all this nonsense?"

"Oh," he said, blithely, "nothing. Just one of my odd fancies."

"No, seriously. Are you hitting on me?"

I couldn't decipher the look that flitted across his face, but his voice was casual enough as he said, "Of course not. We had a deal, right? And Adam is a nice guy; I'm not about to poach on his turf. No, it's just that . . . I never thought I'd like you this much, or that you'd be this much fun to be around. Or this irreverent. Jane is . . . Well, you know my issues with Moonbeam. I figured you'd be just another one of the same, only . . . Well, you know what they say about assumptions. I made an assumption about you, based on . . . Well, let's just say things I had heard."

"Oh, God, you mean the stupid dreams!" I blurted, and he looked amused.

"Yeah, I suppose you could put it that way: the stupid

dreams." He laughed faintly. "Anyway, I figured I knew who you were, but I was wrong, and I'd like to apologize. I was a bit of an ass when you first arrived—"

"A bit of one?" I interrupted again, and he grinned.

"Okay, a lot of one. But I'd really like it if we could forget about that and just be friends. Deal?"

"Deal," I agreed, suddenly feeling conflicted about everything. Here was Lucian, firmly closing a door I wasn't entirely sure I wanted closed. But who was I kidding? I had Adam—and enough issues trying to figure out my damned dreams without adding even more confusion into the mix.

Besides, fifty-five million was the kind of number that could sway heads even more firmly grounded than mine. So who was to say my sudden charitable feelings toward him weren't due more to his net worth than any more intangible qualities?

"And can I just add," he continued cheerfully—and incredibly ironically, considering my recent chain of thought, "how wonderfully refreshing it is to spend an evening with a woman who has no designs whatsoever on my fortune? I know this sounds unspeakably arrogant, but every woman I've been with— with the possible exception of Lauren, who had her own set of issues—I swear saw dollar signs instead of me. I think I became an asshole out of sheer self-defense. If you treat 'em badly and they still stick around, then they're in it for something other than the charm of your personality."

"Or complete lack thereof."

"In a nutshell." He grinned.

"Damn, I never thought I'd be glad to be an impoverished grad student, but it suddenly seems to have its good points."

"You have no idea!" he said passionately, and another facet of Lucian's personality suddenly snapped into focus. It probably would be pretty ego-crushing never to know if people actually liked you, or the price tag attached to your butt. Lucian had the looks and charm—when he actually bothered to turn it on—to attract any woman he wanted. The problem seemed to be keeping them once they found out his story. Or rather, keeping them from sucking his soul away.

"It was the reason I ran out on you at the Atheneum that night," he added. "Stephanie—who was bearing down on me with the vengeance—was the worst of the lot. Her one goal in life is to be a rich man's wife, and I fit the bill perfectly. Especially since I was prettier to look at than the rest of her prospects." And rather than seeing this as further evidence of his arrogance and self-absorption, I now heard the deprecating wryness beneath the words.

"I take it she told you that?"

His voice was dry. "Often. 'Rich and pretty,' she would crow. 'Aren't I the lucky one?' Took me nine long months to get away."

"But . . . you can't have been living here that whole time?"

He was silent for a moment, decanting the last of the wine into our nearly empty glasses. There was enough for only a dribble each, and then he peered at the empty bottle mournfully. "What time is it?"

"Fifteen minutes to closing time."

"Then that doesn't give us enough time to kill another bottle, does it?"

"Sadly, I don't think so."

"Damn."

"Yeah. We don't even have time for dessert."

"Says who?"

"Says the fact that they're gonna throw our asses out of here in fifteen minutes?"

"Ah, come on, you don't want any twee pastries or similarly pretentious desserts."

"I don't?"

"Not when I can do you one better."

I grinned. "I don't know. I won't be happy unless you say—"

"Homemade ice cream? Rich and sinfully creamy."

"Now you're talking! Well, either that, or coming on to me again in some bizarre, food-related way."

He laughed. "We've already been through that. But let me get the check. And wasn't I right about the food?"

"Trust a Frenchman," I said. "Although . . . Now that I think about it, the French aren't so eager to claim you Quebecois, are they?"

"Not even close," he said cheerfully, and summoned our extra-attentive waitress over. A less cynical woman than I might have said she was simply trying to make sure our table was vacated and cleared on time, but I had seen the glances she cast Lucian's way. She had been angling for attention all evening—and very much in vain, to my delight.

We left the restaurant and walked along the balmy evening streets toward the docks. Darkness had fallen while we were in the restaurant, though it was still tinted with the purple of twilight, and the streetlights glowed gold against that dusky arch of sky. I thought back to what Adam had told me, shortly after we met, about how George Pollard Jr., who had commanded the doomed *Essex,* had become the town's lamplighter and nightwatchman. Deemed forever cursed by a superstitious community, he never went out to sea again. Now, every time the streetlights flickered into life, I imagined him, stooped and grey, making his way along the lanes, lighting the lamps so his fellow citizens could see.

Briefly, I cast a glance back at the Jared Coffin House, its warm brick façade making it sink like velvet into the night. And, for an instant, I remembered it, too. Except that I couldn't have. It was built in 1845, and Obadiah had left the island in 1843, never to return.

Best not to think of that.

"So, what, you only date the ultrarich now?" I asked Lucian instead, as we walked.

"Net worth only greater than or equal to my own," he teased. "Yeah, nice in theory, but not so good in practice."

"Why?"

He turned to me, his light eyes flashing silver under the streetlamps, and gave a feral grin. "Have you ever *seen* Paris Hilton in action?" he said, and I laughed.

"I may be the only guy in the world to ever admit this," he added after a moment, "but I like some brains with my beauty. But that's not even the worst of it. Quite apart from the stunning superficiality of the amazingly rich, most of those women have no desire to marry beneath them. So, here I remain—outside one of the finest homemade ice cream stores in Nantucket. Drowning my sorrows in triple fudge chunk."

"Hey, that's my line!" I said, and he grinned.

"Then after you." And he gestured me into the busy, bustling store.

CHAPTER 20

As I had promised Lucian, I ended up with the ooey-gooeyist chocolate selection in the store, piled into a home-made waffle cone, while he went with the comparatively conservative choice of black raspberry.

"But I *like* black raspberry!" he said, when I teased him about it.

Still, he was correct about one thing. The ice cream *was* practically as good as sex: rich and creamy and downright seductive.

"Do you know that there's a chemical in chocolate that mimics the effect of being in love?" I said idly as we continued to walk toward the docks. The ice cream was gooey enough that I had to eat it out of my cone with a plastic spoon. Lucian was so right; this was infinitely better than tiramisu or crème brûlée.

He grinned over at me. "Quite apart from the fact that chocolate contains multiple chemicals . . . Does this mean that you are going to start coming on to *me* now?"

"Dream on," I said contentedly, letting the sinful choco-

late melt across my tongue. It was amazing, how one chocolate cone could suddenly make everything all right with the
world.

We had, at this point, walked out almost to the end of the
public docks, where the huge ferries disgorged their loads of
tourists and eighteen wheelers by day. The slips were empty
now, and no one else seemed to favor this deserted part of
town for their wanderings. So we took a seat on the edge of
the wharf, dangling our feet out over the water, with the WEL-
COME TO NANTUCKET sign at our backs. I looked out over the
curve of the harbor, its half-moon arms stretching out to either side of us, peppered with the pinpoint lights of the
houses in the night.

"So, it's out there, is it?" I said, gesturing with my cone.

"What's out there?" Lucian demanded with an arch of
one dark, sardonic brow. Of course he couldn't follow my
madly skittering thoughts.

"The sandbar."

"Ah, yes; that. The sandbar that—in part—brought about
the death of whaling. Yes, indeed, there it lies. Such an innocent cause for death, is it not?"

"Aren't they all?" I said, and didn't understand why his
tone had turned dark.

"Oh, they are not all that innocent. Or all that benign,"
he said, and I wondered if he was thinking about his father.
Then, more lightly, "What were we talking about?"

"Your various girlfriends."

"Right. Which reminds me, I never did answer your
question about Stephanie."

"Which question?" For the life of me, I couldn't recall it.

"About my nine-month extraction," he clarified.

"Oh, and whether you were living here at the time; I remember. So were you?"

"Far from it," he said. "Long-distance stalker extraordinaire, that was our Stephanie. Left me phone messages, sent me letters and suggestive e-mails. I finally managed to put a stop to it—but only by convincing her I was virtually engaged to someone else. A lie, of course, but a necessary one. Only then I show back up here, clearly unattached and unmarried, and she figures I'm ripe for the plucking again. It was either propose to you on the spot, or run!"

I laughed. "I almost might have paid money to see her face—but then if you had sprung that on me without warning, I probably would have slugged you, and that would have unwired the whole moment."

He gave me a mischievous glance. "So you're saying that if I plan to propose to you, I should warn you first?"

"Isn't that just common courtesy?" I countered flippantly. "And what about Lauren? Wasn't she there, too?"

"Ah, Lauren." He sighed deeply, then chuckled. "My one attempt at dating a completely normal girl who not only was not a gold-digger but seriously didn't seem to give a damn about my cash, and she turns out to be one of the most ragingly insecure people I have ever met. Her whole self-esteem was wrapped up in who she was dating. If she wasn't in a valid relationship, it was like she didn't exist. It was like dating a black hole. The others only wanted to possess my money; she wanted a lien on my soul."

He shivered slightly, and I didn't think it was from the ice cream. I grinned. "So, staggeringly normal, then."

"Yeah." He gave that deprecating laugh again. "I seem stupendously impaired when it comes to judging what normal is. What about you? What's your nefarious dating history?"

"Oh," I hedged, embarrassed. "It's . . . nothing, really. You know, the usual. Nothing to write home about."

"What, are you honestly trying to tell me that Adam was the first?" Lucian asked, a look of exquisite teasing on his face.

"Of course not!" I declared, stung, and he laughed at me.

"So, what's the story, then? Come on, you already know all my nefarious secrets. So spill!"

Maybe it was the quiet of the night and the rhythmic lap of waves against the pilings that unlocked my tongue, or maybe I was just on chocolate overload. But I nonetheless found myself divulging things I hadn't told another living being before—not even Jane.

"I've had plenty of boyfriends, but . . . I've always had this weird feeling that I was waiting for someone specific to come along. Every guy I've dated . . . I don't know, it was like I had to put them through some sort of test or something, like they had to prove themselves to me. Prove that they were the person I thought they were—or wanted them to be." I surprised myself with what I was saying. I'd never put all the pieces together before, but I suddenly knew I was speaking the truth.

"So, you're a romantic, then," Lucian said, with a faint sneer in his voice.

"What do you mean by that?"

"You think there's only one right person for everyone."

"Hell, no!" I retorted, and he grinned.

"Really?"

"Absolutely! I mean, it's all situational, isn't it? There must be many 'right' people; it's just a matter of timing." At least, that's what I'd always believed—until now. Suddenly, in light of my previous confession, I wasn't so sure. What had I been waiting for all these years if not The One?

"Yeah, that's what I've always wanted to believe, too," Lucian said cryptically then added, "So, is Adam one of the right ones in the right situation?"

I thought about this for a moment. If I was being honest with myself—and it seemed that tonight I was—I had to admit that Adam still felt like a placeholder, albeit a gorgeous one. And that our relationship seemed to exist more on a footing of mutual self-delusion, with each of us trying to fit the other into the contours of a box best suited to another's form. His was Caroline-shaped. And mine . . .

I glanced over at Lucian's still profile. He was staring contemplatively out over the waves, his face half-shadowed.

Mine just wanted to be friends.

I took refuge in a lie. "I guess so. What about you?"

"People put too much emphasis on fate," he replied obliquely, then added, "I'm sure that, when I'm ready, something good will come along. And for now . . ." He turned to me again and smiled. "For now, there's ice cream. Or there was," he continued mournfully, having disposed of his black raspberry, cone and all.

I still had about half a cone and a good scoop of chocolaty goodness at the bottom, but I was chocolated up to the eyebrows.

"You can have the rest of mine," I offered, extending it, but he just grinned and shook his head.

"Full," he said. "But you can feed it to the fishes if you're finished."

I looked out over the waves, which were splashed with streaks of electric gold from the streetlamps. "Isn't that littering?"

"Don't toss the napkin, just the cone; it degrades. Plus, the fish will eat anything. And just think how happy it will make them. All that chocolate swirling around . . ."

"What, they're all gonna think they're in love?"

He laughed. "Stranger things have happened."

"Well, far be it from me to deprive the fishes." My cone landed in the water with a splash. "What time it is?"

Lucian consulted his watch. "A little past eleven. Why, were you supposed to go to Adam's tonight?"

"He never made any mention of it."

"Good. Then how about if I show you my favorite place on the island?"

"Now?"

"Can you think of a better time?"

Actually, I couldn't. "Lead on, Macduff."

He rose, then extended a hand to help me up. His fingers were cool and smooth against mine, yet warm, too. Though perhaps that was because of the sparks that always seemed to shoot between us every time we were in contact. Except . . . As evidenced by his speech earlier, it was clearly only me that felt them. Yet another example of the basic unfairness of life.

And, indeed, Lucian broke contact as soon as I was on my feet.

"Where are we going?" I asked, to cover my reaction.

"You'll see," Lucian replied with a cryptic smile.

We strolled along under the huge elms which were too isolated here, thirty miles away from anything else, to have succumbed to the Dutch elm disease that had wiped out most of the other trees on the East Coast and beyond. They had been planted in 1851 by Charles and Henry Coffin, and thus things I should not have remembered. Only I thought I did. As we walked, Lucian pointed out various architectural details.

"I love this island," he said at one point. "The houses, particularly. Such clean lines, such simple elegance. If I ever designed something, it would be something like . . . What?"

I was staring at him, remembering Obadiah's joy in creation. "Have you ever thought about being an architect?"

He grimaced. "God. Not you, too."

"What do you mean?"

"Another helpful soul, trying to save me from being a wastrel. Don't worry, Kitty's already got that corner of the market."

"Frankly, I couldn't care less if you never do a single useful thing with your life! I only brought it up because . . . well, you seem to have a real feel for the thing."

He peered over at me in surprise. "I do?"

"I think so, anyway. So, have you considered it?"

He shrugged, almost sheepishly. "I've flirted with the idea. But don't you have to go to school, or something?"

"Yeah? And so?"

He shrugged again.

"You're not exactly ancient, Lucian. Besides, with your millions, you'd probably weather graduate school better than the rest of us."

"There is that," he agreed cheerfully.

After a few minutes, and despite a fairly circuitous route, I realized we were heading back to Kitty's.

"Hey, I thought you were showing me your favorite place on the island," I protested.

"I am," he answered complacently, as we entered Obadiah's front yard.

"A fine way to get rid of me at the end of an evening," I complained. "Very subtle. Who is she, and what time are you supposed to be meeting her?"

"What?"

"Ha, ha, Lucian. Claiming to take me to your favorite place on the island, and then just taking me home?"

He grinned in obvious amusement. "Well, perhaps it *is* my favorite place on the island."

"Yeah, except that I was expecting to see something new."

He laughed. "And who's to say you won't? Come along, Ms. Know-it-all." He unlatched the front door and turned on the light, illuminating the front hall. Everything else was dark; clearly we were the only people home. It felt strangely illicit, being alone with Lucian under these circumstances.

Was Lucian trying to put the moves on me, after all? Because he taken my hand—a hand gone damp and clammy with uncertainty—and was drawing me up the stairs, turning on lights as he went.

"Hey, stop looking at me like I'm nuts," Lucian complained as I paused at the head of the stairs. "I swear, this is a totally legitimate mission. And there will be no violation of previous agreements."

Which I suppose settled *that*. "All I want," I said, with

what I thought was commendable aplomb, "is to know what the hell is going on!"

"Patience," he said with a grin. "Good things come to those who wait, and other such aphorisms. And see? Here we are already."

"The linen cupboard?" I said, incredulously.

"Oh, ye of little faith," he declared, and threw the door open with a flourish.

And, indeed, instead of the nest of sheets and towels I had expected, a dark space gaped before at me. I had a sudden, shadowy impression of bones: ribs or a backbone, rising into the black. *God, the ultimate skeleton in the closet,* I thought slightly hysterically, and then the vision resolved and I was looking at a metal spiral staircase, coiling narrowly up into the darkness. I started getting excited again, because I *knew* this place. Knew it in my bones, like suddenly finding an object you thought you had lost ages ago.

"What is this?" I asked Lucian.

"Attic stair. Hang on a minute; let me get the light before you come up." And he vanished into the darkness.

After a moment, a weak yellow light washed down the stairs, followed by his voice. "Liza? Come on up."

Before long, I emerged into the open space of a wide attic that stretched the width and breadth of the house, interrupted only by the twin thrusts of the chimneys. It was a triangular room, about eight feet high under the point of the roof, then sloping down to where the roof met the walls, lit at intervals by bare bulbs hanging from the ceiling. Well-packed boxes, and some items neatly bagged, scattered the walls.

Lucian stood near the top of the stairs, grinning.

"Come on," he said, then set off across the room. I followed. An iron ladder had been sunk into the side of the nearer of the two chimneys. Above, the ceiling between the chimneys was flat rather than pitched, with a hatch above the ladder.

Quickly, Lucian scrambled up the ladder and a fresh breeze filtered down as he pushed back the hatch. I stepped closer and peered up, seeing the stars briefly glimmer overhead before Lucian's body blocked the hole. Then he was up and over, and his face reappeared in the space, his eyes twinkling. "All right. Your turn."

I laughed and scampered up the ladder after him. As I reached the top, he extended his hand again to help me up, and I emerged into a night that seemed windier by far than on the sheltered street below. My hair whipped about as he hauled me up—and not surprisingly, since there was nothing much to use as a windbreak up here. The other houses were shorter than ours, and I could see all the way down to the harbor when I leaned against the white wooden railing.

"A real widow's walk!" I crowed.

Lucian grinned in the darkness and shook his head. "No self-respecting Nantucketer calls it a widow's walk—nor was it built for the purpose you might assume. It's just a walk, if you please, and if anyone was peering out over the harbor and the ships on a daily basis, it certainly wasn't an anxious wife. More likely the captains and the ship owners, who were more concerned with making sure everything proceeded apace with their empires."

I grinned.

"What?" he said.

"You sound like Adam. Besides, you're right. I just remembered."

"Okay, then, smarty-pants, what was the other function of the walk? Can I assume that your past self remembers that, too?"

"Of course. Chimney fires," I said promptly, looking at the two chimneys that flanked the walk. "How else are you going to put them out except from above?"

"Is that something you remember?"

I turned to him, pushing my blowing hair out of my face. He was leaning against the railing beside me, one elbow brushing mine. His face, I suddenly realized, was very close to my own, and that strange tension was spiking between us again. That strange tension that it seemed only I felt.

"No, I don't remember any fires," I said, a bit breathlessly. "At least, not yet. But that's not the way it works. It's not like every time someone says something to me, I remember living through it. I mean, occasionally it works that way, but mostly it's . . ."

"What?" he prompted as my voice trailed off.

I grimaced. "No, it's silly. Besides, you don't believe in this stuff, anyway."

He was silent for a moment, then countered, "Says who?"

"Moonbeam?"

He smiled. "You have a point there. But tell me anyway."

"Why, so you can laugh at me?" And when he opened his mouth to reply, I quickly added, "And if you try to tell me that it's because that's what *I* believe, then I may have to hit you, because that is just condescending beyond belief!"

He dissolved into laughter again. "See why I like you?"

he said, when he could speak again. "I admit that I may have had vague impulses in that direction, but you're right, of course. So, let's just bring it down to its very basics, which is that I'm curious as hell. Shall we sit?"

The walk was littered with dead leaves and the inevitable smattering of bird poop. "Where?"

"Right. Hang on a minute." He vanished back down the hatch.

I looked out over the town and the harbor, busy and bustling on a Friday night. I could hear the occasional shouts of happy teens, and a few of their more drunken, college-age counterparts. The occasional car whooshed past below, and I thought I could hear the faintest bass thump from one of the nearby nightclubs. But still, there was something inordinately peaceful about being up here above it all, looking down like some benevolent god with only the wind for company.

"I can see why you love it up here," I said without turning, when I heard movement behind me again. "There's something truly magical about it."

"Yeah," a male voice said softly at my back, and for an instant I thought it was someone else—though I wasn't quite sure whom. "I've spent some of my happiest hours up on this roof." But when I turned, it was only Lucian, after all. He closed the hatch behind him and laid a blanket down across the boards. "There: a seat."

I folded myself down beside him. The streets vanished, leaving only a view of the distant harbor, wiping away all traces of the modern town. Suddenly, I could have been back in 1840, before Lucy's death and that last fatal voyage. Before everything had gone to hell.

"So?" Lucian said softly. "Tell me."

"I don't know. It's not like everything comes back in a flood—or even in order, for that matter. I get a drib here, and a drab there. Sometimes something triggers it, and sometimes it comes right out of the blue. And the damnable thing is, I still can't make heads or tails of it. Half the time, I'm still not convinced it's real! I mean, even if it were all past events, that would be one thing, but it's not even that. Sometimes you are there, or Kitty, or Jane."

"What, no Adam?"

"No, just the people in this house. It's like the damned place is haunting me, or like we're all here together for some reason; I don't know. It sounds silly, even to me."

He chuckled. "You know, I'm actually more convinced by the fact that you don't seem to believe it, either. Or don't want to believe it."

"Well, would you?" I argued.

He shook his head gently. "No. It's not an easy thing to wrap your brain around . . . or so I imagine. More disconcerting than anything."

"Yeah, that's a good word. It *is* disconcerting—especially since I've started having daytime visions, too."

"Like the time you walked into the building?"

"Just like that. Sometimes I get just these quiet moments of knowledge, like about the walk, and at other times it's in full surround-sound Technicolor, like I'm actually there. I mean, what would you do if you started having moments like this?"

"If I did?" Lucian laughed faintly. "I think I'd probably spend most of my time in denial. Or perhaps expend a whole bunch of energy trying to prove I was *me,* and not whoever I used to be. But then . . . perhaps that's just me."

"Huh. If I could even figure out who I used to be," I said bitterly, "that would be a start. But not even that will come into focus. Some days I'm totally convinced I'm Obadiah, and other days I'm sure I am Lucy. Plus, Adam keeps telling me that I don't know things Obadiah should, and yet I keep having these dreams about the sea. Why do I keep dreaming about the sea?" That last came out more plaintively than I intended.

"That I honestly can't explain," Lucian said.

"And you can explain the rest of it?" I demanded sarcastically.

He was silent for a long moment, and I looked over at him in surprise. His expression was very serious in the shadows, and his silver eyes, for once, looked almost black. His face was quite close to my own, and for an insane second I thought he was going to kiss me. But instead he said softly, "Do you really want to know the truth?"

It was a good question, and I considered it in similar silence for an equally long moment. Did I want to carry this quest through to its conclusion? Did I really want to know that I was someone else—someone who might be haunted by Lucy Young's death for a very legitimate reason?

I jumped up from the blanket and began to pace the length of the walk, trying to figure out how to respond to Lucian, when suddenly . . . A by-now familiar tingling gripped me, and I knew I had been on this roof walk before. The view formed like a twice-exposed photograph: the modern street overlaid by one more ancient, the latter scented with the smell of smoke, marked with the leap of fire. . . .

"Hey," I started to say, "I think I may have lived though a chimney fire . . ." when suddenly the world tilted, and that hazy second exposure leaped into sharp focus around me.

I am standing on the walk with Rachel, who is now a permanent part of my fractured household. Owen, now six, is clinging to my skirts, his eyes wide with the same haunted terror I saw on the night of his mother's death—for that is how I must think of it now. We are all of us in our bedclothes, and Rachel's cap is askew, her straw-colored hair tumbling haphazardly out. Her hands are clutched tightly to the breast of her dressing gown, and her face is as grey as the ash that floats through the air. It is strange and frightening to see her so disordered, this woman who now runs my house with such a sure hand.

I clutch my shawl more tightly around me—for propriety's sake only, because the July night was already hot and balmy before we retired. Yet, when the mad bombilation of all the church bells on the island, pealing in an inharmonious cacophony, woke us and drove us to our high rooftop, it was to a sight that chilled the blood.

I wonder if this is what the preacher means when he speaks about the fires of Hell, because I cannot imagine Satan's realm being any less an inferno than that which faces me now. Is it this, then, what awaits me? For I am a sinner of the very worst kind. The only question that remains is this: Shall I see more joy in this world? Will I wake one morning to see the *Redemption* in the harbor and Obadiah once again beside me? It is a prospect that seems bleaker with each new season.

Almost three years have passed since he sailed, and there has been no word.

Still, there is Owen. And how can I be sad when my boy still lives—and thrives? To my endless relief, it seems he was young enough not to truly remember that night. That dreadful, awful night . . .

I hug him closer to me. His hand is tangled in my robe. Yet, bold boy that he is, he is already peeping out of my skirts. He pulls away from me, peering around. He is young enough to still see excitement in this spectacle. How I envy him that innocence!

Rachel is moaning, but I find myself staring, transfixed, like a snake before the charmer's tune. I can hear the roar and crackle of the flames from here, feel their heat on my cheeks. The wharves are enveloped in curtains of fire, and half of Main Street is burning, too. The house where I used to live with Lucy, before Obadiah built our current abode, is likewise ablaze. Even as I watch, its roof gives way in a roar, and sparks shoot high into the night. People, in all state of dress and half-dress, run through the streets—though whether to help or hinder I don't know. The town's two fire engines are overwhelmed.

There is a noise like thunder, and flames leap acrobatically into the sky as one of the warehouses explodes. One of the whale oil stores must have caught alight—and for all our native sperm oil is supposed to burn so clean and clear, black clouds billow forth.

"Auntie Rose," Owen says, the babyish lisp almost gone from his voice. He tugs sharply at my hand, to get my attention. "Auntie Rose, why is everything burning?"

"I don't know," I tell him, but I suspect that I do.

This is Armageddon, plain and simple—the wrath of God made manifest. The frantic people seem so small and helpless in the face of this all-consuming wall of fire that I do not see how we can ever stop it. It will devour us all, inexorably—the innocent and guilty alike—and I can't help feeling that it is all my fault, that I have called this inferno down upon us.

When lust hath conceived, it bringeth forth sin: and sin, when it is finished, bringeth forth death.

The wages of sin *is* death, and it is death I see all around me.

When the heaven is shut up, and there is no rain, because they have sinned against thee: yet if they pray toward this place, and confess thy name, and turn from their sin, then hear thou from heaven, and forgive the sin of thy servants, and send rain upon thy land. . . .

But there is no rain; just the fiery sky.

And I am not forgiven. . . .

I return to find Lucian's arms around me, and a street awash with light but not flames. I must have looked as pale and bloodless as I felt, because he said, sharply, "Liza? What's wrong? What did you see?"

"The Great Fire," I said, but I couldn't seem to force my voice above a whisper. "I lived though the Great Fire. I saw the whole town burning. . . ." But that wasn't even the worst of the revelations that this vision had brought me—and as the full implications came crashing down, so did I.

CHAPTER 21

∞

I returned to consciousness again with Lucian slapping my face.

"Hey!" I protested, struggling to sit.

He looked frustrated, but let me up. "Well, what else was I supposed to do? You were out like a bloody light."

"Lucian . . . Do you realize what this means?"

"What what means?"

"I lived through the Great Fire! I saw Main Street burning. Lucian . . . I'm not Obadiah, after all! Or Lucy . . ." I scrambled to my feet. "I need to tell Adam. How do you get this open?" I demanded, tugging at the hatch.

Lucian looked like he wanted to say something, but then his face hardened with a certain resolve and he opened the hatch for me. "There." He said something more, but I didn't hear him through the sound of my feet on the ladder. I ran out of the house, only remembering my purse and car keys at the last moment.

Part of me knew I was being unspeakably rude to Lucian, who had gone out of his way to show me the walk, but Lucian still thought I was half-mad, and Adam believed me. Though God knows how he would react to the idea that I was not his whaling captain after all, but just . . . Auntie Rose.

But who *was* Auntie Rose?

I knew Obadiah as well as I knew my own skin; that much was clear. And I knew Lucy, too. But the reason I could never figure out which of them I used to be was because I was neither. Instead, I was the one Lucy and Obadiah had left behind.

What had Kitty said? A companion? A cousin?

I cast my mind back over all the dreams as I drove. I was lucky the streets were almost empty, because when the revelation hit, I almost crashed headlong into a bunch of parked cars.

I slammed on the brakes and sat there, just breathing for a moment, as it all filtered in. It was like one of those Magic Eye puzzles, where, when you focus just right, a comprehensible image suddenly pops out of chaos, in three eye-catching dimensions. And a hell of an image it was, from a boatload of chaos.

Despite my earlier confusion, I had seen everything from *one* point of view: Rose's. Obadiah's love, Lucy's friend, Owen's mother. Dear God. All one and the same.

I glanced over at the dashboard clock, realizing it was close to midnight. Would Adam still be awake? Would he even be home? How much entertaining did curators take?

I parked—crookedly—in a spot relatively close to Adam's front door. The lights were on downstairs, but that didn't mean he was still awake.

As I had just last night, I pounded on the door. Only, this time, Adam answered, looking at me in silence through the screen. Thanks to the assembled curators, I hadn't seen him in almost a week, and once again his looks caught me off guard: the well-muscled height; the classic chiseled features, softened by that fall of dark curls; the unusual, startling green of his eyes. He was wearing only an old pair of sweatpants, revealing what seemed miles of smooth, tanned skin, like a man carved from polished oak.

My lips curved in an appreciative smile, which died a-borning when I registered the frigidness of his gaze.

"Liza," he said flatly. "What are you doing here?"

"What do you mean?"

"Didn't you have a date?"

"A *date*? Look, can I come in for a minute?" I had no idea what he was talking about, but had no desire to have whatever confrontation was coming while standing on his front porch.

He pulled the door open in silence. He had clearly been unwinding on the couch, for there was a glass, a liter bottle of Coke, half-empty, and a bag of chips scattered across the coffee table.

"What is it?" I asked as he closed the door behind me. "Did I do something wrong?"

"What do you think?" he replied.

"Frankly, I have no idea," I fired back. "I came over here to tell you something fairly monumental, and you're treating me like I've squashed your favorite bunny. So what gives?"

"The Jared Coffin House?" Adam said pointedly.

"How did you . . . What?"

"I saw you," he said.

"You were *there*?"

"Yeah. I even waved to you. But you were utterly oblivious, so wrapped up with Lucian, the rest of the world didn't exist. And a right fool I looked, too. Look, there's my girlfriend—who couldn't care less that I was even present!"

His face was flushed—and I knew it was that latter point that ate at him more than anything. Had we really been that oblivious?

"But . . . it was nothing, Adam! Honestly. Just two friends having dinner."

"Friends? You looked too cozy to just be friends."

"Oh, and you're suddenly an expert on Lucian and me?" I exclaimed angrily. "He wanted something other than Rob's burgers for the night, and asked me to join him. So I did. End of story."

"Really?" Adam looked a little more tentative, a little less self-righteous. "That's all it was? Dinner? Nothing else?"

"Well, unless you count going out for ice cream, walking back to Kitty's, going up to the roof walk, and seeinc the Great Fire," I shot back sarcastically. "But apparently my revelation means nothing in the face of your petty suspicions."

"My . . . Wait a minute. Did you say, 'seeing the Great Fire'?"

His tone was so much that of the quintessential researcher that I had to laugh, despite my anger. "Yes, Adam," I said patiently, "I saw the Great Fire. And let me tell you, it was every bit as apocalyptic as everybody claimed. But quite apart from the horror of the vision—"

"You're not Obadiah," he said, on a breath.

"No, I'm not Obadiah. Does the name Rose mean any-thing to you?"

"Rose *Garrison*?" he said, his beef with me forgotten. I hadn't heard her last name before, but the moment he said it, I knew it was right. "But she's—"

"The forgotten one. She was there, Adam. Through it all. She was right at the center of everything. And while I still don't know how it all fits together yet, I do know one thing: Obadiah is innocent of his wife's murder."

"And how do you figure that?"

"Because . . . because I think that *I* murdered Lucy Young. Or, rather, that Rose did. And is it any wonder her spirit won't rest? How can you live with that knowledge?"

I had voiced my worst suspicion, and it scared me more than I could say.

Adam didn't hesitate; just reached out and held me, his bare chest warm under my cheek, grounding me in the here and now. But eventually, curiosity took over, and after a minute or two he asked, "What makes you think you killed Lucy Young?"

"Because . . ." I shivered, and his arm tightened around me. "I was angry, Adam. So angry. You see, there's more." And I told him everything—at least, everything that I knew. The affair, the child, my fury at Lucy. "Something big went down on the night of November fifteenth," I added. "I don't know what yet, but it changed everything."

He was silent for a moment, contemplating. "You didn't actually see yourself harm her, did you?"

"No, but . . . There's a part of me that just knows, right? That this was my fault, that this is why I am back here. In all the memories, there is so much guilt. Guilt and grief."

"You never told me that before. . . ."

I grimaced. "There are a lot of things I haven't told you."

"Why not?"

"Because half of you still thinks I'm making this all up!" And, to his credit, he didn't try to deny it. "Not that I entirely blame you. Like I said, sometimes *I* think I'm imagining things—or wish I were. In some ways, it was easier when none of it made sense. So, Mr. Researcher, tell me. What do you know about Rose Garrison?"

"Not a lot, sadly. That she was Lucy's cousin. Came from . . . Boston, was it? Or—"

"New Bedford," I said.

"Right, New Bedford. See? You already know more than I do." And he dropped a feather-light kiss on my forehead, resting his cheek against my hair.

"Not yet," I said bitterly, "but I suspect I will soon. What else?"

"That she raised Owen Young. And ran a school out of the house for years. Hey!" He sat up a bit, twisting so he could look down on me. "Perhaps that explains the vocation."

I shuddered, suddenly wondering if Lucian didn't have a point about running very far in the other direction. But all I said was, "Perhaps so."

We were silent for a moment, then, "But that does leave one critical question," Adam said at last.

"And what is that?"

"If you are Rose Garrison, then how do you know so much about whaling, and why the hell are you having whaling dreams?"

I gave a strangled laugh and banged my head lightly

against his chest. "That's the million-dollar question, isn't it? And the answer is that I have no clue!"

"Mmm." Another silence, then, "What now?" he said.

"You mean long-term, or short-term?" I said with a rueful smile.

"Short-term is all I can manage right now."

"Well . . . Are you sleepy?"

"I've been drowning my perceived sorrows in caffeine," he responded, nodding at the half-empty soda bottle.

I masked a grin. "I'm surprised it wasn't beer. Or vodka."

"God, no." He shuddered. "I learned that lesson, after Caroline left. Too many mornings waking up with my mouth tasting like the inside of an old shoe." I laughed, and he added, "So not excessively tired. Why? Do you have something in mind?" And he raised a salacious eyebrow.

"Mind out of the gutter," I said, poking him. "I was actually wondering if you wanted to take a drive. I have to get up early for work, anyway, so I'd rather sleep at Kitty's." Not to mention that I never seemed to dream at Adam's. "But if you'd care to join me . . ."

"Sold," he said. "Let me just grab a sweatshirt." He rose from the couch, stretched mightily, then turned back to face me before he was halfway out of the room. "Oh, and Liza? About the Lucian thing . . . I'm sorry if I overreacted. It's just . . . Well, Caroline was always so very closemouthed about everything that I got used to leaping to conclusions. But I want you to promise me something."

"What?"

"No matter how hard it might be at the time, always tell me the truth, okay? It's just easier in the long run."

And why did I feel a sudden dread at that? "Okay."

"And . . . hey!" His face lit up again. "Maybe on the drive over, you can tell me all about the Great Fire."

The sky hangs low overhead, the clouds as grey and heavy as pewter. The wind buffets the *Redemption,* shrieking through the rigging and shaking the masts and hull and what few sheets of canvas we have raised against the gale. The rain is hissing down in near-vertical sheets, and the men on the decks look half-drowned as they scurry about their business. For we cannot afford to be lax, even on days like today. We are four years into our voyage, and ill luck has dogged our path. A mere two hundred barrels fill our hold, and if we continue along the path it seems that God has deemed for us, this voyage seems doomed to last seven years or more.

The whales are scarcer now than they were in my youth. I had heard other captains complain of this, and I long thought it to be no more than the ramblings of old men. But now, I see it is nothing more than the truth. The old grounds that once spelled our fortunes—that made our tiny island a giant on the sea—are betraying us. And the great leviathans upon whom our livelihood depends are fleeing our ships for new grounds we know nothing of. And we, too, shall have to roam still farther afield, into alien waters.

We visited the Galapagos two weeks ago, to resupply, and our decks are now awash in tortoises, huddled in miserable groups against the rain. Their sweet, succulent flesh will be a welcome change from maggoty hardtack and salt-beef for the men, and unlike the hogs we took on at the Azores, these beasts do not require feeding. They can live a year without food and water, I am told. Unlike my crew, who daily clamor for fresh meat when there is none. But maybe this treat will dispel the misery of the voyage for a spell, make them forget the sparse contents of our hold and the hundred-plus-barrel bull that eluded us when he dived too deep for our lines, forcing the men to cut him loose before they, too, were pulled into the depths.

I feel a sense of doom pervading the ship. The men want to return to their homes and wives. Thomas Kenney, our third mate, was married a few months before we sailed. Now, his first child will not only be born without him, but looks to be well-grown before we return. I alone seem to be immune to this draw. My home life is . . . Well, you know that better than most. But still, I miss the smells and sights of our island, the feeling of flat, dry land beneath my feet. I wonder when I shall see it again.

But perhaps God has not been so indifferent to our fates as it seems, for our luck changes in an instant. The lookout's cry from the hoops comes but a shade before the cries of the men, the sound that falls involuntarily from my own lips. For suddenly we are amidst them, the great black backs of the mighty sperm lifting up to starboard and larboard, to bow and stern. There must be twenty of them at least, from young to old, rising and blowing ecstatically, their short, bushy spouts steaming in the chill of the gale. It is like a benediction from God—from famine to feast, and we are amidst them, at one with them.

I barely need to call the orders; the men are moving to the boats with silent haste, each of them seeing in this miraculous moment a reversal of our fortunes. One by one, the boats are lowered off the davits, touching down onto the stormy sea as gently as possible, to avoid gallying the whales. But they seem not even to notice we are there, amidst the blowing gale.

It is like the day I lost my finger, and yet . . . not. I pray that no one will be harmed today, because we need this so desperately.

I watch from my post, partway up the foremast rigging. With the four mates and their crews away, I must hold the *Redemption* to her course with but the cook and the cooper aboard. The four boats bob amongst the whales; I see Matthew Phinney dart twice, fixing to a large cow—eighty barrels at least. And before she even begins to flounder, Samuel Pearce, boatsteerer of William Stockton's boat, fixes to an even larger cow.

Ninety barrels, by God; I can almost smell our changing fortunes as the second mate's boat takes a midsized whale.

Three fixed on now, and the group begins to scatter, but I see the fourth mate's boat chasing madly after yet another beast, oars churning against the spray. The waves soon hide them from my view, and I find myself again offering prayers. Two of the boats are being towed rapidly in opposite directions, the sleigh ride made all the more treacherous due to the fierce, rough seas. Soon, the tiny boats vanish from sight.

The third beast is not running but fighting, thrashing her tail and trying to smash the fragile boat. Phinney clings to his lines, and I can see Kenney screaming orders, though his words do not reach me. The whale sounds. Through my spyglass, I see the line play out, fast and furious, even the rain not enough to stop the loggerhead from smoking. George Dawes, at the tub oar, is throwing bucket after bucket of water over the lines, trying to stem the budding flame.

God, she is going deep. Please do not let us lose her, as we did the last bull. We need those eighty barrels like a starving man needs food.

Unbidden, the words of Psalm 104 come to my mind, and I find myself whispering them into the teeth of the wind:

> O Lord, how manifold are thy works! in wisdom hast thou made them all: the earth is full of thy riches.
> So this is the great and wide sea, wherein are things creeping innumerable, both small and great beasts . . .

And suddenly I find myself reciting along, a different voice joining the first: female and male combined, and my dreaming mind suddenly jars and shudders, wondering what this is. But the words draw me in, draw me through:

> There go the ships: there is that leviathan, whom thou hast made to play therein.
> These wait all upon thee: that thou mayest give them their meat in due season.
> That thou givest them they gather: thou openest thine hand, they are filled with good.

We finish together, he and I, and suddenly I understand. I know what this is: the first story he ever told me—perhaps the very moment that started it all—his rough voice painting such a vivid picture of the wind and waves that it is almost like I am there. I see and feel and smell it along with him, feeling within me a swelling homecoming. I hadn't realized until now how much I had missed this, these glimpses of a world that is, by necessity, limited by my sex and station.

My brother had told me such tales, when he shipped out on a whaler. Had I married, I should have been one of those wives who went to sea with their husbands. But there was no marriage. When Daniel perished at sea and our father died shortly thereafter, all that was left for me was charity. My cousin Lucy, three years my senior, needed companionship. And I . . . I needed a roof over my head, and could ill afford to be choosy about which roof it might be.

It wasn't a bad life, all told. My cousin had always been like a child chasing after butterflies. What she had seen in the large, cold man she had married, I could never tell; they were as different as fire and ice. If there had ever been affection between them, it had long since eroded through ten years of marriage and four failed pregnancies—though I knew he still did his duties in the marital bed, when he was home. I could hear the creak of the bedropes, the groans of the wooden bed-frame as he strove to give her the living child she so craved.

But Lucy had no feeling for the sea, no desire to share that part of Obadiah's life. Whereas I missed it, more than I could say. So I had, in some desperation, turned to her dark, distant husband. And, to my surprise, found him a gifted, natural storyteller.

"What happened next?" I urge, caught up in his tale. "Did they catch that whale?"

His dour, wind-seamed face lights in a smile that makes

him almost handsome. For the first time, I see the fire in him, the passion, that his dark, narrow face usually masks. And his eagerness to have a willing audience, so lacking in this house.

"Yes, Rose, they did," he tells me. "She comes back up from the deeps, bellowing and thrashing like the very devil, but Kenney gets the lance into her, churning it into her life. And before long there is fire in the chimney, and she goes fin out. The men tow her back to the ship, and we tie her alongside while we wait. And wait. The winds grow stronger, and our despair rises. How will the boats fare in these heavy seas?

"But God must have been smiling on us, for near an hour later, William's boat comes limping back, with that ninety-barrel monster strung out behind. And then, in comes Macy's—Richard Macy, that's my second mate—with something like a fifty-five-barrel whale in tow."

I smile. William Stockton, Obadiah's first mate, is well-known to me. He is a frequent guest in our house—a bluff, barrel-chested man with the demeanor of a lion and the heart of a lamb. He has a wild mane of hair, the broadest shoulders I have ever seen, and eyes as blue as the heart of a flame. His courage and loyalty are legendary, but so is his kindness. He and Obadiah have shipped together since the *Wampanoag*.

"And the fourth mate?" I demand, forgetting my courtesies in my eagerness.

Obadiah laughs: a sound as rough as the seas he has been describing. "Three hours pass. Enough men are now on board that we have started cutting in the first whale. Phinney is in the monkey rope, riding the whale through the rough seas, and it is his voice that alerts us. Jared Owens, fourth mate, is coming in fast, with another great beast behind him. Four whales," he crows. "Four! Not many captains get four whales together. So there we were, cutting in one to the larboard, with three strung out to the starboard, the lines tangling and the sharks gathering, and not one of us getting more than a wink of sleep for nigh on a week. But the seas calmed, and the warm sun shone, and by God if we didn't fill our hold with just shy of three hundred barrels from one day's catch!

"And, after that, the Lord smiled upon us, for the grounds we had been blown onto were rich, and we got over two thousand barrels inside of the next year, and here I am now, home for these three months, and Thomas Kenney got to see his son's fifth birthday. So all is well. And thank you, Rose, for sitting here so patiently, listening to an old captain ramble."

"Not old," I assure him. Though he is sixteen years my senior, he is still only two-and-forty. "And I like to hear it. I used to pester my brother, Daniel, for stories. He was second aboard the *Hezekiah,* when he died. He was hoping to make first, someday, but . . ."

"What happened?" the captain says with unexpected sympathy in his voice.

I feel the familiar shock of loss for my reckless brother. "The very devil of a whale, Mocha Dick himself. He stove in the whaleboat, and three men died. The first mate brought us word."

Obadiah nods sagely. "I know of Mocha Dick. Praise God, it has never been my fortune to meet him, but I had heard of the *Hezekiah*'s encounter. Three years ago, was it not?"

"Yes. My father was never the same after the news. He died of an apoplexy six months later, and I came here. But I miss Daniel's stories. Now, I have nobody to tell me such tales."

"Ah, but you have me, Rose," he says stoutly. "That is . . . if you want me."

"Oh, I do!" I assure him eagerly. I don't mean in that way, not then; that came later. But I think all the seeds of what followed were planted that day, as that story that grew between us. For, in that moment, we each found something we desired: me a teller of tales, and him an eager audience, willing to share his passions.

"Then, Rose," he vows, "I will be your Daniel. I will bring you home, like Nimrod, tales from the sea—as many as you like, and as often as you like. Do you agree?"

"Oh, yes, thank you!" I say, and our bargain is struck. A devil's bargain, I suppose, which will lead us both down a path of danger and temptation, but at that point I could not have cared less.

CHAPTER 22

My drift back to consciousness was slower this time, with Obadiah's voice resounding in my ears. I opened my eyes mere moments before the alarm shrilled. Adam groaned and rolled over, burying his head beneath the pillows.

I couldn't blame him. By the time we'd gotten back to Kitty's and worked off his caffeine, it was close to three in the morning. We had gotten less than five hours of sleep.

I mirrored his groan and batted off the alarm. Then I staggered across the hall to the bathroom, wondering how I was going to make it though an entire day of tours and lectures.

When I returned from my shower, Adam was half-awake, watching me through slitted eyes as I dressed. When I was finished, I leaned over and kissed his forehead, wondering again what I was doing with a guy this gorgeous. Then I dropped my keys beside him on the bed. "Stay," I said. "Sleep in. Just bring the keys to the museum when you're awake."

He mumbled something incoherent.

"Oh, and try not to fight with Lucian if you see him. Remember, nothing happened. I actually ran out on him to find you!"

Another mumble—more contented, this time—and I kissed him again and left. Down in the kitchen, I ate a bowl of cereal and dumped about a gallon of fresh-brewed coffee into one of Kitty's jumbo-sized travel mugs, then headed to work.

When I walked in, Martha took one look at my face, and shuffled the schedule on the fly. I'd been slated to do the whaling lecture in the morning and a tour in the afternoon. Instead, she put me on the desk for the day. When I protested, she said, "You're hands-down my most reliable worker this summer, Liza. You've more than proved yourself. Besides, everyone deserves an off-day."

I thanked her. Surfing the caffeine wave, I managed to make it through the morning. Adam dropped off my keys and brought me a sandwich around noon, then vanished upstairs to his office. About two hours later, he came back down, catching me in a momentary lull in the crowds. He leaned across the desk, grinning like the cat that had eaten the proverbial canary.

"What?" I said.

"I didn't kill Lucian," he told me. "We had breakfast together. He's a good guy." Before I could figure out how to respond to that, he added, "Better yet, I've got news! I popped by the library this morning, then was just upstairs searching some of the online databases. I found out more about Rose."

"You did? What?" I asked eagerly.

"She was born in New Bedford on May twenty-third, 1807. One brother—"

"Daniel," I said. "He was older, right?"

"By about five years. Born March first, 1802. Don't tell me you dreamed that, too?"

"Just last night. Sorry," I said again with an apologetic grin, then had to break off our conversation as a few visitors entered the museum. I sold some tickets and answered some questions, and then we were alone again.

"Sorry. You were saying?"

Adam gave me a slightly rueful smile. "About Daniel. Do you know how and when he died?"

"Well, I can't tell you the exact year, but it was about a year before Rose came to Nantucket."

"Daniel died in 1830. April eleventh, age twenty-eight."

"God, so young!"

"Yeah. And as for method of death—"

"No, don't tell me; this one I know! He died aboard the *Hezekiah*. He was second mate. In the middle of a hunt, a whale smashed his boat and he drowned. Ha! I'm right, aren't I?"

"The genealogies don't tend to be that specific. All I had was 'lost at sea.' But we do have a lot of the crew manifests from the time, and it shouldn't take me long to check the *Hezekiah*. But I'm sure you're right; you've been right about everything else so far."

I frowned. "Well, except for one really weird thing."

"Which was?"

"Damn!" More tourists, more tickets. In the next lull, I said, "Okay, here's the weird part. In my dream, I was telling Obadiah about Daniel's death, and I said that a whale had got him. A whale named Mocha Dick. How odd is that? I mean, I'm just taking that from *Moby-Dick,* right?"

Adam was silent for a long moment, gazing idly at the prismatic folds of the great Fresnel lens, then turned back to me with a grimace. "Well, if I didn't believe you before, I certainly do now."

"So there really *is* a Mocha Dick?"

"Yeah. One of the most infamous sperm whales in the Pacific. Probably where Melville got his title. He was a huge bull whale, known for the huge white scar across his forehead as well as the many boats he crushed beneath his flukes. His first reported attack against a whaleship was in, I think, 1810, near Mocha Island; hence the name. Mocha Island, by the way, is somewhere south of Valparaiso, off the Pacific coast of South America. And Mocha Dick was so infamous that probably a lot of the attacks laid at his door were caused by other whales entirely. But there was no denying that he was a right old bastard of a cetacean, destroying every boat that came against him and completely evading capture until a Swedish whaleship took him down in 1859."

"And the *Hezekiah* was one of the ships rumored to have come up against him?"

"As near as I can recall, yes. I'll have to check that, of course. What about Rose? Do you know about her death?"

I found myself shivering. "No. What happened to Rose?"

"She died here on Nantucket in 1894, at the ripe old age of eighty-seven. Still a spinster, from what I could tell."

I wasn't sure whether to be relieved or appalled. Obadiah had left on his fateful voyage in 1843. Had Rose really waited faithfully for him to return for fifty-one years? It seemed . . . Well, the word "excessive" sprang to mind.

"Want to see her grave?" Adam added, interrupting my train of thought.

"Do you . . . You mean, you know where it is?"

"Not exactly, but I'm sure I can find out. There's a database for that, too—surprise, surprise. I'll do a search. If you are interested, we can go after work, sometime next week."

"Yes, please!" I said. Then, "Oh, crap." A new group of visitors had arrived.

Adam laughed. "Go on, I'm done interrupting your day. And I suspect you need sleep more than a date tonight. But we're still on for Sunday dinner?"

"Yup. See you then."

He leaned over the counter and gave me a quick kiss, then left me to deal with a handful of grandmotherly tourists who apparently found my love life more interesting than any museum.

When I got back to Kitty's at a little past five, the house was strangely silent. Jane, who should have been home at this hour, was suspiciously absent—though the mystery was quickly solved when I saw her note, tacked to the fridge. She was covering an earlier shift for a sick colleague, so would be working a double today, and wouldn't be home until well after 2 A.M.

Poor kid. Still, what was I going to do about dinner? I had gotten used to throwing something together with Jane in the time between our shifts. I poured a glass of soda and was on the verge of going upstairs to shower and change when Lucian came trailing into the kitchen.

He looked almost startled to see me. "What are you doing home? Isn't it your night with Adam?"

I stifled a yawn. "Normally, yeah. But tonight I need sleep more. Last night was . . . Oh, God, Lucian, I totally owe you an apology! I didn't mean to abandon you so abruptly, especially after you went out of your way to buy me a truly lovely dinner and show me the walk, but—"

"To hell with that," he said brusquely. "I was just worried about you. What happened last night? You babbled something about a fire, and then bolted. Are you okay?"

I contemplated this. "Yeah. It was . . ."

"What?"

Revelatory, I wanted to say, but I wasn't in the mood to get into it with Lucian. Fortunately, I was saved from answering by the sound of a key in the lock.

"Hey, who's home?" Kitty called, her voice preceding her into the kitchen. "Jim and I have a yen for dinner at the sushi place. My treat. Who wants to join us?"

Over a feast of rolls and tempura, Kitty said to me, "So, how has your first week of solo tours been going?"

"Great! I feel like I'm really getting into the swing of things. And it's been a blast picking my own itineraries."

I was apparently a natural at this game, and loving every minute of it. Of course, I had an unfair advantage—one that I didn't hesitate to exploit once I learned that I could begin to control it.

At least twice a week, it seemed, there was some question I couldn't answer. Something too specific, or outside the scope of Rose's lifetime. But this past Thursday, I had had an odd experience that changed everything.

It started with a perfectly innocent moment—and a question that under ordinary circumstances might have stumped me. But two older ladies, about in their fifties, were hanging at the back of my tour, as much just observing the town as listening to my spiel. I heard one turn to the other, commenting about the fence posts along Main Street—which, instead of your usual spiky white pickets, were crowned with a smooth top rail. They wondered at the construction. And, unable to come up with a good answer on their own, they turned to me.

It wasn't a fact included in the regular reading material. Or, if it was, I had missed or forgotten it. I was stumped. There was no crime in pleading ignorant, yet before I conceded defeat, this crazy thought popped into my head. What if I could figure it out? Flash back into the past and find the answer? I had never had any conscious control over my visions before, but maybe that was because I simply hadn't tried. So I just sort of opened my mind, and to my amazement found myself walking along a darkened street.

I instantly knew I was older from the faint ache in my joints and bones, the fainter echo of sadness in my heart. Obadiah was long dead. After all these years, I had no hope that he would be coming back. But life went on. It was cold and wet, and the wind was screaming up the street, whipping my skirts around my ankles, fit to trip me. It was always thus with the winter storms. . . .

And, like that, I had my answer. Trying to mask a too-smug grin, I said, "Nantucket is a relatively flat island, and the winds whip strongly across it in a storm. But, because the early settlers knew that, they provided for it. They capped off their fences, so that people could hang on to them in a blow. Neat, huh?"

The tourists agreed, impressed. And I was elated. The very fact of having control over the visions seemed like a triumph of epic proportions.

"So, what was the bonehead question of the week?" Jim now wanted to know. It had quickly become our favorite topic because it was such a great source of entertainment. There was a bulletin board in the staff room at work where all the docents posted the dumbest questions they'd been asked that week. I don't know who started calling it the Wall of Shame, but the name had stuck. And whoever collected the most entries by the end of the summer won a prize. So far, Patricia Cavanaugh was in the lead, primarily because she led the most tours.

But Jim had already heard most of the worst ones, and it had been a relatively gaffe-free week. I confessed as much, adding, "Though there was the woman who thought the Gold Rush was in 1949. That was pretty good."

Lucian looked scandalized. "Can people actually be that stupid?"

"What, do you mean Jane didn't tell you about the tomato?" I said with a grin.

Lucian shook his head, and Jim chuckled quietly.

"Last week, some woman apparently parked her monster SUV smack in the middle of afternoon traffic, completely blocking the street, and ran into the restaurant, demanding that they sell her a tomato because she couldn't be bothered going to the store."

Lucian grinned. "I don't know if that's stupidity, or an excess of privilege. Either way . . . Scary!"

"Still," I temporized, snagging another spicy tuna roll, "I'd rather handle individual stupidity than institutional stupidity. I mean, you wouldn't believe some of the stuff I have to deal with in grad school!"

"And you want *me* to go back to school?" Lucian muttered to me, grinning.

"What was that?" Kitty said, ears perking up.

"Nothing," he said. "Sorry, Liza. You were saying?"

"Just that teaching is becoming positively mired in bureaucracy. If I have to hear any more about 'learners' and 'outcomes,' I'm going to scream! Not to mention AYP and NCLB. Whatever happened to kids and lessons?"

"And I had to walk uphill to school, both ways, in the snow," Lucian added, laughing. "I think twenty-four is too young to become an old fart, Liza."

"No, she's right," Kitty said. "Even my jobs are becoming so mired in acronyms that I can't tell heads from tails anymore."

Kitty, as I had recently learned, volunteered at a number of local charities and aid societies. Because, like Lucian, she was independently wealthy.

I couldn't help hoping that maybe it was catching, like a disease.

"Well, then, death to bureaucrats," Jim said, and we all toasted.

After dinner, Lucian tried to persuade me to join him at Obadiah's, but I declined. I was already yawning my way through the tail end of dinner, so I went back to the house with Kitty and Jim. I had expected to fall asleep right away, but instead I found myself mulling over last night's dreams. In some ways, I had answered Adam's question about why I had the whaling dreams, but Obadiah relating events to Rose still didn't explain the vibrancy of the images. Those dreams didn't feel any less vital or real than the dreams of Rose's own life. I mean, even if she had a good imagination, how had these stories become such a part of her existence that I was seeing them, hundreds of years later? I was still missing part of the picture.

Impulsively, I picked up my cell and dialed Adam.

"I thought you'd be asleep by now," he greeted me.

"Mmm. Close, but I can't seem to shut my brain off."

"What can I do?" he said instantly.

"Nothing that exciting, sorry. Just . . . talk to me about something. Why do you think this is happening? The dreams. Everything. Is this about reparation? Rose's guilt?"

"What do you think?" he said.

"I think I have to stop it, Adam. I mean, if Rose really did kill Lucy, then maybe that's why I'm here. Or why Rose is still here, in me. Maybe whatever she did in the past still haunts her, and therefore haunts me. So if I can just figure out what she is trying, somehow, to tell me, I can make this all stop. Just be me again, and let poor Rose rest at last. I mean, isn't that the classic way to lay to rest the restless ghost?"

"Well, this is not exactly your classic ghost situation, but you could be right. There must be some reason this is all playing out now. And quite apart from the wider implications—which I am definitely *not* going to think about now!—it does makes me wonder." He paused for a moment, then added, "Do you remember what I told you, when we first met, about how there was this woman back in the forties who kept trying to clear Obadiah's name? What if she, like you, was also Rose? What if this pattern just keeps playing out, generation after generation?"

His words sent an almost visceral shock through me. "Dear God, Adam, you're really beginning to scare me! What are you saying? That I'm doomed to do this lifetime after lifetime?"

"Well, until you get it right, maybe. Until you do whatever it is that Rose wants you to do. You said it yourself: It's like something needs to get done, discovered, or brought out into the light."

"So if I go about declaring from the rooftops that Rose killed Lucy Young, how is that going to fix anything?"

"I don't know. And maybe that's not it. Maybe there's something else Rose needs and you haven't seen enough to know what yet."

His words seemed to contain a ring of truth. There was something I still needed to figure out. But I also felt that it was close—so close I could almost smell it, touch it, taste it. Still, I hoped I got my answers soon, and before the fast-approaching end of summer. I was becoming so tangled with the past that a part of me wondered if I would ever be able to free myself. Leaving Nantucket without answers . . . well, I didn't know what that would do to me, but I couldn't imagine it would be anything good.

Yet if Adam was right, maybe I could unlock the mystery and save some future incarnation from going down the same path all over again. Someone had to stop the cycle, after all. So why not me?

But that brought up another issue. What if I was not the only one treading this path? Was it only souls under trauma who returned, or would I one day find myself confronting some fragment of Lucy or Obadiah? Was that why I was here, to find them and apologize?

It didn't bear thinking about.

"Thanks, Adam," I said anyway.

"Did that help?"

"I think so."

"Good," he said. Then, more suggestively, "What are you wearing?"

"A sombrero and lederhosen. Good night, Adam." And I hung up while he was still laughing.

CHAPTER 23

I lie in my bed, the covers clutched up about my chin. It is hard to sleep when they are fighting; I can hear the voices echoing down the hall.

"Why?" Lucy is whining, her voice high and querulous. The opium always brings out the worst parts of her personality: the childishness, the grasping after immediate pleasures. "Why won't you touch me?"

I have heard the substance of this fight before. She finds little pleasure in the marital bed; she has told me this before. But now she desires an act she would otherwise avoid, because of what it might bring her.

"We have been though this before, Lucy," Obadiah says, his voice level; what Lucy sees as cruelty is more like a father's attempt to control a wayward child.

"I want a child!" she now wails, almost screaming.

"You can barely take care of yourself. How do you intend to care for a child?" His words are harsh but true.

"There's always Rose," she wheedles.

"Rose is not your servant," he says, his voice taut. "You'd do well to remember that."

"You don't know what it is like for me!" she cries. "You have no idea. Child after child, death after death."

"I know better than you think." His voice is reasonable, but I can hear the pain beneath it. "You forget, they were my children, too."

"You? You don't suffer as I suffer. You don't care!"

But she is wrong, I know. While she escaped into her poppy haze, I saw his grief at the loss of his seven-month daughter, blinding and bitter. And that, I think, is when I realized that my feelings for him went far beyond what is right and proper. Seeing this hard man brought low, unable to deal with a sorrow he did not know how to express. In that instant—in the fierceness of my desire to enfold him in my arms, to ease his pain—I realized the extent of my secret shame. I loved the husband of a woman who had taken me in when I had nothing. A woman who had treated me with kindness and friendship when so many women in my position became little more than unpaid servants.

Yet he is man for whom death is a daily fact of life. Friends and companions, lost in an instant to the cold embrace of the sea. He has learned to swallow his grief and move on. She cannot comprehend this, and the dichotomy in their reactions tears her apart.

She has started to sob. I can hear the thump of flesh on flesh: her fists, beating on his chest.

"We have been down this path before, Lucy," he says.

"When you are ready to embrace life again, I will do my best to give you what you need."

"No!" she wails, but already I hear his footsteps leaving the room, descending the stair. The door slams behind him, Lucy's fury. I hear her sobbing loudly.

I should go to her . . . but instead I find myself rising from my bed, wrapping my dressing gown around me, creeping silently down the stairs. For, I tell myself, what can I do for her that he cannot? But perhaps that is only a rationalization. My feet want to go where my heart leads me, and that is downstairs.

He sits on the long sofa in the front parlor, in the dark, his head bowed into his hands. He does not look up as he hears my steps. But when I hesitate at the door, he says, still not raising his head, "I am sorry if we woke you. Come in, Rose."

I enter, taking a seat on the far side of the sofa. My heart is pounding wildly. I am too bold; it is too improper. Alone, with him, in the dark. But I am drawn to his pain like a moth to a flame. If there is anything I can do to ease his burden . . .

At last he raises his head from his hands. It is dark—but not so dark that I can't see him, the glitter of his eyes.

His gaze meets mine, locks, and I feel my breath sucked away. It is all there in his eyes, everything that I have both hoped and feared to see for so long. He stares at me like a drowning man, offered a rope. Like a starving man, offered a feast. His gaze devours me, and I am gasping, breathless from but a look.

"Rose," he says softly.

I am humbled by the desire in his eyes. Humbled—and

awed. I had no cause to hope, no right. And now I am terrified and elated all at once.

Sometimes, over the past few months, he has looked at me with a fire burning in his eyes. And I have wondered: Is it truly for me that those eyes burn, or just for anyone who might show him a modicum of interest and sympathy?

But now I know. That fire is all for me.

He takes a deep breath, the sound seeming to shudder up from his very soul. "Do you ever wish for things to have been different, Rose? Do you ever wonder about the path not traveled?"

"You mean like if Daniel had not died?"

"Precisely. Just like if Daniel had not died."

"Then I would never have come here. And I would never have met you."

"And that would have saddened me. Right now, you're the one bright light in my existence. Sometimes I wish . . ." He breaks off, frowning.

"What?" I prompt, my heart hammering. "Sometimes you wish what?"

"Nothing." He sighs. "I am an old, broken man, with no right to his dreams."

"Not old," I whisper boldly. "And not broken. Not from where I sit."

I ought never to have spoken, but the pain in his voice tears at me. And even if we cannot act on it, at least he should know that someone in this world finds him worthy of love. Of respect.

Fire flares again in his eyes. "Rose," he says softly, "I am not a handsome man, I know. But—"

"I . . . I cannot," I stammer. It is not my place to think such thoughts, or dream such dreams. Not when Lucy lies between us. "This house, your wife—"

"Yes, my wife," he answers darkly. And then persists: "But Rose, if there were no house, no wife—just us two in a void, where our actions could hurt no one, let alone God—what would you think of me then?"

"Then," I manage to say, "I would think you one of the finest men I have ever known." For it is nothing less than the truth.

He is silent for a long moment, then reaches for my hand. His touch burns all the way up my arm. I nearly jump with the force of it.

"Thank you for that, Rose," he says. "That means more than I can say."

I cannot say what would have happened next between us. I hope we would have stayed strong, stayed separate, but there is a rustle in the doorway. He drops my hand. Lucy is standing there, her hair shining in the pale moonlight, the tracks of tears on her hollow cheeks.

Even in distress, she is lovely. How can he look at me in the way he has when she eclipses me like the sun eclipses a pale star? She, with her hair the color of moonbeams, and her eyes as blue as cornflowers in the field? Her skin, even now, is as smooth and pale as cream. Beside her, I am a small dark thing.

"I am sorry," she says, her voice that of a repentant child. "You are right. I am ready to live again. Will . . . will you help?"

"Always," he says, and rises to take her hand.

"And Rose, too?" she pleads, gazing at me with limpid doe-eyes.

"Rose, too," I say, and she manages a shaky smile.

He puts an arm around her shoulders, leading her upstairs—pausing only briefly to shoot me a hard, burning look over his shoulder.

She weeps and rages as he denies her the poppy. She sweats, and tosses, and soils her sheets. And he is hard and implacable— a tower of strength and denial. The ordeal lasts nearly a week, with us sleeping in shifts, Lucy the center of our mutual world.

"How can you keep doing this?" I ask him at one point.

"Because it is the *least* I can do," he said. "It is my fault, Rose. All of it. I should never have married her, should never have brought her to this island. She would have been happier elsewhere, married to a different kind of man. But I did not realize that until it was too late. So I have tried to make her happy, as best I can. Yet, even in that, I fail. It is the loss of my children that drives her to this. How *can* I do less?"

"You're a good man, Obadiah," I tell him, but he shakes his head, broken.

"If I were a good man, I wouldn't want, so badly, that which I cannot have. No, I'm not a good man. But at least I can be a strong man—and that I shall be, Rose."

Still, there is a moment, one night, as she sleeps— momentarily at peace—when exhaustion drives us together. I am too weak to deny him comfort, and so we hold each other, our arms hard about one another, for almost an hour. No more than that, but it is enough.

And slowly, Lucy comes back to herself.

I wake, shivering. Of course, I knew how the story ended—at least, some of it. I knew that Rose and Obadiah eventually succumbed to their temptation. And that, somehow, Lucy paid the ultimate price for that forbidden love. But still . . .

What must it be like, to love someone that deeply? The palpable fire between them, even unconsummated, just emphasized again how pale everything felt with Adam. Would I, like Rose, come to love him in time? But the more I shared Rose's dreams, the more I came to understand what love meant, what love *was*. And it wasn't anything I had known as Liza.

I sighed deeply and rolled over to look at the clock: 4 A.M. I rolled back—then was halted by the sound of voices outside my window: Jane and Lucian, returning together.

Jane's voice, drifting erratically upward, was filled with a bubbling excitement. "I can't believe . . . ," she was saying. "After all this time . . . Who would have guessed it?"

"Certainly not me." A low laugh, and I lost the rest of Lucian's reply. Then, ". . . a woman of many surprises, Moonbeam."

"You, too," she responded. "Who would have guessed . . . such hidden depths?" Something else I couldn't hear, then, "How long have you known?"

I felt a sick, sinking feeling creep through me, unable to believe what I was hearing. But there seemed to be no doubt about it, especially when Lucian answered, "Pretty much since . . . start of the summer." And ". . . in denial, of course, but . . . You?"

For once, Jane's reply was crystal clear. "About the same. And, God, who would have thought it? *Us?*"

A low laugh, then, ". . . pretty unbelievable, I admit. But I'm tired of denying . . ."

I could guess what he was tired of denying. Jane had another conquest, and God, why did this depress me so much? I felt tears prickle in my eyes.

How long could the silence go on? Were they kissing out there? They must be kissing; otherwise, they'd be talking again by now. . . . God!

". . . what are we going to do?" Lucian said, at last.

"You can't . . . too early to tell . . . not ready to . . ." Jane's voice held a hint of panic.

"Don't worry . . . won't tell if you won't . . ."

A low laugh, a giggle, then more silence—during which I tormented myself with all sorts of images. Eventually, the downstairs door clicked open, and I expected them to come upstairs together, but some sort of discretion must have prevailed because, pausing only briefly outside my door, Jane proceeded alone to the bathroom. I wondered what she would say to me tomorrow. Despite her promise to Lucian, Jane was never one to kiss and not tell. And I'd have to be happy for her; I *would* be happy for her. She deserved a good guy, and Kitty must have known what she was talking about, all along.

Hooray. Hooray for all.

A silent tear trickled down my cheek, and I made myself think of Adam, but all I could think of was Rose and Obadiah—so deeply, hopelessly in love.

A second tear joined the first, and I told myself angrily that it didn't matter, that it wasn't Lucian I wanted; it was just what Rose and Obadiah had had. What it seemed Jane and Lucian now had. And that was true, right?

Lucian's footsteps finally echoed on the stairs, and I heard the door to his room bang shut. I waited in dread to see what Jane would do—wondering if, like Rose, I would be a helpless audience to something I really didn't want to hear. But fortunately, she passed by, entering her own room instead.

A long while later, I managed to drift back to sleep.

I don't know how I made it through work the next day. To my shame, I was in far from top shape during my morning lecture, muffing several obvious points. I felt dreadful for misleading all the nice tourists, but I just couldn't help replaying Jane and Lucian's conversation in my head, trying to determine if there was any way I could have misinterpreted it.

But no, even on the seventeen hundredth repetition, it seemed as clear as ever. And indeed, no sooner had I walked in the house than Jane pounced, dragging me up to my room and banging the door shut. Then she bounced down on my bed and sat there, staring at me.

She was glowing in a way I had never seen her glow before, her dark eyes almost radioactive with joy, her pale, clear skin becomingly flushed. Her sleek black hair was freshly brushed, and it even seemed to shine with a healthier gleam than before. The healing powers of love. I felt a complete wreck in contrast, sweaty and dragged out from a bad day at work. Quite apart from the mental distraction, it had been a scorcher, and I had been out for two hours in the afternoon, squiring sweating groups of tourists around. No wonder Lucian preferred the perfect Jane package to the vastly more flawed Liza variety.

I clamped down on the jealousy that threatened to overwhelm me. I *would* be happy for her; I would.

"Oh, Liza," she burst out, "I'm so glad you're finally home! I've been waiting all day to talk to you, because the most wonderful thing has happened! I still can't believe it, because it came so totally out of the blue, and I can't really even give you any details yet, because it is all so new and so uncertain and I both don't want to jinx it and, well, there are other reasons, too, which if I tell you will give it all away, but—"

"True love, I take it?" I said wryly, not mentioning any names. If she wanted to preserve the illusion for whatever unfathomable reason, then let her do so. I wasn't going to pop that bubble.

"Oh, God, Liza," she exclaimed, grabbing my hand and squeezing almost to the point of pain before letting go. "I know I've always pooh-poohed the concept—the ultimate sexual tomcat, that's been me—but I've never felt this way before, *ever,* and that's got to mean something, doesn't it? I mean, it all just feels so . . . utterly *right,* if you know what I mean! Like . . . I don't know, like we were meant for each other, or something. Does that sound completely insane?"

I shook my head slightly, remembering my dream. That was what Obadiah and his Rose had felt; I had felt it, viscerally, that perfect meeting of souls. It was what Cecil and her Tom had, too. Until recently, I hadn't believed in The One, but now I wasn't so sure.

I knew what Rose had felt with Obadiah, and I knew what I felt with Adam, and they weren't the same. Not even remotely. And the thought made me feel ineffably sad.

"Yeah, I think I do know what you mean," I said, thinking of Obadiah and Rose.

She grinned and said, "Of course, you have Adam. Who should be here soon, so I'll get this over with. But, oh, Liza . . ."

Her expression was so goggle-eyed that I had to laugh. "All right. How long has this been going on?"

"Only since last night, really," she confessed. "I mean, we've known each other for a while, obviously"—*God, how stupid does she really think I am? Who else could it be?*—"and I have to admit that I had been gradually growing a bit of a crush on him this summer—I mean, who wouldn't?—but I had no idea he even felt the same way. I mean, it's too bizarrely incongruous for *us* to be together! Except that last night . . . Well, I was flirting a whole bunch after work, and probably being a bit provocative—I mean, you can't get the cow to completely change her spots, right?—and then he—"

"What?" I prompted, when she paused, and she snorted a laugh.

"Can you believe I'm actually embarrassed about telling you all this? Me, the queen of the kiss and tell? I mean, I even told you about the weird guy with the handcuffs and everything, and this wasn't even close! Except . . ." She frowned charmingly.

"This is real?" I supplied, and she nodded.

"Yeah. Feels more private somehow. And I'm sorry for all the cloak and dagger, by the way. I'll tell you who he is soon, I promise, but . . . I can't just now; you understand, right?"

"Yeah, I understand. Tell me as much as you want to."

Which, as it turned out, was rather a lot. I heard about that first kiss, which caught them both so completely off guard. "It wasn't supposed to be like this," the guy in question had told her, and Jane had agreed. If she had expected anything—which she really hadn't—it would have been just another of her usual summer flings. Yet, when he kissed her, it was like lightning had gone through her, and she just knew; this was The One. (I thought of Rose, trembling under Obadiah's touch.) And then, when they made love—in the back room of Obadiah's, when everything was dark and shut down—it was like he knew exactly where to touch her, how to touch her, like he knew what she wanted before she did herself.

It was far less than Jane's usual account, but still she tormented me with details, and I tried not to picture her and Lucian together, in the warm, illicit darkness. Childhood rivals who had finally found love . . .

What do you do if you think someone else's One just might be your One, too?

"So," she said, eventually, "do you mind if I bail on our Monday chick day this week? We kind of want to have a real date, now that we've both realized . . . Well, you do understand, don't you?"

I assured her I did.

"You're the best, Liza!" she said, leaning over to hug me. "I'm so glad that we both came here, and that we both found people this summer. How amazing is that?"

I made a sort of noncommittal noise, and she released me, peering at me dubiously.

"What's wrong, Liza? Are you and Adam really okay, or is something going on?"

"No, everything's fine."

"You sure? Because you know you can always talk to me if something is up."

That was vintage Jane, always trying to fix other people's problems no matter what was going on in her own life. I smiled at her. "I know. Thanks. But really, it's nothing," I lied. "Adam and I are fine. We're great."

"And you really are happy with him?" She was regarding me with a strange intensity.

"Yes, I'm really happy with . . . Why?"

"What do you mean?"

"I mean, why are you asking me all this? You've suddenly gone all weird. What's so important about my relationship with Adam?"

"Because I want you to be happy, of course!"

"As happy as you are?" I said dryly.

"Don't be a cynic." She laughed. "Yes, as happy as I am. I mean . . . You'd tell me if something was wrong, right?"

Okay, I got it. It was a friendship test. Jane wasn't exactly a girl's girl; she probably just wanted to make sure that her new relationship wouldn't cost her her best friend. I could relate to that. "Yes, I'd tell you," I assured her. "Don't worry; we're always going to be friends."

"Of course we are!" she said, almost snappishly. "That's not . . . Oh, never mind; it's not my place to say, anyway. It's just . . . There are always options. You know that, right?"

I started to laugh. "Okay, now I am just plain confused. Can we talk about something else?"

"I'll try," she promised with a grin.

"Good. Now, go," I said, giving her a push. "I'm not fit for polite company until I've had a shower."

"Hey . . ." she said.

"What, you want to be polite company?" I teased, and she laughed. "Now, scram!"

Fortunately, the shower gave me the perfect opportunity to compose myself before dinner. And I had to admit, the masochistic, self-tormenting part of me was very curious to see how tonight's dinner played out, and if she and Lucian would be able to keep their secret in the same room, with company.

They did far better than I'd expected. If I hadn't known, I would never have guessed that anything was afoot. Okay, there was a bit of excess coyness, and occasionally Jane would poke Lucian, who would then glance over at me and bristle up for no apparent reason, or Lucian would raise an eyebrow her way and she would go red as the tomatoes that Kitty was chopping up for salad, but otherwise it was not much different from their normal, teasing banter, and Kitty only once said: "What is *up* with you two tonight?" and then not even really in a speculative way, but more in kind of an irritated tone, as they got underfoot.

Odd. I had never imagined that either of them was that good an actor. Hidden depths, I suppose.

"Are you okay, Liza?" Kitty said to me at one point. Jim was in one corner, doing something esoteric to some steaks, and there was an amazing-smelling sauce simmering on the stove, not to mention the odor of fresh-baked buns permeating the kitchen. Jane and Lucian were side by side at the table, sipping wine, and I was kind of hanging back, leaning on the counter, absorbing it all.

"Why? What do you mean?" I asked her, startled.

"Well, it's just that you're not usually so quiet, and so . . ."

"Observey," Jane put it. "You've got your camcorder eyes on tonight, Liza."

"Despite the fact that I don't think 'observey' is a word," Kitty said, "my niece is absolutely right. You seem to be troubled by something tonight. Is it Adam?"

. "Why is everyone so concerned about my relationship with Adam today?" I said, glaring at Jane. She just shrugged.

"Why do we have seven steaks?" Lucian interrupted, peering over at the counter.

"That's the way they came in the pack," Jim said. "Why?"

"Can I have the extra?"

"Only if you flip me for it," Jim said, and that put an end to Jane's interrogation, as Jim and Lucian entered into a two-out-of-three coin-flipping match.

"You rigged that," Lucian complained when he lost.

"I also bought the steaks," Jim reminded him with a grin. "But because I'm . . . uh, a nice guy," he added, patting his belly as Kitty shot him a sharp look, "I'll give you halvsies."

Lucian brightened, and Kitty laughed. "Yeah, it's a good thing you are a nice guy; you know what the doctor said. Now, come on over and join us, Liza. You are—what is the phrase you young people use these days?—freaking me right out?"

"Beastin', Aunt Kitty," Lucian drawled, and everyone laughed.

I came over to the table, and Jane poured me a glass of

wine. The morning's glow was still in her face, and I was amazed that no one else saw it.

The conversation eventually got stuck on a bit of local gossip—something to do with Jim's store, and some outrageous customer demands; I wasn't following the full details, because I was too busy trying to determine if Jane and Lucian were playing footsie under the table. There was certainly something suspicious going on—though, truth to tell, it looked more like actual kicking. In fact, I thought I once saw Lucian suppress a yelp as Jane let fly . . . which didn't really seem like the relationship of one's dreams, but who was I to judge?

Then, clearly in response to something Jim had just said, Kitty exclaimed, "You have no idea what it is like," in much the same tone that Lucy had uttered, "You don't know what it is like for me!" in my dream, and my world suddenly tilted and fell upside down.

It wasn't just the similarity of tones and phrases; it was . . . well, it was everything. Not that they looked anything alike: Lucy with her moonlight hair and childlike insecurity, and dark-haired Kitty with her oh-so-solid sense of self, but still . . . The revelation hit me with the force of a freight train, and I just *knew.*

Lucy was Kitty, and Kitty was Lucy, and—by all that was sacred—I wasn't here alone!

It was like reuniting with an old friend you haven't seen in twenty years. The old face is different from the young face, but within five minutes, it's like they had never changed, had never grown older. You just knew that these two dissimilar faces both belonged to the same human being.

And that was just how it was with Kitty. I had no evidence to back up my certainty, but a certainty it was. As it hit me, I staggered and half rose, my wineglass falling from a suddenly slack hand to shatter against the tabletop, red wine spilling everywhere like blood.

"Liza? What's the matter?" Kitty exclaimed.

Simultaneously, Jane's voice rang out with, "My God, what's wrong?"

"Are you okay?" Lucian said softly, in my ear. I hadn't felt him move, but now realized he was holding me gently, steadying me.

His face was very close to my own, and there was a strange, glittery excitement in his eyes.

How could I tell him what had just happened? He would never believe me.

How could I tell anyone?

"Sorry, sorry," I bluffed, straightening myself out of Lucian's grasp and thinking as fast as I ever had in my life. "It just, I thought I saw a mouse, and—"

"Mouse?" Kitty exclaimed, her voice rising slightly. "I thought I got rid of them all last summer. Jim . . ."

He immediately rose and, kind man, began searching the area in which I had seen my fictional mouse, while Kitty, ever practical, mopped up my mess of spilled wine and glass and checked me over for cuts.

"Are you sure you're okay?" she said. "You still look kind of pale."

"I . . . I hate mice," I lied, unable to stop staring at her. Granted, the timing was suspicious; I had only thought of this possibility last night, and now here was proof? Yet it also felt so right, so true, I was amazed that I hadn't seen it before.

I wondered if she even knew, if she had any idea of just what had driven her to purchase this particular house. And why. She had never been exactly happy here before. But maybe Adam was right. Maybe it was about repeating the patterns generation after generation until someone eventually got it right, broke the cycle, and moved on.

So who had broken Kitty's cycle?

But it certainly explained some things. Like why—at some level—she had believed my odd ramblings about reincarnation. And why everything in the kitchen was somehow in the same place as it had been, back when Lucy lived here. When *I* lived here.

"You're shivering," Kitty said. "You really don't like mice, do you?"

"Since when?" Jane declared, sounding puzzled. "Liza was the one who killed our mouse this winter, when I went all to pieces."

Oh, God, someone save me, I thought. I should have remembered I was a terrible liar.

"Right," Lucian said. "I'm taking Liza out for a quick breath of fresh air. Back in a sec." And he spirited me out of the house before anyone could comment further.

CHAPTER 24

So," Lucian said, when we were out in the comparatively cooler air of the early evening, "this particular phobia has nothing to do with mice, does it?"

The salt-tang of the air, and the golden light slanting low off the rooftops, was doing a lot to restore my equanimity. Thus, I was able to say, with a certain degree of asperity, "How do you know?"

He just gave me one of his lazy smiles. "Because you don't strike me as the type to freak out at the sight of small furry rodents."

"And Kitty does?" I countered tartly.

"Touché. And I'd probably even believe you, if Jane hadn't already told me the story about the mouse in your kitchen in Madison. Your amazing sangfroid featured heavily in the account. So, what gives?"

A pithy little phrase about frying pans and fires popped into my head, and I sighed. "I thought this was a rescue."

"In a sense," he said enigmatically. "So, again, what gives?"

I thought about that for a moment, then said, "I'm not telling you."

"Why not?"

"You wouldn't believe me, anyway."

"Why? Is it this reincarnation thing again?"

"Of course."

"So, try me. You might be surprised."

"I very much doubt it."

"So now what? You're going to go running off to Adam again, like you did on Friday night?"

I flushed. "I already apologized for that. And besides"—I checked my watch—"Adam should be here in about ten minutes. So if this really is a rescue, then just let me sit here quietly for a moment and think, okay?"

He shrugged and moved off, strolling to the far side of the fenced-in front yard, giving me the space I needed physically, if not mentally. My mind was still spinning. What did it mean, for me to be in the same house as the woman I may have murdered here, over a hundred years ago? Was that the reason I was present, to make some sort of reparations to Kitty? But that didn't seem right. Kitty seemed so supremely oblivious to what she had been, reparations wouldn't make sense to her. But there had to be a reason we were both here at the same time, even if I was the only one who knew it.

Lucian was right. I needed to talk to Adam. . . .

"Hey, Adam," Lucian said dryly, wandering over from the other side of the yard. "You're early. Come in. Or rather, sit here with Liza for a while. She's had a bit of an unspecified shock. I'll go tell everyone you're here." And he vanished into the house.

"I don't think he likes me much," Adam said after he'd wheeled his bike into the side yard and chained it against the fence.

I laughed shakily. "I wouldn't worry. There are days I don't think he likes anyone very much. Jane's going to have her hands full with that one."

"Really?" Adam peered at the house, as if he could still see Lucian's retreating back. "Lucian and *Jane*? I can't see it."

"Nor I, but something's going on. Jane's been dropping big hints ever since I got home. Which reminds me. Are you free tomorrow night? She just canceled on me."

"Absolutely!" he said, and I drew a sigh of relief. We'd go to his house. The last thing I wanted was to run into Jane and Lucian, happily on the town. Best to just hide out completely.

"Now," Adam said, coming closer and drawing me up against him in a hug, "what is wrong? What sort of unspecified shock was Lucian being so cryptic about?"

I snorted a laugh into his chest, which was wonderfully broad and comforting under the circumstances. "He was only being cryptic because I refused to tell him about it," I said.

I sensed Adam's grin. "But you are going to tell me?"

I nodded and did, spilling the whole story.

Adam listened in silence, then said, "Yeah, you're right; I have no idea what to say. But I think you're right in feeling that it is one more piece of the puzzle. And it's not like you understood any of the other pieces, until you put them in context. But maybe . . . Well, maybe this is what it was all about, seeing Lucy happy, realizing that she doesn't blame you for what you think you did, that the blame has always only ever lain with yourself. I mean, if she can forgive you, then maybe you can forgive yourself."

"And then the dreams will be gone, just like that?"

"I guess you'll find out tonight, won't you? Is it okay if I stay, or do you need to be alone?"

"Oh, Adam," I said honestly, "you're way too nice for me!"

"God, don't say that." He shuddered visibly. "That's what Caroline always used to say. Too nice for me; that's the relationship kiss of death. Please, take it back!"

"Okay. Consider it done," I said lightly, but once more wondered just what was holding us together, beyond my obvious appreciation of his looks, and his tendency to see me as good research material.

Then Jane called us to dinner, and I didn't have to think at all anymore.

I am sitting in the parlor with Lucy. It is a warm spring day, and a fresh breeze is blowing in through the open windows, whisking away the clouds of a cold, lonely winter. It is hard, sometimes, with only the two of us in the house. Lucy is easily bored, and in constant need of entertainment. When the weather is fine, we can at least stroll outside, or visit the shops. But in the cold, dark months, there are days when her constant need for distraction and attention is like being tormented by a small, eager puppy.

But today is good. Today she has a letter from home, filled with breezy gossip that distracts her. She is reading it aloud, urging me to an excitement I don't feel about people I have never met. But I can't begrudge her the moment. She has been good to me, in the year and half I've been a resident of her household. And I can see why. It must have been hard to be here all alone, in the long years her husband is at sea. He had already been gone four years before I arrived, only his infrequent letters letting her know he still lived.

For all that he is master of the household in which I now reside, I have never seen him. Though I have seen his portrait—a hard, severe visage that always makes me shudder. What will it be like, when he arrives? If he arrives . . .

Lucy's voice stutters, stops. I glance up, startled, and there, framed in the parlor door, is a figure so large, so black, that I stifle a gasp.

For an instant, I think my imaginings have conjured him. But then he shifts, and I know he is real.

He is both nothing and utterly like his portrait. I had expected him to be both shorter and wider, but he is tall and lean as a mast. The face is leaner, too—no doubt due to the privations at sea—but his beard is a fierce black bush, hiding any expression. His deepset eyes are as dark as the night, his hair like a raven's wing. He has a sea-chest slung effortlessly over one shoulder.

His eyes flash from Lucy to me, and I feel myself shivering. How has my silly, frivolous cousin married such a hard, dark man? How can one even laugh with such a presence in the house?

For an instant, nobody moves. Then the man who can only be Obadiah Young slowly lowers his trunk to the ground. With a squeal, Lucy drops her letter and flies to him. It is like a butterfly fluttering at a rock. And I find myself close to laughter, because he suddenly looks so bemused, so uncertain what to do with this woman who is his wife.

"You're home, you're home!" she cries—though whether in joy at this presence or just in delight at another distraction, I cannot tell.

"Lucy," he says, dropping an awkward kiss on her forehead. But then, how can he know how to deal with a woman he has not seen in five and half years?

He turns to me. His dark eyes meet mine: curious, assessing.

"I am Rose," I find myself blurting. "Lucy's cousin."

"I know," he says, his voice lighter than I had expected. "I received Lucy's letter. Welcome to our home." His face does not echo his words, but he still holds out a hand and, apprehensive, I rise to take it. He is even taller and more fearsome from up close. His eyes glitter darkly as he leans over, drops a formal kiss on the air just above my skin. I find myself shivering. Then the scene shifts, and . . .

Rose." William Stockton is grinning at me, his bold, brash face gentle as he leans over, drops a kiss on my cheek. "It is always a delight to see your face."

Pleasure fills me at his presence. But, at the same time, part of me gasps at his words, his voice. To Rose, he is Obadiah's first mate and strong right hand, just as he always has been. But to Liza, the hidden observer, I know the spark beneath the flesh. I have met him before—though it was not until I saw his past face that I knew.

Jim.

Good lord, the players are mounting. How many of us are here, waiting for the final act to unfold? And what does it mean?

But even as I stagger under the realization, Rose is opening the door wider, gesturing him inside. "William. Welcome."

Lucy is beside herself with excitement, for there is company tonight. We are hosting a dinner for Obadiah's two top mates. Stockton I know, but I have yet to meet Matthew Phinney, the new second.

I leave William to his captain as I help Rachel to ready the table. When a knock comes on the door again, it is Lucy who answers, in her element now that she is the center of attention. William goes to greet the newcomer, and Obadiah passes briefly through the dining room, as if to check on my progress. Rachel is off in the kitchen and I am straightening cutlery when I feel Obadiah's hand in a long caress down my backside. I turn, meet his eyes. A look passes between us, intimate as a touch. We have long since succumbed to temptation, Obadiah and I.

I know he will visit me tonight, as Lucy sleeps, and I feel a tingle run through me. It is shameful to feel this happy, but oh, how I am loved!

"Shall I bring in the guests, Rose? Is all in readiness?" he asks, his voice formal despite the twinkle in his eyes.

It is—and so in they come. Lucy and William, and a young man with sandy hair and an open expression. He is clearly a bit awed at being in such a grand house, in such company. I mask a smile.

"Matthew Phinney, my new second mate," Obadiah is

saying, performing the introductions. "Rose Garrison, my wife's cousin and companion."

I take Phinney's hand; he kisses mine awkwardly. And, when he looks up to meet my eyes, I feel the second shock of the evening.

I know this one, too. *Jane!*

But the dinner is a success. William is the perfect guest, and at times I find myself wondering what the world would have been like if he had married Lucy and I Obadiah. For he treats her with an elaborate courtesy, and she glows in his presence as she has not shone in years. Perhaps, for her, it is just her love of attention. But I have a feeling, for him, it is more. Our gentle William has a certain look in his eye when he regards Lucy, speculative yet tender. Though he would never act on it, never betray his closest friend. Unlike me . . .

Still, for the evening, I pretend it is so, that we belong to others. And my smiles quick and ready . . . until I notice Matthew Phinney's eyes fixed on me, wide and admiring. There will be trouble here, I think, and shudder. . . .

And the scene shifts yet again. I am clinging to the banister at the top of the stairs, my grip all that supports me, for my legs do not want to hold me. I cannot move; I can barely breathe.

There is a trail of blood all the way down the stairs, and at the bottom of it lies Lucy, on the landing, like the unstrung puppet I have seen so many times before. She is bleeding from a gash over her forehead, and she has cracked the side of her head against the wall. There is too much blood, pooling out from under her cheek.

In numb dread, I watch it puddle, then cascade down the step.

Her hands scrabble for purchase; her eyes are wide with terror.

"Rose," she says. "Rose, I can't feel my legs."

I am not surprised. Her body is twisted into unnatural angles, frightening in its motionlessness.

"I'm sorry, Lucy," I say, pointlessly. I can feel myself shaking.

"Rose," she says. "I'm dying, aren't I?"

If I could move, I would nod. But I cannot move. I cannot even unclench my hands from around the banister. I cannot feel anything save a crushing guilt, an aching sorrow.

It should never have come to this. Never.

"Yes, Lucy."

"I'm scared," she whispers. Then, more strongly, "Help me. Help me! Please . . ."

But there is nothing I can do to help her. Even if I could move, she is beyond my help. She is beyond anyone's help.

"Rose, please . . ."

All she wants, I know, is to be held. To feel some human contact, some affection. It is all she has ever wanted.

But I cannot do it. I cannot.

Slowly, I release my grip on the banister, sink to the top step.

Her voice grows more frantic, her pleas more strident. "Help me. Rose! Why?"

Oh, Lucy. You'd know why, if you'd but think. But then, you have never loved him with the fierceness that I have. How could you?

"Rose . . ."

I cannot go to her, but I cannot bring myself to leave her, either.

And so I sit there—for minutes, for an eternity—until her pleas and struggles fade, and the light slowly goes out of her eyes.

And when she is dead . . . only then do I let myself weep.

I wake into the darkness of my room, sobbing, sweating, my heart pounding.

I was right, and Adam was wrong. This was my death, my responsibility. I sat there, doing nothing, and watched her die. And why? So that I could have Obadiah? Or was there something more?

I rolled against Adam, curling myself against his sleeping back. He was warm and safe and solidly of this world. And not, God help me, of the other.

"Caro?" he said sleepily. "What's wrong?"

I suppressed a bitter laugh, through my tears. "Nothing, Adam," I said. "Go back to sleep."

CHAPTER 25

I slept late the next morning, after Adam had gotten up for work, but it was a fitful sleep. I couldn't get the image of Lucy out of my mind. I tossed and turned for a while, then finally rose. It was not until I was steaming myself under the shower that I remembered the first part of the dream—and shivered again, despite the hot water. Jim and Jane? My closest friend, once my suitor? And Obadiah's best friend, who had seemed to love Lucy, now dating her latest incarnation?

Yet, what did it all mean? Like Kitty, Jane and Jim seemed oblivious to the fact that they had ever worn another face. I envied them. I was becoming so mired in Rose's existence that I wondered if I would ever be free of her. And yet, their example proved it was possible to shatter the chains of your past. That a veil could be drawn over previous lives, previous identities. And that gave me a desperate kind of hope.

On the other hand, what was even more noticeable than these presences were certain critical absences. Where was Obadiah? And Adam? Were they one and the same? And if so, why didn't I feel for Adam a fraction of what Rose felt for Obadiah?

It didn't make a lick of sense.

And I had watched Lucy die. . . .

Okay, I really had to find something to do. But without Jane to distract me, I suddenly didn't know how to pass my day. The last thing I wanted to do was see her and Lucian out on the town, but I also couldn't hang about my room all day, hiding. So eventually I drove out to Dionis Beach, hoping against hope that Jane hadn't had the same idea.

To my relief, she hadn't. So I set up my solo camp, and that helped. After a few hours of sun, sea, and sand, the world snapped back into perspective again. Especially when I began to examine the situation more objectively.

I still couldn't say what had happened, definitively, that night in the hall. I hadn't seen myself push Lucy, just the aftermath of what could have as easily been a fall. And Rose hadn't exactly been rational at the time. Even I could feel her shock and horror, in the dream. She was covering for something, that much was clear. But for murder, or for something else? And if so, what else?

Fortunately, the ringing of my cell phone distracted me. Adam.

"Where are you?" he said.

"Dionis. Why?"

"Are you okay? You seemed pretty upset this morning. What happened last night?"

"Well, for one thing, the dreams didn't end," I said sourly.

"Yeah, I rather figured. So much for that theory. Well, what did you see?"

"I don't want to talk about it."

"That bad, huh?"

I grimaced. "There is one thing, though," I told him. "More players have gathered." And I explained about Jane and Jim.

"Weird," he said on a breath when I had finished. Then, more cheerfully, "So, who am I?"

"You don't seem to be anyone," I told him. Which wasn't exactly diplomatic, so I hastily added, "Yet."

"Mmm." He was silent for a moment, then added, "Hey, are we still on for tonight? I've got some good news."

I felt my heart beat a little faster. "About Rose?"

"No, about me, actually," he said, and I instantly felt guilty. "Though speaking of Rose, do you still want to see her grave?"

"Absolutely! And what's your news?"

"I'll tell you later," he said. "Pick me up at five?"

"Done," I said, and hung up, feeling infinitely more cheerful.

At twenty past five, showered and changed, I pulled up in front of the museum and popped the trunk. Adam, grinning, shut it again, then folded himself into the passenger seat.

"What, no bike?"

He shook his head, then leaned over to kiss me. "We'll pick it up later. You're late."

"I know. How can a town, like, five streets wide have so many traffic jams?"

He grinned. "Hence the bike. Come on, I'll direct you."

"Where are we going?"

"Mill Hill cemetery."

Jane had been right about parking around the island being a bitch, but eventually we found a spot. And, with Adam consulting a map he had clearly printed off the computer, there it was. Or rather, there she was. Rose Garrison. It was just a simple stone, lichen-covered, and bearing only her name and dates, but I felt my eyes mist at the sight. More than anything, seeing her stone made it all seem real. Made *her* seem real.

Adam, I noticed, had withdrawn and was wandering among the gravestones, leaving me alone for a moment with Rose.

"Hey, Rose," I whispered, resting my hand briefly atop the sun-warmed stone. "What happened that night? Why are you still here? I want to help you, but I don't understand how. What are you hiding? And why can't you rest?"

Of course, she didn't answer, but I felt a sudden peace steal over me. I still had a month. I would find the answers, for us both.

"I'll fix it, Rose." I vowed. "I'll let you rest. I've seen Lucy, and she's happy. She's with William now, at last. And Matthew Phinney—he and I are friends. He brought me here, to fix things." Though why Phinney should care, I didn't know. "I don't know where Obadiah is, but hopefully he's happy as well."

I glanced over at Adam, who was still wandering the nearby paths, valiantly ignoring my whispered commentary. I felt myself grin.

"It's okay, Adam," I called. "I'm not completely insane."

He flashed his boyish grin and sauntered over, still looking ten years younger than his age in his well-worn jeans and grey T-shirt.

"I feel like I should have brought flowers or something," I said as he joined me.

"I know the feeling," he admitted. "But you probably should see who else I found."

I hadn't realized his wandering had a purpose. "Who?" I said, feeling a sudden dread.

He led me in silence over to another stone—sunken and even more lichen-covered than Rose's. Again, there was no inscription; just the stark name and dates.

Lucy Dalton Young.

I turned briefly to Adam. "Did you know she was here?"

He shook his head, his curls glinting auburn in the sun. "I didn't think to check. But on the drive over, I started wondering, so I thought I'd have a look around while you . . ."

"Stop being so diplomatic. I'm talking to dead people. Hell, I *am* dead people!"

He wrinkled his nose.

I grinned. "Not so appetizing when you put it that way, is it?"

"Not by half! But speaking of appetizing, I believe I promised you dinner. Want to go out, or stay in?"

"In, please," I said emphatically. I didn't want to go near any of the local restaurants, any one of which could be haunted by Lucian and Jane.

"Right, then." He put a hand on my shoulder, slid it down until it rested in the hollow of my back. "Shall we?"

"In a minute," I said. "You go ahead. I'll meet you at the car."

He gave me a somewhat searching look, but the minute he was out of sight, I dropped to my knees, resting both my hands on Lucy's headstone. And suddenly I felt like I *was* Rose, kneeling over Lucy's grave. For an instant, the world wavered, and I saw a fresher stone, flowers. My skirts, puddled around my feet.

"I'm sorry, Lucy," I whispered, the words pouring from me. "I never got to say it, but I'm sorry. It might not have been the right choice I made at the time, but it was the only one I could make. And if I had to do it all over again . . . I might still have made the same choice. For his sake. But it was still the hardest thing I ever did, to leave you there, scared and in pain. And I hope that someday you understand. And forgive me."

But there was no answer save the sighing of the wind through the grass, so eventually I rose and joined Adam.

I don't know why Adam had given me the option of dining out when he had clearly prepared for a dinner in. He had a bag of chicken marinating in the fridge, fresh lettuce and tomatoes, and a tube of Pillsbury rolls. I whipped up the salad and baked the rolls while he fired up the grill, and we ate out on his tiny back lawn while the day slowly faded around us.

"So, what's your news?" I asked as we lingered over beers in the soft purple twilight. It should have been romantic in the extreme, all a girl could want. So why was I quietly tormenting myself by wondering what Jane and Lucian were up to? I could see them sipping wine in the candlelight of some phenomenally posh and romantic restaurant, she with her cap of sleek dark hair, and he with his laughing silver eyes. They would raise their glasses, toast, their gazes like a kiss. . . .

"Remember the curators?" he said with a grin.

I shook myself back to reality and nodded. It felt like eons ago; had it really been only last week? "What about them?"

"One of them runs a museum on Long Island. He wants to update some exhibits, and came up to see how we had renovated our museum. He was so impressed that he wants me to come down and see their facility, then meet the board and offer some solutions. If I'm lucky, it may even mean a year's consultancy, and the chance to help spruce up another museum. The bad news is that I have to go down to New York next week, but still . . . Pretty cool, eh?"

"That sounds fabulous! Congratulations, Adam."

We discussed museum trivialities for a while, his eyes shining as he outlined some of the things he hoped to suggest, and I could see how excited he was about the possibilities this position offered. I wondered if Lucian would ever find this: the glowing satisfaction in doing something you loved. For that matter, I wondered if I would. Was I taking a teaching degree only because it was what Rose had done?

Maybe Lucian was right. Maybe this was a thing to be feared, to be avoided. How much of me was me, and how much was still Rose? Where did one break off and the other begin? The more I thought I had answers, the more tangled I became.

"You seem distracted," Adam said after a while, and I realized I had completely tuned him out.

"Sorry," I said—something I seemed to be saying a lot today.

He shot me a self-deprecating twist of smile. "Never mind. I was probably boring you anyway. I rented a couple of DVDs. Want to watch one of those, instead?"

But even that didn't work—though maybe simply because the silly romantic comedy he chose kept reminding me of Lucian and Jane. My mood sank lower, until finally he said, "Okay, I'm probably going to regret this in the morning when I have to wake up early for work, but let's go." And he jumped up off the couch, holding out his hand.

"What? Where?" I demanded, shaken from my reverie.

"Adam Gallagher's patented Cure For What Ails You," he said. "I'm going to take you to my favorite place on the island, guaranteed to reverse any bad mood. Come on."

His favorite place on the island, huh? I thought back to my night with Lucian, and couldn't help saying, somewhat tartly, "We'd better not be going back to Kitty's."

"What?"

"Sorry. Nothing," I said.

"Right," Adam said. "That's it. Car keys."

"What?"

"Give me your car keys." And he held out his hand. "You're definitely in need of the cure, but I'm driving."

So, where *are* we going?" I asked once we were underway.

"You'll see," he said.

It was too much like Lucian's cryptic comment, in all respects. And we might not have ended up at Kitty's, but I knew our destination all too depressingly well.

"Adam," I said, with what I hoped was commendable

reasonableness, "I've been to Dionis Beach before. I was here just this afternoon, remember?"

"Shows what you know," he said, parking the car and shutting off the engine. He got out, tucking my keys into a pocket, took off his shoes, and held out his hand. "Walk with me?"

I shucked my shoes in turn, and I have to admit, it wasn't a bad idea. There was only a sliver of moon to light the way, and the three-mile stretch of Dionis was dark and peaceful behind its dunes. We walked up the beach for a ways, holding hands, the sand still warm under our toes, and we might as well have been alone in the world. The only sounds were the wind through the dune grasses and the rhythmic crash of the waves against the sand.

I was so seduced by the mood that I was almost startled when Adam stopped, dropped my hand, and said, "Right. This will do."

"What? I—"

Off came his shirt, and a second later, his shorts thumped to the sand. "Come on," he said. "What are you waiting for?"

"Huh? What are we doing?"

"Mind out of the gutter," he chided with a laugh. "We're swimming."

"But I don't have a suit."

His grin flashed out, brilliant in the darkness, and his underwear came off with a flourish. "No suits needed. Come on!"

"But, Adam . . . What if someone catches us? People know you here; you're one of the curators of the museum."

"I am also," he added reasonably, for all that he was stark

naked in the dim moonlight, "thirty-four years old and out with a beautiful girl who has never skinny-dipped in the ocean before."

"Hey! How do you know?" I demanded indignantly.

"Because you still have no idea what I'm about to show you. Race you?" And he was off, running down the beach to the water's edge—Mercury in the moonlight.

I laughed and stripped, dropping my clothes atop his, and I have to admit, he was right about this, too. The water was silky cool against the hot night, and slid over my skin with a sensuousness that I had not expected. It caressed me everywhere.

I swam over to Adam where he bobbed on the waves, his head breaking the surface like a seal, his dark curls dripping into his eyes.

"Ready?" he said, eyes luminous and grin wide in the dark, and I agreed eagerly, not sure to what, but feeling frisky all the same. But instead of swimming closer, he just added, "Look," and drew his hand through the water. In its wake, luminous green flecks flared and died—aquatic fireworks.

I gasped, distracted from my lustful musings, and brushed my hands through the water in turn, setting off my own wave of eerie dancing sparkles.

"What is it?" I breathed.

"Bioluminescent plankton. Pretty amazing, huh?"

I swirled a finger through the water, harder, trailing cold fire.

"This is too cool! How did you know about this?"

"I discovered it years back, on a vacation to Cape Cod with Caroline. She wouldn't skinny-dip, so I swam alone. And discovered this—which almost made up for it." He smiled. "See? I told you. Good for what ails you."

But there was only so much time one could spend making plankton glow before it started to pale—or at least, so I found. But then, maybe I was more distracted than Adam by the flow of the water against my naked skin. So I floated on my back for a bit, legs spread, nipples upthrust and peaked to the night, hoping to draw him in, but he seemed oblivious.

Were I Rose and he Obadiah, he would have swum up between my legs, hot mouth teasing. . . .

With a growl, I flipped over and swam back to Adam, determined to stage my own seduction. But while he quickly rose to the occasion, the buoyant water offered no purchase, no friction—the fantasy definitely better than the reality. But Adam was hot and hard against me, definitely not thinking of plankton now, so he swam us both back to shallow water, where he could stand. His wet skin was like silk under my hands as I wrapped my arms around his shoulder and my legs around his waist, sliding down his body until I took him into the hot, heated core of me.

"Okay," he whispered as I rode him in the waves to my first orgasm, "*now* I'll be embarrassed if someone catches us."

I laughed and ground against him again, but it was still too buoyant for the friction we both now needed. And so I ended up on my back on the hard sand where the waves met the shore, the water lapping over my calves and butt as he drove into me, both us of panting.

Then suddenly, he paused.

"What?" I exclaimed, mindless now.

"No condoms," he groaned. And before I could tell him it

was probably okay, he pulled out, then fell back down on me, running the length of his penis in two hard, forceful strokes straight up the outside of my vagina—not entering, but nonetheless touching everything in his passage, from lips to clitoris, bearing down hard at the top of each stroke. And as he ground against me at the top of the second stroke, I came again, twining my legs about his thighs and clamping him to me.

He, in turn, shuddered in my arms, and I felt a hot wetness flood across my stomach. . . .

I stiffened abruptly. And like a flashbulb going off in my face, I suddenly knew I had been here before. Not with Adam, but I had made love like this many times before. In fact, all but once . . .

A montage of images barraged me, too rapid to make out individual scenes, but each ending the same way—with Obadiah spilling himself onto the sheets, my stomach, anywhere but inside me: the price of our forbidden love. Only once had I felt his hot wetness fill me—but once was enough. . . .

"Liza? Are you okay?" Adam demanded.

I was gasping, I realized, and not from aftermath.

I forced myself back to the here and now, twining my arms around him. "Great. Perfect."

He seemed apologetic. "Sorry about the mess."

"No sweat. There's an entire ocean to clean it off. Shall we?"

Two nights later, and back at Kitty's, I see the rest of it.

There is another price we must pay, Obadiah and I. For Lucy is still his wife, and Lucy still wants a child.

And Lucy must never suspect.

Fortunately, her interest has waned of late, in all things. After she lost her sixth child, I was not able to wean her, completely, off the milk of the poppy. Maybe I am not as strong as Obadiah. Or maybe there is a secret, shameful core of me that knows it is easier to keep her quiescent, dependent. She is mellower then—and when she sleeps in its embrace, Obadiah and I have no fear of discovery.

And yet her obsession sporadically flares, and then we are all in hell. She must participate in an act she dislikes, Obadiah must play the stud (and how she whines and weeps when he cannot perform!), and I must listen to the whole act, a captive audience in my bed down the hall.

He is full of loathing for himself in the aftermath, torn between the betrayal of his marital vows to Lucy and the betrayal of his love for me. He is a man whose very nature is defined by faithfulness, and it tears him apart that he cannot hold true—to either of us. Our next coupling after such a night is always harder, rougher, as if we both seek to expiate our sins in the other's flesh. Once, unable to wait for night, he recklessly took me up against a wall behind the stairs, both of us still fully clothed. And the force of his passion was such that he had no time to pull out, spilling himself for the sole time inside me.

After, he was chagrined. "You must promise me, Rose— promise!—to tell me if anything happens."

Only, by the time I know it has, it is too late; he is at sea. And Lucy catches me, one too many mornings, retching over my chamber pot.

"Rose! Are you with child?" she exclaims.

I nod, miserably. But just as I am about to confess the whole thing, she continues, "Is it Matthew's?" For Obadiah's second mate has been courting me, of late, and he is greatly persistent. I am not sure how to discourage him, this honest, forthright man I have come to like and respect, if not to love. Can I hurt his feelings that way? Better still, could I come to love him? How much easier all our lives would be if I could feel a fraction for him of what I feel for Obadiah. . . .

And so I string him on, clinging to that last, desperate hope. And Lucy has seen my lie as the truth.

I should not do it, I know, but I fall on that lie like a starving woman on a feast.

"Yes," I fib, sealing all our fates.

I will later wonder if everything that followed could have been averted, had all the many betrayals not mounted and festered.

Her face hardens with an un-Lucy-like resolve. "I will save you," she declares. "As you saved me." And hugs me tightly. "I promise, Rose."

I hug her back, twisting in my guilt like a fish on a line. But a day later, she has her plan. I had never suspected Lucy of guile, but now I am not so sure.

When it is no longer possible to hide my condition—if I even keep the child, for Lucy has seen too many losses to have faith in that—we will leave Nantucket for a visit to Martha's Vineyard. We will leave as ourselves . . . and arrive as each other. Though we look not a whit alike, it will not matter, she assures me. No one there will know that Lucy Young is as fair as moonlight, that Rose Garrison is small and dark. "I could pass for a Rose, could I not?" she says, preening.

So I, as Lucy, will bear Lucy Young's child. And Obadiah's son will be his in deed as well as name. Our secret—the devil's bargain that will forever bind us.

And as for why we will go, she just smiles sunnily. "Women get all sorts of silly notions when they are expecting. What is one more among many? Perhaps a change of scene will be good for me, stave off the losses I have suffered before."

Almost as if she has convinced herself that it is really she who is expecting, that this child I carry is truly hers.

CHAPTER 26

Work kept me busy over the next few days, the flood of tourists an ever-increasing commodity. But my tours were going remarkably well—especially since my strange little trick of vision proved replicable. It was like the more I learned, the more access I had to this strange, other world of the past. And the more I practiced, the more adept I became at piercing the veil.

Or maybe that was just the lie I told myself. Maybe the truth was somewhat more sinister. Maybe the web of the past had caught me so firmly I could no longer escape. And the sticky threads of guilt and sorrow were binding me so close to my predecessor's life that the line between us was becoming vague and indistinct.

Nonetheless, I remember one tour—I think it was the following Thursday—when someone asked me what the island had looked like during the 1849 Gold Rush, and if I knew which houses were still standing from that time. I thought about this for a minute. Yeah, I remembered the Gold Rush—the gradual emptying of the streets of all the young men until the place had felt a ghost town. And the great sadness I felt, every day, when the noble ships one by one failed to come home, when the harbor slowly fell into disrepair.

Keeping that image in my mind, I did a quick flash, and—with a little conscious effort—was able to compare the two images, like a double-exposed snapshot, laid one atop the other. And duly pointed out to the interested viewers everything that was the same.

To avoid completely freaking anyone out, however, I neglected to tell them which houses had been painted which different colors. . . .

As the days passed, past and present became so blurred that I began to feel there was only one Nantucket fact I still didn't know, and so I turned it into a joke at the start of every tour—maybe just to save my own sanity.

"How many billionaires do you think we have on this island?" I'd ask the eager tourists.

There was always a moment of silence. Sometimes, the more inventive folks threw out numbers, but I remained mute. Then, invariably, someone would ask: "How many?"

"Honestly, I have no idea," I'd reply with a laugh. "I've heard numbers ranging anywhere from twenty-five to a hundred, but no one can seem to agree on the absolute figure. Still, a hell of a lot for so small an island."

And that became my great Nantucket unknown—which was not bad, for a tour guide. Of course, I was also lucky that most of the history everyone was most interested in had occurred during my first lifetime.

Nonetheless, my name was getting out there as the tour guide to go to, and I felt a certain shudder of dread when

Marian offered me both a slightly increased workload and a substantial raise, saying, "I've been hearing nothing but good things about you recently. Everyone keeps saying that it's almost like you were there!" She had no idea—though, of course, I accepted both offers gratefully.

But the divide continued to blur, and I found myself strolling down the street with Matthew Phinney one day, instead of my tour. My hand was on his arm, and I was laughing at something he said, and at the same time wishing he would not look at me with eyes quite so full of longing . . . when I came around to find my whole tour group staring at me oddly.

One motherly woman, certain it was heatstroke, pressed her bottle of water into my hands and wouldn't abandon me until I had finished it.

If this weren't bad enough, Jane was still running about with that radioactive glow of love, oblivious to the world, but Lucian had taken to actively seeking me out, including me. Perhaps he just felt that, since I was Jane's best friend, he should be mine, too. Regardless, it was both a torment and a delight.

When Jane was at work, he would carry me off. Sometimes to Obadiah's for a drink, sometimes elsewhere. One Friday night, he even carted me off on the quintessential date night: dinner and a movie. There was no talk of going dutch. Lucian swept up the dinner check before I could so much as glance at it, and even paid for the movie tickets and a large tub of popcorn and a soda (two straws). Admittedly, I might have felt it was more significant had I not had prior knowledge of his substantial fortune, but still . . . In all ways but one, it might have been a date—and a beautiful distraction from my growing preoccupation with Rose. But though his silver eyes twinkled at me with barely disguised mischief, and his wicked tongue kept up his usual string of provocative comments, he never touched me. I mean, unless you counted our hands occasionally bumping in the depths of the popcorn tub—which, annoyingly, kept sending more of a jolt through me than it should.

And if this wasn't a sign that I had fallen, hard, for Jane's boyfriend, then I don't know what was. But I loved talking to him, in a way I had never loved talking with anyone before. I loved the firework fury of our conversation, striking sparks off each other's hides. I loved his biting, dry wit. I even loved our occasional hot flares of argument—though I loved our agreements more.

Adam was like a comfortable old shoe. Lucian was . . . Well, Lucian was like donning a brand-new pair of four-inch stiletto strappy sandals, with shiny gold leather and maybe some rhinestones: sexy as all get-out, and making you feel like a million bucks, but always with the dread in the back of your mind that, an hour later, the balls of your feet would be aching, and you'd have a wicked blister somewhere on the side of your big toe. Because, after all, there had to be a price for strutting around like this.

But though it passed all my joking definitions of a date in college—that he asked, drove (albeit, my car), and paid—it wasn't. And not only because, by that definition, I'd had uncountable dates with Jane. But because that one critical component was missing. For though he drove me home, and even walked me to my door—which, in our circumstances, was the door to my bedroom—he merely left me there with a cryptic smile, and a look in those quicksilver eyes that I couldn't interpret.

Still, I found myself smiling as I washed up and climbed into bed. And if there must be dreams, I thought as I fell into sleep, then let them be pleasant ones. . . .

There are some days that are just meant for singing. It is true that outside our wide windows, winter is closing in. The days are growing shorter, and the sun seems colder, even at midday. But still I feel like a bird in spring, for Obadiah has returned!

A boy from the docks has brought the news—beloved messenger!—and soon I shall see him again. That dear, dark visage that no longer looks so forbidding to me, so severe. I have missed him with such a fierceness in the three years that he has been gone that I know it must be love. I wonder . . . Has he thought of me at all, while he has been away? I remember the occasional looks between us, the last time he was home, that led me to think he wasn't so indifferent to me as he should be. . . .

But no, I mustn't think like this, for Lucy is buzzing like an excited bee, and this . . . This is her husband, for whom I pine. Her husband!

A wave of guilt washes over me, sobering in its chill. I cannot think like this. I cannot.

I must take myself away. Whether from the room or from the house, I cannot say. But my nebulous thoughts are interrupted, my nobler impulses halted, by a dark silhouette in the door.

My heart starts beating faster; my feet are frozen to the

floor. Not so Lucy, who does what I have longed to do, but cannot: runs into his arms. His arms close about her reflexively, and I look down at the floor, unable to watch. It is torment. It is . . .

Something draws my gaze back up. Perhaps it is just a desire to torture myself with the sight of what I cannot—must not!—have. Or maybe a part of me senses the truth. All I know is, when I raise my gaze, it is to find his dark eyes fixed on me with a look of such intensity, such longing, that I cannot breathe.

Lucy is in his arms, but the look that passes between us is as strong as an oak, as hot as a flame. . . .

And then the moment is broken as Lucy breaks away, flits off to the kitchen to make sure Rachel has enough supplies for a feast. And we are alone.

Neither of us seems able to move.

He tries to speak, clears his throat. His voice sounds as rough as gravel. "Rose. Are you well?"

"Very well," I say, wondering at our insipid words when this sinful heat is flaring between us. "Was it a profitable voyage?"

"It was. But I found myself keen to get home." A more tentative look, hardened by determination. "I—"

"There is fresh mutton, and Rachel will make a trifle!" Lucy declares, breezing back in.

But throughout that long, long day, I feel his eyes on me, and find my eyes rising to his—only to skip away like a rock off a pond. Dinner is a torment; after dinner worse. I cannot bear the thought of them together, in his room or hers. I know little of what men and women do together, when alone, but a treacherous, unaccountable heat flares low in my belly, and I find myself trembling.

I cannot go upstairs, hear his groans, the creaking of their bedropes. So I stay downstairs. I help Rachel tidy the kitchen, shut the door behind her as she departs for the evening. I blow out the candles and the oil lamps—save two, which I leave burning in the parlor. I have mending to do, I tell myself; Lucy is hopeless at the task. But no sooner have I taken up my needle than I sense a presence in the door.

Obadiah—his collar loosened, his hair slightly tousled.

I had not expected him down so soon.

He looks tired. But he just stands there for a moment in the doorway, staring at me.

"Obadiah?" I say eventually. "Is all well?"

He heaves a sigh at this, enters the room. He takes a seat in one of Lucy's delicate chairs, stretching his long legs out. It looks almost comical—this tall, dark man in the small, frilly chair—but he seems oblivious. "You did not tell me about the opium," he says.

It is not an accusing tone he uses, merely a weary one. But I feel a stir of guilt, regardless. "I'm sorry," I say.

He shakes his head slightly, like a horse shaking off flies. I can't tell if it is denial of my words, or his way of brushing away an unpleasant thought or truth.

"It's not your fault, Rose. There was another child, wasn't there?"

I nod, feeling a stir of sorrow. "She lost the babe at three months."

There is another long silence—he is not looking at me now—and I am suddenly aware of the stillness of the house around me. We are so alone, down here. We might be man and wife, sharing a quiet domestic moment, were it not for Lucy, upstairs.

When he raises his head again, there is a glitter of tears in his eyes. The loss is a distant one for me now, almost three years in the past. But I forget that he has not yet had a chance to grieve.

Without much conscious awareness of what I am doing, I find myself rising, going to him. I kneel beside him. After a moment, I lay one hand, lightly, on his knee.

He grabs my hand in both of his, crushing it, and that heat flares between us again. I am so close, I can smell the masculine scent of him: musky and potent. I want to run, but I cannot. He still has hold of my hand, and my feet are rooted to the floor.

Impulsively, I curl my fingers around his, reach out my free hand to touch his cheek, as I have longed to do for so many years and months, now. His dark, wiry beard is softer than it appears.

His hands, still holding mine, draw me closer, draw me up into his lap, there in Lucy's silly, frivolous chair. And then he drops my hand and gathers me against him, my head cradled against his breast—where I have wanted to be for so long that it frightens me. Because it feels so right, so safe.

I can feel his heart pounding under my cheek—matched, I am sure, by the frantic rhythm of my own.

"Rose," he says. "If only it were otherwise." And I know he is not talking about the child anymore.

"I am a wicked, evil sinner," he says, shifting slightly so that he can look down on me. His hand—his rough, callused hand—comes up to stroke my hair and cheek, so gently I want to weep. "I have coveted forbidden things, all through these long, dark years. Rose . . . before I left, I had dared to hope that you were not completely indifferent to me."

I swallow hard. "No. Not indifferent."

"Might I, even now, dare to hope that you regard me with affection?"

"More than you know," I whisper.

His eyes seem to go darker. That black gaze melts; it burns. I feel myself shaking.

"I want you, Rose," he says, "in a way I have never wanted anyone before. Do you understand what I am saying?"

I may be virgin still, but I am thirty-one years of age now; I am not quite so innocent as he fears.

"I do," I say, feeling bolder in the face of his declaration.

He groans slightly, then dips his head, lowering his lips to mine. It is only a tentative touch at first: light, gentle, his beard teasing my cheeks. And then, dear God, a fire ignites between us, and he urges my lips open beneath his, his tongue delving, plundering, and I am moaning into his mouth in awe at the exquisite sensations.

When at last he tears himself away, chest heaving like a bellows, he stares down at me with a mixture of consternation and amazement.

"Rose," he says, his voice almost a whisper now, "if I were to come to your room tonight, would you turn me away?"

He has granted me the choice, but I can no more turn him away that I can stop breathing. "I would not," I whisper.

"Then the decision lies with me. Shall I be strong, Rose, and do what is right? Or shall I be weak, because I cannot imagine being strong any longer?"

"Do as you will," I whisper, and when he releases me, I flee. There will be time for the mending later. . . .

And I find myself wondering, as I hasten up the stairs, if he will indeed come to me, when Lucy lies at the deepest part of her slumber. . . .

I wake again, suddenly realizing I knew how that one ended. The first dream I had had in this house.

He came, indeed. And Lucy's doom was set in motion.

But really, was it any surprise? Rose and Obadiah had loved each other for five long years—never touching, never speaking the words—hugging their secret passion close. How long can you fight that sort of temptation?

I thought about it a lot on Saturday, but it was not until I was close to sleep that I had the biggest revelation. And as Adam and I were tucked up in my room after dinner on Sunday night, I mentioned it.

"So, do you know what is the strangest thing in all of this?" I asked him.

He shook his head. He was lounging on my bed in nothing but his pair of silk boxers, looking incongruously male under the lacy canopy, but I found the sight oddly distancing.

"I was thinking last night about the dreams—and about the whaling dreams in particular. And how, once I knew I was Rose, I seemed to stop having them entirely."

"But isn't that natural?" Adam said, with a frown, clearly not happy at the path my thoughts were taking. "I mean, now that you know you're not Obadiah, and those couldn't be your memories . . ."

His voice trailed off, and I smiled—albeit a bit grimly. "You begin to see it now, don't you? The massive fallacy right at the heart of all this. On one level, Rose knew the stories because Obadiah told them to her—though I still don't think that's all of the picture. There's some other reason she remembered them, that they were important. But that's not the real issue. Recently, we've both been assuming that this was all about guilt, and the expiation of guilt. And yet, all through it, I've been forgetting the most essential thing of all."

"Which is?"

"Think about it, Adam. What started this whole quest?"

"Your whaling dreams. But . . ." And then his eyes widened, and I knew he saw it, too.

"Exactly. My dreams of death aboard the *Redemption*: nightmares fueled by guilt. And that all made sense, back when I thought I was Obadiah. I was guilty of something, and dreamed it caused my doom. What could be clearer than that? But I never was Obadiah, was I? I've been Rose all along. So why the hell is Rose dreaming of Obadiah's death at sea, over and over and over again? I've explained everything else, but not that. If it was really about Rose murdering Lucy, then why didn't I dream that? Why did I keep dreaming about a whale sinking the *Redemption* instead?"

"Hmmm. Tell me again about the dream," Adam said, frowning. "Everything. All the details." And when I had complied, he looked thoughtful.

"What?" I said.

"The cold. Sperm whales live in temperate waters, not Antarctic ones."

So, yet another fact I had gotten wrong. "And what does *that* mean?"

Adam shook his head slowly. "Once again, I don't know. Except that it seems you are still missing pieces of the puzzle."

CHAPTER 27

∞

On Monday, as if nothing had happened last week to rock her world, Jane and I were back on the beach—Surfside, this time. Thanks to the fickle weather gods, most of the eastern seaboard had woken to a wicked heat wave. The coolest place to be that day—apart from an air-conditioned interior, which Kitty's house was not—was probably out on that stretch of sand, under the shade of our umbrella, catching whatever breeze we could off the water.

On Tuesday, when I came sweltering downstairs, ready for more of the same again, I was shocked to find Lucian waiting for me. He was leaning against the front door with beach chair in hand, in a posture of studied casualness.

"What are you doing here?" I accused, frowning.

He straightened with a smile. "Give a guy a break from the heat, huh, Liza?" he said. Then, clutching both hands around the frame of his beach chair, he gave me Big Eyes so unabashedly that I started laughing.

"Okay," I conceded, "but you're the one wrestling the umbrella into the car!"

He did so—with far more grace and efficiency than I had ever managed. When it was stowed, we drove out to Madaket.

I didn't know why Lucian had accompanied me. It certainly wasn't for the pleasure of my company. Once we had set up the umbrella, positioned our chairs in the tiny island of shade—maximally oriented to get the best breeze off the water—and stripped down to beach wear, he barely said a word to me. So perhaps it was just as he had claimed: he wanted a break from the heat of the house.

Which was fine by me. Not expecting company and in deference to the heat, I had trotted out in my skimpiest of skimpy bikinis, and now I felt distinctly exposed, though Lucian was pointedly not looking at me. Still, when I was certain that Lucian's attention was elsewhere, I couldn't help sneaking surreptitious glances at him. And I have to admit, the sight was pretty stunning. While Adam was built, Lucian was . . . well, about as perfect as it got. Lean but not too lean; muscular, but not too muscular. He had this sort of whippetlike quality, a lithe, quicksilver body that more than matched his startling eyes.

My cheeks flamed—and I glanced up to find him looking at me with a rather cryptic expression. I quickly looked away.

I was actually kind of relieved when the dying light drove us off the beach and back home. No sooner were we in the door than Lucian rushed off, banging the door to the downstairs bathroom behind him—no doubt hurrying to prepare for his incipient date with Jane.

When I got home on Wednesday evening, Lucian came sauntering out of the kitchen just as I was walking in. It was still beastly hot; the sun was slanting in through the windows, bathing the house in a brilliant golden light. And the moment Lucian's dark hair caught the sun, the world slipped and slid, and I was elsewhere, a small boy running, shrieking, past my legs.

I looked down at Owen with a smile, then back up at Obadiah, who was doing a credible imitation of a bear as he chased his delighted son down the hall. He met my gaze and flashed me a grin. I smiled back, feeling a deep satisfaction at the sight.

Small arms clasped my calf as a tiny voice piped, "Auntie Wose, Auntie Wose, he's gonna catched me!"

"Is he?" I said, laying a hand on the dark head. "Surely not!" And for an instant I was a pillar in their game as Obadiah feinted to one side, then the other, and Owen hid behind me. Then the boy broke loose with a scream and started running, and Obadiah scooped him up, swinging his son up over his head while Owen squealed in delight.

I smiled—marveling at the contrast between the tall whaleman and the tiny boy, both so clearly besotted with each other.

It wasn't always so. I remembered the day when Obadiah came home, and Lucy nervously thrust what she firmly believed to be another man's son toward him. Terrified by the stern, dark visage, Owen started howling. And when Lucy set him down in dismay, he tottered straight to me as fast as his tiny legs could carry him. He buried his face in my skirts, wailing. I picked him up and cradled him, quieting his cries, but Lucy needn't have worried. Obadiah was transfixed. He adored his son on sight—and within two weeks, that affection was returned fourfold. The two were inseparable now—and how Lucy never guessed the truth was a mystery to me, for those two faces were the spit and image of each other, albeit years and oceans apart.

Yet, improbably, my secret remained safe.

When Obadiah set the boy down, Owen careened off. And, in the sudden moment of silence, Obadiah turned to me. "Thank you, Rose," he said.

"For what?" I asked, my heart stuttering. Surely, he hadn't discovered . . .

But no. All he said was, with a smile, "Thank you for being so good to my boy. He loves you dearly, I know. And it must be hard. . . ."

A bitter twist of irony tugged at my heart, but I kept a straight face as I said, "It is no hardship, Obadiah. I love him as if he were my own."

I felt a tearing inside as he said, quietly, "Would it were so."

Then Owen was back, a windstorm on legs. "Again, Papa. Again!" And Obadiah went lumbering off after him.

It seemed that Lucy had been correct in her instincts that a child would change everything. After Owen arrived, the house was a happier place, filled with smiles and laughter. Lucy seemed to mature overnight—and, to give her credit, she genuinely did love my boy. But who could not? He was such a smart, sunny child that everyone adored him. And seeing his parents' delight in his presence . . . Well, it was almost like they had a real marriage, for the first time in years.

The only snake still left in the garden was me. I tried to

stay away from Obadiah; I did. But seeing him daily wore down my resistance. Eager to spend more time with his son, he even postponed his next voyage. It cost him his third mate, who sailed with another, more speedy, captain. But William and Matthew stuck by him. William, because he could not imagine serving another master, and Matthew . . . because of me. He was determined to win me before the *Redemption* sailed on what Obadiah had vowed would be his final voyage as captain. And as for me . . .

I was almost inclined to let him have his wish. I liked Matthew. He was kind and gentle. And if he didn't make my heart beat so quickly as Obadiah . . . Well, maybe no one was meant to have that much joy in one lifetime. For a few brief years, I had known true love. Maybe that was enough. Maybe I should accept Matthew's hand, and leave Obadiah and Lucy to what they should have had all along. A gift I had bought them, with the fruit of my womb.

Payment enough for betrayal . . . or was it?

I came to abruptly, to find Lucian snapping his fingers in my face, his eyes very close to mine. I felt a sudden moment of disorientation. For an instant I had expected him to be taller, more imposing. But perhaps I was only used to looking up at Adam. And Obadiah . . .

"That's it," Lucian said in some disgust. "You clearly need a drink. Go get changed; we're going out."

And so he carted me off to Obadiah's and fed me a burger, then plonked me down at the bar, where Jane was still glowing like a signal fire. And the place was noisy and joyous enough that I forgot my strange mood, and even missed my cell phone ringing. When I got home a little past midnight, I noticed I had two messages. A quick check of the caller ID confirmed both to be from Adam—one from yesterday afternoon, and one from this evening.

I didn't bother listening to the messages; it was too late to return the calls, anyway. Besides, I was feeling confused enough about Lucian's bizarre, platonic assault on my defenses—and troubled enough by what seemed to be my increasingly frequent jaunts into the past—that I didn't feel capable of handling the confusion right now.

But Lucian wasn't done with me yet, as Friday night proved. For again, no sooner had I walked in the door than he sprang, saying, "Get changed. And wear something nice."

I admit to being a bit dubious, but I complied. And when I came down again wearing my emerald chiffon top and a rather short, tight black skirt with my bronze strappy sandals, his eyes went briefly shuttered and unreadable—though I could have sworn I saw him mask a smile.

He was looking frighteningly swank as well, in black dress trousers and a dark grey summer-weight jacket over a silver-grey dress shirt. No fool, Lucian; he knew how to exploit his coloring to its best advantage. But all he said to me was, holding out one hand: "Keys." So I duly passed over my car keys.

Our goal, it seemed, was one of those fancy atmospheric restaurants that practically dripped romance—the very kind I had been masochistically envisioning him and Jane at last Monday night. There were candles, and balloon glasses as big as my head for a sinfully fine red wine that would probably have cost me a week's salary. And because I was obliquely annoyed enough at him for not telling me what the hell he was doing,

I had no compunction about ordering the most expensive thing on the menu. So I did.

There were no lingering glances over the candlelit table; no wordless toasts still stuffed with meaning. Lucian was his usual entertaining, snide, and somewhat inscrutable self. And to hell with it if I couldn't figure out what he wanted.

There was a moment, though, between dinner and dessert, when Lucian's face suddenly went quiet, and he said, more seriously than I had expected, "Liza . . ."

Only my phone chose that moment to go off, erupting into a loud chorus of "My Humps" that Lucian, the bastard, must have programmed into it while I was in swimming on Tuesday. I glared at him across the table, then madly fished in my purse, briefly checking the caller ID—Adam—before punching it off.

"Lucian, damn you . . ."

He looked torn between laughter and consternation. "Well, had I known it was going to interrupt me so effectively, I might have chosen differently," he said, with a self-deprecating grin.

I couldn't help it; I started laughing.

Then the waiter arrived with the dessert cart, and the moment—whatever it had been—was gone.

Adam called on Saturday, a few minutes before closing, as I was finishing up for the day. I tamped down a surge of guilt as I answered. I had yet to return any one of his calls—or even fully listen to his messages. And while I told myself I was busy, the truth was far more insidious. Hearing Adam's voice would only remind me how much I had come to want Lucian—and that last parallel to Rose's life wasn't one I was willing to face.

Was I, too, doomed for wanting the wrong man?

Still, I was aware it was bad form to keep ducking Adam, so when he said, "Can you come over?" I agreed with alacrity.

I arrived to find him looking happy and windblown—odd, for such a sweltering day. He grabbed me up in a huge hug. "Did you miss me?" he said.

"Of course!" I said, reflexively and guiltily, still thinking of Lucian.

He suddenly broke out in another huge grin. "Guess what?"

"What?"

"I got the job!"

"What job?" I said blankly.

He frowned slightly. "The one in Long Island? The consultancy?"

"Oh! Was this the week you were gone?" I said without thinking—then immediately realized my mistake when his face went still and silent.

"Adam, I'm sorry. I . . ."

He was silent for another long moment. Then finally, he said, "This isn't working out, is it?"

"I . . ."

"I suppose I've known it for weeks," he continued, before I could make whatever excuse it was that I was considering. "Pretty much since I saw you and Lucian at the Jared Coffin House. But I've always been good at denial. I kept trying to convince myself that it was all okay, that I was just imagining it, but . . . It's Lucian, isn't it? I've seen the way you two light up around each other."

"I . . . What? We do?"

"Yeah. Most of the time, I don't even think you realize it. But I have eyes. It *is* Lucian, isn't it?"

"It's not Lucian," I said, with commendable steadiness, despite the huge knot of sadness that seemed to grip somewhere under my sternum. "I told you, he's dating Jane."

"Are you sure?" Adam asked incredulously.

"Pretty damned sure. And it's really not about that, Adam. If there is anyone at fault here, it's me. I just . . . I've gotten so caught up in all this stuff that's been happening to me, and—"

"I'm not part of your story."

It was such a stark, brutal truth that I felt it like a blow. But he was right.

"You once promised me," he continued, "that you'd be honest with me. I need to hear the truth now. I'm right, aren't I?"

It was harder than I had ever imagined to voice it. "Yeah. You're right. And I'm so sorry, Adam."

He was silent for a moment, then said, with a certain, deliberate steadiness, "I think we should both be honest, and call this relationship over. Do you agree?"

I found myself nodding. "I adore you as a person, and you're hands-down the best-looking guy I've ever dated. But we're not right together; you know it, and I know it. Besides—" I took a deep breath. He had asked for honesty, and there was nothing more honest than this. "—you're still not over Caroline—and until you figure that one out, you're going to be of no use to any woman."

"Hey! I am *not* hung up on Caroline," he protested.

"No? Then why can we never have a conversation without her name coming up? And why do you still have photographs of her all over your apartment?" I saw him cast a guilty glace at the mantelpiece. "You're a great guy Adam, but—"

"Don't. Just . . . don't. I've had enough damning with faint praise to last me a lifetime. And don't tell me I'm too nice, or too good, or too stable. I just don't think I can hear that anymore."

For an instant, I thought he was near tears. I leaned over and kissed him lightly on the cheek, feeling miserable. Despite my conviction that something was missing, I hadn't realized how hard this was going to be. "Actually, I was going to say that you saved my sanity this summer. You deserve great happiness, Adam, but I'm not the one to give it to you. I know that now. And I'm sorry, more sorry than you can know. But—"

"Just promise me one thing," he interrupted.

"Of course. Anything," I vowed recklessly.

He gave a little laugh. "Dangerous words, those. What if I take advantage?"

"But you won't."

"Mmm." He was silent for a moment. "And that's part of the problem right there, isn't it?"

I didn't have the vaguest clue what to say, but he was absolutely right—not that I would ever admit that to him.

Fortunately, he continued before the silence turned awkward. "Just promise me you'll tell me how this all turns out. I've come this far; I'd hate to miss the grand conclusion. When you get your answers—if the dreams ever stop—you'll let me know. Right?"

"Of course I will," I said, and hugged him impulsively. It was an odd embrace, both awkward and familiar. "I really am going to miss you, Adam. I know that sounds facile, but—"

"We've been through a lot together," he said. "I'm going to miss you, too. You're a good person, Liza; you deserve the best. I hope you find what you need."

"You, too," I said, meaning it. Poor Adam; he really was too enormously nice for his own good.

I started to stand, but he laid a hand on my arm, holding me back. "And Liza . . . thank you."

"For what?" I squeaked incredulously.

"For the truth. That took courage, and I . . . Well, I appreciate it. Caroline—" He smiled ruefully, glancing again at the photo on the mantel. "Caroline just snuck out while I was at work."

"I'm sorry." Then, indignantly, "That was a pretty shitty thing to do!"

"Yeah, it was. I'm sure she had her reasons—"

"Adam!"

"No, this is not another instance of me being too nice for my own good. I'm not quite *that* much of a doormat. Caroline was . . . I suspect she had even larger secrets than you." Another pause, and then he laughed. "Talk about having a type. How pitiful is that?"

"Not so pitiful. You make a good white knight, Adam."

"Pity you didn't need rescuing."

"Someday, you'll find the right woman to rescue, I promise."

"And what makes you so sure?"

"Because, if there's one thing I've learned this summer, it's that there *is* one right person for everyone. Rose taught me that."

"So you're searching for your Obadiah?"

"For my sins. And someday, you'll find your Rose."

"Mmm. Though, you know, you might be on to something with that Caroline comment. Here I was, trying to at least have a Caroline-free breakup, but . . ."

I smiled. "No dummy, me. I knows unrequited when I sees it."

"Well, for what it's worth, I think you're wrong about Lucian."

"Whatever makes you say that?"

"I dunno. Just a hunch."

I didn't let myself think of that, just bade Adam farewell and drove back home, feeling both heartbroken and relieved at the same time.

Kitty was in the kitchen, chopping cold chicken, when I arrived. "It's too hot to cook," she told me, "so I'm making chicken salad for dinner. Have you eaten?"

I shook my head.

"Then join me," she said. "It'll just be us girls tonight. Lucian's out, and Jim's doing inventory. You don't mind?"

"Actually, I'm delighted," I said. I had been thinking a lot lately of Adam's theory, wondering if I was supposed to be making reparations to Kitty—although Kitty didn't seem to have any inkling of who she had used to be—and this suddenly seemed the perfect opportunity. I didn't often have a chance to talk to her one on one, and the last thing I wanted was to make a big production of it by pulling her out of a crowd.

But how do you go about apologizing for possibly killing someone in a past life?

I scraped my hair back as I thought about it, twisting it up and tying it into a knot at my neck.

Noticing, Kitty said, "The heat's supposed to break early next week. Everyone says a big storm is coming that will blow it all out to sea. Which will be lovely—except that we'll have to pry Lucian out from under the couch again."

"You mean he really is that scared of storms?"

Kitty grinned. "He's worse than most dogs I know—but don't tell him I said that! Do you like celery in your chicken salad?"

"Whatever you want," I said, and she fetched a few stalks, chopping them expertly. "Can I do anything?" I added.

"Talk to me," she said, which I suppose was the best opening I was going to get.

"Sell, if you don't mind me asking you a question—"

"Fire away."

"I was just wondering . . . I mean, I don't want this to sound rude, or anything, but ever since I've met you, I've always admired your . . . well, your lifestyle, your independence. I've never met a woman who seemed so centered, so grounded. And I guess I was just wondering . . . I don't know, how you got there. Have you always been like this, or did you, well, learn something along the way?"

Crap, how stupid did that sound? Except that she actually seemed to be thinking about it, laying her knife down for a moment.

"You don't ask small questions, do you, Liza?"

"I'm sorry. If it's stupid, we can talk about something else."

"No, no. There's no such thing as a stupid question. And

I sometimes forget what it is like to be young. You and Jane . . . Well, it's been such a pleasure having you both in the house this summer—two amazing young women on the verge of discovering their lives. It's made me remember what it is all about. And I think it's an admirable thing that you want to be independent." She looked at me closely. "You realize that I already think of you as family. It's like I've known you my whole life."

You have no idea, I thought.

"Is this about Adam?" she said.

"Hey! I mean . . ."

She grinned. "Didn't expect me to turn the tables, did you? Well, I'm not exactly blind; I see that something's been going on. You here, alone, on a Saturday night? But tit for tat. I'll answer your question if you answer mine."

"You're scary," I told her, and she laughed.

"Age and wisdom, my dear."

"Fine. Then deferring to that . . . you go first!"

"Touché. Okay. The first thing is, I had it easy. It's easy to be independent when you don't actually *have* to work."

"Yeah, Lucian says much the same thing."

"He told you that?"

"Yup. What?" I asked, in response to her cryptic smile.

"Nothing. But you are partly right, in that it is as much a state of mind as anything else. And I'd love to be able to tell you that there was some moment of epiphany that brought me here, but sadly I think it's just how I'm built. I've always just had this sense that it was more important to figure out who you were and to be happy in yourself than to depend on someone else for your happiness. I mean, if you're with the right person, I suppose it could be wonderful—I mean, it *is* wonderful!—but I've always had this sense that I'd rather be by myself than be with the wrong person. I mean, look how long I waited for James to come along."

"So are you and Jim going to—?"

"Marry?" She grinned. "Hell, no! Not that I don't adore him, but I'm too old and set in my ways. I *like* my independence; it's important to me. Does that begin to answer your question?"

It did. She might have had no memory of being Lucy, but something in her had clearly reacted to Lucy's circumstances. Lucy was a helpless, dependent woman, trapped in marriage to a man who loved another. Clearly she was not going to let her future selves make those same mistakes.

So, maybe my suspicions weren't so far off. Maybe souls did come back, and maybe we were each fated to find each other again and again so we could learn from our mistakes. Or, at least, let go and move on.

I found myself wondering how long it would be before the future Lucys truly learned to trust again. I hoped Jim would help. He had always been Obadiah's true friend and strong right hand; maybe he would now be Lucy's as well.

"Yeah, actually it does," I told her. "And thanks."

She smiled. "I also know that my choice is not valid for everyone, Liza. Don't think you have to avoid commitments, just because it might become risky."

"Is that what you think is going on?"

"You tell me. All I know is that Adam is a lovely young man, and that you're here alone on a Saturday night. So, what gives?"

"We broke up," I admitted.

"Really? Why?"

"You don't ask easy questions, either, do you?" I said, and laughed. "You know, you're right; Adam really is a very nice man. I'm just not sure . . ."

"What?"

I felt myself flushing. "Well, I'm just not sure I'm a very nice girl."

"Trust me," Kitty said, "you are. But I know what you mean. Something was missing."

"Yeah. He's sweet, he's gorgeous, the sex was good, but . . . I don't know. . . ."

"Not spectacular?" she supplied.

"Exactly. And now you are going to tell me that spectacular isn't everything, and—"

She actually snorted. "Whatever makes you think I'm going to say that? My dear girl, spectacular is everything! Why else do you think I waited so long for James?" And her eyes twinkled delightedly at me.

I choked.

"Oh, good heavens, I've rendered you speechless! I never thought I'd see the day. No, if Adam wasn't right, then Adam wasn't right. In fact, I can't say I'm entirely surprised. I honestly thought this would come to a head a lot sooner than this."

I stared at her, incredulous. "You *knew*? How?"

She just raised an eyebrow.

"God damn! Did I mention you were scary?"

"Twice," she said, laughing. "And, you know, if my expert opinion makes any difference, I think you made the right decision."

"About Adam?"

"Yes. I wasn't lying when I said I liked him; I *do* like him. But you and he . . ." She shook her head slightly. "You need something different. And, unless I am very wrong, you are going to find that sooner than you think."

"Hey! What do you know that I don't?"

She chuckled. "I've got thirty years on you, kid; I suspect the things I know that you don't run to volumes. But you've got a good head on your shoulders. You'll figure it all out in time." Then, to my vast surprise, she added, "I always say, one of the great advantages to being single is that you get to choose your own family. And, like I said, you've been part of mine for a long time now. You'll come out all right, I promise you."

I felt a huge smile break out on my face. Hell, if that wasn't complete forgiveness, then I didn't know what was.

Lucy and I, it seemed, had made our peace.

But, as proved by that night's troubled dreams, Rose's trauma still endured—and I still had no idea how to fix it.

And summer was creeping inexorably to an end.

CHAPTER 28

When I got home on Sunday, I could hear Jane rattling around in her room. So, taking a page out of her book, I knocked twice on her door, then entered.

"Got a minute?" I said.

She looked up, her face pinching slightly in worry. "Yeah, what's up? Anything wrong?"

I folded myself down onto the foot of her bed—her usual position. "I don't know if you'd call it wrong or right, but I figured you should know. I broke up with Adam yesterday."

"You *did*? I mean . . . Sorry, you did? Are you okay?"

I laughed. "I assume from your initially gleeful tone that you think it was the right thing, too?"

She looked suddenly suspicious. "What do you mean, 'too'?"

"Kitty," I clarified. "Apparently, she saw the whole thing coming."

"*Kitty* did? Damn." Jane was silent for a long moment.

"So, do you think I did the right thing?" I asked her eventually.

"Not my decision, babe. Do *you* think you did the right thing?"

"Yeah, I do. I mean, he's a great guy and all—and I'll miss having unlimited access to a body that amazing"—She grinned—"but, yeah. It was never going to be anything . . ."

"Earthshaking?" she supplied.

"Exactly."

"And earthshaking is worth waiting for," she said. "Believe me."

"That's about what Kitty said, too."

Jane shrieked with laughter. "See? Didn't I tell you you'd love Kitty? Didn't I tell you she was just like me?"

"Yes, and you were right—as usual. Even though she didn't have green hair. So, I take it your thing is going well, then?"

She got such a rapturously glowing look on her face that I felt the ugly, green snake of jealousy bite. "Oh, yeah. And I'm sorry I can't tell you any more yet—I hate keeping this stuff from you!—but hopefully soon. I mean, if it were just my secret, no sweat, but—"

"No, I totally understand," I told her. "Plus which, I've pretty much already figured it out."

"You have?" she exclaimed, astonished.

I nodded. "And I hope you are both very happy." It was true; I did. Though it still made me feel wretched.

"Oh, we are. And will be. But what about you? Are you really okay about all this? I mean, I'm not going to have to buy you gallons of ice cream and mop away your tears, am I?"

"Since when have you ever had to buy me gallons of ice cream and mop away my tears?" I responded scornfully.

She raised an eyebrow.

"Okay, forgetting the PMS. And that never involved tears."

"No, just the ice cream." She sighed. "And here I was hoping we might actually have one truly girly moment. But alas."

"Yeah, sorry, babe. But I don't think either of us are cut out for the girly thing."

She laughed. "Go, us. So, no Adam at dinner?"

"No Adam at dinner."

"Well, like you said, I'll miss the eye candy. But, if it makes any difference, I also think you made the right decision. He was damned cute, but . . . not full-on Liza material. Not really."

"Oh, and you'll let me know when the full-on Liza material comes along?"

"Already on it," she said, twinkling. "C'mon, let's go spoil our appetites with ice cream, anyway. Anyone who's been through a breakup needs ice cream."

"Even if they are the breaker, not the breakee?"

"Why the hell not?"

"Good point. All right, then, you're on."

We made a valiant stab at destroying our appetites, and dinner did feel a little weird without Adam there. But no one said anything, and we all attempted to act as if everything were normal.

I again spent part of the meal surreptitiously watching Jane and Lucian for signs of their burgeoning relationship, but they were still being immensely discreet—save for the occasional bouts of kicking and giggling (Jane's side), and kicking and scowling (Lucian's), which seemed par for the course these days.

It was a bit awkward at work the next week, as Adam and I kept running into each other unexpectedly. But fortunately, my new increased tour schedule meant I was out of the building more often. Which would have been good, if the heat wave wasn't clinging stubbornly to the island like a smothering blanket, far longer than the weather guys had anticipated. So I dragged around the streets, trailing a pack of limp tourists, and none of us were entirely happy.

I also found myself missing Adam almost every night, when I'd wake, alone, from the dreams . . . although I still knew I'd made the right decision.

But what probably made me saddest of all was Lucian. Because as soon as he heard that I had broken up with Adam and was back on the market, he withdrew completely. No fancy dinners, no movies, no teasing banter. Apparently, I was okay to be friends with only as long as my affections were firmly engaged elsewhere.

And my anxiety was growing. Wednesday was August first. I had all of two weeks left on Nantucket, and I still seemed no nearer a real solution. The dreams were getting worse, not better, the grip of the past stronger. The thought of leaving Nantucket without answers terrified me, because I had this unshakeable feeling that I simply wouldn't survive it.

But, three days later, it all came crashing in. And, as usual, it started with a dream.

I am standing in Obadiah's study. He has recently turned half of the downstairs into the place where he and William will work, once the final voyage is completed. It is early evening, the sky a thick, crepuscular purple outside the windows. Rachel has just finished lighting the lamps, and a warm glow permeates the room, though it cannot dispel the chill in my heart. A storm is brewing; I can feel it. Both outside this house and in.

Lucy is upstairs, napping, and I have taken the opportunity to come downstairs, to confront Obadiah. What is between us can go on no longer. I have already begun my long-planned speech when the outer door of the house bangs shut—Rachel, trying to make it home before the storm. There will be no witnesses save Lucy, and she sleeps.

"What do you mean, you are leaving?" Obadiah glares at me across his desk, his voice a heavy whisper.

"Just that." I try to keep my tone, reasonable. I will not let my heartbreak show. "Tomorrow's dawn, you sail. Matthew has asked to call on me tonight. I know he is going to ask for my hand. Obadiah, I am going to accept him."

"You can't!" he says, his voice breaking in anguish. "Rose, no. Please. You and Owen are the only things that give my life any meaning—"

"You have a wife, Obadiah," I remind him. "And a son." *Mine.* "It is time you became a family, as you were meant to. And as for me . . . Matthew loves me. And I deserve the chance at a life of my own."

The agony on his face is breaking my heart. "Rose, you

can't. I need you. I *need* you! Don't tell me you don't feel it, too."

"I can't," I say. "Not anymore."

"Do you love him, then?" His voice turns bitter, hard with betrayal. He wants to hurt me, as I am hurting him. He rises, comes around the desk.

"No," I whisper, fighting back tears. "No, I don't."

"Then why?" he howls, primal agony.

"Because." I am sobbing openly now. "I can't do this anymore. I cannot be at your side every day, loving you and getting nothing in return but snatched moments. It's tearing me apart, Obadiah. And in time, it will destroy Lucy and Owen as well. For all of our sakes, you must let me go."

"How can I, Rose? You are my life, my being. You are the reason I wake up, and the thing I dream about as I fall asleep. How can I do without you, for all these long years? *How?*"

His agony tears at me, but I am right. He knows I am right. "You once told me that it was up to you, to be strong. Well, now it is my turn. For both our sakes. Please, Obadiah, let me be strong!"

He crumbles then, that tall, proud man, falling to his knees before me. His arms tighten around my waist; his face is pressed into my belly. I feel the strong shoulders shake; the hot tears soak my skirts.

I tangle my hands in that thick, dark hair, my heart breaking. Surely, this cannot be the last time I touch him, hold him. But it must be; it must.

I sink down to my knees in turn, sliding down his body, until our damp, tearstained faces are pressed close. And then

I am kissing him desperately, hungrily. Once more, dear Lord. Once more, and then I will let him go.

He pushes up my skirts, frees himself from his breeches, and then he is in me, on me, thrusting hard and desperately, as if trying to imprint this moment on his memory forever. While I wrap my legs around his back, clutch him to me. As my climax claims me, I look up to see Matthew's face pressed to our window, his expression one of horrified disbelief.

I stiffen. "Obadiah," I gasp, pointing.

He angles his body away from me, turns to the window. I feel him wilt within me, and from his string of curses, I know this is no illusion. He leaps away from me, pulling my skirts down as he does so, and stuffs himself back into his breeches as Matthew backs away from the casement.

"Go after him, Obadiah," I say. "Please!"

He casts me an agonized look, then complies, straightening his clothes as he flies out the door after his second mate and drags him inside.

By that time, I have gotten my skirts in order, and I meet them in the hall. Matthew's face is incandescent with pain and betrayal, and Obadiah looks old and defeated.

"I am so sorry, Matthew," I say. "I know there are no words, truly, but . . . can you forgive me?"

The sky chooses that moment to open, a deluge pouring down from the heavens. Lightning flashes; thunder booms. God, passing judgment on our sins.

"How could you?" Matthew asks, his voice breaking. "I loved you! I wanted to wed you! And all the time . . ." His voice is thick with disgust. "How could you betray me like this?"

"Matthew, I—"

"You filthy whore!" he is screaming. "Jezebel! Harlot!"

Obadiah is about to hit him; I can tell. But God help us all, it is Lucy who intervenes, flying down the stairs like an avenging angel. The thunder and our screams must have woken her.

"How dare you?" she cries. "After all you have done! It was your filthy lusts that got her in that way. But I saved her. I saved her!"

Matthew stares at her in incomprehension, and I feel a mounting dread. "I know not what you are talking of, madam," he snaps. "All I know is, I arrived to find them rutting like beasts on the floor!" His gesture encompasses Obadiah and me.

There is a long moment, so thick you could cut it, then Lucy's face cracks. "Is this true?" she demands in a broken voice. I don't know which one of us she is appealing to; her eyes flit between us both.

But it is Matthew who answers, his voice still thick with hurt. "I saw it with my own eyes. It is a fact."

Obadiah has gone still and silent. Now he grabs Lucy by one arm, whirling her to face him. "What do you mean?" he demands.

"Don't touch me, betrayer!" she shrills.

"What do you mean?" he repeats, more harshly. *"How did you save her?"*

"It was her child," she sobs. "Hers—and his!" And her finger points, unerringly, at Matthew Phinney.

I can see Matthew's anger evaporating, as understanding slowly dawns. He looks pale and shaken, suddenly realizing he has ripped a wider hole than he intended. Secrets are spilling forth, like flour from a sack. Inexorable. Blinding.

Obadiah's face is exultant. He releases Lucy, swings to face me. "He's yours," he says. "Owen. Yours and mine!"

I nod. I can do no more, say no more.

Lucy has crumpled to the floor, huddled around her knees, sobbing. Matthew looks white as a ghost. And Obadiah has clutched me in his arms. "Ours," he crows. "Ours! My love, my love . . ."

When I say nothing, he finally puts me down. I meet Matthew's hurt, shocked eyes. "How long?" he whispers.

"Too long. I am sorry. I am so—"

Lightning flashes again; thunder booms.

"Mama!" comes Owen's cry, terrified, from upstairs.

Matthew laughs, hollowly. "Which one of you is it?"

With a dignity I did not know she possessed, Lucy picks herself up off the floor. She is still crying, but silently now. She will not look at me. "I will go," she says. And slowly starts climbing the stairs, as if her feet were made of lead.

Matthew, too, wheels in silence and heads for the door.

Leaving Obadiah and me again alone.

He pulls me to him, kisses me fiercely. "I'll go after him," he said. "He's a good man. I'll make him understand. You . . . Go to Lucy."

I am silent. After a moment, I nod. And, as the thunder booms about me, I head up the stairs. . . .

And wake, gasping. That was it, I knew. The night. Less than an hour later, Lucy would be dead. But how. *How?*

The final piece still eluded me. But though I tried, valiantly, sleep would not come. I tossed and turned until my alarm went off, then sleepwalked through my day. All I wanted was to get back to sleep tonight, hoping—knowing—I would see the final piece of the puzzle that had been hidden for so long.

I could feel the air gathering around me, as heavy and tense as it had been in the dream.

"I think it will rain tonight. Finally!" Kitty said over dinner.

Kitty. Lucy.

"Liza, you're freaking me out!" Jane said, shaking me by one arm.

I'm sorry, Matthew, I wanted to say. *I'm sorry I wasn't what you needed*.

Even Jim was peering at me, concerned. Kind William, always a tower of gentle strength.

"Should we put her to bed, do you think?" Kitty's voice, concerned. "At least she can sleep late tomorrow."

It was a Sunday, I recalled. No work tomorrow.

It was Lucian who came to my defense. Lucian, with his quicksilver eyes. "Let her be," he said. "She'll be fine. Trust me."

I only hoped he was right. But to my joy, sleep came quickly. And with it, the dream.

CHAPTER 29

I am standing at the head of the stairs. Oil lamps flicker from the walls, and from a table in the hall. I have come upstairs, but Lucy is not here. She is in Owen's room, comforting our son.

Before long, the door opens; she emerges. Her eyes are wide and haunted, filled with pain. I can see the tracks of tears on her cheeks—and the ghost of girlhood in her features.

"How?" she asks pitifully. "How could you do this to me? I trusted you. I . . ."

Her voice breaks, and guilt washes over me like a wave.

"Lucy . . ."

"How?" Her voice cracks, breaks. "Traitor! Viper!"

There is a storm raging around the house—a companion to the one in my head.

Her lips draw back in a snarl; her fingers hook into claws. And she flies at me—kicking, flailing.

I am stronger than she is; I cannot fight her. Besides, I understand her pain, her rage. And so I let her beat her fury against my flesh.

"Go away!" she is crying, her words punctuated by her ineffectual blows. "Go away, and never come back!"

Then a door flies open, framing a small anguished face. Owen—so small and vulnerable in his white bedgown. His eyes are wide with horror at this sight no child should see.

"Mama!" he cries. "Mama, no!"

And we both freeze.

Lightning flashes; thunder booms. I did not think it was possible to feel any greater loathing for myself than I already do, but now it rushes in like a wave, drowning me. I am choking in a sea of bitter gall. For in all my desire to do the right thing at last, the one person I never considered was my son.

His eyes are fixed on me—desperate, pleading.

If I leave, it will break him, irreparably; I know this now. And suddenly all my thoughts of nobility look foolish and self-serving. We have entered into a devil's bargain, Lucy and I, one we can never untangle. Not without someone paying the price. But dear God, please let it not be Owen!

I step forward, but before I can move more than that step, Owen flies into action.

"No, Mama, no! You mustn't send Auntie Rose away!" His voice still carries a trace of his childish lisp, I notice, and then he is on her, all his rage and fear released in one mighty burst. He shoves out both hands and pushes her, hard.

She is so stunned by this attack that he actually topples her. She falls, hard, against the banister; I hear her head crack against the newel post. And then he is nestled in my arms, my boy, who has always seemed to sense, deep down, which one of us loves him more.

I hug him to me, numb, as he buries his head against my

legs and wails, terrified by both the storm and the furious emotions.

. . . *Lucian?* a part of me thinks, but is quickly silenced.

Trembling from pain and shock, Lucy rises to her feet, hanging on to the newel post for support. Blood sheets down her face from a cut above her eye. There is blood and a bit of hair stuck to the post. But it is the look in her eyes that strikes me to the heart. The betrayal is even worse when it comes from Owen. Owen, who has chosen between us, as clearly as a child can choose.

She has lost her husband, and she has lost her son. Both to me.

"Lucy . . . ," I say.

"Take him," she whispers. "Take him to bed. Please."

"Are you . . ."

She forces a smile. "I'll be fine. Owen, baby, Mama will be fine. Go with Rose, now."

I pick him up, and he buries his face against my bosom. He will not look at Lucy, which seems to me a blessing. In the darkness of his room, it takes a long time to calm him. He clings to me, until I assure him, a dozen times and more, that I will not leave him. I will never leave him. And I know it is true. There can be no more right thing, not for me.

When he finally sleeps and I emerge, Lucy is sitting at the top of the stairs, blood still leaking sluggishly from the cut on her head. She looks up, numb, as I close the door behind me, and our eyes meet for a long, anguished moment before her gaze loses focus. She lifts a trembling hand to her forehead.

What have we done, Lucy?

"You can stay, of course," she says. "I . . . You can stay."

She grabs the banister to pull herself erect. I see her swaying with pain and dizziness.

Instinctively, I reach out to her; I have been taking care of Lucy for a long time. But she is not yet ready to forget or forgive. She flinches away from my touch and stumbles. As I watch in horror, she tumbles backwards, down the stairs.

And . . .

The ship is rocking, the waves slapping iron-fisted against the hull. A cold wind is screaming out of the south, blasted up from the Antarctic, chapping the cheeks and watering the eyes. There is nothing but ocean on all sides, as dark and forbidding as the backs of the leviathans when they finally surface in swirls of water and spouts of steam. Overhead, the sails creak ominously, taut under the strain of the fierce wind. A momentary lull slackens the canvas, then it snaps into place with the sullen crack of a slavemaster's whip.

The ocean, my dreaming mind tells me, is a harsh mistress, hard and unforgiving. But it is also the cradle of life. The cradle . . . and the grave.

From the slender hoops in the mast high above, the lookout gives the call, his voice high and thin in the screaming winds: "Thar she blows! She blows!"

It rises off the port bow like some beast of legend, water pouring off its scarred black back like waves off a rock. Its breath, moist and hot in the chill air, hisses forth: the fires of Hell unleashed.

Frenzy erupts with the lookout's cry. The deck boils with motion as the ship begins its slow, ponderous turn into the path of the whale. The whaleboats are flung from the sides; men pour like rats over the rails. The boatsteerers take up position in the bows, their harpoons flashing silver in the pale light of the morning sun, ropes coiled like torpid snakes beside them.

Senses are heightened at such a moment. The familiar salt-tang of the air rakes at the throat with caustic fingers. And the voices of the crew echo back and forth like macaques in the jungle: all noisy cacophony, devoid of sense.

"Hold fast the course!" Obadiah cries, and I hear the desperation in his voice.

Oars are shipped, the whaleboats skimming across the water like bugs across a pond. The rowers are well-trained, the oars a poetry of synchronized motion. Rise, dip, stroke, and rise again.

The whale, too, dips below the surface, then rises, blowing. The dark, squarish head, the stubby ridges of its dorsal hump, reveal it to be black gold: the elusive sperm—the rarest and most valuable of the cetaceans. Kings are anointed with its oils. And under its flukes, scores of whalemen have met their Maker.

The cries go up from the men, echoing eerily in the chill air. The whaleboats gain speed, fleeting after the leviathan. Harpoons are poised for the toss, their deadly points gleaming. And we who are left behind, riding above the waves as the leviathan rides below, wait in taut anticipation, nerves belled out like canvas before the wind.

Why am I here?

Why?

Once again, the whale breaks the skin of the sea. The lead

boasteerer poises, casts. The weapon soars, a silver arc, the lines singing out behind it. And then again, in quick succession. Both shots are true. Barbed and deadly, the points sink into a mountain of black flesh. The lines snap taut. And the monster rises. Not just breaking the surface this time but thrashing upward in a wake of foam.

The toothed jaw clashes; the beady eye gleams with rage and pain. Higher and higher the monster rises until it looms over the small boat like a wall of storm-tossed water. Will it drop once more and attempt to flee the harpoon's sting, towing the whaleboat behind it like a child's toy, or will it rise up until it almost clears the surface of the waves then dive down deep, our last view of it the mocking flap of its mighty tail?

But this time, it is the third and most sinister possibility that occurs. The vast, black body twists in midair and descends on the boat like a hammer on an anvil, crushing it as if it were no more solid than a nutshell.

The toothed jaw clashes, shearing through the second boat so that it falls in halves, spilling human cargo like seeds from a pod. A mighty flap of the tail annihilates the third.

It is hard to see if there are any survivors in that welter of wake and foam, nor is there time to evaluate, for the whale is turning. The harpoon juts from its back like a pin, the lines streaming behind it like a banner as it comes.

And then that vast, squarish head is hammering into the side of the ship. I hear the crack of timbers, feel the wallow that lets me know the ship is wounded. It is not enough, though. The whale comes again, striking up into the hull. I can feel the ragged hole it makes, as if my vessel is an extension of my body.

For my sins, I think, as the water floods in and the ship founders.

Rose . . .

I am twisting with guilt like a fish on a line, even as the waters flood in and the ship begins to split. The boards groan, then tear apart with a tortured scream. Soon, the frigid waters will embrace me: the only lover's touch I deserve.

The ship shudders again beneath the beast's assault. It is not, I know now, a whale. It is some avenging demon out of Hell: my fate and my punishment.

Yea, though I walk through the valley of the shadow of death, I will fear no evil . . .

Except that I do fear. I can smell its stink upon me, sour and acrid in my sweat. I can taste it on my tongue.

For thou art with me; thy rod and thy staff they comfort me . . .

But it is too late for comfort now. Too late for repentance.

"No!" I cry. "No! No . . ."

"No!"

To this day, I am still not sure if it was my own shout that awakened me, or the deep boom of thunder outside my window—so loud, it rattled the glass in the panes. Scant seconds later, lightning flashed, cold and harsh, bathing the room in white-blue light.

I sat up with a start, my heart pounding almost as loud as the storm. I had figured it all out, solved all the puzzles. That was supposed to end the dreams, yet I was back to the beginning again, as if I had learned *nothing.* Why was I being tormented this way?

"It wasn't your fault, Rose!" I cried aloud. But the storm swallowed my words in another bang of thunder, and only the lightning answered.

We were in the heart of the storm, I realized. The rain was coming down in heavy sheets and the wind was whistling around the house. It screamed in through the crack of the window I had left open, blowing in enough rain to soak the carpet.

I hastily rose and wrestled the window shut, ignoring the water that lashed at me. My emotions were as chaotic as the weather. It was a little past four in the morning, but the last thing I wanted to do was sit alone in my room, with my thoughts thrashing as wildly as the trees outside my window.

I tugged on the pair of sweatpants I had left on the floor last night. Then I eased open the door to my bedroom and padded out into the hall.

The storm sounded wilder out here, magnified down the length of the vestibule, and I wondered how Lucian was faring. Would he really be under the furniture, as Kitty had claimed?

I made my way downstairs, guided by the flashes of lightning. I don't know what drew me to the living room. It seemed eerily silent and empty—until lightning revealed a dark figure hunched in one corner of the couch like a gathered ball of darkness, and I nearly screamed aloud.

Darkness claimed the room again, but my faint whimper had not gone unnoticed.

"Liza?" a voice said—familiar, if disembodied, in the darkness.

"Lucian?" I gasped.

"In the flesh," he confirmed, and when the lightning

flashed again, I could see him huddled in a dark robe, his usually sleek hair tousled. "What are you doing up?"

"Dreams," I said. "And you?"

"Storm."

"So, you really *are* scared of storms?" I asked, moving closer. His answer was drowned by another boom of thunder.

I didn't need verbal confirmation. I was close enough to see that he was sweating, his eyes wide and white-rimmed with terror. When I sat down beside him and stretched out a hand, he seized it in a death-grip that wrung yet another squeak out of me.

He grimaced and eased the pressure.

"Why? Is it really because you were born in a storm?" I asked.

I could barely see the glitter of his eyes through the darkness. "No, quite the opposite. It's because I died in one," he said, and the shock that went through me rivaled the flash of lightning that followed, freezing the room in an odd moment of suspended animation.

"Around the Horn," he added. In the shadows, his eyes were not silver but as dark as obsidian.

"August sixth, 1846," he continued meditatively. "The worst, most frigid devil of a storm I had ever seen. Snapped the masts clean off, one by one, then tore the ship in half. Not a man survived."

"But . . . It's August sixth today, isn't it?"

"Indeed August sixth, 2006. Sometimes life's a bitch, eh? One hundred and sixty years, and it still hasn't gotten any easier."

"But . . ."

"I was coming home, Rose," he continued. "I had a full hold, and I was coming home."

"Oh my God!" I said, on a sob. *"Obadiah?"*

At least he had the grace to look sheepish. "Hello. Been a while."

"Only a hundred and sixty-three years!" I was practically screaming now, unaware that tears were streaming down my cheeks until he reached out and brushed one of them away. "How long have you known?"

"Oh, I suspected something for most of my life. But I probably put it all together when I was about fifteen."

"So you mean this whole summer . . ."

"I knew the whole time, yeah. I recognized you the instant you stepped into Kitty's kitchen. Why else do you think I acted like such an ass for so long?"

"But . . . You told me . . ." I could barely get the words out. "That night, at Obadiah's, when I asked if you were anyone . . ."

"I lied. So sue me."

"What do you mean, you *lied*?"

"Ouch! Stop hitting," he said, grabbing both my arms this time, and I felt the deep shiver that ran through him as the thunder boomed again. "And I mean just that; I lied. Give me a break, Liza! Do you think any of this has been remotely easy? Being a teenager is hard enough without adding in a massive identity crisis to boot. I've spent my whole life dealing with the fact that I was not myself. How do you think that feels? How do you come to terms with who you are as Lucian when a huge part of you knows you are this guy called Obadiah instead? Which is which? Which is *me*?"

"But . . ."

"Okay, let me put it another way. Do I want to kiss you right now because you are Liza, or because you used to be Rose?"

"I . . . You want to kiss me?"

He ghosted a laugh. "Trust a woman to muck up the priority system. Yes, I want to kiss you—rather desperately, if the truth be known. But the reason I waited is the same reason I lied. Because now I know that I don't want to kiss you just because you used to be Rose and I used to be Obadiah; I'm not that much of a mindless slave to fate. Instead, I want to kiss you because you are Liza—in all your great, wonderful, Liza-ish glory—and I am Lucian. Yes, I knew you as Rose, but I fell for you as Liza. And, to me, that makes all the difference in the world."

As I stared at him, he added, "Besides, I almost spilled everything that night on the roof, when I asked you if you wanted answers. Remember? That's got to count for something—even if you were more keen to get to Adam than hear my reply."

"I . . ." My rational brain was failing under the onslaught of his words and his nearness. "But what about Jane?" I managed.

"What about her?" he replied, sounding almost annoyed. "What the hell does Moonbeam have to do with any of this?"

"Well, except for the fact that she was Phinney—"

"Caught that, did you? Smart girl." He was slowly pulling me onto his lap, and my resistance was only token. But still . . .

"Aren't you dating her?"

"Dating her?" he exclaimed. "It would be a cold day in

hell before I dated Moonbeam—and not just because of who she used to be."

"But I heard you! She said—"

"Jane," he said calmly, "is dating Rob Winter."

"Rob *Winter*?" I exclaimed. "But he's—" *Gay*, I was going to say.

"Most decidedly not me," Lucian finished. "Damn it, Liza Donovan, you are the most perverse and irritating woman I have ever met! As you said yourself, it's been one hundred and sixty-three years. So are you going to keep talking, or kiss me?"

"Kiss you," I said, and did.

And, damn, but Kitty and Jane were both right about stupendous. It was totally worth waiting for.

CHAPTER 30

Though the storm still raged about the house, Lucian rose in silence from the couch and, once again holding my hand, drew me up the stairs. We were both still a little breathless as we walked.

"Where are we going? To my room?" The thought filled me with quiet joy. Was this what I had been waiting for, my whole life? It was, I was beginning to suspect, certainly what I had been waiting for all summer, ever since I first saw him standing in the kitchen.

"No, *our* room," he said, pulling open the door and gesturing me in. And he was right; it was. It was where we had first come together, and where we had spent so many of our best hours.

There was a look of such exquisite mischief on his face, his mouth curving up into that knee-melting grin, that lucky me finally got to do what I'd wanted to do all summer and kiss the expression right off his face. He hauled me close, and oh, yeah, he had missed me, all right—I could feel his arousal against me; it sent a wave of liquid fire through me. His body, beneath the robe, was as lean, hard, and wiry as his predecessor's. "Do you recall our first night here together?"

"How could I not? I was so scared, and so excited all at once. And you were—"

He laughed softly. "Shall we see if I still remember how to torment you? We've got all night."

"Or at least what's left of it," I said.

"No, we have hours, yet." Then he pulled back a bit. "You're mouthier than Rose, you know that?"

"And you're glibber than Obadiah," I countered.

He laughed. "You know, to hell with Rose and Obadiah! Have I told you how much I adore you, Liza? Since the moment you first stepped into that kitchen, I knew you were the one for me. In fact, if you hadn't been Rose, I would probably have beaten Adam into a small but bloody pulp and carted you off long ago. It was only my stubbornness about not falling into the same old patterns that held me back."

I grinned. "Have you seen Adam without clothes? I don't think he's so easily taken as all that."

It felt odd—but oddly right—to find myself gazing straight into Lucian's eyes. "Don't remind me," he said darkly. "But I still think I could have taken him—from righteous indignation over stealing my girl as much as anything."

"You do, huh?" I said, practically purring.

"Well, okay, you judge," he said, and dropped the robe.

He was still wearing a pair of silky boxers, but otherwise it was the body I remembered from the beach—only so much better now that it was mine for the touching. For the exploring.

I grinned.

"What?" he said, not at all self-conscious.

"Now I get to see what I couldn't, that day at the beach. Drop them," I commanded, indicating his shorts.

He grinned and complied. He was already erect—not quite so prodigious as Adam, but definitely something I could get used to seeing for the next, oh, sixty to seventy years or so. . . .

I stepped toward him, and the next thing I knew he had a leg behind my knees and had dumped me on my back on the bed—which, fortunately, had been updated to a nice, cushy queen over the years, instead of the narrow, ascetic mattress of Rose's day. And before I could get my mental balance back, he had me out of both T-shirt and sweats, as if by magic.

I had momentarily forgotten I was dealing with such an accomplished ladies' man. Suddenly, I hoped I'd measure up to the legions of other women who had come before me. Half of whom would probably be lined up outside the house tomorrow to fight me for him.

I sublimated my insecurities into a tease. "Slick, Lucian."

"You ain't seen nothin' . . . ," he began, and immediately set my fears at rest when he apparently ran out of words just staring down at me.

"What are you grinning about?" he said, lying down beside me and skimming a hand up my body.

"Nothing. It's just that . . . You barely said a word to me, that day on the beach!"

"Give a guy a break, Liza! I was in a state of incipient arousal all day. There you were, looking all phat in your skimpy little bikini, and—"

"Hey!" I said, punching him.

His lips quirked in a smile. "I assure you, I mean that in the purest gangsta sense. Pretty. Hot. And. Tempting." He punctuated each word with a kiss. "Although, in your case, I'd probably have to modify it to e-hat."

"For?"

"*Extremely* hot and tempting," he elaborated, with another twist of grin. "Those swim trunks, as you may have noticed, leave little to the imagination. I've never thought so hard about cold showers and mathematics in my life!"

I chuckled. "Not to mention sabotaging my phone."

"Not to mention. But hey, I had to distract myself somehow. And it's not my fault you have Bluetooth. It was either that, or humiliate myself publicly. So I chose to humiliate myself in private instead."

"What do you mean?"

His eyes twinkled. "Why do you think I went racing off so fast when we got home? There was no option but to go do unspeakably nasty things to myself in the bathroom until I calmed down. See what you drive me to? The sacrifices I have to make in your name?"

"Poor baby," I teased, feeling a surge of pure womanly satisfaction. *I* had driven the unflappable Lucian over the edge? "I'm sure it was a hardship."

"You have no idea!" he countered passionately, and I grinned.

Given the heat and hardness of what was currently poking into my side, I felt I had a rather good idea, indeed.

"Smug, are you? Then maybe I can give you something to really grin about." And he lowered his mouth to one nipple while one hand drifted down between my legs.

And God, he was good. It was like he knew exactly when

and how to touch me—as maybe, in fact, he did. I tried to touch him in turn, but he just batted my hand away and kept teasing me with lips and hands until I was going to jelly beneath him.

"So, are you grinning yet?" he whispered, his voice hot and rough in my ear. "Or shall I, I don't know, try something else? You hungry? Maybe I should order a pizza . . ."

I laughed—although the sound was a bit strangled. "You can do whatever you want. Just . . . *don't stop!*"

He chuckled, then shifted his mouth and kissed me, his tongue plundering above as his fingers ravaged below.

I was panting and quivering by the time he released me from the kiss, if not from his relentless, knowing hand. "Isn't there . . . supposed to . . . be foreplay?" I managed.

"What do you call this?" he asked in turn, also breathless, but more in control than I.

"Can't be foreplay if it . . . Ah!" I came hard against his hand, then collapsed back onto the bed bonelessly. "Leads to the main event so quickly," I finished, a bit sheepishly.

He raised an eyebrow. "Didn't I say we've got all night? And we're not even close to the main event yet, I promise you!"

Of course, he was right. I had never been put though my paces quite so thoroughly. Lucian seemed to know instinctively what I wanted: hard and fast first, then languorous and slow. Had Rose been like this, too, or had he somehow just grown attuned to me, to Liza?

Still, there was something to be said for a man with experience—both past and present. He used his body like a precision instrument—and played me like one as well. When he first entered me, it was with such exquisite control, the strokes so perfectly timed, that I thought I was going to die. But it wasn't just a question of showing off his prowess, either. He seemed to take an almost inhuman glee tormenting me— speeding up to pull me to a peak, then backing off again, stroking slow and languorously until the urge began to fade a bit, then pulling me back up with him again.

"You're the very devil," I told him during one of the lulls, and his silver eyes laughed at me. "How many more of these do you have in you?"

"How much time do you have? I'm a Frenchman, after all; I have a reputation to maintain."

But this wasn't about how long he could last; I could see that from his face. It was about how long he could stoke my fires before I could finally take no more.

Quite a while, as it happened. By the time we approached the sixth peak, I urged him on and he responded, and I came so strongly, I actually thought the top of my head was going to explode. I was also aware of his deep groan of satisfaction as he followed me into oblivion.

This, I suspected, went way beyond spectacular.

He collapsed against me, then rolled off to the side, cradling me against him while he efficiently disposed of the used condom with his free hand. Then, we just lay there panting for a moment, our sweaty limbs entwined.

"Damn," he said at last. "I never knew it could be like that. I mean, okay, I did, as Obadiah, but never as me."

"What," I said smartly, stroking a hand along his side, "never in all those times with all those women?"

"Never once," he said, leaning over to kiss me briefly.

"Really?"

"Scout's honor. It was all mere mechanics."

"Skillful mechanics."

"French," he said. "Reputation." And tweaked a nipple. I laughed. "But you," he added. "You I really want to play with. And for you, not because . . . I don't know, I'm proving a point or something. Though I am good with points . . . I mean, aren't I?"

"Exceedingly good with points," I assured him, stroking his now less-pointy bit, and was delighted to feel it stir a little, like a sleepy bird, under my hand. "But what was up with you, these past few weeks?"

"What do you mean?"

"First, you take me out on a series of bizarre non-dates. And then you drop me like a hot potato. What gives?"

He had the grace to look sheepish. "I was mounting a campaign of dirty warfare, my love. I knew full well Adam was out of town, even if you'd forgotten. So I figured I'd win you over, make you drop Adam. I was going to say something at dinner that night, proposition you, but then I went and got caught in my own damn trick with your phone—which yes, serves me right, I know. And then you dumped Adam, and what was that going to make me, the rebound guy?"

He paused for a moment, then grinned. "So Moonbeam read me the riot act. If it makes you feel any better, I was planning on making my move next week. Only Fate took a hand, and here we are."

I ran a hand over the drying sweat on his chest. "But I still can't believe you didn't say anything! I spent this whole summer on a quest, and you could have told me what was up the first day I arrived?"

He laughed slightly and tightened his arm about me. "And what fun would that have been? You had to figure it out yourself, much like I did. Besides—you had Adam."

I pushed myself partway out of his arms. The storm, I noticed idly, was dying, the rain growing gentler and the thunder fading away. "Is that why you've been such a prick all summer?"

"Not all summer!" he protested, sounding offended. "I was happy for a while. Figured I'd shown fate who was boss. But then I got all jealous again, and . . . yeah, okay."

"I spent the whole summer convinced you thought I was nuts!"

"Well, what was I supposed to say?" he asked, sounding aggrieved. "'Yes, I believe every word you say, but I'm not telling you why?' You found out what you needed to know—"

"And more!" I said, suddenly excited. I sat up, looked down at him where he lay sprawled among the sheets. "I saw the whole thing, Lucy's death. And . . . Hey, did you know that Kitty was—"

"Lucy?" He smiled. "Remember the fucked-up childhood? Try dealing with the memory that your oblivious godmother used to be your wife." He shivered deeply. "Now can you begin to see why I wanted to run as far from all of this as possible?"

And he looked at me with such deliberate piteousness

that of course I had to administer kisses and consolation, and . . .

When we finally came up for air again, the storm had all but vanished.

"Lucian," I said.

"What?"

"I didn't kill her. Lucy, I mean. It was an accident." I told him what I had seen, in that last dream, and when I had finished, he pulled me to him and held me in silence for a long moment.

"I'm so glad," he said, at last, into my hair. "I never knew what to think about that. I mean, I would have protected you, but I was never sure. You were in shock that night, not making any sense. I didn't know what to think."

"Me, either." I said. "But we're innocent." I sighed. "Still, I thought that once I found that oup, the dreams would stop."

"And they haven't?"

"No. That's what woke me up tonight. I had the whaling dream again, the one that started it all. The one where you die . . . Oh!" I suddenly remembered his words, the ones that had started this whole conversation. "I made that one up, didn't I? Fused what I knew of the *Essex* story with your tales of the sea, and . . . invented this fantasy of doom for you, because of everything that had happened. A whale never sank the *Redemption,* did it?"

"No," he said gently. "Like I told you, I died around the Horn. On my way home to you."

And that's why I had some of the details wrong, like the cold. Because I had created this apocalyptic fantasy that was totally false in all its particulars.

"God, I've been so wrong for so long," I exclaimed.

"I don't know," he replied with a catlike grin. "You seem pretty all right to me." And he ran a caressing hand up my side, making my skin tingle with desire. In the way only Lucian—or Obadiah—could touch me.

Above us, the rain pattered a gentle staccato on the roof.

"You're not sleepy yet, are you?" he said, his eyes twinkling suggestively in the gloom. And when I shook my head, he grinned and reached for me again.

It was, all in all, a revelatory night. We made love four times before dawn lightened the sky, and each time was better than the time before. How could I ever have thought Lucian was a Puritan? Adam was a nice boy, and made love like a nice boy. But Lucian was raunchy, inspired, and quite frankly inventive.

And by the time I finally drifted off to sleep, I was as happy and as sated as I had ever been in my life.

But Fate, it seemed, had one last vision for me. It picks up where the other left off, as I sit at the top of the blood-covered stairs, staring down at Lucy's corpse.

It is an hour or so later. All that remains of the mighty storm is a gentle patter of rain against the windows, but still I have not moved. I have run through all the scenarios in my mind; I know what we must do. If there's an inquest, an investigation, Owen's part will come out. And I cannot do that to him, to my boy. I cannot let him know that, however indirectly, he has killed the woman he knew as his mother. For now, if we play it right, it can pass as an accident. And Owen will have a future.

And so I wait for Obadiah to come home. I hear the door open, his tread in the hall. His gasp as he sees Lucy crumpled on the landing. "Rose? Rose! Are you safe? What happened?"

I stand, lean down over the banister until I can see his face. His dear, beloved, horrified face.

"I'm fine. There was . . . She fell, Obadiah! She fell—"

"I'm coming up, Rose—"

"No!" I say sharply, forestalling him. "You can't. You mustn't It must . . . It must look like an accident. There is no other way."

His brow furrows, and I can see him thinking. I do not care if he thinks I did it. My life is over. It is Owen's I must protect, at all costs.

"What happened with Matthew?" I ask, to distract him.

He climbs as far up the steps as he can without treading in the blood, gazing up at me. He has never looked old to me before, for all the difference in our ages, but he does tonight.

"We talked," he said with a sigh. "I told him everything. How much I love you. How much I have loved you, always. He is not happy about it, but he understands." He takes a deep breath, then adds, "I also told him that I set you free. And I mean it, Rose. When we are back from this voyage—and, God willing, it will be soon—it shall be your choice. If you want to go to him, I will not stop you. But if you want to stay with me . . .

"I will marry you, Rose. Make you my wife in the eyes of God and the law. If it is what you want."

I don't know what I want, other than for this nightmare

to be over. But that means . . . he must sail, tonight. And I cannot hold him, kiss him, bid him farewell save with cold, ineffectual words.

I feel a tear slide down my cheek.

"Rose?" he says, his voice worried.

"I love you, Obadiah," I say, "but you must go. You must." His sea-chest is already packed and downstairs. He brought it down this morning, so Lucy and I could tuck some final items in amongst his possessions. It will have to be enough.

"I don't understand," he says. "I . . ."

"If you trust me at all, then trust me when I say that this is how it must be. I will go up to sleep, with Owen. When Rachel finds Lucy in the morning—undisturbed, no footprints in the blood—I will say she must have fallen, in the night. We will all be safe, then."

"But . . . is this the way it must be? Is this how we part? With not even a touch, a kiss, between us?"

His face is anguished.

And then I hear Owen's voice calling my name. "Auntie Rose? Auntie Rose?" Anxious, perhaps, that I have gone, despite my promises.

"I'm coming, Owen," I call, then add, to my love—my one and only love, "I must go to him. Farewell. Come back to us. Come back safe."

"I will," he promises. There is an agonizing moment when he stretches his fingers up, and I stretch mine down, as far as they will go. An unbridgeable two-inch chasm yawns between us.

"Tell my son about me," he pleads. "Don't let him forget, while I am gone. You know the stories."

"I do," I say—and this, I suddenly know, is why they stayed with me, Obadiah's stories, told to Owen down the years, until they become as much a part of the fabric of my life as my own experiences.

"Auntie Rose?" Owen sounds more awake, more frightened. I cannot allow him to leave his room and see . . .

"I love you," I say. "Go!"

"I'll be back, Rose," he vows. "I swear, on everything my soul holds dear: I will return for you, if only to hold you one more time."

"No matter what?" I plead.

"Through hell and fire, sea and storm," he swears. "No matter what it takes, or how many years, Rose, I will come for you."

There is fire in his eyes, and I feel the tears rolling down my cheeks.

"Then I swear, too. Through hell and fire, sea and storm, I will wait for you. I will be here when you return, no matter what it takes, or how many years."

And I know—I *know*—he will be true.

Liza? What's the matter? You're crying. . . ."

The soft voice—a whisper in my ear—brought me out of sleep. Lucian's arms were about me, his body still twined warmly with my own.

"I . . ." I reached out a hand to my cheek, feeling the wetness, then touched his face, running my fingers along his cheek, his jaw, his lips. "You came back," I said, amazed. "After all those years, you really did come back!"

Lucian smiled at me, his face alight with joy, and—could it be?—love. "Yes, I came back. Only took me a hundred and sixty-three years, but I came back for you, as promised. How could I not? If only to hold you, one more time."

"So is *that* what all this has been about?" I said. "The promises Obadiah and Rose made, before he sailed?"

"Finally remembered that, did you? I was wondering. And, yeah, silly as it might sound, I rather think it is. In fact, I wouldn't be at all surprised if this was the end of the dreams—for both of us."

"So it wasn't about guilt or grief, or atonement. It was simply about . . ."

"Love," Lucian finished. "If you want to call it that."

"You know, I think I do."

"Good. Because . . . me, too. I've kind of adjusted myself to the fact that we're linked—at least, for this lifetime." He quirked an eyebrow. "Where I am Lucian Obadiah. I wonder if Kitty even had the remotest idea?"

"I suppose she must have," I said. "Somewhere deep in her subconscious."

"Yup. Pity your mom didn't . . . What?" he said, dragging my flaming face back up out of his chest. "What aren't you telling me?"

"My full name," I muttered.

"Which is?"

"Shit. Are you really going to make me say it?"

He raised an eyebrow.

"Rosalind Elizabeth Donovan," I choked.

He burst out laughing. "The universe really has a sick sense of humor sometimes, doesn't it? Well, Rose . . ."

"Yes, Obadiah?"

He grinned, and hit upon the very fact I'd been trying to hide from Jane for all this time. "Hey, your initials spell Red. Can I call you Red?"

"Hell, no! And anyway, your initials spell Lot. Hey, does that make me—?"

"—Lot's wife?" he finished, and grinned. "Probably. Eventually. But we've got years ahead of us, yet. Years and years and years. Still, consider yourself warned."

I laughed.

"What?" he asked.

"I don't think you're allowed to give a warning several years in advance of the event."

"No? Pity."

"Is it?"

A French phrase flowed out of him that sounded suspiciously like what he had said to me once before. So I swatted him—hard.

"Ow!" he complained, rubbing his shoulder. "What was *that* for?"

"For shame, spouting obscenities at me at such a moment."

He looked puzzled. "Obscenities?"

"Like you said in the kitchen, what fun is speaking a foreign language if you can't curse in it? Or . . ." Enlightenment dawned. "Were you lying about that as well?"

He actually had the grace to look sheepish.

"Okay, so what does it *really* mean?" I persisted.

Those silver eyes of his glowed. "Something entirely

more complimentary, I assure you." He measured me. "You know what, Liza?"

"What?"

"We talk too much."

He had a point. And with Lucian, there were any number of advantages to silence . . . which he now proceeded to show me.

CHAPTER 31

At a little past one, we heard a knocking on the door.

"Right, game's up!" Jane sang out cheerfully. "Everyone knows, so you might as well come down. Besides, Kitty's made pancakes."

"For lunch?" Lucian said, raising one eyebrow at me.

"It's never too late for pancakes," Jane declared. "Now, render up Liza, or am I going to have to come in there and fetch her?"

Lucian dissolved into laughter at my stricken expression, then rose and tossed me my T-shirt and sweats while I spent a moment admiring his lithe nakedness. It was every bit as good in the bright light of day.

"Um . . . what do you mean, everyone knows?" I called out as I hastily threw on my clothes.

I could hear Jane outside, choking back a snort of laughter. "Kitty peeked in to check on Lucian after the storm, to make sure he was all right. And surprise, surprise, he's not in his bed. So she got worried. Then she peeked in on you, and there he was. There you both were, apparently. So, are you coming out, or not?"

I turned and shot Lucian a dirty look.

"Your door, your lock, Red," he protested innocently, unable to hide his grin.

"Don't call me Red!"

His grin widened, and he gave me a kiss effective enough to stop all protests, then pushed me out the door.

Jane was leaning against the wall outside the bathroom. She straightened at my appearance, grinning fit to split her face. "Pancakes can wait," she declared, pouncing. "You're coming with me." She pulled me into her room, then shut the door behind us. "Well?" she said pointedly.

I went bright red, and she whooped. It took about half an hour, but she got the whole story out of me: Lucy's death, Rose's innocence, and Lucian's secret identity.

"I'm so glad," she said when I was finished. "I'm so glad you got your answers. I always had this odd feeling, from the very first moment I met you, that I should help you—that I *could* help you, like, I don't know, it was my duty or something—but who knew it would all turn out so well?"

"Who knew, indeed?" I said, looking at her anew. Poor Matthew Phinney. I remembered his horror when he realized what he had unleashed. I guess he finally got to make amends.

"But . . . doesn't it all seem a bit, I don't know . . . mawkish to you?"

"What, at the end?" she said. "You mean: all for love?"

I nodded, embarrassed.

She grinned. "A few months ago, I might have said yes,

but now . . . Now I actually think it's sweet. Hell, I'm a born convert to high romance myself."

"Yeah, which reminds me . . . Rob *Winter*?"

"What? So, he's older, but he's amazing, and . . . Oh my God, you totally thought he was gay, didn't you?" And she poked me.

"Well . . ."

"For your information, he was married. With two kids. In the process of finalizing the divorce when . . . you know. *That* was the reason for all the secret agent stuff. This place is no better than any other small town when it comes to gossip, and he didn't want anything complicating the final stages—especially in the minds of his kids. But it's all through, now, and . . . Kids! God. Can you imagine me, a stepmom?"

"Stepmom?" I exclaimed. "Is it that serious?"

Her smile was luminous. "Yeah, I think it is. I mean, we're not getting hitched tomorrow or anything, but yeah, I think this one's a keeper."

I shook my head in amazement. "Well, I'm delighted for you, of course, but I *so* had no idea!"

"Then who . . . Oh. Lucian blabbed." She frowned slightly. "But I thought you had figured it out."

I smiled ruefully. "Yeah, I thought I had. I thought you were dating Lucian."

"Lucian?" She shrieked with laughter. "Good Lord above, what ever made you think *that*?"

"Well, I heard you, that night, coming home," I confessed. "You know, all your talk of 'who would have believed,' and 'us,' and—"

"You are such a goose sometimes, Liza! No, he caught me

giving a rather . . . enthusiastic good night to Rob, so I had to confess. And the conversation ran somewhere along the lines of 'Who would have believed that two cynics like us could fall so hard?' Me for Rob, and Lucian . . . for you. Why else do you think I've been kicking him under the table every Sunday night since then—especially after you broke up with Adam? He's nuts about you, and I've been trying to get him to make a move. Looks like he finally did."

"Looks like," I said, and grinned. "So, pancakes, huh?"

Jane looked offended. "What, no details?"

"Hell, no!" I exclaimed. "He's like, what, your god-cousin or something? No way, too close. No details."

She pouted briefly, then brightened. "Just tell me one thing, then."

"Jane—"

She grinned. "No, it's an easy one. Just answer me this: Is it the amazing you've been hoping for?"

I laughed. "Yeah, it definitely is."

"Then my job is done," she said, and reached out to hug me.

That Sunday, Jane proudly trotted Rob Winter over to our family gathering, and she was right; he was wonderful. As for Lucian and me . . . We never seemed to run out of things to say, or ways to touch each other, and I had never been happier. In fact, I could almost feel myself radiating a disgusting, happy glow out onto the world that I tried in vain to hide, but to no avail. For the first time in my life, I was at home and at peace, and it felt wonderful.

Lucian was right; the dreams did not return. And while my memories of my past life didn't vanish, they faded into a comfortable background glow that no longer carried any urgency. I wondered if eventually, they would seem no more than a fondly remembered dream. But for now, I didn't mind letting whatever imprint of Rose still lingered on my soul share in my newfound happiness, because it was due to her dedication that I was here at all.

Rose and Obadiah had waited 163 years to be reunited, and it was up to us—Lucian and Liza—to make sure their sacrifice had been worthwhile. I had a feeling we wouldn't disappoint.

As for Adam, I kept my promise. I met him for coffee one afternoon, a few days before I was slated to leave the island, and told him everything. When I got to the revelation about Lucian, he smiled somewhat ruefully, and said, "I told you he wasn't dating Jane."

And so the summer drew to a close. School would start again soon. I had a reservation on Monday morning's ferry, and a long drive to Wisconsin ahead of me. I hated the thought of leaving the island, but I had a life to get back to. That Lucian was now part of that life made it seem full of unexpected promise.

On Sunday, August nineteenth, Kitty outdid herself throwing us a farewell bash. She and Jim—with Rob's help—had been cooking all day to make our send-off special. And it was. It was sad and joyous all at once, and God, would I miss this family I had found.

But Kitty was right; there were many different kinds of families, and the ones you chose for yourself were no less valid

than those you were born into. So, there we were: Kitty and
Jim; Jane and Rob; Lucian and me. It was a gathering made
even more poignant for Lucian and me by our shared realization of how we had all been together before, and no doubt
would continue to be together again—whatever faces wc
wore, or however little we remembered—for many lifetimes
hence.

Admittedly, neither us still had any real idea of what this
all meant about life's many mysteries, although we had talked
about it extensively, but I chose to see it as an affirmation of
the truly important things in life, like friendship. And love.

For a moment, in the comfort of the kitchen, it almost
seemed like our past ghosts were with us, too: Lucy and
William Stockton, and even poor Matthew Phinney, smiling
back at us in calm acceptance.

Until Lucian and I got off onto a debate about *Firefly,* and
everything got noisy and riotous and normal again.

We were only partly aware of Kitty rising and clinking on
her wineglass to get our attention. "If you two will stop talking long enough to let someone else get a word in edgewise,"
she admonished with a grin, and Lucian chuckled. "It is both
with profound joy and great regret—oh, God, I promised myself I was not going to cry!" Jim reached out and squeezed her
hand, and Kitty snuffled a laugh. "As I was saying, it is both
with profound joy and great regret that I officially call the
Nantucket summer of 2006 to a close. Having you here for
the summer has meant more to me than I can possibly say, and
brought me more joy than you can know. Jane, you and Rob
have a bright and brilliant future ahead of you. Rob, it has
been an honor getting to know you, and welcoming you to

the family. And as for you two"—she twinkled over at Lucian and me—"I can't tell you what great pleasure you give me! From the first moment Liza walked into this house, I had a feeling this was meant to be. And seeing it now is like . . . destiny. Liza, you are a remarkable young woman, and I can't imagine a better match for my precious godson. And you, Lucian, are a reprobate who has gotten far better than he deserves. You know that, don't you?"

"That I do!" he responded fervently.

"So, I suppose that all that is left to say is travel safely, and come back next year, all of you!"

"Well, that'll be easy," Jane put in brightly, "given that I am not leaving."

We all laughed, and I shot her a secret smile. I'd miss her like hell, but my new roommate had a few significant advantages.

"Let me know when you're back," Jane added to me, "and I'll help get my lease transferred into your name."

"Are you sure that won't be a problem?" Kitty asked.

"If it is, we'll just find another place," Lucian put in. "It shouldn't be hard. You know," and he grinned at me, "I'm going to enjoy keeping Liza in the style to which she will eventually become accustomed."

"Lucian," Jane confided to Rob, who was looking puzzled, "is independently wealthy. Rich as Croesus, actually—whoever Croesus is."

"The king of Lydia," Rob said immediately, "who reigned . . . oh, somewhere in the 500 BCs; I forget the dates exactly. But the Lydians under King Croesus were believed to be the first people to mint coins for money." And when we all stared at him, he added, "Sorry, former classics major."

"And you're running a restaurant?" Kitty asked.

Rob grinned. "Of course. What else do you do with a classics degree?"

"So, what about *your* housing?" Kitty asked, peering over at Jane.

She looked innocent. "I promise not to be too much of a bother. I'll get my own place soon, but while I'm looking, don't let the fact that I'm here cramp your style, or anything. I mean, you can go back to having loud, noisy sex if you want—"

"Jane!" Kitty exclaimed, but she was laughing.

"And, on that note," Jim said, his face still slightly red, "shall we propose a toast? To—"

"Family," Jane supplied. "The kind you pick yourself, which is always the best kind anyway. Right, Aunt Kitty?"

"Amen," her aunt said, and we all drank.

The following morning, I hugged my new family good-bye on the wharf. The ferry was looming before us, accepting its usual load of eighteen-wheelers into its capacious hold. Then, dashing a surreptitious tear or two out of my eye, Lucian and I drove on board.

It felt like the end of an era, but the start of a whole new one, too. One circle had closed, but an even grander one was opening before me. And with Lucian at my side, all things seemed possible.

We parked and locked the car, then climbed to the top deck. It was cooler now than at the height of the summer, and the wind sweeping off the water made me glad I had listened to Lucian's advice and brought my jacket. I shrugged into it, then brushed the hair out of my eyes and turned to Lucian, who was grinning at me, his silver eyes shining.

Down below, on the docks, Jane had produced a huge homemade banner from somewhere. It read: GOOD LUCK, LUCIAN AND LIZA. She had Kitty and Rob each holding a corner, and was capering madly behind it, bouncing and waving. It seemed odd, to see her without her multicolored hair, but Jane was Jane, and who knows? She might surprise Rob yet.

I waved back, once more trying not to cry. I was going to miss her something dreadful.

Lucian's arms slipped around me as I waved, and I leaned back into his comforting warmth. The ferry's horn let out a mighty blast. Slowly, the great doors descended, and we began to steam out of the wharf. Lucian and I waved until the dancing Jane was no more than a speck in the distance; then he turned to me.

"So," he said, "Wisconsin, eh?"

"Yup," I confirmed. "Madison, Wisconsin."

"Lots of cows there?"

"Yup. And cheese. And my parents." And when he raised an eyebrow, I added, "No causal connection."

He laughed. "That's good, because for a moment there, I was worried." Then his mouth quirked in a wry grin as he added, "The things I do for love. Do you realize I've never lived that far from the sea before?"

"You'll survive. And besides, it's only for one more year, anyway. Then we can go wherever we want. I can teach anywhere in the world . . . and isn't Yale supposed to have a good architecture program?"

"I have to get in first," he said.

"Oh, you will. You can be awfully motivated when you put your mind to it. So, I'll teach, and you'll build, and—"

"The world is our oyster?"

"Or something equally nautical, yeah."

"The world is our sperm whale?" he suggested with another of those knee-melting grins.

"Ick! That's disgusting, Lucian."

"Look who's talking. You never had to see one being tried out. Or smell it."

I grinned. "You know, I suspect Adam would have given his left arm for even half of what is in that head of yours."

"Adam," Lucian said, scowling slightly, "can lump it. I spent enough time this summer coveting what he had. Fair's fair on the turnaround."

We stared out over the waves in silence for a moment; then Lucian turned to me and said, "So, Rosalind Elizabeth Donovan, was this summer everything you had hoped for?"

I looked over at him—his face already so familiar to me, with those startling silver-grey eyes, his straight, dark hair blowing in the breeze, and his mouth curved into the beginnings of a cynical smile.

I grinned back at him. "Yes, Lucian Obadiah Theriault, it was." And it was no less than the truth. I had never imagined that one summer could change your life so completely. I had felt like my life was a puzzle with all the pieces jumbled randomly. In two short months, I had fitted it together, piece by piece, until a fully comprehensible image stared back at me. And now, unburdened by the past, I could go anywhere, do anything, be anything. I had never felt more free in my life.

And with Lucian at my side, I had a feeling that anything was possible.

"So, on we go," he said, almost echoing my thoughts. "Wind at our backs, faces to the sun, and all that jazz?"

The ferry was steaming steadily along, the wind of its passing blowing our hair back from our faces, and the sun cast our shadows long before us, like arrows pointing toward the future. I grinned.

"Something like that, yeah," I said. "And this time, together. Took a while, but we made it."

"Amen," he said, and kissed me.

His every touch still went through me like a spear. I wondered if that would ever change; I hoped not.

When we finally broke the kiss, I turned to look behind me, but the dim grey shoreline of Nantucket had vanished completely against the horizon and there was nothing to be seen on any side but the rolling waves, as if we were indeed aboard the *Redemption* in the middle of the vast Pacific, waiting for the whales that would bring us home again. I almost expected to see one rise, blowing ecstatically, its short, bushy spout blooming against the horizon.

But no, that was another era, and when I turned back again, I knew there was another land in front of us, waiting. And whatever that land brought us, I knew it would be good.